William Francis Allen

Essays and Monographs

Memorial Volume

William Francis Allen

Essays and Monographs
Memorial Volume

ISBN/EAN: 9783743305021

Manufactured in Europe, USA, Canada, Australia, Japa

Cover: Foto ©Andreas Hilbeck / pixelio.de

Manufactured and distributed by brebook publishing software
(www.brebook.com)

William Francis Allen

Essays and Monographs

·ESSAYS AND MONOGRAPHS

BY

WILLIAM FRANCIS ALLEN

𝔐emorial 𝔙olume

BOSTON

PRINTED FOR THE EDITORS, BY GEO. H. ELLIS, 141 FRANKLIN STREET

1890

TABLE OF CONTENTS.

PREFACE.

In this volume, we have aimed to collect from the writings of Professor William Francis Allen papers upon educational, religious, literary, and historical subjects, illustrative of the breadth of his scholarship and his keen interest in all that makes for better living. To these we have added the more important of his monographs upon Roman, Germanic, and English institutions. Space forbade printing selections from his political papers, and from the interesting and valuable mass of material in manuscript and print upon the South, written during his residence there in the later years of the Civil War. The Bibliography, however, gives a complete list of his published writings, including all his review articles, with unimportant exceptions; and it is to be hoped that at some time his papers on the South may be brought into a book.

These selections, written at different times, and lacking the final revision of his own hand, must not be taken as the last word he might have wished to speak; yet so careful was his workmanship that we do not hesitate to print them as we have found them. We believe that students will gladly read the helpful words he penned, and that American scholars who were proud to count him among their number will appreciate this collection, illustrating his acute, judicious, and comprehensive investigations.

We have had the valuable assistance of Mrs. Margaret Andrews Allen and Dr. Charles H. Haskins, of Madison, in the revision of proof-sheets and the preparation of the Index. Professor Joseph H. Allen, of Cambridge, Mass., has assisted in revising the proofs of the Bibliography. Our thanks are also due to the publishers of the several magazines from which articles in this volume are republished, for their generous permission to copy such material as we wished to include in the collection.

DAVID B. FRANKENBURGER,
REUBEN G. THWAITES,   } *Editorial Committee.*
FREDERICK J. TURNER,
JOSEPH H. CROOKER,

MADISON, WIS., Dec. 1, 1890.

MEMOIR OF
WILLIAM FRANCIS ALLEN.

WILLIAM FRANCIS ALLEN.

BY DAVID B. FRANKENBURGER.

THE ancestry of William Francis Allen gave promise of a man. For more than three hundred years the Allen family had been farmers, English yeomen and then New England Puritans. William Francis was a lineal descendant, of the seventh generation, of James Allen, who in the year 1639 came over from Great Britain and settled at Dedham, Massachusetts. He was afterwards one of a company that in 1650 settled and incorporated the town of Medfield on the Charles River, the territory of which was originally part of Dedham. The land then allotted to James Allen was the beginning of the "Allen farm," and has been in the continuous possession of his descendants to the present time.

The "Allens of Medfield" fitted perfectly Emerson's description of the typical farmer — "men of endurance, deep-chested, long-winded, tough, slow and sure, and timely." They were stalwart men, cheerful and friendly.

But the simple living and honest toil of these farmers must, in the economy of nature, come to flower and fruit; and, on August 15, 1790, was born Joseph Allen, of the sixth generation, who, while possessing in a high degree the Allen traits of endurance, cheerfulness and good fellowship, was yet unlike the rest of his family in being slight of body, and in having a passion for books. He was graduated from Harvard College in 1811. Among his classmates were Edward Everett and Nathaniel L. Frothingham. In 1848, his Alma Mater conferred upon him the honorary degree of S.T.D. — "the first among the Allens who received the honors of old Harvard. He studied for the Unitarian ministry, and in 1817 was settled at Northborough, a little village in Worcester County, Massachusetts, about fifty miles west of Boston. On February 3 of the following year, he married Lucy Clarke Ware, eldest daughter of Rev. Dr. Henry Ware, of Cambridge. The Wares came over from England in 1630. The family were distinguished for gentle graciousness, poetic insight, and intellectual vigor, but lacked the robustness and good fellowship, the perennial cheerfulness and interest in practical affairs that so distinguished the Allens. They remembered Greek conjugations more readily than the details of housekeeping; they were one of the academic families of New England, being a part of the colonial aristocracy. With few interruptions there lay back of Lucy Clarke Ware seven generations of ministers.

Joseph Allen and Lucy Ware, after they were wed, travelled from Cambridge to Northborough in a sleigh through a driving storm of snow and rain; and there for more than fifty years they broke the bread of life to the country folk, and reared their family. Here were born to them seven children, three daughters and four sons. Of the sons, Joseph Henry, Thomas Prentiss and William Francis graduated from Harvard. Joseph Henry became a Unitarian minister and later lecturer on Ecclesiastical History at Harvard; he is also the author of several standard works on church history. Thomas Prentiss became a minister and an educator. Edward A. H. was a graduate of and afterwards a professor in the Rensselaer Institute, Troy, New York.

In the quaint old church at Northborough the children of Joseph and Lucy Allen have set in the wall a tablet on which is inscribed this: " Joseph Allen, a faithful counselor, a wise instructor, a leader in the work of Public Education, a helper of many in times of need, a lover of flowers and of little children"; and this: "Lucy Clarke Allen of serene, patient and cheerful spirit; in daily life humble, scrupulous, self-denying; of deep convictions in matters of public right, of thoughtful, loving kindness to the poor and suffering."

William Francis Allen was born at Northborough, September 5, 1830. The course and quality of his life were early foreshadowed. To show how much the child was the father of the man, we quote from a letter of his sister Elizabeth: "William had very winning ways as a little child, sunny, affectionate, lively; he never required to be amused. He seemed to think it incumbent on him to entertain visitors if no one else was present. He never refused to sing, if any one asked him; it was as natural for him as to speak. One day mother was amused on coming down to see callers to find William entertaining them with a very sentimental song he had somehow learned. 'My heart is breaking for the love of Alice Gray' had a droll sound from his lips, as he was only three years old. . . . He had an excessive shrinking from pain and suffering, and we know how this sensitiveness soon developed into sympathy for others. His peculiar mental traits showed themselves very early. He used to explore father's book-shelves, where he found treasures of old books of history which would have repelled most children, especially from the old-fashioned print and spelling, which never seemed to trouble him." His father read Shakespeare aloud to the family, and William before he was seven years old had written a tragedy himself. His sister says: "It was quite complete in every detail, with plot and sufficiently defined *dramatis personæ*. We found many other little writings of his in verse, usually rescued from his pockets in the wash, and with them many lists or items from history — lists of sovereigns, dates, battles, etc."

"His interest in politics," writes his sister, "was awak-

ened during the famous Harrison campaign, when he was
ten years old, and it grew with his love of history.   He
wrote a political song to be sung at a Log Cabin meeting
that year. . . . He was happy-hearted, little dependent on
circumstances for enjoyment, yet he was not impossibly
perfect.   The tendency to carelessness and forgetfulness
in every-day matters, which often carried trouble to others
as well as himself, was felt as a serious fault, requiring
effort and energy to overcome." (That Professor Allen
was one of the most thoughtful and orderly of men is a
witness to his effort in overcoming this fault of his boy-
hood.)   "When he was fifteen, he had a slow fever, and
the day on which the doctor remanded him to his bed was
Thanksgiving.   How hard it seemed to us all to see him
leave the lively circle! and one and another would insist
on going to his room to cheer his solitude, but he was as
resolute to send us away, assuring us that he had a nice
time thinking.   He could not bear to think any one
troubled on his account."

The small salary and growing family compelled the
keeping of a home school at the Northborough Parsonage,
where the neighboring youth and the pastor's children
were prepared for the active duties of life, and for college.
The home school began when William was four years
old, and closed when he was fourteen.   Here he was prepared for college, with an additional year at the Roxbury
Latin School.   He entered Harvard in 1847, and graduated in 1851.   The winter of 1848–49 he taught school
at Lancaster in his native county, and the following winter at Fitchburg.   His vacations were usually spent at
home.   From a letter to a classmate in the summer of
1849, we get a glimpse of his vacation.   He says : "I have
been employed in manual labor (rather homœopathic that),
reading novels, visiting, singing and playing.   We have
got hold of some fine music of Mozart, Haydn, etc., and I
enjoy a perfect elysium in raising my voice to unheard of

pitch and sinking it beneath gloomy Acheron. I have been making violent efforts to play one of Beethoven's Waltzes on the piano, in which I succeed as well as might be expected. I pass pleasant minutes, too, in learning to play some of my mother's inexhaustible fund of Scotch tunes on the flute." He writes at this period of Burns, and of Channing, whose writings did much to shape his religious thinking.

After graduation, he was for three years a private teacher in the family of Mrs. Waller, in New York City. His life here was very pleasant; he made many friends, spent much time in the picture galleries of the city and heard the best operas and concerts. He is now twenty-one, and is thinking of a profession. He writes: "You will be gratified to know that I have decided to adopt the ministry. My great objection to it was that so many of my relatives had entered it that I did not wish to have it appear that it was a matter of course or of prescription. But I thought it my duty to look only at my obligation as a man, and not as an Allen or a Ware. And I thought there was a need for ministers, so I shall study theology. That I am decided upon." But seven months later he writes, "I do not feel competent yet to fix on a profession, although once I thought I had." His reasons for not entering the ministry probably were (1) the fear that his eyes, never very strong, would fail him, and (2) the hostile attitude of the Unitarian clergy towards Theodore Parker, whom he greatly admired.

The pleasant years went by. The impulse of the scholar was strong in him ; he longed for opportunity for broader study, and on September 7, 1854, two days after he had completed his twenty-fourth year, he sailed for Europe. The purpose of this voyage he tells in a letter to a friend: "My plan is to set sail in September and spend two years or more in Germany and Italy. If I can, I shall pass through England ; but, as I mean to be very economical both of time and money, I may have to save that for another trip. I want to understand Greece and Rome — their history and incidentally their language — feeling sure that, if I get a good knowledge of these, I can turn it to account in some way. My great fault has always been in being superficial. I do not know any one thing well, but I am determined that I will." Theodore Parker said, "In our Democracy nearly every man gets a mouthful of knowledge, few men get a full meal." Mr. Allen longed for a full meal, and determined to get it.

He landed at Liverpool, September 27; made a brief stay in England; visited Kenilworth Castle, Westminster Abbey, the British Museum, and a few other places of like interest; and then on October 11th sailed for Hamburg, and then to Berlin on the 14th, and five days later he matriculated in the University.

From Mr. Allen's diary, extending over more than forty years, we learn what he did, but not what he thought. "A diary," he said, "is for facts, and not for sentiment." The occurrences of nearly his whole life are there written down, very briefly, in neat, unspotted pages. In his diary at this period, we find a table of lectures attended by him at Berlin; we quote the lecturers and their subjects: "Haupt (Tibullus), Boeckh (Plato), Gerhard (Pausanias), Lepsius (Egypt), Curtius (Ancient Geography and Ancient History), Brugsch (Herodotus)."

To give a glimpse of his diary and to show the way his days passed at Berlin, we quote at random : —

"*October* 23, 1854.— Heard Haupt and Boeckh (three hours). To reading-room. In afternoon to Picture Gallery and Raumer's lecture. Called on Mr. White. In evening wrote.

"*October* 24.— To Professor Lepsius and Boeckh's lectures. In afternoon to Professors Curtius and Twesten. In evening wrote, and read Boeckh's 'Staatshaushaltung der Athener.'

"*October* 25.—Walked. To Trendelen urg's lecture, reading-room and Gerhard on Pausanias. With Goodwin to Picture Gallery. Hennings Garden."

"*November* 18.—Strabo. Herodotus. Grote and Bunsen. In afternoon called on Draper, and heard Bötticher on Ancient Temples. To tea to Professor Curtius."

"*November* 20.—Strabo, Grote and Herodotus. Brugsch sick. To opera with Goodwin —'Der Freischütz.' Thayer called. Bunsen."

"*November* 30.— Herodotus and Bunsen. Cut Lepsius and Brugsch. In afternoon read Burns. At 6 Thanksgiving dinner. Gilman [D. C. Gilman, President of Johns Hopkins University], Williams, 3 Bigelows, Draper, Chase, Goodwin, Bullions, Thayer and I."

"*March* 24.—Curtius. Chase called. Called with Goodwin on Professor Lepsius, with Goodwin and Dean on Alex. von Humboldt. Finished Curtius, and walked with Thayer to Stettin Bahnhof, etc. Met Vischer. In evening to tea at Fräulein Solmar's." The " Goodwin " so frequently referred to in the diary was his companion throughout his European trip, and is William Watson Goodwin, since 1860 the professor of Greek Literature in Harvard.

On the 31st of March, 1855, Mr. Allen left Berlin, and, stopping at Wittenberg, Leipzig, Weimar, and Wartburg Castle, journeyed to Göttingen and was matriculated, April 16. The professors most often named are Hermann, Wiezeler, Waitz, and Hoeck. He remained at Göttingen until October 2, 1855, when he started for Rome. On his way he stopped at Magdeburg, Berlin, Dresden, Prague, Venice, and Florence, and reached Rome November 7, where he remained until February 12, 1856. These three months he spent mainly in studying the topography of Rome, building up in his mind a picture of the city as it was in the time of the Cæsars. Then he went to Naples, and to Athens, spent thirteen days

in making a tour of the Peloponnesus, then to Marseilles
and to Paris. He remained in Paris for two weeks, then
to London, and sailed for home May 8, 1856, arriving in
Boston June 15.

From 1856 to 1863 he was the Associate Principal of
the West Newton English and Classical School. These
were not unprofitable years. They were years of reading,
writing, of living interest in men and institutions, of a
closer study of the new territory mapped out during his
two years in Germany.

On July 2, 1862, he married Mary Tileston, daughter of
Rev. Henry Lambert, of West Newton. In November,
1863, Mr. Allen, in the employ of the Freedman's Aid
Commission and accompanied by Mrs. Allen, went South
to begin the education of the Negroes at St. Helena
Island, off the coast of South Carolina. In a series of letters, which passed from household to household of his
family, he sets forth their experience. The plantations
had been swept and garnished. The houses were still
standing, but all the appliances of civilization were gone.
Robinson-Crusoe-like, they set about making themselves
comfortable. The empty windows were fitted with glass
brought from the North, and Mr. Allen painted the sash
with a mucilage brush. The handle of an old kettle-cover
was hammered into a door scraper with a brick for an
anvil; a stout barrel with the upper half partly sawed away
furnished the frame for an easy-chair; an old carriage
axle much bent and two cart-wheels were the basis of a
nondescript vehicle, and when the old white mule was attached the turnout was complete and fantastic. They had
a riding-horse whose " powers surpassed her inclinations."

The old house grew by degrees comfortable, and the
school was opened. All ages came, the children in the
morning, the men and women in the afternoon. Here
was an opportunity for the historian to note the decay of
the old order of things and the rise of the new. Men

and institutions were in the throes of a readjustment. To teach these ignorant blacks was in one sense a work of charity; and yet it was not unprofitable from an intellectual standpoint to this pupil of Lepsius and Curtius. He saw the significance of the changes going on around him. The dialect of the Negroes, their half-civilized, half-barbaric songs, their music as it was in slavery days and as it was then being modified by their new environments — all these things were a perpetual source of interest to him.

Mr. Allen and Mr. Charles P. Ware, his cousin, took down from the lips of these freedmen the music and words of their songs as they planted corn or picked cotton or waved to and fro and clapped their hands in the shout. These songs with others were published by Mr. Allen, Mr. Ware and Miss Lucy McKim, afterwards the wife of Wendell Phillips Garrison, under the title " Slave Songs of the United States." To this little volume Mr. Allen, as senior editor, wrote a highly interesting introduction, discussing at length the origin of the songs, and the linguistic peculiarities of the Negro dialect.

On the 12th of July, 1864, Mr. Allen came North, Mrs. Allen having preceded him several weeks. He remained at the North until the first of September, when he went as agent of the Sanitary Commission to Helena, Arkansas. He was here brought into official relation with the Union forces, the contraband camps, the hospitals and the colored schools. The history of the whole Sanitary Commission is told in his journal: the distribution of potatoes, pickles, onions, etc., in camp and hospital; the begging through Northern papers for sanitary supplies, the distribution of reading matter, the arrogance and red tape of military authorities, and through all the pathetic scenes in hospitals, and the destitution and grotesque humor of the contrabands in camp and school.

He came North in February, 1865. On March 23 his wife died, leaving an infant daughter, Katharine, born

February 17, 1865. On April 14, five days after Lee's surrender, he began a series of letters from Charleston, South Carolina, whither he had gone as Assistant Superintendent of the Charleston Schools. He lodged in the stately old home of Chancellor Dunkin, who was a classmate of Mr. Allen's father. There were ninety teachers, and the number of scholars enrolled was four thousand. Mr. James Redpath was the superintendent ; but, owing to the pressure of other duties, almost the entire work of superintendence and management of the schools fell upon Mr. Allen. His letters discuss the great problems of reconstruction, just then coming into definite form, the temper of the ex-rebels, the possibilities of the freedmen, who, as he says, "thought more of their new rights than of the new duties they brought." After the close of the schools for the year Mr. Allen came North, expecting to return in the fall.

It is hoped that Mr. Allen's family will yield to the many requests made for the publication of these Southern letters, and thus make a substantial contribution to the history of the closing days of the great Rebellion.

During the summer he received a call to the chair of Ancient Languages at Antioch College, Yellow Springs, Ohio. This he accepted ; but, owing to a bitter religious strife in the Governing Board, Professor Allen left at the close of his first year, and accepted a position in the Eagleswood Military Academy at Perth Amboy, New Jersey. In 1867, he accepted a call to the chair of Ancient Languages and History in the University of Wisconsin. A year later he received a call to the chair of Latin in Cornell University. He weighed the matter carefully, and finally decided to remain in Wisconsin, because there he could probably soonest devote his entire time to history. His chair was changed in 1870 to Latin and History, and in 1886 to History.

On June 30, 1868, he married Margaret Loring, the

daughter of John Andrews, Esq., of Newburyport, Massachusetts. She bore him three sons, Andrews, William Ware, and Philip.

"The life of a scholar," says Oliver Goldsmith, "seldom abounds with adventure : his fame is acquired in solitude." The story of the life of Mr. Allen from this time to the end is that of the scholar ; he is the busy college professor and the tireless student. In the summer vacations he usually went East, reaching Harvard for Commencement week, and spending July and August among his friends around Boston. He made a trip to the Yellowstone Park in the summer of 1884, and went for a tour through England and the south of Europe from April to August in 1885. These, with occasional trips in Wisconsin and neighboring States, to deliver lectures or addresses before societies or colleges, alone broke the steady flow of his life in the University. Such a life as that must be measured by its spiritual power as well as by its material product — a life that can best be known through its impress on others, as we know the ife of Arnold of Rugby or Mark Hopkins of Williams.

As a teacher he had profound learning, great ability in classification and arrangement of facts and principles, a rare power of exact statement, a simple sincerity that stooped to no pretence, and a love of truth that inspired to lofty endeavor. He was born a teacher, born with a "joyous readiness in communicating his acquisitions." But it was especially as a teacher of history that he excelled. "No historical fact is of any value," he said, "except so far as it helps us to understand human nature and the working of historic forces." He urged the students to go to the sources ; discarded text-book recitations and, so far as possible, regular lectures in favor of the topical system of study, and of the examination of original authorities. Under him students learned to study a subject rather than a book. He was a pioneer in this method

of teaching history. Says G. Stanley Hall, President of
Clark University, "The marvellous amount of work,
always of the highest kind, which he was able to turn off,
and the almost epoch-making modification in the teaching
of his department, which he has been so largely instru-
mental in bringing about, make his loss, especially coming
as it did before his work was done, a very grave one to
American scholarship." The student from the high school
or academy, who had studied the dry details of battles and
dynasties, and nothing more, gained in the study of history
under Professor Allen new interest and enthusiasm.

But it was something more than mere learning or great
intellectual ability that drew young men and women to
him. It was his sincerity, his unselfishness, his nobility
of soul, a certain moral attraction akin to gravitation,
that made him a joyful experience in their lives. His
character begot a tender, reverent affection for him in
all who came under his instruction. "Our loss in his
departure," said the student editors of the *University
Badger*, "is no greater than our gain in having once enjoyed his presence. To meet him and come to recognize
his wide research, his profound learning, his perfect sincerity, his unswerving devotion to the truth, was an inspiration. No man could come within his circle without
a spiritual uplift. To sit before him daily, to observe
his steady search for the true, the beautiful and the good,
to feel his sympathy for the right, to watch the pure
flame of his intellect till Promethean fire leaped from it
to your own, *that* was a liberal education. His very face
showed that whatsoever things are true, pure, lovely and
of good report, these were the subjects of his thoughts."

It was his delight to meet the Alumni and old students.
And on every journey, in whatever secluded place, as out
of the ground, they would rise to grasp his hand ; and
such gladness shone in their eyes that you would think
he had at some time done each a peculiar personal favor,

His correspondence with them was voluminous. Of no other professor in the University, perhaps, were aid and advice so frequently asked. His large private library was, in a broad sense, a public one — "the annex" it was called. From every quarter came requests for assistance: one is starting a reading club, and submits the plan and course for criticism and suggestion; another desires him to lay out a special course in historical reading. He, in some sense, directed and controlled a university above the University.

Mr. Allen's work as an author shows a remarkable versatility and prodigious industry. The bibliography published herewith exhibits his work in detail. I can here but indicate the lines of his literary activity. First, in the editing of Latin texts : with his brother Prentiss he published in 1861 a "Classical Handbook"; in 1868–69, with his brother Joseph he published a "Latin Reader," "Latin Lessons" and the "Manual Latin Grammar." His "Latin Composition" and the "Germania and Agricola of Tacitus" were published in 1870. He also furnished the historical and antiquarian matter for the text of various works of Cæsar, Cicero, Sallust, Ovid and Virgil, published by himself, his brother Joseph and Professor Greenough. A few months before his death he completed an edition of the "Annals of Tacitus" for the College Series edited by Professors Tracy Peck, of Yale, and Clement C. Smith, of Harvard.

He was a prolific essayist and reviewer. When only seven years of age, he was a constant contributor to a child's paper written fortnightly for a society to which he belonged; and he early became a contributor to the best magazines, writing usually on social, political and historical subjects. He did much literary work for *The Nation.* Beginning with its fourth issue, hardly a number appeared until his death without something from his pen. Most of his work as a reviewer appeared in its pages. Says *The Nation* of December 12, 1889: "His range as a reviewer was very wide, embracing ornithology, political economy, history (ancient and modern, European, Oriental and American), English literature and the classical languages and literature. *The Nation* in particular feels that in his departure it has lost a part of itself."

Wendell Phillips Garrison, one of the editors of *The Nation*, in speaking of Professor Allen as a political writer, says: "His historical studies, though by inheritance congenial to his mind, were pursued with other aims than mere intellectual amusement, and led up to principles of private conduct and maxims of government. I do not think our literary men, as a class, are divorced from politics in the nobler sense; but it is somewhat uncommon for them to give public expression to their political ideas, and engage editorially in current debate through the press. It is not every one, indeed, who can command the different styles needed for the two kinds of writing, excessive cultivation of either of which tends to unfit a man for the other. Professor Allen was not, perhaps, equally at home in both; but he practiced both at will and successfully. His interest in national affairs never abated; he was a dispassionate observer and a true independent."

He was one of the founders of the Wisconsin Academy of Sciences, Arts and Letters, and at nearly every session the programme was enriched by his contributions. He was also one of the founders of the Madison Literary Club. Of his papers before this club, Dr. John Bascom wrote: "He always bore us by his manner, his appearance and the matter of his paper, into the clear, sweet air of knowledge, and gave us a spiritual lift in the world of insight and reflection. We felt under his words, as when gentle winds strike indolent sails, a sense of motion and the hope of better things. The serene spirit with which he came to urgent, practical questions, taking simply and quietly the honey of truth from its deep cups and secret places, was a marvel to us, often full of more passionate, even petulant, endeavor."

As a scholar he was versatile and yet profound. His purpose in 1854 to know one thing well was steadily adhered to. To know the history of Rome, "to know its events, its personages, its literature, its thought in every department, political, religious, philosophical, its science, its industry and art, and then to be familiar with the manifestations of all these in the every-day life of the people, the manners and customs, the dress and furniture, the institutions and modes of procedure, the transient phases of thought and tricks of speech"—all this he proposed to himself. For thirty-five years he studied primitive institutions, their rise and development under all possible environments ; the primitive life of Rome and of the Middle Ages became mutually interpretative; the customs and manners of the Romans were studied by the side of those of the Greeks, the Teutons and the Orientals.

He left no adequate memorial of his scholarship. Said *The Nation,* " In this domain [history] he never had the leisure to produce a work commensurate with his knowledge and powers." At any time for ten years before his death he was ready to write an enduring historical work; but his work in the University left him neither the time nor the physical strength. What he has written might properly be termed "Chips from a Historian's Workshop."

In 1878 he delivered, in the Johns Hopkins University, a course of twenty lectures upon the History of the Fourteenth Century. He published at various times the historical monographs in this volume, which have won for him the high regard of scholars both at home and abroad. For several years he reported for the *Revue Historique* the important historical works published in America — a work of considerable importance and magnitude, now being done by the department of history at Johns Hopkins Uni-

versity.   On the night before he died he finished reading
the proof of his most important work, "A Brief History
of the Roman People," a text-book for high schools and
colleges, the plan and scope of which had been outlined
as early as 1861.   To verify his work, he made his trip to
Southern Europe in the summer of 1887.

He fostered original research ; saw with joy the treasures of the State Historical Society of Wisconsin increase
from year to year, especially the materials of history — the
journals and letters of the first traders and pioneers and
of the discoverers and conquerors of the great North-
west ; the records of Indian life ; the brief annals of the
early settlers in county, town and village histories.   A
crumpled, faded letter or manuscript was to him a joy,
if it threw but a ray of light upon the past.   With such
accumulations, he believed that at the University would
arise a great school of American History.   Professor
Tracy Peck pays this fitting tribute to Mr. Allen : "His
great attainments in several fields of research, his catholic
taste and interests, the openness and alertness of his
mind, his joyous readiness in communicating his acquisitions and the genuine modesty and nobility of his character made him a permanent honor to scholarship and to
life."

The Rev. Joseph H. Crooker writes of Mr. Allen as a
Unitarian : "Mr. Allen, while an earnest and loyal Unitarian, justly proud of his religious heritage and enthusiastic for the spread of our gospel, yet cared more for the
truth than for mere names, and he was vastly more anxious to bring in the kingdom of heaven than to win con-
verts to his own theological opinions.   He was absolutely
free from the sectarian spirit, he judged every religious
body in a generous and appreciative manner, he saw the
good in all our churches as though himself a communi-
cant, he thought of believers in creeds radically unlike
his own at their best, he had a profound respect for the

religious opinions and even prejudices of others which re-
strained him from both criticism and dogmatism respect-
ing religious matters, and yet he was a man of firm convictions, which he carried frankly and openly through all
his life, always anxious that people know his position,
always anxious to co-operate in every possible but appropriate way for the advancement of liberal Christianity
and always interested in the progress of our faith among
young people — a man who combined in even balance as
rare as it is beneficent the poise of a rationalist with the
zeal of a Churchman, the critical temper of the student
with the abundant enthusiasm of a philanthropist. . . . He
had no religion apart from his daily life. He did not have
a religion : he himself was essential religion ; for the interior principle which shone out from him, as continuously
as light from the sun, was love to God and man. He
never assumed any superiority, and he was never denun-
ciatory, and yet he moved among us as a genial day of
judgment. He was gentle and unobtrusive ; and still he
made himself a persuasive monitor in the hearts of the
multitude, because his piety was so deep and genuine."

He was for seven years president of the Wisconsin Unitarian Conference, one of the founders of the Unitarian
church in Madison, and, since its organization, a member
of its board of trustees. His philanthropy found expression through the Madison Benevolent Society and the
Wisconsin Humane Society and in a thousand acts of
gracious kindness to students and neighbors. Every man,
woman and child who knew him was his friend and
lover.

Professor Allen was generally in good health. In January, 1888, he had a severe attack of pneumonia, which left
his lungs in a sensitive condition. The 3d of December,
1889, he contracted a severe cold, but was not considered
seriously ill. He was confined to his bed, but continued
to work, reading the proof of his " History of the Roman

People." On the evening of December 8, he completed the proof-reading, saying, "It is finished." He was still cheerful and hopeful, and expected to resume his work in the University in a few days. He passed a disturbed night ; in the morning he made some pleasant remark, then quietly fell into that sleep that knows no waking. In compliance with his request, he was buried in the beautiful cemetery at Madison, near the great University where his life-work was done.

Such was William Francis Allen. Nature kindly gave his blood a moral flow, the elements in him were so mixed as to produce a man. We should be grateful for his having lived, even had he done nothing that survived. "Common souls pay with what they do ; nobler souls with that which they are." Like the good Ben Adhem, he loved his fellow-men, and so added to the sum of human joy that, "were every one to whom he did some loving service to bring a blossom to his grave, he would sleep beneath a wilderness of sweet flowers." His face had caught while here the light of other worlds. As some sweet odor consumes itself in its forth-giving, so the earth life of the great scholar and teacher, the ideal citizen, neighbor and friend, spent itself in beautiful beneficence. He was a type of the coming man, a hint of the day when justice and culture and beauty and reverence shall dwell in their fulness among men.

Upon a marble tablet in the First Unitarian Church of Madison is the following inscription : —

In Memory of
WILLIAM FRANCIS ALLEN
1830–1889.
Twenty-two Years a Professor
in the
University of Wisconsin.
The first President and for eleven years
A Trustee of this Church.

*   *   *   *

A man of varied, exact, and broad scholarship.
A teacher of creative power and original methods.
A wise, sincere, and generous friend.
A citizen, active and efficient
in all movements for
Education, Reform, and Philanthropy.
A Lover of Flowers, Poetry, and Music.

———

Gentle, Strong, and Pure.

———

Erected by the members of this Church.
1890.

ESSAYS.

A DAY WITH A ROMAN GENTLEMAN.*

IT is a little surprising, considering how accurate is our knowledge of the poetry, philosophy, and art, the wars, religion, and political institutions of the ancients, that we have so vague a notion of them as men and women — find it so hard to imagine how they looked, dressed, and lived, how they spent their time, what they thought and talked about, in common every-day affairs. The Greeks and Romans are, after all, very unreal to us — hardly more than names which represent and embody certain conceptions of art, literature, and thought. We know them only in the monuments they have left — the books, statues, and temples; and we scarcely think of them as actually living, any more than these. We see statues of Pitt and Washington, robed in a costume which we know they would have shuddered at; and it is hard to conceive that Demosthenes, Sophocles, and Augustus actually looked as we see them represented in marble. A boy who has labored through Cæsar, Cicero, and Virgil, has an indistinct idea that these men he has been reading about spent their lives in waging war, sitting in the Senate, and founding cities, offering solemn sacrifices to the gods, or attending gladiatorial shows and the games of the Circus. He cannot imagine to himself people *talking* Latin: that stately tongue seems to him to exist only in periods and hexameters, and to disdain the sordid uses of petty traffic or the trivialities of fashionable small-talk. Nor do books or antiquities help him much. They give, it is true, the dry facts, and these are indispensable materials to a knowledge of the life; but they are only materials, after all — the body without the soul.

* From *Hours at Home*, vol. 10, p. 389 (March, 1870).

Nevertheless, the Romans did have a private and domestic life ; their character had a light and amiable aspect,
as well as that sterner one which is more familiar. They
ate and drank; dressed and bathed; had their clothes
washed and mended, and their shoes patched ; wore wigs
and false teeth. The boys played with marbles, tops,
hoops, and balls ; the women gossiped and went shopping;
the men speculated, drove bargains, and shaved notes,
quarrelled, jested, and flirted.

Nothing helps so much to realize the daily life of the
ancients as a visit to Pompeii, the city buried by an irruption of Vesuvius, eighteen hundred years ago, and now at
last restored to light. Here you enter gateways through
which Pompeian gentlemen drove with their wives ; you
tread streets, paved with solid stone, rutted with the
wheels. You enter the doors of houses, over the floors of
elegant mosaic, and stand within the walls, in some
cases under the roofs, where men and women of that distant age lived. You see what sort of rooms they lived in,
the taste with which their walls were adorned — not
gaudy, mouldering wall-paper, but exquisite paintings,
with colors still bright and forms still distinct. You
might see the furniture, too; but it has been removed
to the museum. You enter drinking-shops and bakeries,
baths, temples, theatres, forum and exchange, and see the
marks of daily life about you — the defacements of ordinary use, even the scribblings and caricatures on the
walls. In the great museum of Naples you see the articles that have been removed from these houses — chairs
and tables of most elegant shape, in bronze or marble (the
wood, of course, has perished), kettles, jars, saucepans,
steelyards, pitchers, cups, strainers, frying-pans, jelly-
moulds, even carbonized loaves of bread; combs, pins,
needles, thimbles, locks and keys, saws, planes, spades,
pickaxes, chisels, lamps — in short, nearly all the com-
monest implements of every-day use are found there,

many of them the very counterpart of ours, and many much more elegant than we ever see.   But these are only the appendages of life, not the life itself.

Whoever shall desire, a hundred or a thousand years hence, to obtain a vivid and accurate picture of the daily life of us who are living now in the middle of the nineteenth century, will not look for it in the historians and poets alone.   From Macaulay and Motley, Longfellow, Browning, and Tennyson, he will get one view of it ; and, if he could look at it but from one side, that, no doubt, is the one he would choose — just as we would not, if we could, give up the records that we possess of the higher thought of the ancients in exchange for the most intimate acquaintance with their outward habits and manners. But he will not need to stop at this ; he will go to our newspapers, novelists, and caricaturists to piece out the partial knowledge of our age which he has obtained from the higher walks of literature.   Now of Greek and Roman literature we have hardly anything which represents prose fiction and periodicals ; and this is the chief reason that life in antiquity is not made to look natural to us, as ours will to our posterity.

The ancients were not, it is true, entirely destitute of these two branches of literature.   There are still extant two or three Roman novels, rather low and grotesque in character, and giving only a very limited view of society ; invaluable for the picture of life which they present, if we bear in mind that this picture is at once partial and exaggerated.   There was a sort of newspaper, too, in Rome during the Empire, a daily register of all matters of general interest, issued by public authority and called the *Acta Diurna.*   Tacitus, the historian, alludes to it when, apologizing for the barrenness of events of a certain year, he adds that he might have filled up space with a description of the new amphitheatre ; but that sort of thing is for the newspapers : it is below the dignity of history.   And again, in his eloquent account of the death of Thrasea, the most illustrious of the victims of Nero, the sycophants who accuse Thrasea of treason tell the emperor, in order to inflame his jealousy and suspicion, that in the provinces and the army the journal is read chiefly in order to see how Thrasea votes in the Senate — what measures he disapproves. The satirist Juvenal, too, in describing the cruelty of a noble Roman lady, says that she has her slaves flogged in her presence, while she herself is gossiping with her crony, or admiring a new dress, or reading the news. This morning journal was no doubt copied by hand from the official copy by persons who made this a regular business, and furnished, like books, to wealthy nobles or sent abroad. Would that somebody had thought it worth his while to preserve a file of them for our eyes! After all, they probably contained only a meagre chronicle of events, and would have served us very little in getting at the domestic life of the Romans.

The poets, especially Martial, and the letter-writers abound in the information we are in search of. The light, fashionable poets, not aiming to rival the lofty strains of Homer and Æschylus, but to tickle the ear of the crowd, fill their writings with the jests and repartees and familiar allusions which make up the small-talk of the day. The comedies of Plautus and Terence introduce the men and women of that age before our eyes, and give us their conversation, witty or trivial, often earnest and abounding in matter. But the private letters of Cicero, Pliny, and others are still better fitted to give us an idea of the personality of the best representatives of the Roman character; for Plautus and Terence lay their scenes chiefly among the uncultivated classes; Propertius and Martial delighted in dissolute and fashionable society. But the private correspondence of Cicero and the Younger Pliny is very voluminous, interesting, and instructive. From this we learn of the family relations of these distinguished men, their warm friendships, their elevated thoughts and sentiments, their genial and playful social intercourse, their manner of doing business and their mode of life. Whoever is disgusted with the indecency of Ovid and Petronius, or shocked at the bloodthirsty proscriptions of Sulla and Octavianus, or the terrible scenes of the amphitheatre, should turn to these letters of Cicero to his wife and brother and friend Atticus, or those of Pliny to the Emperor Trajan and the historian Tacitus, to have his faith in humanity quickened.

It has been remarked that, next to the failure to recognize the common element of humanity in different communities and at different ages, there is no more fundamental mistake than not to recognize the essential differences in these different communities and ages. And, when we compare the Greeks and Romans with the civilized people of the present day, we find, perhaps, no more vital cause of contrast — even more striking, perhaps, in manners and customs than in thoughts and feelings — than this: that we are farther removed from primitive barbarism than they, by a difference of several hundred years. The Romans were as great barbarians five hundred years before Christ as our ancestors were a thousand years ago. The savage fierceness which only shows itself at rare intervals among Europeans nowadays, when humanity seems cast aside for a time, and man makes himself a beast — as in the French Revolution, the Indian revolt of 1857, the military prisons of Andersonville and Belle Isle, and the massacre at Fort Pillow — this fierceness never wholly disappeared from the Roman character. Humane gentlemen, like Cicero and Pliny, were the exception; for a few such as these the Stoic philosophy had accomplished what Christianity has done for the mass of men in modern times; but of the majority of the Romans it may be said that, with all the externals of civilization, they were through and through barbarians. Napoleon

said, "Scratch a Russian, and you find a Tartar." So
with the Romans : the polished, merciful Augustus was
only the treacherous, bloody, lustful Octavianus under another name. "It is noble to be avenged on one's ene-
mies" — this was the sentiment of that model of Roman
matrons, Cornelia, mother of the Gracchi.

This semi-barbarous nature of the Romans, this nearness
in time to the forests in which they had their origin, has
wider and more varied effects than one sees at first sight.
The Roman house, for instance, never departed very far in
principle from the simple cabin in which it took its rise.
There was always the one central room, or hall, out of
which the smaller rooms opened — the *atrium*, from *ater*,
black, because its walls were blackened with smoke —
which was at once kitchen, dining-room, bedroom, and sit-
ting-room, just as is the case in the log cabins of the present day. But the Romans never wholly outgrew this.
When they built larger houses, the atrium was always
the chief feature. They had separate sleeping apart-
ments, but here stood the symbolical bed; they had their
cooking done out of sight, but here remained the symbolical hearth; they had banqueting-rooms, courts, colon-
nades, boudoirs, and spacious parlors, but the atrium was
always the centre of the house. Here the Roman noble
received his clients and friends ; here were the images of
his ancestors, and all his family heirlooms. The narrow
chink in the roof through which the smoke escaped was
widened into a broad *impluvium;* the smoky rafters became cedar beams, carved and gilded, and supported
sometimes by marble columns ; the earthen floor was
laid with mosaic, statues stood between the columns,
and the central space, open to the sky, was paved with
even blocks of stone — so the poor dark atrium of Cincinnatus and Fabricius was transformed into an open
court, surrounded with cloisters. But, however elegant
might be the later ornaments of the hall, there was still

always room for the simple waxen images of the fore-
fathers and the rude wooden statuettes of the household
gods.

Neither did the Romans ever make common use of
chimneys or windows. The hole in the roof was still the
outlet for the smoke in most private houses. It must,
however, be remarked that in that mild climate the usual
heating apparatus was an iron or bronze pan for charcoal,
such as is still in use in Italy, and that large houses were
warmed by pipes of hot air, running under the floor, like
our furnaces. The windows were small and high, and
usually closed with wooden shutters. It was not an object with them to look at the street, or, if they ever
wished to do this, they made use of balconies : the windows were only for light and air. About the time of the
Empire, windows of mica came in use, and glass was also
employed for this purpose, although not extensively ; for
cups, vases, etc., it was a common material, and was manufactured with great skill.

Again, take the dress. What is the Roman *toga* but
the Indian blanket? somewhat altered in shape, to be
sure, and worn in a peculiar and distinctive manner, but
unmistakably inherited from that period when a single
piece of woollen cloth was the sole garment. Indeed, even
in the earlier years of the Roman Republic, we read of
persons clad in the toga alone. Afterwards the *tunic* was
introduced, a garment almost precisely like the sleeveless
shirt, with a belt about the waist, which also served as a
purse; and, until toward the close of the Republic, this,
with the toga and a pair of shoes, formed the entire dress
of a Roman gentleman. The toga was a large blanket of
unbleached wool, approaching the shape of a semicircle,
but broad in proportion to its length. One end was thrown
from behind over the left shoulder, hanging down over the
left arm, and reaching nearly to the feet; it was then
brought round from behind under the right arm, the curv-

ing edge hanging nearly to the ground, and the other end thrown back over the left shoulder. The right arm was in this way left free, the left being quite covered. To wear the toga, and wear it in this formal and artificial manner, was the peculiar right of a Roman citizen; and great pains were taken by fops to make it hang gracefully, in folds prepared and pressed out over night. And not merely was it the exclusive right of a Roman citizen to wear this, but it was a breach of decorum for him to be dressed in any other way, when performing his duties as a citizen. The officer sent to announce to Cincinnatus his appointment as dictator found him ploughing in the field, *nudus*, or "naked," meaning by this, perhaps, in the tunic alone. "Clothe yourself," said the messenger, "that I may lay before you the commands of the Senate." Then he directed his wife to bring his toga from the house, washed himself, put on the toga, and listened to the message. In later times the citizens were less scrupulous about this. It is related of the Emperor Augustus that, seeing one day in the assembly a crowd of people dressed in the *pallium* (a Greek garment), he repeated indignantly the words of Virgil, *Romanos rerum dominos gentemque togatam* (the Romans, lords of the earth, and the race that wears the toga), and ordered the ædiles thereafter to admit no one into the Forum or Circus without a toga — much as, in the Rome of the present day, no man is admitted to certain festivals without a dress coat. Again, Cicero, in his fiery invective against Mark Antony, contrasts the manner of his own entrance into the city with that of his enemy: "I came by daylight, not in the dark; in shoes and toga, not sandals and cloak" — the shoes and toga being the fit and becoming dress of a Roman Senator, while sandals and cloak were indications of foreign manners.

A clumsy garment like this, worn in so formal a style, might make an imposing appearance in the Senate, as it certainly gives dignity and grace to a statue; but it must have been sadly in the way when there was anything to be done, especially anything that required the use of both hands. In point of fact, it was purely a show garment, laid aside when there was any work to be done; in the army it was exchanged for a military cloak. Moreover, it was worn only by citizens; and the Roman citizens for the most part practiced no handicrafts — it was slaves, freedmen, and foreigners that carried on the petty trades and mechanical arts at Rome. The poor citizen — ignorant, needy, vicious, it might be — was entitled by virtue of his citizenship to live without labor. He received corn gratuitously, or for a nominal sum, from the State; he fastened himself upon some wealthy patron, and was fed by him; but work he would not. He was a Roman citizen — one of the lords of the earth. To attend the public assemblies and courts of justice, the gladiatorial shows, the theatres, the baths, and the games in the Circus — these were the lofty employments in which he passed his days, and to these the sweeping toga was no hindrance. But as soon as his duties as a citizen were over, or if he had any manual task to perform — and tilling the earth was always a respectable occupation, however despised the tradesman and mechanic might be — the Roman doffed his uncomfortable garments of state. When he entered his house, he exchanged his shoes for sandals or slippers, and put on an easy gown of any color to suit his taste. So in bad weather, or travelling, he wore a rough cloak and a hat.

De Quincey says, in one of his brilliant but overwrought descriptions: " The Roman was the idlest of men. ' Man and boy ' he was ' an idler in the land.' He called himself and his pals ' rerum dominos gentemque togatam,' the gentry that wore the · toga. Yes, and a pretty affair that ' toga ' was. Just figure to yourself, reader, the picture of a hard-working man, with horny hands, like our hedgers, ditchers, weavers, porters, etc., setting to work on the highroad in that vast sweeping toga, filling with a strong gale like the mainsail of a frig- ate. ... Had there been nothing left as a memorial of the Romans but that one relic, their immeasurable toga, we should have known that they were born and bred to idle- ness. In fact, except in war, the Roman never did any- thing at all but sun himself. ... The public ration at all times supported the poorest inhabitant of Rome, if he were a citizen. Hence it was that Hadrian was so astonished with the spectacle of Alexandria, 'civitas opulenta, fæcunda, in qua nemo vivat otiosus' (a rich, populous city, in which no one lives idle). Here first he saw the spectacle of a vast city, second only to Rome, where every man had something to do. ... This pro- digious spectacle (so it seemed to Hadrian) was ex- hibited in Alexandria, of all men earning their bread in the sweat of their brow. In Rome only (and at one time in some of the Grecian states) it was the very meaning of *citizen* that he should vote and be idle." *

In this proud contempt for labor we see another illus- tration of the nearness of the Romans to barbarism ; it is exactly the characteristic of savages.

The complete dress, then, of a Roman Senator was tunic, toga, and shoes — a marvellous contrast to the complicated suit that is worn by Mr. Gladstone or Gen- eral Grant. But the less hardy generations of the Empire found this insufficient. Many, even, during the Republic, wore two tunics, and leggings reaching not quite to the knee — pantaloons were despised as a barbarian institu- tion, and a mark of effeminacy. About the same time hats began to be more generally worn, and we are told that Augustus, simple and conservative as he was in his

* Two or three inaccuracies in this extract may be noticed. The hard-handed farmer did wear the toga, but of course not when working on the highway. Again, it was not until late in the Republic that corn was distributed to the people, and even then only at a reduced rate at first, and not enough at that to support a family without labor.

tastes and habits, always wore a hat in the sun to shield
him from its rays. The dress of the women was originally the same as that of the men. But in course of time
the *stola* was established as their distinctive garment —
an outer tunic reaching to the feet ; over this a shawl
(*palla*) instead of the toga, and generally sandals instead
of shoes. If they wished to cover their heads, they used
a shawl, or at most a hood, such as men also wore sometimes in bad weather. The wife of a Roman nobleman
cost him nothing for bonnets !

The civil and political institutions of the ancients be-
tray still more unequivocal marks of their nearness to
barbarism, especially in the remarkable degree in which
the primitive patriarchal institutions remained in force.
Whatever might be the station or power attained by a
Roman citizen in his public career, he was at home, so
long as his father lived — and his wife and children as
well — a slave of that father; nor could he himself become a *paterfamilias*, or head of a family, until his
father's death. Nay, more, not only did the father possess this authority, but it was out of his power to divest
himself of it, except by the fictitious process of selling
the son as a slave, with the understanding that the purchaser would manumit him. Even this did not make the
young man free. He reverted again to his father's authority; and, in order to make his emancipation complete,
it was necessary to repeat this process three times.
Then, thrice sold and thrice manumitted, he stood a free
citizen, and a *paterfamilias* himself. This power ex-
tended even to life and death. A Roman magistrate —
vast as his power was — dared not put a citizen to death
without formal trial. Cicero himself never recovered
from the obloquy that he incurred by venturing to pun-
ish with death the leaders in the conspiracy of Catiline
without due form of law; and yet he was backed by all
the authority of the Senate. But at that very time

Aulus Fulvius, a man known to us by this one act alone, exercised, unchallenged, unrebuked, and irresponsibly, this power denied to the consul, by beheading his own son, in his own court-yard, by his own sole authority.

Another ancient custom, still more prevalent among the Greeks than the Romans, reveals the element of barbarism still more startlingly — the common and recognized practice of infanticide. When a child was born, it was for the father to say whether it should be reared or not. It was laid at his feet, and, if he lifted it up — *sustulit* — this was interpreted as an expression of his willingness to undertake its support. In one of the comedies of Terence, an old bachelor, remonstrating with his married brother that he is too penurious toward his two sons, says, " You lifted them both up, knowing just what means you had, with the expectation that what you had would be enough for both of them." If the father did not "lift up" the child, he was considered to have disowned it ; and it was put to death, generally by being exposed in a forest and suffered to perish. An old law of Rome forbade exposing boys unless deformed, or the eldest daughter — with younger daughters the practice was common, for women were of little account in those times, as is illustrated by the fact that girls had no distinctive names. The sons were Marcus, Publius, Lucius, Titus ; but their sisters had nothing but the family name : Cornelia, Lucretia, Licinia, numbered first, second, and so on, as many as there chanced to be.

Still, the Roman women were not wholly without honor. Their position was far superior to that of any other women of antiquity, both in the respect shown them and in the character by which they earned this respect. The typical Roman matron is a fitting mate of the typical Roman Senator ; there is the same heroic, lofty spirit and intrepid bearing in her, too, as in him, not unmixed with the characteristic fierceness of the nation. Cicero mentions several women whose refined culture, especially in the use of the Latin language, was noted, and had exercised a powerful influence upon the male members of their family. And Roman history is illustrated by the names of women in whom strength of character was not inconsistent with the more womanly graces — from Cornelia, the mother of the Gracchi, to Arria, the wife of Pætus, who, when her husband hesitated to put himself to death at the command of the tyrant, herself plunged the dagger in her own bosom, and handed it to him with the words, " Pætus, it does not hurt."

> "When Arria from her wounded side
> To Pætus gave the reeking steel,
> 'I feel not what I've done,' she cried,
> 'What Pætus is to do I feel.'" *

It may be that we do not habitually do justice to the family relations of the Romans; their sternness and fierceness overshadow their finer qualities. But family affections appear to have been very strong and tender, especially between brothers, as we see in Cicero's correspondence with his brother Quintus. The marriage relation was also, with the best Romans, a very happy one. And here is a striking and noteworthy fact. There is throughout ancient literature hardly a trace of the passion which we call peculiarly "love." Marriage was a concern managed entirely by the parents, who exercised the power, as they had the right, to betroth son or daughter as they pleased. The young lady lived a very retired, secluded life indoors, hardly seeing any male acquaintances; and as for falling in love, forming an attachment which should result in marriage, the thought hardly occurred to her. But although the marriage relation was thus entered into, not from personal inclination, but from a sense of duty, with no people has it been held more sacred, and have there been more shining ex-

---

* Martial, Hoadley's translation.

amples of a true and happy union, than among the Romans of the Republic. The reason was that a religious sense of duty governed both husband and wife. There was no nonsense of elective affinities, and spiritual attraction, and uncongeniality of temper, to destroy harmony and happiness; but both parties to a contract not made by themselves, but which they deemed an irrevocable one, felt themselves bound by every consideration of manly honor and womanly devotion to do their full duty in the position in which the gods had placed them. Until luxury and corruption had crept in and undermined the very foundations of morality, this was the nature of wedlock — the strong foundation on which the Roman family rested; and even through all the debauchery and degeneracy of the Empire we never fail, now and then, to catch a sight of beautiful examples of genuine Roman manhood and womanhood united in a marriage bond as holy and indissoluble as in the palmiest days of the Republic.

It may perhaps be of interest at this point to copy the inscription upon the sepulchre of a Roman matron — it is the stone which speaks : —

> " Brief, traveller, is my message — pause and read it.
>   The poor stone covers a beautiful woman.
>   Her parents named her Claudia :
>   With single love she loved her one husband;
>   Two sons she bore — one she left behind her on earth,
>   The other she buried in the bosom of the earth.
>   She was becoming in speech and noble in mien ;
>   Cared well for her household, and span.   I am finished — Go."

Another feature of family life remains to be mentioned : the slaves, so important a portion of the Roman household as to be called peculiarly " the family." American slavery gives no adequate idea of Roman slavery. The slaves in this country were of a different race and a different color, vastly inferior to their masters in ability and

education.   In Rome, on the other hand, by the side of
natives of various barbarous tribes, who were employed
only in the rudest branches of industry (a class which
corresponds in character and position to the American
slaves) — by the side of these there were slaves brought
from all the most polished nations of the world — Greeks,
Egyptians, Syrians, Asiatics — and their functions in the
household were commensurate with their talents and
attainments.   The steward of the estate, the tutor of the
children, the librarian, the secretary — all were slaves.   A
wealthy Roman possessed troops of slaves of all kinds —
it was his pride not to be obliged to go beyond his own
farms and his own " family " to supply all his wants.   But
in nothing was the native barbarity of the Romans more
glaringly exhibited than in their treatment of these un-
fortunates.   The vindictive excesses of passion which are
related as the rare exceptions in the treatment of the
negroes of the South were every-day affairs with the
Romans.   If the life of the Roman citizen could not be
touched, that of the slave was cheap enough.   Nor was
the brutal passion of the master satisfied with killing — it
must be death by torture — by the cross — or it might be
by being thrown into the fish-pond to fatten the lampreys.
After a servile insurrection in Sicily, twenty thousand
slaves in that one island were crucified along the high-
ways.

The horrors of Roman slavery — more terrible than it
is easy for us to conceive of — were, however, somewhat
mitigated by the commonness of emancipation.   The
freedmen, or emancipated slaves, were so numerous as to
form a class by themselves, and a very important one.
But although free, and thus no longer exposed to the
grossest abuses of slavery, the freedman still remained in
a relation of dependence upon his former master, and was
known not merely as freedman (*libertinus*), but as *his*
freedman (*libertus*).   His relation to his patron did not

differ materially from that of the client, only that he was considered bound to perform for him whatever services were in his power, almost as when he was a slave. Nothing is more common than to meet with accounts of freedmen who acted as the confidential servants or agents of their patrons ; and this, it would seem, without any regular remuneration, except their favor and patronage, and the hope of a legacy. The slave gained by his emancipation, therefore, principally the right to own property and the exemption from abuse, not the freedom from the obligation to service.

It has been said that the freedmen were practically on the footing of *clients.* Every poorer man in Rome found it necessary to attach himself to some one of the nobles as his protector, and, so to speak, his representative. Rome was through and through an aristocratic State. The idea of equal rights for all would have been a strange one in those days. It was only through the favor and assistance of some powerful noble that any inferior citizen could hope for redress in any grievance, or justice in any suit. Every nobleman was by virtue of his position a lawyer, as well as a statesman and a soldier ; and it was his duty to protect his clients, to defend them in any case at law, and to act for them in all important affairs. Both parties were benefited by this ; for the noble derived much of his dignity and influence from the number of his clients.

Having thus given a general outline of the Roman household and its members — the *paterfamilias*, the wife, the children, the slaves, freedmen, and clients — let us take up the history of a single day, to see how this family lived. Two or three ancient writers have given us detailed accounts of the manner in which the day was spent; the briefest of these, and the best fitted for our purpose, is contained in an epigram of Martial, a popular poet, who lived about a century after Christ. It should be premised that the Romans divided the day, from sunrise to sunset, into twelve equal hours, varying, therefore, in length at the different seasons of the year.

> "Two hours the clients crowd your stately halls;
>   The third the lawyers bellow themselves hoarse.
> Work till the fifth, the sixth for quiet calls,
>   Then through the seventh all business runs its course.
> The eighth hour baths and exercise you need;
>   The ninth hour spread your table; and your friends
> Listen, the tenth, while you my verses read,—
>   What were a feast unless the Muse attends?"

We will now follow out this programme hour by hour. Let us personify our account, and call our nobleman by the aristocratic name of Paullus Æmilius.

The Roman rises early — commonly by daybreak. It does not take him long to make his toilet. The bathing and shaving come in the afternoon; and there are no strings or buttons to fasten, no collar to put on, no cravat to tie, no waistcoat, pantaloons, stockings or underclothes, no watch or pocket-knife, no hat or gloves. He slips himself easily into his tunic, and fastens around his waist a belt which has a money-pouch attached to it. A slave ties his shoes and folds his toga gracefully about him, and he steps from his bedroom into the atrium, already crowded with eager and obsequious visitors. Here is a tenant of one of his farms, come to pay his rent; here a freedman in attendance, to see if his patron has any commands for him; here is the steward of his villa, with his monthly report; here is a yeoman who owns a small piece of land near his villa, and has attached himself to his wealthy neighbor as a client — he comes bringing a gift of a fat capon, and tells a story of some outrage committed by the bailiff of another nobleman, and begs for protection; here is a city client, who is involved in a suit at law, and comes to consult Æmilius; here is a crowd of needy parasites, whose whole living is derived from the daily allowance given them by their patrons ; they present themselves at more than one hall every morning, and the bargain is reckoned a fair one — the consideration and distinction derived from a numerous body of clients, and their votes when the patron is a candidate for any office, are well worth the trifling cost of their gratuities. In attending upon these visitors an hour or two passes. An educated slave no doubt attends his master to take notes, if necessary.

The morning salutation being over, Æmilius partakes of a slight breakfast of bread and figs or olives — alas! the Romans knew not coffee, nor buckwheat cakes, nor waf- fles, nor rolls and butter. If the morning was chilly, and they wished a warm breakfast, there was the favorite *calda*, wine mixed with hot water, probably spiced, and sweetened, if at all, with honey — for sugar they had not. After this frugal breakfast, Æmilius betakes himself to the Forum, or market-place, to attend to the business of the day. Every town or city of the ancients — like every European town of the present day — had its open square, or market- place (*forum*), as the centre of all business, public and pri- vate. Around this, or in its neighborhood, were the most important temples and other public buildings. Here courts of justice and public assemblies were held, originally in the open air. The public assemblies, indeed, were always held in the open air. The courts of justice sat in later time in the Basilica, an open hall, used also by the mer- chants as an exchange. Æmilius, therefore, proceeds to the Senate, if the Senate is in session to-day — for, being a permanent body, all its members residing in Rome, it sits only when there is business to be transacted ; if there is no Senate, to the Basilica which his father had erected, to attend the trial of a case in which he is interested ; or, if there is a public assembly, to the Forum, to hear Pollio or Messala address the people ; or, if there is neither Senate assembly nor court, he attends to his own private con-

cerns, lounges in the Basilica or on the Forum, and talks
with his friends on the news from Parthia or Spain, or on
the prospect of an outbreak between the triumvirs, Mark
Antony and Octavianus.

In this way the hours of the forenoon pass, and at
noon, or soon after, the business of the day is over. All
this time, the narrow, crooked streets, lined with high,
irregular houses, abutting directly upon the street, with
no sidewalks, have been the scene of the extremest bustle
and confusion, with the dealers in various commodities
carrying about and proclaiming their wares. Carts, too,
are allowed in the city during the morning hours for purposes of trade; but carriages are never permitted there,
except to ladies or on rare festal occasions. Whoever
does not wish to walk must be carried in a litter or ride
horseback. The hurry, bustle, and confusion of the streets
of Rome are frequently mentioned by ancient writers, and
probably the streets of modern Cairo or Constantinople
give a fair notion of them.

At noon, therefore, we have a cessation of business,
which is not resumed unless there is some special occasion. The second meal, *prandium*, is now taken, which
appears to have been much the same as the first, only
somewhat heartier, often with some meat or fish. Like
the first, it might be taken wherever a person happened
to be, generally with no formality. Frequently no table
was set at all, and sometimes it was entirely omitted. It
is therefore incorrect to call the *prandium* "dinner," which
is, as De Quincey urges, "the *principal* meal of the day,
the meal upon which is thrown the *onus* of the day's support." Let us call it *luncheon*.

How, meanwhile, has the wife of Æmilius, the matron
Cornelia, passed her forenoon? It is hard to say. The
life of women in no age or country admits much variety,
least of all that of virtuous women among the ancients.
As a lady of the old Roman stamp, she has employed her-

self, no doubt, in superintending the labor of her slaves: the rooms were to be cleaned, the floors swept and polished, preparations to be made for the evening's festival. If she does not spin and weave with her own hands, like her ancestors, she has been fully occupied in overseeing her slaves that did. For there were no Lowells and Manchesters in those days: all the noblemen's articles of clothing were made here in his own house. This huge pile of wool came from the backs of his own sheep, on his Apulian pastures. On this loom you see a toga near its completion — woven in one piece, heavy and fine, with a soft nap like velvet — already narrowed towards the end, to show its rounded form. On this other is a piece of cloth to be made into a tunic. A broad stripe is woven in it, of wool dyed in the costly Tyrian purple, intended to run up and down in front of the garment, marking Æmilius as a Senator: this is the *latus clavus*. In this other room is a company of slaves making up garments, either for their master's use or coarser ones for themselves. In these employments Cornelia finds that the morning does not drag upon her hands; and while her two boys, Lucius and Marcus, are at their school, reading Homer or writing rhetorical exercises in Latin, her daughter Æmilia [Emily] accompanies her mother in her labors, gives her what aid she can, and learns how to manage a household, in order that, when married to the young Licinius, to whom her parents betrothed her the other day, his house may be cared for in a manner worthy a Roman nobleman.

But let us turn for a moment from our chaste and virtuous Cornelia, a Roman matron of the old stamp, and read the description which Lucian gives of the fashionable ladies two centuries later : —

"If any one should behold these ladies at the moment that they wake in the morning, he would certainly believe he saw a monkey or a baboon, to meet either of which on going out in the morning we are accustomed to con-

sider a bad omen. For this reason they shut themselves
up so closely at this time that no man's eye can see
them. . . . She is at once surrounded by a circle of
officious nurses and attendants, who make it their business to revive upon her countenance its faded beauties.
To wash the sleep out of her eyes with fresh spring water,
and then betake herself briskly and cheerfully to her household duties — what an absurd and old-fashioned notion!
No, there must first be all sorts of ointments, powders,
and essences. The performance has quite the look of a
public display. Each maid and attendant has a special
part of the toilet to attend to. One brings a silver wash-
basin, another a pitcher, others mirrors and caskets —
boxes enough to make up the stock of an apothecary.
And in none of them is there anything but falsehood
and deception — in one teeth and coloring for the gums,
in another black eyelashes and eyebrows, and other tricks
of the toilet. But the greatest art and the greatest time
are spent upon the hair. Some, who have the madness
to change their natural black hair into blonde or golden,
color it with ointment, which they then suffer to dry in
the sun at mid-day in order to set the color. Others, who
are content to wear their hair black, spend their husbands'
entire income upon it, and let all Arabia Felix breathe
from their locks."

Not so very different from some fine ladies of a later
day, even to the dyeing of the hair yellow — a custom
which the Roman ladies adopted in admiration of the
northern nations, which they had just come to know.
Nor was false hair uncommon: one of their poets
writes: —

> " The golden hair that Livia wears
>   Is hers — who would have thought it?
> She swears 'tis hers, and true she swears;
>   For I — know where she bought it."

But what does Lucian mean by the unsavory comparison with the baboon? Why, this: that the favorite method of the ladies of his day, to preserve their complexions, was to bathe their faces on going to bed in a gruel made of bread and asses' milk. This became hard, dry, and discolored during the night, and the first process in the morning was to wash it away with warm asses' milk — the Empress Poppæa was always, in traveling, accompanied with troops of asses, stated at five hundred in number, to provide her with her indispensable baths. This yesterday's rubbish cleared away, a slave touches up the cheeks artistically with white and red paint, and another shades the eyebrows and eyelashes with a black powder — and the fair face is finished.

It is afternoon now. The *prandium* is over, and the siesta too, if any have indulged themselves in that luxury. No more labor to-day, unless to hard-worked slaves or to lawyers or magistrates whose business will not wait. It is afternoon, and all Rome is taking holiday. What occupation does Martial's epigram give for the afternoon? "Baths and palæstra." But Martial lived in the time of Trajan, and our Æmilius in that of Augustus. Under the Empire, the daily bath was the grand object of life with the enervated, luxurious Romans; and the *thermæ*, or warm baths, were among the most magnificent of the structures of the city. There were several of these, built at different times, the largest perhaps a third of a mile square, fitted up with every variety of luxurious baths and provided with pleasant grassy lawns, with halls for games and gymnastic exercises, with porticos and lecture-rooms for conversation or instruction. To these the people were admitted, either gratis or for a mere nominal sum; and here they spent hours of every day. We may praise the Romans for their cleanly habits; but cleanliness ceased to be the object — it was the mere sensual gratification, derived from the succession of the different kinds of baths in which an idle and dissolute people wasted their hours.

But Æmilius has no such establishments as these to visit; nor is he a mere trifler, to spend the whole afternoon in soaking and scraping himself. Indeed, these establishments were not intended for the rich and aristocratic, who in those days had elaborate bathing accommodations in their own houses, but chiefly for the mass of the citizens, to whom this was a part of the price paid by the emperors for the privilege of ruling. At the close of the Republic there were no free baths on this magnificent scale. Therefore, if Æmilius has no rooms in his own house set apart for this purpose, he is satisfied to go, as his ancestors did, to a barber's shop and have his beard shaved, his hair cut, and his nails trimmed (a thing no gentleman thought of doing for himself); then to one of the *balneæ*, or private bathing establishments, where he takes such a simple bath as suits his tastes.

We may fancy him then, now that the business of the day is over, spending the rest of the afternoon in any way that we fancy. Perhaps he orders his carriage to wait him at the Porta Capena, and he himself rides on horseback, while his wife is carried in a litter to the gate; they mount the carriage, and, driven by a slave — for no Roman gentleman may lower himself by holding the reins — enjoy an afternoon drive over the Campagna, while the declining sun lights up the Sabine mountains with a brilliant purple, and the Alban hill lies in sombre shadow. Perhaps they go along the Appian Way, crowded with travel and traffic, and lined with splendid tombs on both sides; if this is not retired enough, towards Ostia, to get a whiff of the sea air; or to visit a friend's country seat in Etruria, or inspect their own villa at Tusculum. Or perhaps he may prefer to recline in his own parlor, and have a slave read to him a new satire of Horace, or an historical treatise of Varro, or one of Cicero's never tiring speeches.

At length it is the dinner-hour, and the guests begin to arrive — a party of gentlemen, all high-born and wealthy, all rejoicing at the prospect of an outbreak between Antony and Octavianus, and some venturing to hope that the result will be a restoration of the commonwealth. On ordinary occasions, Æmilius dines with his wife and children — it is the only *family* meal. Civilization has not so far conquered the habits of barbarous life as to bring the whole family together to the morning and mid-day meal. These are still solitary, informal, individual, occasional ; but towards evening civilization conquers at last, and, when the work of the day is all finished, brings the whole family to a common table. In olden times they sat at table ; but the later Roman felt himself disinclined for so much exertion, and reclined on a broad couch, leaning on his left elbow, and feeding himself with his hand from the bits of food cut up for him by the slaves in attendance. Forks were unknown — knives were hardly used at the table — spoons, pointed perhaps at one end, were the only implements, except their fingers, which were made before forks ; and was it not an easier and more lordly thing to be spared the trouble of cutting at all, and use the fingers, with a slave at hand to wash them with perfumed water ? Women, however — was it modesty or dignity or self-sacrifice, or was it that the lords of creation ruled it so ?— women did not recline at meals, but still sat, as their ancestors did.

To-day, however, is a banqueting day. Æmilius receives his friends in his splendid *triclinium*, or banqueting hall, while Cornelia dines in the common room of the family, with her daughter, the gentle Æmilia, and the two school-boys Æmilii ; and let us trust that they behave better than boys are apt to do nowadays when left thus, not forgetting that they are destined one day to be Senators and Consuls.

The great banqueting hall contains three broad couches, placed to form three sides of a hollow square, each calcu-

lated to accommodate three guests. Varro, the great
antiquarian and scholar, has declared that the number of
guests should never be less than that of the Graces (three)
nor more than that of the Muses (nine) ; a dictum which
has come down to our days, as a rule which everybody
respects, but nobody obeys.   But at a Roman dinner the
accommodations of table and couches limited the number
to nine.   We will close the door upon Æmilius's banquet — its political conversation must be kept a secret.
In its place, we will copy from a Roman novel — the Saty-
ricon of Petronius * — the description of a dinner, given by
one of the guests : —

"For the first course, we had a hog crowned with pud-
ding, and garnished with fritters and giblets, capitally
dressed ; and there was endive and bread of whole meal,
which I like better than white.   For the next course we
had excellent cold tarts with Spanish honey poured warm
over them.   So I ate no small share of the tarts, and
smeared myself well with honey.   All round these, chick-
peas and lupines, nuts in plenty, and an apple apiece.
I, however, brought away two, and here they are tied
up in my napkin ; for, if I carry home nothing to my
favorite slave, I get abuse.   Ha ! true, my wife reminds
me, had on a side table a piece of bear's ham, and I ate
more than a pound of it, for it tasted quite like boar ;
and, said I, if bears eat a man, with how much more reason
may men eat bears !   Finally, we had cream cheese, grape
jelly, a snail apiece, chitterlings, livers in pâté-pans, chap-
crowned eggs, turnips and mustard, and a dish of kidney
beans.   There was also handed round a wooden bowl full of
salted olives, whence some of the party unfairly helped
themselves to fistfuls."

A brief account, from Suetonius, of the personal habits
of the Emperor Augustus, one of the most finished gentlemen of antiquity, will fitly conclude this attempt to illustrate the daily manners of his countrymen :

* Bohn's translation.

" His economy in furniture and household utensils can
be seen even now [one hundred years later] from the beds
and tables which are still in existence, many of which are
hardly elegant enough for a private gentleman. They say
he never slept on any but an ordinary bed, and with bed-
clothes of a common sort. He did not often wear any but
home-made clothes, made by his sister, wife, daughter, and
nieces. His toga was neither sweeping nor scanty in
dimensions ; his purple stripe neither broad nor narrow ;
rather high shoes, so that he might look taller than he
was. And he never failed to have his outdoor clothes and
shoes in his bedroom, ready for any sudden and unexpected
need. He banqueted frequently, but never except in regular form, nor without careful selection of his companions.
. . . His dinner consisted of three courses, and never, when
most sumptuous, of more than six ; but, although he was
thus economical, it was always of consummate elegance.
For, if the guests were silent or conversed in a low tone,
he would challenge them to a general conversation ; and
he enlivened the feast with singers and stage-players, or
even with pantomimists from the Circus, and quite often
with buffoons. Feast days and anniversaries he celebrated
with great magnificence. . . . The food that he ate himself was small in quantity and of an ordinary quality.
Stale bread and small fishes, and fresh cheese of cow's
milk, and green figs were what he was most fond of. The
earlier meals of the day, before the dinner, he took wherever he happened to be. These are his own words from a
letter. 'We lunched in the carriage, on bread and dates.'
Again, 'On my way home from the Regia, I ate an
ounce of bread, with a few grapes.' And again : 'No Jew,
my Tiberius, fasts more rigidly on the Sabbath than I
have done to-day, for not until after the first hour of the
night [at about 6 P.M.] did I eat a couple of mouthfuls in
the bath, before I was rubbed with oil.' From this carelessness it resulted that sometimes he dined alone, either

before or after the banquet, taking nothing at the table.
He was likewise very temperate in the use of wine. . . .
Instead of drinks, he took bread soaked in cold water, or
a slice of cucumber, or a head of lettuce, or a fresh sour
apple of winy flavor.   After luncheon, when he had dressed
and put on his shoes, he took a short nap, holding his
hand before his eyes.   After dinner he went at once to
his study.   There he remained until late at night, making
out either wholly or chiefly the records of the day.   Then,
going to bed, he slept not more, at the outside, than seven
hours, and that not continuously, but waking three or four
times in the interval.   If he could not get to sleep again,
as sometimes happened, he called a reader or story-teller,
and worked often until after daylight. . . . In winter he
wore fur tunics, with a thick toga, with an undervest
fitting close to his body ; his legs and thighs were also
covered.   In summer he slept with open doors. . . . He
could not bear the sun, even in winter, and never walked
in the open air without a hat. . . . He gave up field exercises of arms and on horseback immediately after the civil
wars, and took instead to playing ball ; afterwards he rode
in a litter and walked, wrapped in a blanket, leaping at the
end of the walk."

The Paullus Æmilius whose day we have endeavored
to reconstruct from fancy is no fictitious character.   He
was a nephew of the triumvir Lepidus, and was consul
in the year thirty-four before Christ.   Very little is known
of his history, and it may be he did not deserve the character we have ascribed to him, of a Roman of the old
type ; but one would not willingly believe that it was a
mean or wicked man to whom were addressed the tender
verses of Propertius, in the name of his deceased wife : —

> " Cease, Paullus, to entreat my grave with tears —
>   The black gate opens to no human prayer.
> When once the shade in Pluto's halls appears,
>   The road is ever closed that brought it there.

" Now to thy care the pledges of our love,
 Even from my ashes, fondly I commend.
The father now a mother, too, must prove,—
 Let my caresses in thy kisses blend.
Be cheerful, if thou canst, when they are by:
 Alone and in thy chamber mourn for me;
And if thou seest my form, and deem'st me nigh,
 Believe that she thou lov'st will answer thee."

RELIGION OF THE ANCIENT ROMANS.*

THE "Mythology of the Greeks and Romans," as it has heretofore been taught in our school-books and used as material in modern literature, is in truth neither Greek mythology nor Roman mythology, but an incongruous mixture of the two — Grecian fable with Roman nomenclature. So long as it was purely a matter of fancy and of literary concern, there was no great harm done. Everybody understood what was meant by the Olympian Jove, the Eleusinian worship of Ceres, and the temple of Diana of the Ephesians, better, indeed, than if we had said Zeus, Demeter, and Artemis. But with the present century has come in a new school of philology, which has abandoned the merely literary treatment of such themes for one rigidly scientific, and which has discovered that names are not an indifferent matter in science; in fact, that in such a field of inquiry as this the name is often the key to the entire investigation. Max Müller, indeed, the leading authority in this new school, asserts "that mythology is simply a phase in the growth of language," an assertion in which we may recognize an important truth under an exaggerated form of statement. Perhaps there was a little pedantry in the first zeal for calling the Greek divinities by their right names; but it was at bottom a genuine, if blind and pedantic, striving for scientific accuracy. And now that Comparative Mythology has come up as a science, we can see that one of its first and most essential requirements was to distinguish with precision between the religious systems of these two related peoples, and that the first step towards this was to use names rightly. So long as Poseidon was called Neptune, and

Ares, Mars, the foundations of the new science could not be laid.

This first step has now been well-nigh accomplished. Very few persons of any pretension to scholarship insist any longer upon confounding together two independent sets of deities under common names. But while the Grecian gods have recovered their true names, and Grecian mythology has thus been placed upon a sound basis, the discarded Roman names have ceased to have a meaning to us. We know Zeus and Hera and Athena now: we have known them all our lives, it seems; but who are Jupiter, Juno, and Minerva? Roman mythology is hardly better known—at least among English and American scholars—than it was fifty years ago; that is to say, hardly at all.

When mythology was purely a matter of art and litera-ture, so that, as remarked above, it mattered very little whether the god of fire was called Hephaistos or Vulcan, Roman mythology was also a matter of little consequence, for the reason that it afforded very little material for art and literature. Moreover, it was not strange that the best scholars were almost wholly ignorant of it, for the reason that the facts with regard to it were so hard to get at, scattered in out-of-the-way authors or hidden under a mass of irrelevant matter. The Roman poets for the most part do not give us Roman mythology, but Greek. Even Ovid, in his *Fasti*—the only work of Roman liter-ature which makes a pretence to embody the traditions of national mythology — draws quite as much from Greek as from Roman sources; and it is often impossible to say, even where he appears to be giving us pure Roman le-gend, whether he is not, after all, making up a story. Thus the graceful story of Anna Perenna, in the third book, is evidently his own work, suggested by the identity of the name in the fourth book of the Æneid with that of the Latin goddess; and all we get from this long episode, towards an understanding of the genuine Roman faith, is the description of the usages and habits of a popular festival, from which we may draw our own conclusions as to its origin.

In the scientific discussion of mythology, on the other hand, Italian traditions are of the first importance. Indeed, it may be doubted whether their scientific value is not enhanced by the fact that they were not subjected to the distorting and transforming influences of poetry. Hartung, in his "Religion der Griechen," points out that the original and genuine traditions of Greek religion are to be sought, not in the poets, but rather in such works as the Itinerary of Pausanias. The poets and artists took the crude myth and moulded it and modified it to serve their purposes. Pausanias dryly describes institutions and usages of immemorial antiquity, and from these we can learn what the *people* actually believed and how they worshipped. Now, our authorities for Roman mythology are mostly of this character. It was for the most part let alone by the poets, save in the single instance of Ovid's *Fasti*, a work which is of priceless value in this investigation, for the reason that it gives us just what Pausanias does, a description of forms and customs. What it contains more than this may be of service and may not; at any rate, it needs to be sifted; but these descriptions are genuine. Next to Ovid's *Fasti*, in our materials for this study, will perhaps come Augustine's *De Civitate Dei*, which contains a summary of the views of Varro, the most learned Roman antiquarian, introduced by the Christian writer for the purpose of being refuted. Besides these we have little more than scraps and fragments. Varro's treatise *De Lingua Latina* is partly preserved, and is of the highest value, so far as it goes. Of Verrius Flaccus, the next antiquarian in merit, we have a portion of an abridgment by Festus, in a terribly corrupt and mutilated condition, and an abridgment of

Festus by Paulus Diaconus. The commentary of Servius upon Virgil comes next in order ; he was not himself an antiquarian of the rank of Varro and Verrius, but he copied many a curious bit of information into his hotch-potch of a commentary. So did Aulus Gellius too, whose *Noctes Atticæ* may indeed rank above the commentary of Servius. Besides these, we have some late writers, like Macrobius, a few allusions and statements in that poet of genuine learning, Virgil, in Cicero and the Elder Pliny, and not a few inscriptions of value.

These materials, it will be seen, are, after all, not so very scanty : it is a question whether we are not, in some respects, better informed as to the original religious institutions of the Romans than as to those of the Greeks. Neither is this material altogether so dry and unedifying as might be supposed ; nor is the Roman mythology wholly destitute of stories of love and adventure, such as those in which the Greek mythology abounds. Many of their gods were married : Mars and Nerio, Neptune and Salacia, Saturn and Ops, were faithful pairs. The pleasant story in Ovid (*Met.* xiv. 623) — how Vertumnus sought the love of the shy Pomona ; how, changing his form — he was the counterpart of Proteus — he appeared successively as a reaper, a mower, a vine-pruner, a soldier, etc., and then as an old woman, who lectured and warned the maiden, finally in his own youthful form and won his bride — this story and numbers like it may be dressed up by the poet, but can hardly have been wholly invented by him.

Nevertheless, it must be confessed that stories like this are not characteristic features of the Roman religion ; that it did not encourage flights of the imagination, but was serious and earnest, running to observance and ceremonial rather than to fable. It was remarked by an eminent German scholar that the Romans had no mythology, only sacred antiquities (*gottesdienstliche Alterthümer*) — an as-sertion which has enough truth in it to serve as a general description. This expresses the most fundamental distinction between the Greek and Roman religious systems; but it will be interesting, and indeed essential to our discussion, to inquire in what further particulars they differed from each other—that is, what different development the two related nations gave to the same original faith.

In a previous article I described this original faith, common to the ancestors of both Greeks and Romans, as starting in "the immanence of the divine power, inhabiting, inspiring, and vivifying every living thing, nay, every inanimate object, and every action of life; . . . a sort of pantheism—a belief, not in one God pervading all nature, and identified with nature, but in millions of gods, a god for every object, for every act." Pandemonism Preller calls it. In anthropomorphizing, or investing these divinities with personality and human shape and attributes, consisted the development from fetichism to polytheism; and it is the special excellence and glory of the Greeks that this anthropomorphism was so complete, and that the Greek Olympus contains no man-bulls or cat-headed monsters by the side of the perfectly human Zeus, Apollo, and Aphrodite. The Centaurs and Minotaurs of Greek mythology were few in number and of subordinate importance.

The Romans lacked the high æsthetic sense which preserved the Greeks from the puerile bestialities of Oriental mythologies. On the other hand, they had their own protective in an even higher and nobler quality. Their conservative and practical temper led them to cling to that primitive mode of regarding the divine power which the Greeks lost sight of in the individuality of their deities. The Greeks, out of the original *numina* or δαίμονες, had created their marvellous Olympus of living gods and goddesses — their ideal of perfect humanity. The Romans, on the other hand, were capable of only a very moderate degree of anthropomorphism. Their gods were persons, it is true, but they were not, as a whole, invested with any very marked human attributes; and it was found easier to keep up the habit of imputing individual acts to distinct deities than to extend the sphere of activity of the gods they already had. Hence the multitudinousness of their pantheon. No other nation, perhaps, would have conceived of a special divine spirit, existing merely for the purpose of causing Hannibal to turn his back on Rome when already in sight of the city. The Romans, indeed, might have given the credit of it to Jupiter or Mars, and invested him with a new attribute and built him a new temple. Instead of that, they chose to build a shrine, on the spot which Hannibal last occupied, to the *Deus Rediculus*, the god who caused the turning about. But the most remarkable illustrations of this practice are found in the *Indigitamenta*, or books of religious formulæ, and other remnants of the old worship. Every act of life had its peculiar divinity, to be invoked in its proper time and place. There were some sixty or seventy of these, who presided over the growth of the human body alone : *Vagitamus*, who opened the mouth of the infant for its first cry; *Cunina*, who guarded the cradle; *Educa*, who taught the infant to eat; *Potina*, who taught him to drink; *Ossipaga*, who knit the bones, etc. Then for husbandry there were *Nodutus*, who caused the joints of the stalks to grow; *Volutina*, who wrapped them in their leaf-sheaths; *Patclana*, who opened the wrappings, that the ear might come out in due season; *Hostilina*, who made the crop even in its ears; down to *Runcina*, who presided over the pulling of the roots from the ground. These were not strictly gods, even in the polytheistic sense of the word, but *numina*, or attendant spirits.

But, above all — and this is the source of what is purest and noblest in the Roman religion — they delighted in recognizing the divinity that inspired every virtuous thought and act — the worship of abstract qualities. It was a necessary accompaniment of this characteristic that harmful spirits and vicious qualities should also be recognized and worshipped; but it is a remarkable and honorable fact that the Romans were never led astray by this to an overweening service of evil deities. They propitiated Vejovis (the bad Jove) and Febris (Fever) and Mephitis (Malaria); but there was no devil worship or service of Moloch: so far from it, indeed, that they did not even feel sure who Vejovis was, although they regularly sacrificed to him. (Ovid, *Fasti*, iii. 435, ff.) The Romans had an unwavering faith that the powers of good were superior to those of evil. This worship of abstractions went probably far beyond that of any other mythological system, and is the most striking and characteristic feature of the Roman theology. Other mythologies possess it in a degree: the Athenians built temples to Unwinged Victory and to Health. But the Romans, besides Victoria and Salus, had Honor, Pudicitia, Fortuna, Pax, Libertas, and Concordia among their most honored deities. Indeed, several of those gods who rank as personalities were abstractions at the outset. Minerva was the abstraction of mental power (*mens*); Mercury, the abstraction of traffic (*merx*); Janus, the god of opening (*janua*); and Saturn, the god of sowing (*satus*).

On the other hand, while the Romans went far beyond the Greeks in the worship of abstractions, they lost in a much greater degree the worship of elementary spirits, which had been in reality the starting-point of each theology. Ouranos, Gaia, Okeanos, were reverenced by the side of Zeus, Demeter, and Poseidon; but the Romans had only the personal gods, Jupiter and Neptune, Bona Dea and Dea Dia, while Tellus (rather than Terra) did not hold a high rank in their worship. This fact illustrates the different development of the two peoples. Both started with the worship of elementary spirits; in both the spirit of the firmament, Zeus or Jupiter, naturally took the first rank, and other spirits of water, fire, earth, etc., were personified by his side. Then, when these had become completely anthropomorphized, and their origin was forgotten while their power was reverenced, the imaginative Greeks repeated the same process, and created new deities of earth, sky, and water, by the side of the old; while the practical Romans turned themselves to the contemplation of the human virtues, or provided for the whole range of human sentiments and actions by regarding each of them as produced and controlled by an indwelling spirit.

The Romans again, aside from what passed as history, lacked the demigods and heroes who make so large a part of the Greek system, and who, one would think, would be peculiarly congenial to the Roman temper of mind. And, as a matter of fact, this proved to be the case; for among the earliest Greek deities whose worship was engrafted upon the Roman tradition were demigods like Hercules and the Dioscuri, heroes like Æneas and Evander. Almost the only native Italian deity who is reckoned among the heroes is Semo Sancus, or Dius Fidius, who had two or three temples at Rome, and who was frequently identified with Hercules, for no other apparent reason than that both were commonly adjured in oaths — *me hercule*, *me dius fidius*. But why the god whose very name, Fidius, implies that he was the spirit of faith, and of whom not a single legend is narrated — who is as purely an abstraction as Concordia or Spes — should be called a *hero*, it is at first sight hard to see. His second name means nearly the same as the first: *semo* is *spirit*, *sancus* is usually connected etymologically with *sanctus*, holy. But Sancus or Sangus was really an object of tradition, being the alleged founder of the Sabine nationality; and it was natural, perhaps, that he should be identified with this favorite of Greek tradition, Hercules, whose name and worship were spread far and wide along the Mediterranean. Just as he was identified with the Sabine Sancus, his name superseded that of the Latin Recarenus, the slayer of Cacus in the original legend ; and in the East he was adopted by the Phœnicians as their god Melkarth under another name.

This conservative temper, which, as we have seen, was the source of what was best in the Roman religion by keeping alive the faith in the immanence of the divine power, had, however, its weak side, and was equally the source of the worst peculiar feature of this worship; that is, its excessive formality. All Roman history illustrates this. The service is vitiated, and the games must be renewed, says Cicero (*Har. Res.* xi. 23), "if the pantomimist makes a sudden pause, or the flute-player interrupts his blowing, or the boy stumbles or loses hold of the chariot, or lets the reins fall, or if the presiding ædile makes a slip of the tongue or a false motion with the cup of libation." Cases were known in which the same rites must be begun over again fifty times before they were accomplished in due form. Or take the formalities required in the case of the *Flamen Dialis*, or priest of Jupiter, next the *Rex Sacrificulus*, the highest priest in the hierarchy (Aul. Gell. x. 15). In the first place, he must be of pure, patrician birth, of parents married by the ancient patrician ceremony of *confarreatio;* he himself must have married a virgin by the same ceremony, and his wife bear the title of *Flaminica.* He must not ride a horse, nor look upon a marshaled army outside the *pomœrium* (that is, except when it entered the city in a triumphal procession), nor take an oath, nor wear a solid ring, nor a knot in any part of his clothing. His hair must not be cut except by a free man, and the cuttings of both hair and nails must be buried under a tree of good omen. He must not touch nor even name a goat, uncooked meat, ivy, or beans, nor must he touch dough when fermenting. A bound prisoner brought into his house must be set free, and the chains removed, not by the door, but by the *impluvium*, or opening in the roof. So, if a person who is to be scourged falls as a suppliant at his feet, the scourging must be remitted for that day. He must not touch a dead body, nor take part in a funeral, nor enter a tomb. He must not strip his body except under a roof. The legs of his bed must be smeared about with mud, and he must never be away from it three nights together.

Unquestionably, all these points had a meaning and an object once, and are simply an illustration of forms kept up with strictness long after they had lost their vitality. What is peculiar to the Romans is the multiplicity of them, and the painful precision with which the smallest details were insisted upon. The religion of the Greeks and Romans consisted, as Zumpt has pointed out, not in doctrine, like that of the Hebrews and Persians, but in faith and ceremonial; and its very life depended upon maintaining the forms pure and unimpaired.

Now that we have discussed the great distinctive features of the Roman religion, let us proceed to consider some special classes of religious ideas, which will best illustrate the character of their faith and worship and the points of resemblance and contrast with those of the Greeks. We shall then be prepared to glance at their religious system as a whole — their theogony and Olympus, if we could use these words for so jejune a creation — and to trace the history of their religious ideas and forms of worship.

It has been said that the primitive Roman worship was directed to the divine spirit dwelling in an object or inspiring an action or process of nature — the thought that lies at the foundation of fetich worship. We meet, indeed, with not a few real fetiches in the developed worship of the city. Of this nature were the plants sacred to the several gods — the oak of Jupiter, the myrtle of Venus, the *sacer fauno foliis oleaster amaris* (Virg. *Æn.* xii. 766), and the animals sacrificed to them — the boar to Mars, the cow to Diana, the sow to Ceres. Such was the sacred fire in which the divinity of Vesta was conceived to reside. So with the *ficus ruminalis*, under which Romulus and Remus had been found in infancy, and which was believed to have been afterwards conveyed to the *comitium* by divine power. Still better examples are the flint-stone kept in the temple of Jupiter and used in oaths (*per Jovem lapidem* was a common oath, Cic. *ad Fam.* vii. 12); the *lapis manalis*, kept by the temple of Mars, and carried through the city when rain was needed; best of all, the lance (or lances) of Mars, kept with the sacred shields in the Regia. It was a most portentous omen when this lance moved of its own accord, and one to be consulted upon by the highest powers of the State. When war was declared, the commander entered the sacred building, struck the shields and then the spear, crying out, *Mars, vigila !* "Mars, awake !" Neither is the principle of that form of fetich wanting which has received the name of *totem* — a fetich appropriated to a tribe and transmitted by hereditary descent, as is found especially among the North American Indians. At least among the cognate Italian tribes we recognize the Hirpinians as receiving their name from the wolf (*hirpus*) of Mars, and the Picenians from the woodpecker (*picus*) of Mars, which had guided them to their new homes. The *Hirpi Sorani*, or wolves of Soranus, will be mentioned presently.

There are some traces among the Romans of that serpent-worship which plays so important a part in some religious systems. The *genius*, or indwelling spirit of the man, appears under the form of a serpent, as is illustrated by the occurrence when Æneas sacrificed at his father's tomb (*Æn.* v. 84). Propertius (iv. 8) describes an oracle at Lanuvium, to which the seekers approached down a dark opening, and fed hungry serpents with the hand. If the maiden is chaste, she returns in safety, and the husbandmen joyfully shout that the year will be a fruitful one. Of wilful indecencies the Italian religion was, in its original forms, almost absolutely free, although many such grew up in after time.

Fairies and elves, the graceful creation of northern mythologies, were foreign to the notions of the Greeks and Romans. The Greeks made up for this with a wonderful abundance and variety of nymphs and other beings, completely human in bodily aspect, and with no magic powers, but the living embodiment of the simple powers of nature. The Roman equivalent for the nymphs were the *Viræ* or *Vires*. These were joined with Diana in the worship at the Nemean sanctuary, but are otherwise a wholly shadowy existence to us, not even having made their way into poetry; their name, however, has been developed into the better known *virgo* and *virago*. The companion male beings, on the other hand, the fauns and silvani, are better known, and represent for us not merely the Greek satyrs, but the weird creatures of northern mythology. Faunus, "the favorer," is the old god of nature, a chief personage in the earliest mythology. As having the ear to the secrets of nature, he is a prophetic god; as the father of the Italian theogony, he was transformed into an early king. In his whole nature he corresponds very closely with the Greek Pan, and, like him, was multiplied, in the popular conception, into a class. The name, therefore, which at first was that of the chief god of nature, was afterwards applied to the lesser gods of the wood and field, corresponding in this sense to the Greek satyrs. The same is true of Silvanus, always an inferior being to Faunus. The *fauni* and *silvani*, then, were often playful or malicious beings, like the dwarfs, alps, and scrattles of German fairyland. To protect against their pranks, the children wore the *bulla* and other amulets. Especially was Silvanus to be dreaded after the birth of a child; and mother and infant were protected by three deities, Intercedona with an axe, Pilumnus with a mortar, and Deverra with a broom, to personate whom three men went about the house at night with axe, mortar, and broom, cutting, pounding, and sweeping the thresholds. There were also the vampire *strigæ*, who sucked the blood of infants in the cradle. Against these Carna or Cranea, the goddess of the hinge, was invoked, who touched the threshold and door-posts with a bough of arbute, sprinkled the doorway with charmed water, and threw out the entrails of a young pig, saying, "Birds of the night, spare the vitals of the child; a little victim is slain for the little one. Take this heart for his heart, I pray, this flesh for his. We give you this life for a better one." Then she puts in the window a twig of white thorn, the plant sacred to Carna, and the child is safe.

The Romans did not originally incline to *mysteries*, such as those of Eleusis, Samothrace, Imbros, and Crete, in which the Greek religion abounded. Leaving out of consideration the rites of Cybele, Bacchus, and others, which were purely exotic and of late introduction, there were still, however, a few native mysteries, very early in origin and very widely reverenced. There were secret rites to Angerona, in the temple of Volupia — in allusion, says Hartung, to the anguish which is turned to rapture. The best known, however, and most important are those of Bona Dea, the *good goddess*, whose very name is a mystery, although she has been identified with Fauna, Ops, and others. It is probable that she represented the fructifying powers of the earth, and her festival was on the first day of the month of *increase* (Maius), whence also she was called Maia. Her mysteries, however, were celebrated in December, in the house of the highest magistrate, by women alone, and appear in later times to have acquired a wild and orgiastic character. The sacrilege by which Clodius managed to witness these rites, and the uproar it made in the State, can only be compared to the famous mutilation of the statues at Athens. It is too familiar an event to need more detailed mention; neither need we conclude that the fearful picture drawn by Juvenal of the license of these rites is even approximately true for the times of the Republic.

Although mysterious rites did not much abound among the Italians, yet there were several *mysteries*, that is, secrets — the secret name of the city of Rome, which was concealed in order that no enemy, by learning it, could call forth (*evocare*) its protecting deities; and those of several classes of gods, to guess which a great deal of learning and ingenuity has been expended. We may safely conclude that what was a secret then will be a secret now. And in reference to such classes Preller says (p. 549), " In general, it must be assumed that all gods of lesser rank which were conceived as pure spirits (*dämonenartig*), and for this very reason were named and invoked only as classes, originally had no personal names, either in Greece or Italy." It will be worth while, however, to examine a little more in detail points which are so characteristic of Roman modes of thought.

The *Dii Consentes* and *Dii Involuti* appear to belong rather to the system of the Etruscans, who were peculiarly fond of dark and sombre articles of faith. And yet it appears clearly from Varro that the Consentes had temples in Rome (*L. L.* viii. 71), and that their statues, twelve in number — six male and six female — stood on the Forum. They might therefore be identified with the Twelve Olympian Gods; but we are expressly told that their names were unknown, and we must bear in mind that this idea of twelve chief gods is Greek, not Roman. The list of them, given by Ennius —

Vesta, Minerva, Ceres, Juno, Diana, Venus, Mars,
Mercurius, Jovi', Neptunus, Vulcanus, Apollo —

includes several, as will be shown presently, who are essentially foreign deities. On the whole, it seems most rational to assume that there was really no secret here. The Dii Consentes were the council of Jove, having no individuality, and therefore no names of their own. The Involuti are conjectured by Gerhard to be represented in an Etruscan relief, as two partially veiled figures, sitting back to back, with the backs of their hands placed before their mouths. We shall not probably be wrong in identifying them, as Gerhard does,* with the Fates, as a council higher than that of the Consentes. The Etruscans taught (Seneca, *Nat. Qu. ii.* 41) that Jove hurls his first thunderbolt alone, to inspire terror; the second, which hurts, but heals, by the advice of the twelve gods (the Consentes, no doubt); the third, which blasts and destroys, *adhibitis in consilium dis, quos superiores et involutos vocant.*

The names of the *Penates* were also a secret, both those of the city, and especially the *great gods* worshiped at Lavinium, which Æneas was supposed to have brought with him. But the word is of pure Latin derivation, and it is not likely that the alleged connection with Troy or Samothrace was anything but a theory, started when the Greeks and Romans came into contact with each other along the coast, like the whole story of the colonization of Æneas, and the stories of Evander, Hercules, Sancus, Catillus, etc. Very likely the Penates of Rome were the secret gods of the city, connected with its secret name. Another much disputed name is that of the *Dii Indigetes,* generally rendered the *native gods* — a rendering which is correct as far as it goes. It is applied to such characters as Æneas and Cæculus, the native heroes, ἐγχώριος, of Lavinium and Præneste respectively. But it appears to imply something more than nativity, or even divinity; it carries with it the conception of the spirit, or *numen* — the *genius* — that dwells in the place and the people; a connection almost as close as that of father of the race.

A still more puzzling class are the *Novensiles*, or *Noven-siles*. In the formula of invocation used by Decius when about to devote himself (Liv. viii. 9) they are mentioned: "Janus, Jupiter, Mars pater, Quirine, Bellona, Lares divi novensiles, dî indigetes, divi quorum est potestas nostrorum hostiumque, diique manes," etc. These are all deities either of high rank or peculiarly Roman, or specially connected with the act of self-devotion. Janus was invoked first, as on all occasions; then the three great national gods, Jupiter, Mars, and Quirinus; then the goddess of war, the deified ancestors, the heroes, the shades. From the position of the Novensiles, by the side of the Indigetes, these have been supposed to mean respectively the native gods and those which were originally foreign, thus deriving the word from *novus*, new. This is Hartung's view, and was held by the ancient writer, Cincius. Varro and Piso, however, say that they were Sabine gods, and the name has been found on inscriptions in the Sabine country. It seems more natural, therefore, to derive the name from *novem*, nine, and to consider them a special group of deities introduced from the Sabines, whose functions had some natural connection with the act of devotion. It does not seem likely that these two terms would be used on this occasion in order to include all existing deities, especially after so peculiar a list has been enumerated as that given; and at any rate it would be strange that we have no other instance of the use of *novensiles* and *indigetes* in this distributive sense. May it not be doubted also whether the native, *indigetes*, would not have stood first in this case? I am inclined, on the whole, to the view of Manilius, that they were the nine gods who, according to the Etruscans, had the power of hurling the thunderbolt — a meaning quite appropriate to their occurrence in a formula of devotion.

In nothing were the Romans more distinguished from the Greeks than in the mode of seeking the will of the gods. They had no Apollo, whose frenzied hierophants uttered oracles under a divine afflatus. But the formal auspices which the magistrates consulted, and which were interpreted by the college of augurs, were among the most characteristic of the institutions of the State. Everything was simple and definite, and reduced to rigid rules. It was not all birds, at all times, that conveyed the will of the gods, but only certain ones, when the magistrate consulted them with well-defined ceremonies. It was to him only that the auspices were sent; the augur was but the skilled interpreter who was called in to explain phenomena, but who had no power himself to seek for the signs. This resulted from the fundamental principle that the State rested upon the divine will, as declared in the auspices. The auspices belonged to the citizens as a body — that is, to the patricians; the chief magistrate for the time being had them in his possession; but, whenever there was a vacancy, the auspices, the embodiment of sovereignty, returned to the patrician body, where they remained until a new magistrate, installed with the consent of the gods, was again the depositary of them.

The Roman or patrician auspices, thus carefully and jealously maintained, were, however, but the specially Roman development of the Italian system of augury. The plebeians had their auspices likewise, and the other Italian nations, different from the Roman, but no doubt analogous. They observed, for instance, different birds, and gave a different interpretation to the same sign. Individuals, too, could interpret for themselves the signs that came in their path, and there were many other methods of ascertaining the future besides the flight of birds, the appearance of animals, and the path of the thunderbolt. Another public oracle, the Sibylline Books, must not be forgotten; but it will be treated of in another place. The haruspices, a low class of Etruscan soothsayers, who foretold by consulting the entrails of animals sacrificed, must be carefully distinguished from the augurs, who were a body of statesmen and gentlemen of the highest rank. The serpent oracle at Lanuvium has already been spoken of. Faunus, the good god of nature, was wont to whisper his secrets in dreams, or call them out to his worshipers, as is described in the seventh book of the Æneid (v. 81). Sanctuaries of Fortuna were likewise frequented for this purpose. The most famous was at Præneste, where lots were drawn from a box. It has been surmised that the elegantly engraved boxes, peculiar to Prænestine art, were in some way connected with this oracle. Another was at Antium, celebrated by Horace in the thirty-fifth ode of the first book — *O diva gratum quæ regis Antium.* Of the superstitions of the later Republic and Empire I shall speak presently.

From the general religious conceptions we will pass to the consideration of the special objects of Roman worship, and the changes in their religious institutions and ideas. Probably there is no nation which illustrates the transformations of faith so well as the Romans: first, because in their case these transformations were very extensive and remarkable ; secondly, because we are unusually well informed in regard to them, and can trace them with great distinctness and accuracy.

The primitive religion of the Romans consisted of two elements — that which they inherited from their remote ancestry and possessed in common with other Aryan peoples, and that which was developed for itself by the Italian race after its separation from the Greeks. To the first class, besides the general conceptions which have already been spoken of, belonged the worship of Jupiter (Ζεὺς πατήρ), Juno (Διώνη), and Vesta (Ἑστία), and perhaps nothing more. Even here the Romans had hardly more than the names in common with the Greeks ; the conceptions and forms of worship were wholly their own. The other class, that of distinctively Italian deities, forms a peculiarly interesting group, one which is, however, not always easy to analyze. Many of these, whose worship was of great importance and popularity in the earliest times, were afterwards forgotten or cast in the shade by Greek and other foreign divinities. For instance, it may fairly be claimed that any god who had a *flamen*, or special priest, held a tolerable rank at one time, although it would not necessarily follow that he had the highest rank. Now we do not possess the complete list of flamens, but we know that besides the three of chief rank — those of Jupiter, Mars, and Quirinus — and those of Vulcan, Flora, and Pomona, the gods of fire, flowers, and fruits, there were flamens of the river god (Volturnus), the harbor god (Portunus), the goddess of the Palatine, the original seat of the city (Palatua), of Carmentis, a goddess of spells and song, and of Furina and Falacer pater, whose functions are not known. It was in the sacred grove of Furina, not of the Furies, that Gaius Gracchus was killed; Falacer pater is connected by Hartung with the Etruscan word *falandum*, heaven, as being therefore only another name or another form of Jupiter. This is all that is known, or conjectured, about these two deities; but it is a fair inference that all these, even those who were quite insignificant or actually forgotten in after time, were leading gods in early ages.

Besides these gods who dwindled or vanished in historical times, there were not a few who were insignificant at first, and acquired high importance afterwards by being identified with leading Greek deities (as Venus, Ceres, and Mercury), or whose attributes were entirely altered in this identification (as Liber Pater and Saturn). For Saturn was originally only the god of sowing; and he had nothing in common with the Greek Kronos, except the tradition of great antiquity. It was related that he had reigned in the most distant periods of time, before Jupiter was known; but no original Italian myth made him the father of Jupiter.

Jupiter, as the god of the heavens, was the chief god in early as in later times; and the vine, which depends so much upon the weather for its fruitfulness, was under his special charge. Bacchus was only a late importation from Greece; and Liber Pater, with whom he was in after times identified, had originally nothing to do with the vine or with drunkenness, but, with Libera, presided over the bearing of children. But, if Jupiter was recognized as the greatest of all gods, Mars was the favorite object of worship, the national god, not only of the Romans, but of the Italian race as a whole — just as a Catholic people, without impugning the supremacy of Jehovah, will take Saint James or Saint Denis as its special patron and protector, and the object of its dearest affections.

Mars, therefore, although the god of killing, was hardly the *special* god of war in early times. This character was merged and lost out of sight in that of the national god of a nation of shepherds and husbandmen; and he was "pre-eminently regarded as the divine champion of the burgesses, hurling the spear, protecting the flocks, and overthrowing the foe" (Mommsen, Book I. ch. xii.). Bellona, on the other hand, was the special impersonation of war. Mars, in this point of view, was grouped with Faunus, Picus, Silvanus, Pales, and other deities of nature; while as civic god of the old Roman city upon the Palatium he was associated with Quirinus, his duplicate, the Mars of the hill city upon the Quirinal.

Jupiter, then, the chief god of all, with Mars and Quirinus, the patron deities of the two cities on the Palatine and the Quirinal, which were united together to form Rome, were the great triumvirate of early times. By the side of these there were worshiped Faunus, the good god of nature (in February), Terminus, of boundaries (also in February), Ceres, the goddess of growth, and Pales, of the flocks (in April), Neptune, of the sea (in July), Consus (from *condo*) and Ops, of the harvest (in August),

Vulcan, of fire (in August), and Saturn, of sowing (in December). Add to these Janus, the god of opening, and Vesta, the goddess of the hearth, and we have, with the omission of some less important names, the original Roman pantheon. What is most striking in this is the number of purely Latin names of great importance in after times which are wanting. At this time Juno was perhaps nothing but the *numen* of women, the counterpart of the male *genius;* Minerva was only an *indigitamentum,* of memory ; Diana, a leading Latin goddess, was hardly recognized in Rome ; Venus was of quite subordinate importance ; and Mercury was hardly known, if at all.

The changes made in after time in the objects of worship may be referred to three heads — Italian influence, Greek influence, and Oriental influence. For, although the Romans were themselves a pure Italian people, and possessed those elements of faith which were common to the Italian race, yet each community, like Rome itself, had its special rites and divinities, many of which were, one after another, adopted by the Romans. Etruria has the credit of having supplied the Romans with many articles of faith; but the more is known of its people, the more barren its institutions appear. The Capitoline trio, Jupiter, Juno, and Minerva, whose worship marks the Tarquinian dynasty, is often referred to Etruria; but Varro expressly tells us (*L. L.* v. 158) that they had a chapel upon the "Old Capitol" (on the Quirinal) earlier than that upon the Capitoline. At any rate, we have seen that Juno was a primitive Græco-Italian goddess, and was certainly known before this time, at least as the indwelling spirit of women. Minerva, too, is a purely Latin name (*mens*) ; and her worship was specially in the hands of the Nautian gens, which was of Alban origin. Varro (*L. L.* v. 74) reckons her among the Sabine deities. It seems impossible, therefore, to say what religious movement was connected with the establishment of this trio. But, whatever it may have been, these three from this time appear at the head of the Roman Olympus. The political bearing of the fact is suggested by Marquardt's theory (vol. v. p. 47) that this new institution was to form a religious centre for the now united State, corresponding with the important constitutional changes that took place at this epoch. As the patrician city had its Jupiter, Mars, and Quirinus, the plebeians had the temple of Diana on the Aventine. It was the work of the Tarquinian dynasty to unite these two elements into one; and with this work the founding of the new temple and worship may have been connected. At any rate, it is at this period that both temples were founded — that of Diana and that of the Capitoline Jove. To this period belongs, likewise, the commencement of the custom of having images of the gods, according to Varro's statement (Aug. *Civ. Dei*, iv. 31) that the Romans worshiped the gods one hundred and seventy years without images.

As to Diana herself, it is hard to determine her precise character, further than that she seems to have been a feminine form of Janus (Dianus). She had a renowned sanctuary at the Lake of Nemi, near Aricia; and it was probably from the similarity of her worship here to that of the Tauric Artemis that it came about that Diana was identified with Artemis. The *Rex Nemorensis*, or priest of Diana, held his place by the sword — by killing his predecessor in single combat; and he must maintain it in the same way — an exploit which none but runaway slaves undertook in later times.

When the power of Rome grew, and she came to absorb all her neighbors into herself, many other local deities were incorporated into the Roman system. The Penates at Lavinium and Fortuna at Præneste and Antium have been already spoken of. The Sibyl Albunea at Tibur, and the Dioscuri at Tusculum, belong rather to a later period. One of the most important of this class was Juno Sospita Mater Regina, who had a famous sanctuary at Lanuvium and lesser ones at Rome; it was in her temple that the serpent oracle described above was found. This goddess has perhaps more reality to us than most of her class, from her mention in Cicero's Oration against Milo, and from her peculiar statue in the Vatican, with shield and spear, clad in a goatskin, with pointed shoes, and a serpent at her feet.

Still another was the worship of Soranus on Mount Soracte, who, as a god of light, worshiped on the top of the mountain, was identified with Apollo — *Sancti custos Soractis Apollo* (Virg. *Æn.* xi. 785). But he was also identified with Dis Pater, god of the lower world, by reason of a sulphurous vapor which exhaled from a hole in the mountain side, and of the peculiar rites with which he was worshiped, partly described by Virgil in the passage cited. For once, when the service was going on, wolves came and snatched the flesh of the sacrifices; and, when the shepherds pursued, they were led to this cave, where the sulphurous exhalations were so strong as to kill those who came nearest. Then, as a punishment for pursuing the sacred animals, a pestilence broke out, which, as an oracle told them, could only be checked by the people themselves becoming wolves (Serv. Æn. xi. 785). From this they were called Hirpini (from *hirpus*, a wolf), just as the Hirpinian Samnites had received their name from following the guidance of a wolf when they went off to find a new home. The wolf ceremony was, like the Roman Lupercalia (also from *lupus*, a wolf), a purifying one; they ran naked and unhurt through blazing fire at their annual festival. This rite is described by Strabo (v. 226) as occurring at the grove of Feronia, at the foot of the mountain; and there was undoubtedly a close connection in this place between the two divinities. But Soranus was merely a local deity, the god of the mountain

Soracte; while Feronia was one of the most widely reverenced goddesses, whose worship is traced in many parts of Italy, from Verona in the north to Latium in the south and the Vestinians in the east. She seems to have been a goddess of nature, like Flora, but in some way came to be especially connected with popular traffic. Her three principal groves — at Soracte, at Anxur or Tarracina (*ora manusque tua lavimus, Feronia, lympha*, Hor. *Sat.* i. 5, 24), and at Trebula Mutuesca — were all famous for the throng of traffickers from all parts who gathered there; they were genuine fairs, where pedlers and showmen resorted, as they do nowadays to cattle-shows and camp-meetings. It was a disturbance at one of these fairs that led to the war of Tullus Hostilius with the Sabines (Liv. i. 30).

It would be interesting to describe some others of the primitive rites of the Romans, connected with their original character as a farming and pasturing people; such as the worship of Dea Dia in May by the Arval Brothers, one of the oldest and most illustrious of the patrician sodalities, and which was kept up long into the empire. Many inscriptions, illustrating their usages, have been discovered at their sanctuary, five miles from the city, where they still continue to be found from time to time. Then there was the procession to the grove of Rubigo (rust) in April, at which the flamen of Quirinus offered the prayer recorded by Ovid (*Fast.* iv. 911): "Harsh Rubigo, spare the growth of Ceres, and let the smooth top tremble above the ground. Let the crops, nourished by the favoring heavens, grow until they are ready for the sickle." The worship of the Lares and Manes, too, would throw much light upon the religious notions of the people: the *genius*, or indwelling spirit of the man, took its place after death among the *Manes;* the deified ancestors were *Lares*, while the spirits of the impious flitted from place to place, tormenting the wicked and themselves finding no rest; these were *Larvæ* and *Lemures*. The word *Lares* came to have a rather wide compass; and we find that Alexander Severus had images in his chapel (*lararium*) of Abraham, Christ, Apollonius of Tyana, Orpheus, and others, besides his ancestors (*Æl. Lamp. Alex. Sev.* 29). But we must hasten on to the later developments of the Roman faith.

The first great change wrought by foreign influence was in the direction of the Greek, partly in introducing new deities, partly in modifying the conceptions of the old. It was really a revolution to invest Jupiter, Mars, Minerva, and Neptune with the attributes of Zeus, Ares, Athene, and Poseidon, and to foist the whole Greek mythology, with its ideality and sensuousness, upon the dry, earnest, pure theology of the Romans. Cicero and Cato did not believe that their gods had ever done the acts that were ascribed to them; in the time of Camillus nobody could have believed it, because these were so wholly at variance with the national mode of thought. The influence that came from the later intercourse with Greece was not a legitimate and salutary one. It was not Sophocles or Socrates, not even Homer or Praxiteles, that introduced Grecian thought to the Romans; it was the dregs of philosophy — not divine philosophy — the fancies and sensualities of art, when its spirit had disappeared — not the imaginative reason — that came in to help corrupt a people that was going to ruin fast enough by itself.

This, however, belongs to a later stage of Greek influence. The early Greek influence was good, or at all events not bad. For some three hundred years we watch a succession of new gods and goddesses, borrowed from Greece. In some cases, they were plainly foreign deities, and the name as well as the religion is new. In others, some Roman divinity was found, often of wholly subordinate rank, and raised at once to importance and dignity by being clothed with all the attributes and associations of some one of the twelve great gods of Greece. To the first class belong Apollo, Hercules, Castor and Pollux, and Æsculapius ; these are in every respect foreign, although Apollo was identified with Soranus, and Hercules's shoulders were made to bear all the heroic traditions that had sprung up on Italian soil. There are as many of the second class. Diana has already been spoken of, and her resemblance to Artemis is enough to explain the identification of the two, especially in the fact that the Latin nymphs, the Viræ, were peculiarly connected with her. Mercury again, originally hardly more than an *indigitamentum*, or impersonation of the act of traffic, became Hermes, the messenger of the gods, the contriver, the god of eloquence, the conductor of the souls of the dead, merely by virtue of the one function that the two had in common. Venus, the abstraction of sensuous pleasure, and at the same time (in these simple rural days) a goddess of the garden, in the same way became Aphrodite.

Still more important is the case of Ceres. She has been shown to have been one of the original nature-deities of the Romans, but her worship was simple and public. Whatever sentiments of mystery were connected with the observation of nature were embodied in the worship of Bona Dea and perhaps Dea Dia and Dis Pater (the god of the lower world). It was to one of these, then, that the Greek mysteries of Demeter, Dionysos, and Kore should have been attached. Instead of that, Ceres was taken, joined with Liber and Libera (an utterly incongruous combination), and made the centre of a new worship, purely Greek, and conducted by Grecian priests, while at the same time the old festival of Ceres was kept up by the side of the new. The original Latin Ceres was now wholly overshadowed and obscured by her new functions as Demeter ; so that she appears from this time on as an essentially Greek divinity. The name of Proserpine, the goddess of the *Indigitamenta*, who causes the young plant to creep forth from the ground, has so close a resemblance to Persephone, the daughter of Demeter, that she, too, was made into a Grecian goddess, and joined with Pluto as queen of the lower world.

It is Marquardt's view that all these elements of Greek religion were introduced by method, and as part of a system, of which the Sibylline Books were the authority, the *Quindecemviri sacris faciundis* the managers; that is, that the purchase of the Sibylline Books marks distinctly a new era in the Roman religion, and that the two systems went on side by side — the Pontifices at the head of the native system, the Quindecemviri of the foreign. It is certain that the Sibylline Books were of Greek origin, and that in most cases of the introduction of the Greek rites it is explicitly stated that it was done by the direction of these books. One feature of the new system was the *lectisternia*, or festivals, at which the statues of the gods were placed on couches at tables spread with a banquet.

The Greek forms of worship mentioned above were all established at Rome before the Second Punic War. Although they were essentially foreign, and in some cases in the hands of foreign priests, yet there was nothing in them (apart from the myths) really inconsistent with Roman ideas; and they were kept well in control by the authorities of the State. With the Second Punic War, when that baleful Greek influence described above began to be powerfully felt, commences a new series of foreign rites of a new character, attended by the most disastrous consequences. In the case of Apollo, Diana, Ceres, Æsculapius, and even Venus, there had been new ceremonies and at worst mysteries. With the arrival of Cybele, the Great Mother, begins a period of orgies and debasing superstitions. The circumstances attending the introduction of this worship are too well known to need repetition; but it cannot be made too plain what a contrast this frenzied Oriental worship, with its bloody symbolism, its begging priests, its wild dances, and its trumpets and cymbals, made to the old Roman and even the earlier Greek rites. We can well understand how suspiciously these narrow-minded but clear-sighted Senators must have stood aloof from it. But this was only a beginning. Soon after followed the rites of Bacchus, private in origin and celebration, even more wild, orgiastic, and indecent. The Senate did its best to check the growth of these practices, but it was too late. Already the simple, pure, formal, strictly national religion of Rome was dead ; and there was nothing for it but superstitions and philosophies.

In saying that the Roman religion gave way to superstition and philosophy, it must be remarked that this was a natural transformation, and in certain aspects a salutary one. The nature-religion of the Greeks and Romans was, in its essence, capable of only a very limited development ; that of the Romans was peculiarly narrow and inelastic. It was essentially a State religion, well adapted in its formality and strictness, to a people whose whole individuality was merged in that of the State. And whatever elements of worship were popular and spontaneous in their origin and character were pure outgrowths of that simple, unimaginative observation of nature and deification of its powers which were natural to the Italian people. As the character of the nation developed, its religion was transformed by successive stages. The first of these has already been traced. It is connected with the sway of the Tarquinian dynasty, when Rome first became conscious of her destiny, and from being a single Latin city assumed the dignity of a State. This individual member of the Latin confederacy is now found not merely in possession of the hegemony in Latium, but in a relation of equal alliance on the one side with this confederacy on the other. At this same time, the political institutions expanded, and the patriarchal patrician organization began to be superseded by the principle of territorial nationality. With this political revolution there was naturally connected a religious one, which has been already described as consisting in the establishment of the supreme Capitoline triad, and in the introduction of Greek rites and forms of faith, through the Sibylline Books. Now, these changes, it must be remembered, were not at all hostile to Roman nationality. They were, in truth, an expansion of it. The purity of the nationality was in no ways impaired, but went on manifesting itself with more and more vigor for centuries. Whatever the Romans borrowed at this time either remained completely exotic, under the charge of Greek priests, or was completely assimilated, so as to become an integral part of the Roman faith.

With the Punic Wars comes in a new stage of growth, when the Roman people ceased to be purely Roman and became cosmopolitan. The change was one in capacity as well as in modes of thought. The early Roman had no needs or aspirations which his native religion could not satisfy. His calm, rigid spirit was not disturbed by doubts and anxieties as to the future, or tormented by the perplexing problems of older States and society, or attracted by the enthusiasms and orgiastic rites of more excitable peoples. With the conquest of the world all this was changed. It was partly that new elements of population flowed from all quarters into the capital of the world, partly that the Romans themselves had a wider field of view opened before them, and were more powerfully influenced by the thoughts and usages with which they were brought in contact. With their old narrowness and formalism they lost, it is true, their old simplicity and purity; but they gained in insight and impressibility. Matthew Arnold speaks of the pagans of this time as "people who seem never made to be serious, never made to be sick or sorry." But this view is one-sided. They were sick and sorry, they did feel those longings and aspirations which are so characteristic of modern times; and these puerile, fanatical, and often disgusting superstitions, which mark the downfall of the ancient faith, are only the indications of a demand for, and a seeking after, something higher and better.

The old Roman religion could not satisfy the new needs and longings of this new Roman people, because it had neither elasticity nor sympathetic power. It fell short as well of the intellectual demands of the time. It was abandoned, therefore, both by the masses, who were ready to believe, but needed some more vital faith, and by the cultivated, who had ceased to believe. The one class had recourse to superstitions, the other to philosophies. Three schools of philosophy gained a strong foothold among the cultivated classes of Romans — the Epicurean, with those who rejected all intervention of the gods in human affairs; the Stoic, with the more earnest and devout believers in a divine providence; while the Academic school afforded intellectual discipline and interest to those who thought the whole subject beyond the scope of our intelligence. With the Epicureans associated itself all that was contaminating and destructive to morals and society; the Stoics quickly identified themselves with whatever survived that was noble and heroic, and we owe to them some of the most striking examples of devoted patriotism and disinterested virtue that history contains. To this period belongs Euhemerism, that school of philosophizing which considered the gods to be nothing but deified men.

With all this the established religion fell into neglect. It is true that much of it preserved a certain popularity and respect by becoming identified with Greek fable. The Greek mythology satisfied some of the new longings of the community — those which were repelled by the formality and sterility of the old worship ; and some of the Roman gods, invested with new attributes and made the heroes of adventures and exploits that their early worshipers never dreamed of, were still the objects of reverence. But whatever was distinctly Roman rapidly disappeared, with the exception of rites which, like the Lupercalia and the festival of Bona Dea, were in a degree fitted to satisfy the new needs. Names of gods were forgotten, temples fell into decay, consecrated places were filled with rubbish and filth, the most honored priesthoods were left vacant, holy times were neglected, and sacred observances were despised. Even Cato, the Censor, wondered that one haruspex could look another in the face without laughing ; but this belonged to the age, not to Rome alone, for Hannibal indignantly asked King Prusias, when he refused to fight because the sacrifices were not favorable, whether he would rather put trust in a bit of veal than in an experienced commander. Cæsar indeed does not appear once in his whole career to have consulted the sacrifices.

With the Empire came in a temporary reaction. Augustus, conservative in all things, was especially so in religion, and from him dates a restoration of the old temples and a more zealous observance of the old rites. So far as the State was concerned, the decay of the Roman faith was arrested. At the same time the new *régime* was inaugurated by new observances, significantly connected with the Empire and the Julian dynasty. Sacrifices were offered thrice in the year to Peace, temples erected to Mars Ultor (the avenger of Julius), and Venus Genitrix (the mother of the race) ; and Augustus even aimed to make Apollo, rather than Mars, the special deity of his city.

Meantime, while the old religion was neglected and the higher classes were sedulously cultivating philosophy, the masses had taken refuge in Oriental superstitions. As the earlier epoch, that of the Tarquins, had received its character from Greece, this later one was influenced by Asia — the early source of religious inspiration to the Greeks, as well as the cradle of the later Christianity. It is not necessary wholly to despise the frantic rites of Cybele, or even those of Bacchus. They were perverted, as emotional religious observances are always in danger of being — as were those of Bona Dea herself — to an instrument of corruption and licentiousness. But, unquestionably, at their introduction they did satisfy a human want for which the hereditary religion made no provision. If Catholicism finds its purest expression in the ecstasies of Saint Francis, if the most successful Protestant denominations stimulate the wild excitements of revivals and camp-meetings, we need not criticise the ancients too severely that they fed their religious cravings with fanaticisms, many of which differed from those of modern times rather in the object of the worship than in the forms and spirit. It was the best they could do. I am not concerned here to speak of the abominations to which they led — no more revolting than were attributed to the religious organization of the Knight Templars or than are known of the Anabaptists of Münster. I care rather for what is true in these superstitions than for what is false.

In a religious aspect, we are already at the transition period which divides the ancient pagan world from the modern Christian world. The Greek and the Roman religion had each run its course, and Asia was now called in to contribute the vital element which they lacked. The worship of Cybele, of Isis and Serapis, and of Mithras, attempted to give to humanity, although in an ignoble and distorted form, precisely those truths which Christianity brought home to the heart of men — immortality and the unity of the godhead. And if Christendom borrowed some of her most sacred institutions from the earliest Roman forms, if the Roman Catholic ritual and ceremonial are in many respects only the ancient Roman ones over again, and the festivals of the Church have many of them come straight down from republican times, yet these are but matters of form. In more essential spiritual points we find a frequent parallelism between the accepted doctrines of Christianity and that mixture of Roman and Oriental religion which had sway in the later Republic and the early Empire.

In the article upon the religion of the Greeks, already referred to, I pointed out the connection of the myths of Persephone, Adonis, and Osiris with the death of the year, and its revivication in spring, and showed how these myths became the symbol and expression of the idea of immortality. The Romans had hardly anything in their primitive religion which could be made use of for this purpose ; or, rather, it would be more correct to say, they did not possess the creative imagination which would develop their simple ideas into a sympathetic faith. Even when they introduced from Greece the combined worship of Ceres, Liber, and Libera, and Eleusinian mysteries along with it, it was left wholly to Greek priests, and would appear to have soon become wholly formal and lifeless. The worship of Cybele, introduced at the time of the Second Punic War, assumed a more popular and enthusiastic character, although even this failed to be fully developed until the time of the Empire, when the rites of the "Great Mother" became still more orgiastic, and were made the expression of a lively religious enthusiasm. In its essential features the new March festival of the Great Mother bore many resemblances to Easter. It was at just the same time of the year, when the day at last gets victory over the night, and the new spring rises to life from its long sleep. The festival lasted several days, chief among them being one of mourning and fasting, to which followed, on the 25th of March, a day of joy, when the dead Attis was raised to life from the grave.

The same idea was expressed in the Egyptian religion of Isis, which was one of the most popular in Rome at the time of the Christian era. The death of Osiris at the hands of his enemy Typhon was like the abduction of Persephone by the god of the lower world; the sad search by Isis for her lost husband was that of Demeter for her daughter; and, when the lost one was found at last, the worshipers broke out in shouts of joy, "We have found him; we rejoice with thee!" In this Egyptian myth, as transformed by the Alexandrian Greeks, Osiris became Serapis, who lived on as king of the lower world; a somewhat different phase of the belief in immortality from that which is seen in the worship of Cybele. In the worship of Isis we mark for the first time a tendency to give personality and a name to that supreme deity, ὁ τὸν ὅλον κόσμον συντάττων, whom so many philosophers and thinkers had already recognized. "Thou, goddess Isis, who alone art all things," says an inscription; and her enthusiastic votaries claimed for this goddess that she was, in truth, the supreme divinity.

We must not make the mistake, however, of recognizing in a supreme divinity such as this the strict idea of one god, like the Jewish Jehovah. Polytheism does not differ from monotheism in the accident of number alone, but in the very conception of the divine nature. By *deus* the Romans meant only a supernatural being, who could help or harm men, and who might be an object of reverence; what we understand by a *spirit.* Thus the spirits of the departed were *dii manes;* that is, when the *genius,* or indwelling spirit of a man, passed from his body, it became a god. Primarily there is no necessary inequality among these spirits, only a difference of function; and it was the greater or less importance and extent of these functions, or the accident of local worship, that gave one god a higher position in rank and power than another. Thus Jupiter, the god of the sky, whose powers had so wide a sway and whose sphere embraced that of all others, naturally became the chief god, both with Greeks and Romans; while Mars, from the accident of his being the special god of the Italian race, held a much higher position than his Greek counterpart, Ares. But Jupiter was only the strongest of the gods: he was not god in the monotheistic view. When the Greek and Roman philosophers spoke of a divine power which was really supreme in the universe, they rarely called it Zeus or Jupiter, but Fate, or Necessity, or simply God.

On the other hand, monotheism is not at all incompatible with a multitude of divine beings, such as the Romans would have called *dei*. The Jews had their angels, the Catholic Church has its saints, even the Protestants hold fast to the existence of angels, devils, ghosts, and witches. "The difference between monotheism and polytheism," says Hartung, "lies noways in the number of supernatural beings, but in the relation of this plurality to the unity.... In the former necessity has given way to freedom, in the latter freedom is confined under necessity"; that is, "the heathen gods have necessity over them, not in them; under it they act after their wills, endowed with like conditions, but higher powers than men," so that Jupiter was only the first among equals.

The symbolism of the myth of Isis and Osiris — the same as that of Demeter and Persephone, Cybele and Attis, Aphrodite and Adonis — is the deepest and tenderest in the whole range of mythology; and the truth of immortality expressed in it is one of the dearest to the human heart. Probably there was something in the Egyptian costume and ritual that took a peculiar hold of whatever was sensitive in the Roman people, and at any rate this worship seemed to them to embody all results of the centuries of Egyptian wisdom and learning. However that may be, it was the popular religion in the early Empire;

and Isis and her husband — under his new name Serapis — not unnaturally gathered about them most of the enthusiastic and sympathetic elements of faith. With him were identified all the highest attributes of deity, with her all the womanly qualities, like the Virgin Mary in the Catholic system: their devotees went so far as to claim that all the chief gods and goddesses of various nations — those who might themselves have been called the sole God — were only these under other names and in different form. This was not pure monotheism, but rather an effort to raise one out of the pantheon to a higher rank than the rest, by removing his rivals. On the other hand, it was a step towards monotheism, and satisfied the monotheistic cravings, so far as they consciously existed at that time. It has been already said that this was a transitional period, when beliefs were being transformed, and rites from all parts of the earth were brought together and compared. In consistency with this, the conception of a chief god was no longer the polytheistic one ; at the same time it was not yet clearly monotheistic.

The dynasty of the Severi, which formed so important an epoch in the political development of the Empire, was an almost equally important one in religious matters. It marks a new irruption of Asiatic superstitions, chiefly embodied in the worship of the sun, under his Syrian name Elagabalus and the Persian name Mithras. With the Unconquerable Sun, *Sol Invictus*, was associated a still higher form of the growing monotheistic conception than that of Isis and Serapis. The worship of Mithras, with its strange and bloody symbolism, and its claims to represent the unity of the godhead, was zealously prosecuted even after Christianity had become the State religion. Heathenism, in its expiring form, assumed all the attributes and claims of the victorious faith which it could, and thus for a while held its ground against it. To this period belong especially the fastings, expiations, and cleansing rites which form a link between the pagan religion and mediæval Christianity. The most striking of them was the *Taurobolion*, or baptism in the blood of a bull (other animals were also used), which was connected especially with the March festival of the Magna Mater. It was a striking illustration, however, of the growing unity of faith, that this ceremony was not peculiar to any one worship, but was associated with all the forms of orgiastic religion of the time.

Lastly, a word must be said upon the worship of the emperor. This has been a strange puzzle to many moderns, but was in reality not merely a direct outgrowth of the ancient religious conceptions, but a very striking and immediate link between them and those of the modern world. It was not the man Augustus or Trajan that was worshiped, but the divine spirit, the *genius*, which dwelt in them and inspired the great actions of their life. If this *genius* became a god at the death of the poorest and meanest, and was added to the *dii manes*, how much more in the case of great and beneficent sovereigns! The apotheosis of an emperor after his death, even the worship of his *genius* during his life, was neither irrational nor illogical, when once we understand the ancient conception of the divine nature. That the same honors were bestowed upon a Nero and Caracalla may have been fear or flattery; it was, at any rate, an outgrowth of the same mode of thought. But we need not go to the ancients for an analogy. The modern world is perfectly familiar with the spectacle of a man of ordinary powers and passions invested, by the election of a body of men, with a peculiar holiness and sanctity, so that it is conceived that, when he speaks, it is God that speaks through him. No one believes that it is in the man Gregory or Leo that this divinity consists, but that in some way a divine nature has been added to his human nature by a direct and special act of the Almighty. Now, the pope is as much a god, in the eyes of his followers, as a Roman emperor ever was ; that is, not at all, according to the modern definition of the word *god.* The appointment to the imperial dignity was, on the average, hardly more irregular, in respect to fraud, violence, and corruption, than that to the papacy during a great part of its history ; and any one who believes that John XII. and Alexander VI. were clothed with these holy attributes and powers by virtue of the post they held as Christ's vicegerent on earth need not find any difficulty in seeing how the Roman people could believe that Caligula and Commodus were invested with a similar sanctity by virtue of holding a post which at that time and for that people was the highest and most important that could be conceived of.

My aim in this paper has been, first, to point out the essential and distinctive features of the primitive religion of the Romans, and to show how important its study is in the comparative view of religions ; secondly, to show that its overthrow in the later Republic was a necessary development, and that the superstitions which took its place were not merely the best and only substitute they had, but did actually satisfy some of the most earnest cravings of the human heart. The corruptions they underwent were quite as much the result as the cause of the corruptions of society.

Of the works whose titles are placed at the head of the article, that of Preller is, on the whole, the most complete and satisfactory for the use of the student. Hartung is a writer of more originality, and far more suggestive and instructive for the philosophy of the subject. Zumpt's little treatise contains some excellent points ; but it was a popular address, and makes no pretensions to fulness. Marquardt's work is admirably clear and copious in citation, like all his writings ; but it is partial, being purely the antiquities of worship, rather than the religious system as such. Preller's treatise, being later than Hartung's and more extensive, contains material which Hartung has passed over, so that, while quite inferior in insight and suggestiveness, it is superior in arrangement and completeness.

THE PLACE OF THE NORTH-WEST IN GENERAL HISTORY.*

THE hundredth anniversary of the first settlement of English-speaking people within the borders of the North-west, celebrated at Marietta last spring, has called the attention of our people to the importance of this event in the history of our country. It is not the least significant among the centennial celebrations in which these last years have abounded. But perhaps few have observed that we have this year not merely a centennial anniversary, but a bi-centennial, yes, even a three-hundredth anniversary. In 1688 was the English Revolution; in 1588 the destruction of the Spanish Armada — two events which it would be difficult to match in these centuries for significance in the history of free institutions, and even, we may assert, in their bearing upon the history of the North-west.

Three hundred years ago Spain was the first power in the world, a nation arrogant, tyrannical, bigoted, grasping beyond even the customary standard of great powers, possessing an extent of territory and an amount of resources surpassing, I should say, even those of Napoleon when at the height of his power. The territories governed by Philip II. comprised the whole Spanish peninsula, from which he derived the best equipped, disciplined, and commanded army in the world; about a half of the Italian peninsula, then the seat of the highest civilization of the age; the whole of the Netherlands, the most populous, wealthy, and industrious community north of the Alps; considerable portions of what is now France; and the

---

* Paper read before the American Historical Association, in Washington, D. C., December 27, 1888.

New World, from which he received yearly immense treasures of gold and silver. This New World, discovered by
Spanish enterprise, and granted almost exclusively to
Spain by papal decree, had not yet to any appreciable extent been withdrawn from Spanish control. France and
England, it is true, refused to recognize the exclusive
claim of Spain : their explorers are among the most illustrious of the sixteenth century, and both nations had made
attempts at colonization. But these attempts were feeble
and short-lived. In 1588 Spain was the only European
power that held a foot of ground in North America, and
her absolute title was asserted as haughtily as ever.
Florida was occupied by a flourishing colony ; so was New
Mexico ; and the country lying between, explored by De
Soto and Coronado, had been, it might fairly be said,
vindicated beyond a doubt for the Spanish crown. Our
North-west was still unknown, and in the undisputed possession of the savages ; but whoever had attempted to
forecast the future in that year would have said that
Spain was destined almost certainly to extend her empire
over the whole of North America.

This mighty Spanish empire was not overthrown all at
once, nor by any single person or event ; its dissolution
was the work of a number of causes, inducing weakness
in the governing power, and gradually severing from its
rule the greater part of the outlying countries. So far as
we can ascribe the result to individual causes, we may say
that William of Orange was the person who gave the first
serious blow to Spanish domination, but that the event
which more than any other brought to light the inherent
weakness of Spain, and hastened its decay, was the defeat
of the Armada in 1588. It was the fortunate privilege of
England to present herself as the champion of free institutions, and the foremost antagonist of Spain in the events
which followed.

Ten years after the defeat of the Armada, in 1598,

Philip II. died; and less than ten years after this we find both French and English colonies of a permanent character established upon the coast of North America. The Atlantic seaboard, north of Florida, was irretrievably lost to Spain. Florida and New Mexico were still held firmly in her grasp; but the vast territory between, which we now call the Mississippi Valley, remained unknown and unoccupied. The dim and shadowy memories of De Soto's exploration gave no valid title to this territory, because there had been no attempt at permanent occupation. This priceless domain lay ready for the first-comer; and that first-comer was not likely to be Spain, for Spain had lost all enterprise and initiative.

Let us now pass down to the next hundredth anniversary, and inquire what we find in 1688. France had now succeeded to Spain as the leading power of the world. Louis XIV. had taken the place of Philip II. as an aspirant to dominion over the world. The domination of France under Louis XIV. would have been preferable to the domination of Spain under Philip II., for it presented, on the whole, the highest civilization of the age; and, insolent, unscrupulous, and unfeeling as Louis was, his rule did not crush and benumb, as did that of Spain under the Philips. But the supremacy of France, like that of Spain, even if not in the same degree, meant the overthrow of national independence and the extinction of free institutions wherever it went; and the best interests of mankind now called for resistance to France, as a century earlier for resistance to Spain. Now as then the man who headed this resistance was William of Orange,— great-grandson of the other — and the nation was England. The Revolution of 1688, which secured to England her free institutions, at the same time brought her into line with the nations of the continent which were arrayed against the ambitious schemes of Louis XIV., and made her the champion of Europe against French aggrandizement.

Nowhere had France gained greater and more significant successes than in North America. This was, in a sense, the heroic age of the French people; at all events, it was the heroic age of the French Church, and it was now that the French people threw themselves most heartily into the work of exploration, discovery, and colonizaation, as well as of the propagation of their faith. France, as if by right, stepped in and took possession of the vacant tract between Florida and New Mexico, to which Spain had once had a certain claim, but which Spain no longer possessed the enterprise to occupy. The discovery by Nicolet, the exploration by Radisson, Joliet, Marquette, and Hennepin, the occupation by La Salle and Iberville, followed one another with rapidity; and in 1688 France was in undisputed possession of the valley of the Mississippi as well as of that of the St. Lawrence and the Great Lakes. Spain was crowded back to her old possessions on the Gulf of Mexico; England was confined to a narrow strip between the Alleghanies and the ocean, which the enormous empire of New France surrounded upon the north and west. The prophet who had undertaken in 1688 to forecast the future would assuredly have said that North America was destined to be the possession of France.

The Revolution of 1688, placing England at the head of the coalition against France, speedily brought the two nations into collision in the western continent. Frontenac's invasion of New York, Sir William Phips's invasion of Canada, the cruel Indian raids and massacres, the succession of intercolonial wars — these events are familiar to every school-boy, and have been related with graphic detail by one of our most eminent historians, Francis Parkman. It was soon made plain that France had passed the culminating point of her greatness, and that the star of England was in the ascendent. The first great series of wars, known in our colonial history as King

William's and Queen Anne's Wars, ended with the treaty of Utrecht in 1713, by which the entire Atlantic coast was transferred from France to Great Britain. The next great series of wars, known as King George's Wars — the old French War, and the French and Indian War — ended in 1763, with the treaty of Paris, which gave to England all that remained of the French possessions east of the Mississippi. As at the same time her possessions west of the Mississippi were conveyed to Spain, France was by these events utterly stripped of her American territories. It was a collapse of national greatness and aspirations such as the world has seldom witnessed.

Thus England succeeded to France as the foremost power of the world ; and our North-west, having in the sixteenth century seemed destined to belong to Spain, and having in the seventeenth century been an integral part of the dominions of France, now in the eighteenth century found itself in the possession of Great Britain. The events that followed are well known — how this territory was vindicated for the new republic by the arms of George Rogers Clark, and the diplomacy of Jay and his colleagues ; how the sagacious legislation of the Confederate Congress organized it in the spirit of free institutions ; and how then the anniversary year 1788 sealed this series of events by a formal and well-ordered act of organization.

The eighteenth century is not an heroic age. Neither its personages nor its actions are of a character to excite enthusiasm or moral interest. Its wars, illuminated by the exploits of two of the greatest military geniuses of history — Marlborough and Frederick — are not inspired by a single great or fruitful principle — in humiliating contrast with the wars of religion in the sixteenth and seventeenth centuries, or the wars of independence and the revolutionary struggles of the nineteenth. Its diplomacy

aimed at nothing but to deceive and swindle. To us of
the present day its thought seems commonplace, its poetry
flat and prosaic, its society sensual and corrupt. Even
that great awakening of mind which we associate with
Voltaire, Diderot, and Rousseau, repels us by its crude-
ness and sentimentality. But selfish and sordid as the
century was, in its aims and its achievements, there is one
fact that stands out in the history of the balance of power
as an event of more than ordinary importance, the transfer
of the leadership in the society of nations to the peoples
of the North. The significant fact in the dynastic history
of the eighteenth century is the coming to the front of
England and Prussia. The greatness of Prussia was reserved for the present century and generation. In the
eighteenth century its growth was rapid, but its place
remained second to that of Great Britain. England and
the English race now took the lead ; and the leadership
thus assumed is marked by two events of prime importance and significance — the building up of a British
Empire and the American Revolution.

The British Empire, upon which, together with her
maritime superiority, the power of Great Britain, and
her ascendency in the European family of nations, have
rested, may be said to have been the creation of the
Seven Years' War, and to have come into being with the
acquisition of the French colonies in America at the end
of that war in 1763. Not that Great Britain was destitute of foreign possessions before this, or that these were
her only acquisitions at this epoch. She had already
numerous colonies and military posts in various parts of
the world ; and her Indian empire was founded almost in
the same year with the conquest of New France. But
these American possessions so far outstripped all her
other possessions in extent, in resources, and in compactness, that it may fairly be asserted that it was especially
these that made it a British Empire, and that made Great

Britain the first power in the world. North America was now partitioned between England and Spain — between the nation which stood first in power and enterprise and one which had steadily declined in both respects for two hundred years. Mistress of half a continent, with a sluggish and decaying neighbor in occupation of the other half, England enjoyed a prestige and inspired a degree of respect which all the rest of her colonial possessions could never have given her.

We shall see, when we come to speak of the American Revolution, how impossible it is to understand the causes of that event without an adequate appreciation of the fact just mentioned — that the British Empire derived its greatness directly from its American colonies. At present we will turn to the distinctive character of the British Empire itself, in its relation to the European family of nations.

The great fact, therefore, in the dynastic history of the eighteenth century is the shifting of the balance of power, by which England succeeded to France in what we may call the *hegemony*, or leadership, in the European system. This change was not a mere incident, a mere substitution of one unscrupulous and grasping power for another. It marked a radical reconstruction of that European system, a revolution in the temper and character of the domination aspired to. I do not intend to claim for England any higher motives or any less questionable practices than were those of the Continental nations that she superseded; although, as coheirs in the great inheritance of English liberty, we might well be pardoned if we believed that our mother country displayed a cleaner life in her public men and greater honesty in international relations than her rivals on the Continent. But we must be prepared, in the public affairs of every nation, to find a standard of morality lower than that of private life; and in this respect neither England nor America can claim to be

without sin. But this is not the point. The thing to be
noted is that the transfer of leadership from the southern
nations of Europe to the northern meant the prominence
of a totally different type of national life, and the introduction of a new principle of government. It has been
the mission of the Germanic race, which now took possession of society, to preserve and develop the habits and
capacity of self-government, and give them a controlling
place in European society.

It is not my practice to insist overmuch upon inherent
differences in race — a theory upon which a great deal of
nonsense has been talked and written. But that different
races have independent and well-defined traditions and
environment, and a disparity of capacities and powers as
the outgrowth of these, no person can question. In accordance with this we readily recognize that, from some
cause lying too far back for us to comprehend, the Germanic race has been distinguished at all ages for its political capacity, and the possession of vigorous institutions of self-government; that there grew up among the
nations of this race a well-ordered system of government,
based upon the rights of the individual; and that all the
Germanic nations of the North have preserved these institutions in a more or less complete degree of vigor and
efficiency.

The nations of this race were never brought under the
authority of the Roman Empire, and made to exchange
their native system of government for that of Rome; the
victory of Arminius in the Teutoburgensian Forest preserved our ancestors from this fate. I would not be
understood to deprecate the great services to humanity
rendered by the Roman Empire. It was without question
a great good fortune for Gaul to be conquered by Cæsar,
because the tribal institutions, by which the nations of
Gaul were still governed, appear to have received all the
development of which they were capable, and to have

consisted at this time in the unrestricted rule of an imperi-
ous aristocracy, indifferent to the welfare of its subjects
and incapable of progress.   Vercingetorix was perhaps a
nobler and more heroic man than Arminius ; and, at any
rate, the uprising led by him inspires the heartiest human
interest and sympathy.   But, when it failed, we cannot
feel that humanity or even Gaul was worse off for it ; his
success would have been a disaster.   So with most of the
other nations conquered by Rome.   They had passed their
prime, and were stagnating in an effete civilization or
trembling under cruel despotism.   But with the Germans
it was different.   It would have been a great calamity if
they, with their uncorrupted social life and their vigorous
though undeveloped political institutions, had been forced
to become subjects to the Roman system.   Those German
nations which pushed across the bounds, and established
themselves upon the soil of the empire, were obliged to
submit to this fate.   The Goths and Franks lost all memory of their original liberties, and entered into the traditions of the Roman Empire.   But free Germany and
Scandinavia retained their institutions essentially unimpaired ; and with the triumph of England, in the eighteenth century, the Germanic principles of self-government triumphed for all Europe.

For five hundred years the leadership in Europe had
been held by nations which dwelt within the bounds of
the Roman Empire, and had inherited its principles of
unlimited authority and despotic rule.   Italy had first
exercised this influence, not so much by superiority of
material or political force as by her intellectual maturity,
the splendor of her civilization, and the spiritual authority
possessed by her ecclesiastical head.   With the Renaissance of the fifteenth century the nations beyond the Alps
entered into the intellectual life of Italy, which country
now lost its intellectual leadership, while the spiritual
power of the Pope, with a certain authority growing out of

it, as arbiter in international controversies, was destroyed by the religious revolution of the century following. Spain and France, which enjoyed undisputed precedence among nations during the sixteenth and seventeenth centuries, inherited in the fullest degree the traditions and practices of the Roman domination. It was only slowly and feebly that the free institutions of the North asserted themselves successively in England, Holland, Sweden, and Prussia, and wrested a tardy recognition from the autocratic states of the South.

It is not an accident that the moment of the advance of England to the leading place among nations was also a turning-point in the *constitutional* and the *international* relations of these nations. For a hundred years, since the close of the period of religious wars by the treaty of Westphalia in 1648, and of the English civil war the next year by the execution of Charles I. — during these hundred years the sovereigns of Europe had been engaged in unintermitted efforts to enlarge their territories and increase their power. In all this period it is hard to discern any issue in the wars or the diplomatic relations except pure greed, or the desire to place a check to this greed and preserve the balance of power. And in internal affairs the only principle of government was the absolute authority of the sovereign. This principle held sway everywhere except in England, and even in England the more liberal principle of government was to a great extent neutralized by despotic practice. No country in Europe at this epoch was governed more arbitrarily, with a more complete disregard of popular rights, than Catholic Ireland under the rule of the Whig, or Constitutional, party of Protestant England.

After the Seven Years' War, and the Peace of Paris (1763), we meet no more wars of an exclusively dynastic character. Always the rights of the people or of the nationality form an element, and more and more the controlling element, in public relations. Even the Partition of Poland, the grossest and most wanton abuse of absolute power, is a significant event, as for the first time bringing the principle of nationality actively and conspicuously into notice. Then followed the American Revolution ; and the revolutionary period was fairly opened, which has lasted to the present day. In the tremendous struggles of the intervening century there have been many moments of reaction and depression, in which popular liberties have seemed hopelessly lost. But the result of it all is that nearly every country of Europe has, first or last, had its constitution remodelled on the plan of that of England ; and constitutional liberty of the English type has everywhere, except in Russia and Turkey, superseded the absolute system of government which prevailed universally upon the Continent a century ago. I do not assert that these parliamentary institutions have always been well planned and successful in their workings. I do not overlook a certain reaction against them at the present time, not only in the nations of the Continent, but in England itself. The fact itself of their dissemination is none the less noteworthy and significant.

Along with parliamentary institutions and local self-government, equally with these an outgrowth of the democratic temper, the English race stands for the dignity of labor. No more fundamental contrast exists between ancient and modern society than in the absolute denial in the one, and the hearty recognition in the other, of the claims of industry in the organization of society. Industry in the ancient world was left to slaves and dependents : a freeman was disgraced by labor. Now, in those countries of the Continent which have derived their institutions and civilization by an unbroken succession from the Roman Empire, industry has continued to be held in the same contempt ; and, as even the countries of the North have been exposed to this influence in some degree, this aristocratic principle of contempt for labor has had control of society through all modern times, but least of all in England and the countries of Scandinavia. In these the democratic spirit was never extinct; and, when England assumed the leadership among European nations, she ushered in the dawn of an industrial epoch, when the arts and avocations of peace shall take precedence of those of war. Even in the present age of enormous and costly armaments, it is noticeable how every one of these military nations is reorganizing its social system on an industrial basis. Railroads, manufactures, the technical arts, scientific agriculture, control society in France and Italy as truly as in England and America.

It cannot be said of this industrial revolution, as it can be said of the introduction of parliamentary institutions, that it is directly and entirely the work of England. It is the modern spirit, the spirit of the age, closely connected with that Christian civilization which forms the chief difference between modern society and ancient. But the English, having come less directly under the influence of Roman traditions than any other of the leading nations of Europe, and having, therefore, preserved more completely their primitive free institutions and the democratic spirit of which these were the outgrowth, are the foremost representatives and the pioneers of this movement. When Napoleon called the English "a race of shop-keepers," he spoke in a spirit of pagan antiquity, in high contempt of any but military interests. The industrial age has its faults and dangers. The shop-keeping spirit is prone to become mean-spirited, sordid, gross. But the nation of shop-keepers manifested a military energy and efficiency which humbled the great Napoleon himself, and it is a significant fact that Prussia did not lend her hand to the work until her social institutions had been reorganized in the modern spirit by the reforms of Stein.

Another point may be noted in passing. It is not in

the nations thoroughly imbued with the modern industrial spirit, but in those which are ruled by the traditions of the Roman Empire, that that social weakness exists and those social agitations have originated which threaten to subvert our social organization. Germany, the home of Socialism, forms no exception to this assertion. It is, it is true, a Teutonic country, and possessed originally the same free institutions as England ; but it was brought at a very early date by the conquest of Charles the Great into close connection with the Romance nations ; was thoroughly feudalized; and, while never losing entirely its primitive local liberties, was reduced under the rule of absolutism as completely as its southern neighbors. But it is not too much to claim that in the nations of English race, along with inequalities of condition and inadequacy of law, such as are incident to human nature, there is nevertheless a fundamentally democratic spirit in social relations, which affords no hold to anti-social theories. Labor contests there may no doubt be ; but schemes to destroy society itself could never have originated in an Anglo-Saxon community.

The leadership among European nations, secured to England by the Seven Years' War, meant for Europe free institutions and the advent of an industrial age : for America its significance was truly incalculable. Until now the English colonies had ranked third in extent and importance ; now they divided the continent with those of Spain. However magnificent the claims of the English colonies, their actual occupation had been only a narrow strip along the coast ; and, what is more, they were incapable of expansion, so long as Spain held Florida, and France the Mississippi Valley. Now their territories seemed sufficient for an unlimited growth of population. The first great step had been taken towards the realization of the manifest destiny of the Anglo-Saxon race to control the continent of North America. The acquisition of Louisiana, the treaty of Guadaloupe Hidalgo, the Gadsden purchase — all followed almost by an uncontrollable necessity; and, if some of these steps were marked with insolence and bad faith on our part, the injustice cannot now be undone, and to the lands themselves it is an almost unmixed benefit that they have been brought under the sway of the English race.

The establishment of the British Empire in America brought with it English civilization, English law, English political ideas. The practices of local self-government, parliamentary institutions, the supremacy of law over the will of the sovereign, the place of precedence assumed by industrial interests — all these, which we have found to be the distinctive characteristics of the Germanic political ideals as opposed to those of the Romance nations, were by this event made dominant in the continent of North America.

The method of colonization of the two rival nations, as has often been pointed out, assisted in this. The French occupation, thinly spread over an immense area, consisting of scattered forts, missionary posts, and the isolated cabins of roving fur-traders, testified to the sovereignty of the French crown, but had hardly any points of contact with the French people. It was therefore superficial and transitory. Before the Seven Years' War France ruled supreme over the greater part of the continent. A hundred years later it had utterly vanished, leaving no traces but a few names. It had no roots. We have our Fond du Lac and Eau Claire and Prairie du Chien, our *cooleys*, *dalles*, and *portages;* and from these names we know that this land was once a French land. But these towns bear no trace of French origin except their names. English civilization has completely superseded French. For the English colonization was carried on by a slow and thorough process of occupation. Its settlement was compact, orderly, industrious. At every step it was organized in bodies politic, all connected with one another by ties of common origin and common interest. This has been the method of English and American colonization from that day to this — more rapid as new means of transportation and intercourse were available, more superficial when new lands were opened in a quantity disproportioned to the number of settlers; assimilating foreign elements of population and bringing them into active relation to its political system, but everywhere busying itself with the foundation and organization of political communities. In this work we meet with many failures, much inefficiency, much positively bad government; but in this, we heartily believe, is to be found the only sure foundation of the future nation, the only guaranty of future liberty.

Thus the statesmanship of Pitt and the victories of Wolfe secured to our North-west the inestimable treasures of English liberties, English institutions, English civilization. The next stage in our history was the further development of these institutions and the more complete realization of these principles of liberty through the American Revolution.

The characteristic political events of the nineteenth century are the extension of the English parliamentary system to the nations of the Continent, and the spread of the revolutionary spirit — two events which are to a certain extent independent of one another, although both of them are expressions of the Germanic principles of government. In their origin, they are connected with the two great events which, as I have said, marked the predominance of the English race. As the building up of the English Empire gave to England a position among nations so conspicuous and controlling that her parliamentary institutions became the model of theirs, so the American Revolution inaugurated the revolutionary epoch in the world's history, setting an example to the European nations which they were rarely capable of following to good purpose, but which at any rate led the way to the triumph of free principles in the end.

The British Empire was not established without enormous expenditure, both of men and of money. Weakened as France was in national character, in public spirit, and even in material resources, under a king, Louis XV., whose name is a synonym for sloth and dissoluteness, she nevertheless did not surrender her rank among nations without a tremendous struggle. From this struggle England emerged with increased power and prestige, and far from exhausted in resources, but with a consciousness that these resources had been strained to their uttermost, and in such pecuniary embarrassment as she had never experienced before. It is not my intention to narrate events which are familiar to all, or to enter into the analysis of the causes of the Revolution, which, even if they were not already so well understood, do not belong to my subject. But I wish to bring into prominence the fact, which is not so generally noticed, of the close connection between the American Revolution and the establishment of the British Empire. Upon the acquisition of New France by the treaty of Paris in 1763 rested, more than upon anything else, the greatness of this empire; but it was this very acquisition that led, by an inevitable sequence of the cause and effect, to the uprising of the colonies and the severance from the empire of its most important dependencies. The time and circumstances of this uprising are most significant. Says Parkman : " The measures on the part of the mother country which roused their resentment, far from being oppressive, were less burdensome than the navigation laws to which they had long submitted ; and they resisted taxation by Parliament simply because it was a principle opposed to their rights as freemen. They did not, like the American provinces of Spain at a later day, sunder themselves from a parent fallen into decrepitude, but with astonishing audacity they affronted the wrath of England in the hour of her triumph, forgot their jealousies and quarrels, joined hands in the common cause, fought, endured, and won." *

The American Revolution was the second great act in the newly asserted preponderance of the Anglo-Saxon race. With it commenced the revolutionary era, which has been the most characteristic fact of the last hundred years. I am careful not to say that these revolutionary movements were caused by the American Revolution. They had causes enough on the spot, in the oppression and misgovernment inherited from former centuries: the revolutionary era would have commenced in France if it had not commenced in America. Nay, the misfortune was that the European revolutionists did not take example by us. A high enthusiasm, the inspiration which comes from witnessing our success and prosperity — this is pretty much all that the French Revolution derived immediately from ours. But its type was wholly opposed to ours. The American Revolution was a conservative act, directly in the line of English constitutional history. Our fathers claimed that the mother country had forgotten its own principles, and they arose to maintain inherited and traditional rights, to vindicate the historical liberties of Englishmen. In France, on the other hand, there were no such historical liberties to vindicate, or, if there ever had been any, they had been ruthlessly trampled down, and long forgotten. The French people were inspired, in their revolt, by an indefinite craving for something better, they knew not what; the abuses which they wished to be rid of were plain enough, but how to secure themselves against future misgovernment they did not know. The blind groping in the dark, the crude theories, the futile efforts to imitate models which they did not understand and to adopt reforms for which they were not prepared, lend a pathetic interest to the first years of the French Revolution.

* Montcalm and Wolfe, vol. ii., p. 413.

In the republican institutions of the United States the English constitution has received a new development and a somewhat new form. They are a legitimate and healthy outgrowth of the original Germanic institutions. But to England herself the event has been no less salutary in the complete remodelling of her colonial system, which was a result of the American revolt. The colonial system, the principle that the colonies were dependent provinces, existing only for the advantage of the mother country, to add to her glory and help her citizens to amass wealth — this system was the cause of the American Revolution. Against it the colonists claimed that they were not subjects and dependents, but citizens, endowed with all the rights of Englishmen. Here was the issue, which was decided by the arbitrament of war. As a mere question of law, possibly it is not so clear and self-evident as our ancestors thought. Some English writers maintain to the present day that our claim was unfounded, and the alleged grievances gave no ground for resistance. But it is not a mere question of law, but of public polity ; and the significant fact is that the American theory has, in the result, prevailed, and has become an accepted part of the English constitution. The old colonial system was killed by the American Revolution. The greatness of the British Empire was too firmly founded, and had too active germs of youth, to be crippled or more than temporarily checked even by the loss of its most important colonies. It has gone on enlarging and prospering until at the present day it is for extent and resources, even if not in immediately available military strength, the most powerful in the world's history; and in all its wide-spread territories, wherever circumstances permit, the genuine English principle of self-government, the principle that the inhabitants are citizens and not dependents, now prevails. The colonial system, which kept our ancestors in a condition of subjection, and led to the war for independence, is dead.

In treating of the relation of the North-west to general history, it has been necessary to take a rather wider survey than the subject would itself seem to require, and sometimes to speak of the North-west almost as if its future were that of the country of which it forms only a small part. But it has happened more than once that in the North-west, small as it is, we have found the key to problems of a national character. And, in summing up, I wish to emphasize four points, which have formed the principal subject of my paper, and which, I think, will warrant the prominence given to this aspect of our history.

First, the title to the North-west belonged in succession to the three great nations, Spain, France, and England, which, in the sixteenth, seventeenth, and eighteenth centuries respectively, possessed the acknowledged leadership among the European states.

Second, the leadership acquired by England in the eighteenth century was integrally associated with the building up of the British Empire; and the decisive fact in the formation of this empire was the acquisition from France of that enormous tract of territory of which the North-west is the centre—the keystone, as we may call it, of the arch.

Third, the imperial destiny of the United States hung upon the possession of this North-west. But for the military successes of Clark, and the diplomatic skill of our commissioners who negotiated the treaty of peace, in securing just this territory, our domain would have been contracted, our national aspirations would have had no scope, and it is not likely that there would have been the courage to make the purchase of Louisiana and the subsequent acquisitions.

Fourth, the development of our national policy was closely connected with, and, in fact, first took shape in, the ordinance which organized this territory. Our territorial system, our policy of creating new States, our national guaranty of personal freedom, universal education, and religious liberty, found their first expression in the great act which provided for the government of the North-west.

HISTORICAL FICTION.*

A RECENT English review of an American historical novel, "Passe-Rose," says, "The historical novel is at a low ebb; it is unpopular with the highly cultured reader, for it must almost inevitably annoy him with more or less gross and disillusioning anachronism; it is wearisome to the mass of literary subscribers, for it deals with episodes of no present significance and with personages of alien speech and manners; and it is not of very strong appeal even to those who love to have their wine of literature diluted with the water of instructive facts." †

There is much truth in this criticism, which touches upon the two principal defects of historical fiction — its anachronisms and its remoteness from the interests of the present. And, nevertheless, the reviewer gives hearty praise to the book which he is reviewing, and our supply of historical fiction shows no signs of giving out. No sooner is "The Master of Ballantrae" finished in *Scribner's Monthly* than Harold Frederick commences "In the Valley" in the pages of the same magazine, the scene of both stories being laid in the middle of the last century. The present year has besides witnessed the publication of new novels treating of the times of Nero, Charlemagne, Nuremberg in the Middle Ages, Charles II. and James II., and the Christian Martyrs; while the historical novels of Dumas and Victor Hugo have appeared in new and luxurious editions. The historical novel has become a recognized branch of literature: it

* The last piece of completed writing composed by Professor Allen. It was read before the Madison (Wisconsin) Literary Club, November 11, 1889, four weeks before his death, and posthumously published in the *Unitarian Review*, vol. 33, p. 447 (May, 1890).— EDS.

† William Sharp in the *Academy*, July 13, 1889.

meets a want; it is not likely to disappear. Let us then consider what are its merits and its shortcomings, what we can expect from it and what we cannot expect, and establish, if possible, some canons of criticism which may apply to this special branch of literature.

The historical novel is, it must be confessed, a hybrid, being at once history and fiction, dealing both with real events and with imaginary personages and occurrences. It is not my province to discuss the subject of fiction in general — to define the romance, the novel, the tale; to decide the controversy between the realistic and the ideal schools; to determine how far it is allowable to make fiction the vehicle for instruction and controversy. If historical fiction has any place at all, it is as "diluting the wine of literature with the water of instructive facts." It is therefore from the point of view not of fiction, but of history, that we are to examine the subject, to determine whether fiction may properly be made the medium for historical instruction, and, if so, of what nature and within what limitations.

For what purpose do we study history at all? Here, again, as in relation to fiction as a branch of literature, the subject is too large and complex to be treated in the introduction to a short paper. I do not ask whether the study of history is beneficial: that we may take for granted; nor what benefits we may derive from it: this question will be considered as we go on, so far as is necessary for the ends of this discussion. Assuming that the study of history is beneficial, and leaving on one side for the present the consideration just what good we may derive from it, let us turn our attention to the question what historical facts or classes of facts are important to know. The entire field of history is too vast for any one person to master. The facts of which it consists — events, institutions, customs, characters, ideas — are infinite in number and complexity. It is only by selecting certain facts and concentrating our attention upon these, leaving unnoticed the much larger body of facts which, for our purposes, are indifferent, that we can accomplish any valuable result.

The outline of events — dates, dynastic changes, decisive battles, wars of conquest, rise and fall of empires — must be learned as *history:* fictions can have nothing to do with the systematic study of these. But, when we have learned these, what, after all, do we possess? Only a skeleton, to be clothed with the flesh and blood of history. These facts have no more value in themselves than the names and positions of the stars to one who has no knowledge of the constitution and movements of the heavenly bodies; or the minute description of every variety of beetle or lichen, apart from the laws of growth and classification. Except for the gratification of intellectual curiosity, enabling us to understand the allusions in literature to historical names and events, the value of historical study consists entirely in two things: first, it teaches the relations of cause and effect, as they are exemplified in the working of historical forces, the interplay of human passions and interests; secondly, it introduces us to the life of a past generation, so that its thoughts, its emotions, its habits, its concerns, may in a measure become as real to us as that of the age in which we live, and the people whom we meet every day. These we may call the philosophical and the picturesque aspects of history; and I do not know of any other benefit conferred by historical study. No historical fact is of any value except so far as it helps us to understand human nature or the working of historic forces.

Now, the first of these, the study of historical causes and effects, lies out of the range of historical fiction as completely as is the case with the systematic study of events. Both of these — events and their interpretation — may come incidentally into historical fiction, but only incidentally. The methods are totally different. These subjects, especially the relations of cause and effect, must be treated with a certain degree of abstraction, and almost wholly by analysis ; but fiction, so far as it is skilful, avoids abstractions, eschews analysis. Its method is synthetic and concrete, and whatever use we can make of it in historical instruction must be by concrete and synthetic representations.

It is plain that this concrete method of fiction is exactly adapted to the second of the two objects specified, the picturesque aspect of history, the delineations of life and society. But what I want especially to point out is that this is precisely what formal instruction in history, or formal historical treatises, cannot do at all, or can do only very imperfectly. Nothing is so dreary and devoid of life as chapters upon life and manners : they may have some scientific value, like the dried specimens in a herbarium, but no reader or student can derive from them any real, vital notion of how the people of a by-gone epoch lived, how they felt and what they thought. The literary men, statesmen, and philosophers, whose works have survived from earlier times and make up the body of literature, all lived in a world of their own : they have handed down to us a record of their generation which is concerned merely with the higher and more subtle aspects of its life. In this they have done rightly. It is the privilege and the function of literature to withdraw the mind of the reader from the sordid and commonplace affairs of daily life, and lift it upon a higher plane. We would not have had Æschylus, Thucydides, Lucretius, Horace, Dante, Chaucer, Shakespeare, and Milton follow a different path from that which they chose. Any realistic picture of their times which they could have given us would have been at the sacrifice of what the world values incomparably more highly.

But the present age, with its humanitarian sympathies, demands something in addition to this. It does not undervalue Æschylus, Dante, and Milton ; but, just as by the side of Tennyson and Browning there is room for Dickens, Thackeray, and George Eliot, so we crave, as supplementary to the lofty idealism of the great creative minds of literature, something which shall bring before us the men and women for whom these great works were composed. It is for lack of this that these past ages have so little reality for us. The characters of history appear to us always in their stage attitudes : the king perpetually wears a crown, and sits upon a throne ; the orator is perpetually clad in a toga and haranguing the Senate ; the general is presented to our imagination only as drawing up his army in a triple line of battle and bringing up his reserves. We cannot imagine Cæsar, like Grant, standing with his hands in his pockets, and smoking interminable cigars.

Now, no formal study can give us much assistance in obtaining such a realistic picture of life : formal study gives us only the dried specimen, not the fragrant flower. Neither do we obtain much assistance from the writers of past ages. We could almost count upon our fingers the works, prior to the eighteenth century, which present a vivid contemporaneous picture of their age on any considerable scale : some of the Dialogues of Plato, the plays of Plautus and Terence, the correspondence of Cicero and Pliny, the Paston Letters, the Memoirs of Colonel Hutchinson, the Letters of Madame de Sévigné, "Don Quixote," Boccaccio's "Decameron"— books like these are approximately what we seek. They are not complete delineations of society ; but, so far as they go, they give the reader just that sense of reality which he misses in the great works of literature. Apart from these our materials consist of isolated scraps of information and details of art. Of these we have abundance ; but they are, as I have said, of the nature of dried specimens, and need to be brought into combination and inspired with life by the literary artist. The people of these past ages did not care for such concrete presentations of life : this taste, a controlling one in the eighteenth and nineteenth centuries, is an outcome of the modern sentiment that "the proper study of mankind is man," and man in all phases of life.

The greatest lover of historical novels will admit that there would be no place for them in literature if by-gone generations had left behind them such pictures of their own society as the novelists of the present day are preparing for the generations which will come after us. Instead of this we have for the most part only such partial and occasional materials as I have described, out of which we may more or less skilfully fashion pictures for ourselves. The novel is a modern branch of literature. Except for a very few doubtful examples, it does not go back beyond the beginning of the eighteenth century. The student of the eighteenth century can go for a truthful, if one-sided, delineation to Defoe, Fielding, Smollett, Richardson, and Madame d'Arblay, just as he who wishes a picture of Russian life at the present day goes to Tourguéneff and Tolstoï; but, for any period before the eighteenth century, therefore, and for the most part for the eighteenth century itself, we must have recourse to historical fiction if we wish to get behind the scenes, come in direct contact with the men and women of the time, and understand them somewhat as we understand those of our own time. Historical fiction has therefore a large and important field to itself, a field which it is not possible should be occupied by any other branch of literature. Its work is hardly inferior in value, if well done, to that of genuine history; for it affords that insight into the human mind, that acquaintance with the spirit of the age, without which the most minute knowledge of events and institutions is only a bundle of dry and meaningless facts.

But, if historical fiction has a real and important place in literature, its task, nevertheless, is an extremely difficult one; for, in addition to the accurate scholarship of the historian and the constructive power of the novelist, it demands the highest exercise of the historical imagination — the capacity to place one's self in the mental attitude of persons wholly different in training and environment. If it is true that human nature is the same in all countries, classes, and ages, it is equally true that the attitude and furnishing of the mind differ widely in different countries, classes, and ages, and even in the same country, class, and age. Who can say that he really understands the feelings and mental processes of his nearest friends — the members of his own household? How hard it is for even neighbors, separated from one another by education or interests — protectionists and free traders, Calvinists and Catholics, laborers and capitalists, natives of New England and natives of the Mississippi Valley — to place themselves in the mental attitude of one another! How much greater must be the difficulty of entering into the motives, aspirations, tastes, and prejudices of persons removed from us by hundreds of years, by difference in race and religion, accustomed to a totally different environment, mental as well as physical!

To write an historical novel requires, therefore, not merely the equipment of a novelist, an historian, and an antiquarian. History and antiquities merely furnish him with materials for his trade; and of these he cannot have too much. The creative imagination which enables a skilful writer of fiction to construct the framework of a romance, and fill it in with living characters and entertaining incidents, is only half of what he needs. He must have the historical imagination as well, or all that he will get out of his materials will be nineteenth-century characters dressed up in the garb of the age which he is trying to depict.

Here is where so many historical novels break down. The names and the costumes, the historical and geographical accessories, are all there; but the personages are only the men and women whom we see about us every day, and do not feel and think like the men and women in whose guise they are masquerading. I do not say that such books are worthless. They familiarize the reader with historical names and events; and of course the dullest mind cannot fail to catch something of the spirit of the age which it is engaged upon. But the reader does not find himself in touch with the age depicted, as he does when he reads Cicero's or Cromwell's letters, "Tom Jones," or the Memoirs of Colonel Hutchinson.

An illustration will make this more clear. The modern novel almost invariably centres in the passion of love; and the novelist who desires to reconstruct the past naturally carries with him this governing motive of modern fiction into the life of antiquity. This is a fundamental mistake. This sentiment did not exist in ancient times. Love, as the ancients understood it, was a purely physical passion. Affection between husband and wife, parent and child, brothers and sisters, friend and friend, they knew; and I believe no age has exhibited purer and nobler examples of these types of love than the much traduced Romans in their most corrupt period. But the pure and reverent love of young man and maiden was, I believe, inconceivable to them. At any rate, I have never met with an example of it. This sentiment is the outgrowth of two modern forces working in co-operation — the Christian doctrine of chastity and the Germanic respect for women. Neither by itself would have effected it. It is significant that the two most truthful delineations of life in the empire — "Callista" and "Marius, the Epicurean" — are wholly free from this defect, which vitiates all of Ebers's novels, in many respects so admirable; and the incipient love of Agellius for Callista is a delicate recognition of the partially Christian origin of this modern sentiment.

If it is so difficult and so rare a thing for a modern writer to place himself fully in sympathy with another age, so as to depict it, moreover, with fulness of knowledge as well as intimacy of feeling, we see why it is that, with few exceptions, the best historical novels — those which bring their readers closest to the society which is described — are isolated works of their authors. Sir Walter Scott, the creator of this class of literature, and therefore incapable of understanding its limitations, a writer of genius and vast learning, who therefore could attempt successfully more than most men, has covered a very wide field with his historical fiction ; and yet, when he ventured at all out of his own island, it was to depict a single epoch, that of Charles the Bold. Thackeray confined his historical novels to the eighteenth century. George Eliot, Reade, Stevenson, Besant, and Blackmore (except when he treats of the Napoleonic wars) have each chosen a single spot of history ; while Pater's " Marius, the Epicurean," Cardinal Newman's "Callista," Scheffel's " Ekkehard," De Vigny's " Cinq-Mars," and Manzoni's " Betrothed " are the only works of these authors in this line, the only ones, at least, which have gained any reputation. Kingsley, Victor Hugo, and Dumas have covered more ground ; but even they have not ranged over all periods and lands, like James, Henty, Bulwer, and Ainsworth.

The fundamental principle, therefore, which should govern the composition and criticism of historical fiction, is, that it cannot undertake to give instruction in regard to historical events and personages, but should confine itself to the delineation of society and character. It should never be forgotten that its field is not only *history*, but *fiction ;* and that in dealing with historical epochs it should deal with them by the method of pure fiction. I do not say that this rule of criticism is subject to no exceptions : certainly there are very few historical novels which follow it without exception. What I wish to say is that, when actual events and personages are made the material of fiction, there is not only a probability, but almost a certainty, that history will be falsified, and that the reader will confuse the actual occurrences with the fictitious occurrences which are foisted upon them.

When Scott has the army of Montrose guided over the difficult mountain passes into the country of Argyle by Ronald MacEagh and his Children of the Mist, he is giving to a real event, the passage of these passes by this army, associations and surroundings which are not true. There was no doubt some such guide, and the results were such as are described ; but the reader who knows that Montrose and Argyle are real personages does not know how it is with Allan McNab, Dugald Dalgetty, Sir Duncan Campbell, and Ronald MacEagh. His history and fiction are inextricably mixed. Still, the narration, if not *true*, is yet *truthful.* When Tolstoï brings Pierre Bésoukhow on horseback in his civilian coat into the heat of the battle of Borodino, looking round him inquisitively out of his spectacles, both Pierre and the little lieutenant who is shot down by his side are purely fictitious characters, introduced into a real scene, even at a real battery ; but the fictitious characters are associated so skilfully and vividly with the environment of a real battle that the scene does not in reality transgress the principle I have laid down. But when Koutouzow and Napoleon are intro. duced with their staffs before the battle, discussing plans and giving orders, we have represented as historical detail what is only known in general or inferred from the result. Different and wholly indefensible is the act of Dumas in representing the assassination of the Duke of Buckingham as the outcome at once of religious enthusiasm and the intoxication of love : the other cases were truthful, if not true — this is a distortion of historical verity. It is, however, a perfectly possible occurrence, although untrue.

But when Ebers in his "Sisters" makes Scipio Nasica, a haughty Roman nobleman, of the most aristocratic and conservative type, marry a Greek girl whom he has picked up in Egypt, although after the fashion of modern novels she turns out to be of noble birth, he presents his readers with an occurrence which is not only untrue, but impossible, which violates the fundamental principles of Roman social life.

As I have said, it is difficult to draw a line between the legitimate description of an historical environment and the unwarranted narration of historical occurrences. The persecution of Decius forms the background of Newman's "Callista"; the invasion of Hungarians that of "Ekkehard"; the plague at Milan that of Manzoni's "Betrothed"; the French Revolution that of the Erckmann-Chatrian novels; the defeat of the Armada that of "Amyas Leigh"; the English Revolution that of "John Inglesant"; the preaching of Savonarola that of "Romola"; the career of Claverhouse that of "Old Mortality." A novel must have a background of reality, and this can hardly be provided except in some event or series of events related by historians. But so far as possible the actual events of history should provide only an atmosphere, an environment, not a framework.

What is true of events is even more true of persons. Events are impersonal, and, once passed, have no existence except in the memory and the chronicle. But the characters of history were men and women, of mixed natures and actuated by mixed motives, like us; and their actions are as hard to interpret and their motives as liable to misconstruction as ours. To misrepresent these motives, to distort these characters, is a wrong as real as to bear false witness against our neighbor. The neighbor may never know it: the historical personage has passed beyond the power of malice or misunderstanding. His character, nevertheless, is his sacred possession, not to be trifled with by the writer of fiction who finds him a convenient stalking-horse for the portrayal of some phase of life or some combination of moral qualities to which he wishes to give expression.

These considerations may indeed be pushed a little further, even if it may be somewhat fanciful or perhaps whimsical. I remember several years ago being struck with a review, in some periodical, of an historical novel, treating, if I remember rightly, of the Raid of Ruthven: the novel was probably by G. P. R. James or Ainsworth. The reviewer asked indignantly by what right the novelist ascribed motives and actions of an immoral character to persons who were still living in another sphere of existence, who were perhaps cognizant of the wrong done them, whom he might some time meet in another world, and who would then have a right to call him to account. Since reading that review, I have never read an historical novel treating with disparagement of real personages without a feeling that it was an offence somewhat akin to slander towards the living.

The conclusion to which we are led is that historical fiction is a perfectly legitimate and very useful branch of literature : not, as is sometimes urged, a device for sugar-coating the pill of instruction, but the only possible method of conveying one kind of historical information, and that in many respects the most important — direct personal knowledge of the life and thought of a by-gone age. It is, however, an extremely difficult branch of composition, requiring as it does the qualifications at once of novelist, historian, and antiquarian — qualifications which few persons combine for any one age, and perhaps none for all ages. Success is not likely to be attained, therefore, except by confining one's self strictly to some special field of history, which has been made the subject of exhaustive study.

Consider how wide and varied are the acquirements

which the successful novelist must possess for depicting
all phases of life of his own day — the branches of science
he must have mastered, the knowledge of human nature
he must possess, the familiarity he must have with all
the intricate relations of our complicated social life. To
this intellectual equipment the novelist must add a creative imagination, enabling him to conceive characters and
endow them with life, to devise incidents and situations
and make them probable, to compose a story and narrate it in an interesting manner, to represent people talking together naturally and entertainingly. These are the
qualifications of the great novelist.

To these the historical novelist must add a profound and
accurate knowledge of an age more or less remote from
his own in two points of view — history and antiquities.
As an historian he must know its events, its personages,
its literature, its thought in every department — political,
religious, philosophical — its science, industry, and art.
As an antiquarian he must be familiar with the manifestations of all these in every-day life — the manners
and customs, the dress and furniture, the institutions
and modes of procedure, the transient phases of thought
and tricks of speech. No knowledge bearing on the
generation with which he proposes to deal is indifferent
to him ; but there is much of this information which he
must have in his mind without using, for nothing is more
fatal to success than the constant parade of antiquarian
knowledge.

But history and antiquities, it must be repeated, can
only furnish the atmosphere, the stage of action : the
action itself, both in personalities and in incidents, should
be wholly the work of the imagination — the creative
imagination which every successful novelist must possess,
and the historical imagination which enables him to clothe
with life the dead memories of the past, and to combine
an infinite multitude of items of intelligence into a con-

crete presentation which shall possess unity and reality. Events so far as possible, and characters entirely, should be the creation of the author : real events and real personages are as much out of place as they would be in a novel of William Black or Henry James.

I admit that few writers of historical novels recognize this principle, or follow it in practice, but I believe that this is because they have never reasoned out the subject for themselves ; and, as a rule, I believe their works are successful in proportion as they approach it in practice. In a large proportion of the most successful historical novels it is followed in substance. In "Marius, the Epicurean," the most sympathetic delineation of pagan thought ; in "Callista," the most sympathetic delineation of the early Christian community ; in Dahn's "Felicitas," a vigorous picture of the transition from ancient to modern life ; in "In His Name," perhaps the best American historical novel ; in "The Cloister and the Hearth" and "Notre Dame," the comedy and the tragedy respectively of fifteenth-century life ; in Manzoni's "Betrothed," which has been called the most beautiful of historical novels ; in "Lorna Doone," a vigorous picture of sturdy English life in the seventeenth century ; in the "Chaplain of the Fleet" and "Kidnapped," which bring the middle of the eighteenth century before us with remarkable power ; in "Madame Thérèse," and its companions, "Ninety-three" and "The Tale of Two Cities," which all, but in different ways, breathe the genuine spirit of the French Revolution — in these works, if any historical characters occur, they are wholly secondary and incidental. Thackeray's great historical novels, "Henry Esmond" and "The Virginians," introduce a few real personages, but so skilfully and genially that they may be pardoned. Scott constantly sins in this respect; but the creator of a class of literature may be pardoned if he fails to see its limitations, and every reader will agree that he

is at his greatest when dealing with really fictitious characters, which are nevertheless genuine types — like Old
Mortality, Dandie Dinmont, Dugald Dalgetty, and Jeanie
Deans. There are other historical novels of the first
class which depart from it — " Ekkehard," " Passe-Rose,"
" Romola," " Amyas Leigh," " John Inglesant "; but
there are special considerations in each of these cases,
and the historical sense is so strong in their authors that
they have not materially sacrificed the truth. In mentioning some, I must not be understood to exclude others :
there are no doubt many excellent works of this class
which I have never read or even heard of.

It will be permitted me to say a few words upon a
branch of literature closely related to historical fiction —
the historical drama. The drama has in general the
same object as the novel : indeed, the novel occupies
much the same place at the present day which the stage
occupied in former times. Both undertake to portray life
and character ; and one branch of dramatic composition,
the so-called Comedy of Society, does this very much in
the spirit of the novel, and, where we find it, it may take
the place of the novel fairly well, as a presentation of life
and manners. It goes in history about a century further
back than the novel, and is peculiarly rich and instructive
in the Elizabethan age and the period of the Restoration :
the worst phases of life, at any rate, are portrayed in it
with great skill and truthfulness. Unfortunately for the
periods before the Elizabethan, this as well as the novel
is almost wholly wanting ; the plays of Plautus and
Terence — Latin translations of Greek Comedies, and
therefore presenting a picture of life which is neither
purely Greek nor purely Roman — being all the examples
that survive from the ancient world.

Tragedy, on the other hand, belongs to the highest
realms of literature, as a department of Poetry, with
lofty and ideal aims. "Prometheus," "King Œdipus,"

"Medea," "Hamlet," rank with the "Divine Comedy," not with "The Rivals" and "School for Scandal." But modern tragedians are fond of choosing their themes from history. Even Æschylus made the Persian war, in which he himself served, the subject of a tragedy; and many of the finest modern dramas have a similar foundation.

It is evident that historical tragedy, if it covers the same ground, has yet a wholly different aim from historical fiction. It cannot depict every-day life like the novel and the comedy of society : it moves upon a higher plane. Its aim is to trace the working of human feelings and passions, and to do this without taking account of the trivialities and conventionalities of the life which the novelist is obliged to depict. When Shakespeare therefore takes Macbeth for his subject, he is not called upon, as the novelists would be, to present a picture of Scottish society in the eleventh century; when he takes Julius Cæsar, although he is in the main faithful to the historical sequence of events, he is not obliged to give a description of the institutions of Rome such as would satisfy an antiquarian, or even to develop the characters and bring them in relation with one another, so as to satisfy the historical critic. The reader is not disturbed by hearing the roar of cannon in "King John," or by the death of Talbot near twenty years before it took place, any more than by the presence of the Christian Church in "Cymbeline," or the seaports of Bohemia in "The Winter's Tale." We do not care for anachronisms or for mistakes in chronology or in antiquities, because the work is *poetry*, confessedly the production of the imagination; because the aim is not to portray an age, but to develop character, to represent the working of passions and emotions, which do not belong to any one time or set of people, but are common to all mankind.

Perhaps we pardon Shakespeare where we should not

pardon an inferior writer. I do not think we should for give Browning, or Schiller, or Henry Taylor for giving Bohemia a seaport, or for introducing cannon into the reign of King John; but even from them we do not demand the painful accuracy, the truth to local color, which we expect from the novelist. We require them to keep to the facts in chronology and genealogy, and we do not justify them when they make the historical char acter a mere vehicle for the elaboration of their ideas of life and the working out of human motives. Macbeth, Cymbeline, and even Coriolanus have so little historical character that we care very little if the poet treats them as purely ideal personages. On the other hand, his treat ment of Julius Cæsar, Cardinal Wolsey, and Richard III., is, on the whole, historically truthful; and the same may be said of Philip van Artevelde, King Victor and King Charles, and Mary Tudor. But it is treading on danger ous ground, and we cannot help feeling that even in tragic drama it is better to take fictitious or mythical characters. When Browning attempted to present his view of Straf ford's character and motives in dramatic form, he produced a noble drama, but one not true in all respects to history. Schiller deliberately set aside the facts of history, and chose to depict Mary Stuart and Wallenstein not as they were, but as he wished they were.

In this Schiller followed a rule laid down for himself by Sir Walter Scott—that the characters and events of his tory were rough material in his hands, which he might use as he pleased: he was an artist, not an historian, and the result was to be judged as a work of art, not as a treatise. I have shown why I consider this a totally false principle as applied to historical fiction. The objections to it do not apply so fully to the historical drama, because the laws of poetry are different from those of prose; but even in the field of tragedy it is hard to see by what right a poet, in using historical material, can deliberately divest it of its historical character.

PRACTICAL EDUCATION.*

THE cry is for Practical Education; for speedy and tangible results. Life is too short, and its needs too urgent, to waste our time on subtle theories and indecisive preparation. Every word and every act must be made to tell. If the primary and most essential principle of education is to afford a training for future use, nevertheless its results must not lie too far in the future, or be too obscure and uncertain in their working out. We must have in view the practical and pressing wants of everyday life, not the rarer excellences of exceptional character. When we raise the question, "What knowledge is of most worth?" we are answered, That which will best "prepare us for complete living."

Certainly we can have nothing but sympathy with this aspect of education. If an education is not practical, it has missed its first and only end, and there is no room for it in this busy world of ours. An education which leads to no positive practical results commensurate with the cost and pains bestowed upon it is like the road described in Longfellow's "Hyperion," which, after leading over pleasant hills and through smiling meadows and shady woods, narrows at last into a squirrel track, and runs up a tree. Chief of all is the demand a reasonable one in regard to an education provided at the public expense. Here with full right the public may require manifest and wholesome results, and at not too great a distance of time. An institution supported by private munificence has simply to carry out the designs of its founder; may, if he think fit,

* Address before the University of Nebraska, at its fifth annual Commencement, June 19, 1876.

undertake to determine the Homoousian and Homoiousian controversy ; to ascertain who was Hecuba's mother ; or to debate that question of mediæval schools — how many angels can dance upon the point of a needle. There might be waste of time and money, but there would be no breach of trust. But a university founded and maintained by the State must devote itself to departments of education in which the State has a direct and lively interest, or it forfeits its right to exist.

Education, then — a State education at any rate — must, we all agree, be practical. But, when we have said this, we have really said nothing, or rather have only uttered a truism, shaping a definition out of terms equivalent to the word defined. By practical, in education, we mean having ends outside of itself. Now, in so far as education is *training*, its very essence is that it only prepares — that its ends are outside of and beyond itself.

Again, in a sense, every question, however trivial or remote, may have its practical bearings ; even those just instanced, as inquiries of the dryest and most unedifying type, might possibly be found to throw light incidentally upon some discussion of real importance ; and we can never tell beforehand where and in what directions such incidental bearings may manifest themselves. Not even these apparently worthless topics, therefore, can be absolutely excluded from a practical education. They should not be its professed object, but they have a right to come in, if needed.

The real controversy is not, therefore, whether an education should be practical ; it is not even whether its practical character should be clear and manifest, or only remote and incidental : it is as to what those practical ends should be. And, if we sift to the bottom this popular demand for practical education, we find that it really means, in the minds of its supporters, an education with purely *material* ends. The question what will be of immediate use to us here in America, in the nineteenth century, is, in its construction, narrowed down to one pitiful question — What will be of speedy use in making money? Latin and Greek are to be banished from the curriculum because they are not spoken at the railroad stations, and are not used in prices current and quotations of stocks. Philosophy and literature are barely tolerated. Even constitutional law and political economy are looked on askance; do not our politicians manage to govern us with scanty knowledge of the one and none at all of the other? Liberal and even lavish grants are ready for whatever has a practical sound — scientific and industrial schools of every sort, laboratories and observatories — while the branches distinctively devoted to culture are treated with neglect or even contempt.

Now, this education in external nature, these scientific and industrial schools, these laboratories and observatories, are doing an invaluable work in the furtherance of genuine culture — of practical education in the best and highest sense. I would not disparage them; rather I would do honor to them by claiming for them a higher place among educational agencies than their special advocates are apt to recognize. Neither would I deny that, if, of two rival branches of study or systems of discipline, equal in intrinsic educational power, the one is more immediately and readily applicable to the common uses of every-day life than the other, it should be preferred. What I say is that, in a system of education, this should always be a subsidiary point — that disciplinary power, training, should come first, while practical usefulness, in the sense in which the term is generally used, should be only incidental.

And, after all, the practical bearings of scientific studies are not always more certain and obvious than those of their rivals. They abound in inquiries apparently as remote from practical ends as the veriest dry bones of genealogy, chronology, or scholastic theology. Who cares for the exact distance of such and such a star, or the precise markings on such and such a fossil, any more than for Hecuba's mother? Nevertheless, there seems to be a shorter cut from these investigations to the great end of life — money-making — because they deal with solid matter now existing; therefore, our philosophers reluctantly admit them within the field of practical education.

The introduction of scientific studies into our curriculum, and the establishment of special scientific courses in confirmation and further development of them, has been of the greatest advantage to the higher education. These studies afford a certain kind of training at a certain stage in education, which neither the languages nor the so-called "humanities" as a whole can give; and our old college courses, which omitted them, were lame of one foot. But it is not this genuine educational power of theirs that gains them support from the advocates of this modern theory of education. Scientific studies are favored, not because they fit men to do efficient and useful work in the world — to build reservoirs which no spring freshets will carry away, and bridges which no weight will strain, and to weave honest cloths, and dye them with colors that will not fade nor wash out, and thus by genuine science and faithful labor aid in overcoming that besetting vice of a new civilization — superficial and dishonest work — but because their students will speedily earn their livelihood as chemists, telegraphists, and engineers; because they can be made to assist in furthering narrow, personal aims, not because they advance the great interests of society. Thus a false and demoralizing theory has, in spite of itself, been led to accomplish great and enduring good.

I am not blind to the shortcomings of what is distinctively called *culture*. If the tendency of the day is to make education too material, to make it consist exclusively in the acquisition of money-making powers, to

make all higher education purely professional, the opposite theory may lead in its turn to equal narrowness.
Culture, we must confess, is not infrequently fastidious
and hypercritical; irresolute, bewildered in contact with
real problems, unfit for practical life. But this is not the
highest culture, nor is it complete culture. To say all
this is to say that culture can be incomplete and one-
sided; not that it is necessarily so. To return to the
principle with which we set out: a man's education is
not a good one unless it has fitted him for practical
life — not necessarily by putting in his hands the very
tools with which he is to work, but by training him to
the best use of all his powers, and enabling him to choose
a career for which he is fitted. I do not call a literary
fop a man of culture.

But, again, it is easy to bring against culture the charge
of being unpractical; it is not always that the charge is
well founded. Often the highest practical ability fails of
recognition by reason of the low standard by which it is
measured. It is notorious, for example, that men of college education are hardly found in public life nowadays,
while they formed a large proportion of the signers of the
Declaration of Independence and the framers of the Constitution. "See what your culture comes to!" is the cry.
"It does not fit men for public life. Your college graduates cannot compete with the graduates of the workshop, the counting-house, and the farm in the practical
work of politics." But have we gained by the change?
Have we a better type of politicians now than when we
took them from the ranks of educated men? Do they
serve us better? Has the tone of politics improved in
the process? All honor to the Roger Shermans and Patrick Henrys and Abraham Lincolns, who, without education, by ability and integrity, have made themselves illustrious in high stations! But it is not to the discredit of
educated men as a class that they have been found more

and more unfitted for politics in the form which our politics have of late years assumed.

Nor does this unfitness have relation alone to the intrigues and manipulations of party politics. The treatment which great public questions receive at present is not such as to attract men of culture into public life. These are practical questions of the highest type and the widest bearings. But if a man who has made political economy the study of his life undertakes to approach the subject of the currency, for instance, his mouth is at once stopped. This is a practical question, he is told, and not for the like of him, who never handled a thousand dollars at a time in his life: let him leave it for "practical men" to settle, and go back to his books; he may study its theory as much as he likes, but must leave its practical details alone. Here, again, we have a right to put the homely question: How does our new method work? Are our finances better managed? Is our diplomacy in better hands than in those early days of the republic, when we were accustomed to have educated men in places of honor and responsibility?

We are reaping what we have sown. For more than a generation we have deliberately acted upon the theory that education is not required for the greatest business of life; that statesmanship is a game of chance and intrigue; that a man's first allegiance is due to his party, and not to his country. We have sown the wind, and now we are reaping the whirlwind in the complete collapse of our political methods in this anniversary year; in the disgrace of our government, unparalleled among civilized nations; in the almost absolute dearth among our public men of any higher standard of the duties and responsibilities of their office than success of their party.

It is time for us, college men, to stop and consider what is our duty in the matter. The State has created our Universities; or, if it has not created them, it sustains and favors them. How shall we repay this obligation? How shall we make the education which we provide most practical, in the true sense of the word? How shall we make it serve the best interests of the State from which it emanates?

Something, no doubt, can be done directly by inculcating a truer notion of the State and our relations to it. The essence of a republican government is that every citizen has a share in it; and each should have his share clearly defined and actively present in his mind. I do not speak here of the duties of the statesman. The special aptitude and training which fit one for this most elevated career are rare and individual. Those that possess them are called to the service of the State with an urgency that will take no denial. But we are all citizens. We all have duties towards the public that cannot be slighted without bringing a retribution — a retribution which we are now suffering; for, if there is any one truth more prominent at the present time than another, it is that the accumulated disgrace that has fallen upon our nation comes from our having practically surrendered our rights as citizens of a republic, and suffered an irresponsible body of politicians to govern us at their will. I do not say how much of this is forced upon us by the defects of our governmental system. I do not propose as a remedy the hackneyed recommendation to "attend the primaries," for this would be simply to shift the difficulty from one stage in the election process to another. It is enough to note the fact, and leave it for really practical statesmen to devise a remedy.

We should feel therefore that the welfare of our country and the permanence of our republican institutions depend upon a revival of the old feeling that every man is a citizen; that, as a citizen, he has a whole series of duties and obligations which he must be ready to meet; that whether it fall to his lot to assume special positions of trust and power, or merely to exercise his judgment in determining the general line of public policy as embodied in one of the rival parties, and in choosing fit men to carry it out, it is the same at bottom. The function of choice is as high and responsible as that of office; and it is one which comes directly to all of us, while the other belongs properly only to a select few.

What I have said is true of all citizens; it is especially true of us who receive from the State special privileges and training. We are by this placed under a peculiar obligation. The idea of the State developed by a certain school of speculative thinkers, as having merely the function to protect its citizens from wrong, but not to confer active benefits upon them; to keep aloof from all objects of general interest, leaving them to private and individual enterprise — this purely negative conception of the State can find little acceptance in our Western communities. We are committed to a broader theory of governmental functions. Our commonwealths of the West have deliberately adopted the principle of providing an education for their citizens as high and thorough as is within their power, on the theory that the most perfect manhood and womanhood, the best thinking and the most thorough scholarship, are the stuff to make citizens out of.

What we are, therefore, as educational institutions, we owe to the State; and to the State our ripest fruits should be devoted. Our students should graduate with the conviction that it is a mean and sordid thing — I will not say to be dishonest and mercenary in public relations, to use place and honor as instruments of personal gain; I am not satisfied with any so negative patriotism as this — it is sordid and ungrateful, I will say, to receive an education at the public expense, and then devote it to purely private ends; to ply one's profession busily and assiduously, all to put money in one's purse, careless whether the State or the community prospers, careless whether there are special political or social duties that might fall in one's way if one had the eyes to see and the will to act.

I would not underrate the assiduous and successful performance of private and professional work. If every man is a citizen, he is also a merchant, a farmer, a lawyer, or a man of letters ; and his special professional work — that by which he earns his bread — takes a thousand of his hours to one hour directly bestowed upon the public service. Neither are the immediate and direct functions of citizenship the only ones which concern the State as such. If a man is a good merchant, farmer, lawyer, or man of letters, he is so far forth a good citizen. The chief work of a university is therefore only indirect in its relation to civic duties. It employs an hour a day for perhaps two terms in studies which bear directly upon the polity of the State — its organization and its economical interests : all the rest of its time is devoted to educating the man, not to training the citizen. Our attention must therefore be turned to the field of general education.

A perfect and complete education is directed to every human faculty and power, with a view to developing each healthily and harmoniously, and thus preparing the man for all the duties and exigencies of life. A complete education of this type is, it must be confessed, beyond the reach of a State university. A public education must, by the very terms of its existence, in our country and at the present day, set aside an entire category of human faculties, and leave them to other influences. It was not always so ; neither is it so now in all countries, nor necessarily even in our own country in the case of private institutions. A denominational college instructs in the tenets of its own theology, and undertakes to make them the basis of individual morality. The public schools of Prussia give their pupils religious instruction, at the choice of the parents, within certain limits. The universities of the Middle Ages were distinctly church organizations. But the State of Wisconsin or of Nebraska, whether in its primary schools or its University, must confine itself to secular education. This is a condition of its educating at all.

The wisdom of this I do not propose to discuss. It is enough that this limitation has been set, and that it must be observed so long as we maintain a system of public education. Further, although the problem has grown upon us by degrees, so that no one can say at precisely what moment of time our schools ceased to recognize certain theological dogmas, and became purely secular — although, indeed, the process is not even yet entirely complete — it cannot be said that we are without a well-considered principle in the matter. Our system of public education rests upon the assumption that no mischief is worked by this policy, or at any rate that the mischief is more than counterbalanced by the good. It does not deny the necessity of a cultivation of all the human faculties in a complete, well-rounded plan of education, but it holds that private religious associations are so numerous, so well organized, and so active that they may safely be intrusted with the responsibility of the religious education of their own members ; and, if it be argued that there is a certain number of children outside of all religious organizations who, under this method, receive no religious education at all, the only answer can be that, even so, more is gained than is lost ; that the State cannot meet these particular cases, because the State cannot identify itself with any special form of theological belief ; that, if the churches cannot reach these classes, they cannot be reached at all for this purpose, and must go without religious education, but at the same time, if the churches cannot reach them, neither would church schools reach them. Under the present system, they receive, at any rate, a secular education at the hands of the State : under a system of denominational schools, they would receive no education at all, as has until recently been the case in England.

This one-sidedness, this purely secular character, of university education under the auspices of the State, is therefore a necessity of the case; a necessity, be it observed, which is copied by large numbers of denominational institutions, which also claim to be unsectarian, evidently because unsectarian — that is, secular — education is seen to be that now in demand by our people. But it does not follow, because theological instruction is excluded, that moral or even religious influence is shut out with it. No system of education, however bare of dogma, can fail to exercise the most powerful influence upon character. The methods of instruction, the tone of discipline, the daily walk of the teacher and his relations to his pupils, all form a part of their education.

Foremost among these elements, because most prominent in the daily work of education, is the quality of thoroughness. We have been told often enough that we are a superficial nation, and it is quite true; we are superficial in work and in acquirements. Not that it is a very serious charge; it is a defect which belongs to our stage of development rather than to ourselves. It is, for instance, a commonplace of economic science that a new country will endure only a very superficial and so-called *extensive* cultivation of the land. The garden culture of Belgium or the high farming of England — even the degree of thoroughness common in New England and New York — would ruin the farmer of the Mississippi Valley: he does not get so much wheat to the acre, but he gets more money to the acre than he would if he adopted those methods. The slovenly style of cultivation alone possible in countries where a small population is scattered sparsely over a wide region may be an argument against opening new countries to settlement; it is the only thing possible when once a country is opened. Again, look at the handicrafts. The settler that builds a log cabin cannot afford the time to make everything square and even and smooth ; fine carpentry would be out of place. A rude bench to sit on and ill-fitting garments to wear will serve his purposes better than mahogany chairs and dress coats. Or, to speak of substance rather than form, he cannot let his hides remain seven years in the tan-vat, as in the land from which he emigrated. It would make better leather ; but he wants his boots next year, not seven years hence. Take again the professional man. No medical skill is too good when your child lies at the point of death. You cannot have too good a lawyer to defend your legal rights. But a new country must have its doctor and lawyer now. By the time the student is better trained your child is buried or your farm forfeited.

I am not defending want of thoroughness; I am explaining it. A new country cannot afford the best. The best professional men, the best mechanics, the best gardeners, will stay where their services will be more highly remunerated, and the new country must take the best it can get ; and according to the demand will be the supply. Nevertheless, this is an excuse that will not serve a day after the need has passed. It accounts for the necessity of putting up with inferior work ; it does not justify the inferior work, when better could be rendered ; it does not excuse the workman who sets up for himself before he has learned his trade, or the half-educated physician who tampers with the health of his patients ; it is no apology for us if we give superficial instruction or confer degrees upon those who have not earned them. Probably the greatest service which our common schools perform for us lies in this much needed quality of thoroughness. They are — at least in those States in which the school system is most highly organized — excessively mechanical. Instead of opening the pupil's mind to the love and search of truth for its own sake, they oppress him with drudgery and routine; instead of aiming to develop the individual mind and make the most of its special powers, they insist upon cutting all upon the same formal pattern; instead of making it their first object to develop and train the mental powers, they scatter the attention and fritter away the vigor of the mind in an effort after wide and multitudinous knowledge. In a word, their professed object is instruction rather than education, knowledge rather than mental power. These are the faults of the public school system. On the other hand, it has a very high and exact standard of performance; it puts up with no slipshod work; it cultivates that invaluable habit of placing before one's self a definite object of attainment, and attaining it. The American public school system affords therefore the surest remedy for American superficiality.

In the kind of thoroughness in which the public schools excel, the college cannot rival them; nor should it desire to. Its primary object is training; its methods do not consist so much in teaching special things as in guiding the student in the desire and the capacity of learning for himself. But, although the performance is totally different in kind, it should nevertheless be subject to as strict a rule of judgment. Thoroughness in college work does not mean learning lessons by heart and reciting them; it means completeness of investigation, clearness in the perception of relations, exactness of knowledge, and correctness of reasoning. The student who has acquired the habit of never letting go a puzzling problem — say a rare Greek verb — until he has analyzed its every element, and understands every point in its etymology, has the habit of mind which will enable him to follow out a legal subtlety with the same accuracy.

It is in this quality of thoroughness that we find the chief utility of the natural sciences in a scheme of education. The half-accurate student, who leaves a breathing, or an accent, or a change of vowel in his Greek verb unaccounted for, finds that he cannot neglect any such residuum when it comes to analyzing a chemical compound. A flaw in the reasoning process in political economy will simply land one on the wrong side in the currency question, and leave him perfectly satisfied with his ignorance. But in geometry it leaves him high and dry, unable to attack the very next proposition in the book.

Thoroughness and accuracy of knowledge rather than of performance are aimed at by our educational systems, consistently with the principle that our object is primarily training, while the application of the knowledge and the training belong properly to professional education. Nevertheless, apart from professional training, every method of education must have an aspect of execution as well as of acquirement. It is here perhaps that college education is weakest, especially as compared with what is accomplished by the common schools. We may call this feature *art* as compared with purely scientific training ; and, as an art is the practical side of its kindred science, we come here most distinctly into the field of Practical Education.

In the common schools the art is never disjoined from the science. This is indeed the principal source of the mechanism of the system already complained of. The object appears to be not to know a thing, but to recite it, and to recite it in a precise and methodical way. A formula is devised, such as appears most appropriate in statement, and everything must be squared to this formula. The omission or change of a word vitiates the performance. The order of the school-room, the semi-military exactness of the movements, the precision in every trivial detail — all these artificial excellences, the violation of which creates purely conventional faults, illustrate the strikingly practical character of common-school training.

Now, on this side our college methods form an even more striking contrast with those of the public schools than on the strictly scientific side. As we do not merely teach from books, neither do we in our recitations make a point of order, forms, and special sets of words. It is not to be desired that it should be otherwise; we should be in danger of sacrificing the substance to the shadow. At the same time it might be well for us to pay more attention than we usually do, not to special forms, but to style of execution. Gentlemanly and ladylike habits and demeanor; promptness in answering to one's name; correct pronunciation, and exactness in the use of words — a well-conducted recitation is an exercise in all these things. Here again we find that the natural sciences give the nearest approximation to the advantages afforded by the public schools. The precision of their matter and of their processes of reasoning allows and encourages a higher degree of precision in performance than is easily attained in other branches. The languages, on the other hand, afford opportunity for exercise of a freer and more varied character. There is no better practice in English composition than translating from a foreign language; and, if this translation is oral — if pains are taken that the rendering shall always be into good idiomatic English — there could hardly be devised a better preparation for extempore speech, having the advantage, as it does, of allowing the student's mind to rest almost exclusively upon the expression, without concern as to thought or arrangement. Studies like metaphysics and political economy form a further stage in the same direction, and present the greatest advantages, as well as the greatest difficulties, in the acquisition of the difficult art of extempore speaking. For here the mind must be busied upon the thought as well as the expression, and the teacher's attention must be directed primarily — often almost exclusively — to the train of thought or line of argument. A recitation, in short, is a daily exercise in readiness of thought and correctness of expression; and its influence cannot be purely negative. If these qualities are not made a distinct and definite object in recitation, their opposites will be sure to intrude. Bad grammar, inappropriate words, inelegant phrases, vagueness of thought, and incoherency of reasoning, will come without being invited.

It is in this power of acquirement and of work, rather than in the acquirement and the work themselves, that the practical influence of college education should be mainly felt. Not that the two can be disjoined. It is through the process of acquiring thoroughly some specific knowledge that we make ourselves competent to future acquirement ; it is by sedulously doing good work, whether with the hand or the brain, that we acquire the aptitude for doing well whatever work we set ourselves to do. Nevertheless, the distinction is not a useless one. It is the source of one of our greatest mistakes in our courses of study. We are not willing to leave out of the curriculum anything which a well-educated man ought to know ; and as a result we have crowded into our four years a multiplicity of studies, enough, if only moderately pursued, to occupy twice that space of time. It is true the thing of importance is not the special piece of work, but the way in which the work is done. It might be claimed therefore that it makes no difference, so the work is good, whether it is concentrated upon one branch or scattered upon three. We should remember, however, that, in order to acquire any one branch thoroughly, it is necessary to pursue it a considerable length of time. No study can be thorough unless it has time enough devoted to it to enable the mind to grow into it, to adjust itself to it, and suffer its principles to enter into organic relation with itself ; and, further, unless the subject is taken up with sufficient breadth and depth to insure familiarity, not merely with its most obvious facts, but with its more remote and obscure ones. A few weeks devoted to the most exact study of each of three or four different languages will result in no thorough knowledge of any one of them; only certain superficial points of resemblance and difference will be impressed upon the mind.

In view, on the other hand, of a reasonable demand for a wider range of studies than was contained in our old college curriculums, provision must undoubtedly be made for a mere general knowledge of some of the branches taught. Neither is this inconsistent with thoroughness of education, if only it is combined with the more profound and extensive study of certain other branches. "To have a general knowledge of a subject," says Mr. Mill,* "is to know only its leading truths, but to know them not superficially, but thoroughly, so as to have a true conception of the subject in its great features, leaving the minor details to those who require them for the purposes of their special pursuit." "The amount of knowledge," he adds, "is not to be lightly estimated which qualifies us for judging to whom we may have recourse for more." To recur to the illustration just used, the thorough study of one language, joined with the general study of others, will perhaps combine the advantages of the old narrow system with the new demands for a wider range of acquirement as well as is practicable in the limited amount of time at our disposal. The true principle for our college courses is, it seems to me, to concentrate the work largely upon a few leading branches, differing in the several elective courses, and to supplement these with as large a number as need be of extra studies, pursued for only a very short time and with a view to merely general knowledge. Every course of study, for example, should embrace a good, thorough, and extensive knowledge of some one foreign language: with this as a foundation, a very slight amount of instruction in other languages — if only accurate so far as it goes — will be sufficient. Whoever has this can take up the study at any time he pleases, and follow it further to good advantage by himself.

---

* Address at St. Andrews, "Dissertations and Discussions," vol. iv. p. 396.

But the chief practical value of thorough training lies in its moral rather than its intellectual side. Character even more than scholarship is the aim of a liberal education. To be able to do good work is one thing : to be willing to do none but good work, in the consciousness of duty to one's neighbors, one's country, and to God, is another. Without this sense of duty the power, however great, and even supported by strong habit, is no guaranty for practical efficiency. It is the men with intellectual powers well developed and highly trained, but not guided and inspired by right and duty, that do the most mischief in the world. An education that gives the one, and leaves the other out of view, is not merely defective — it is positively mischievous, because it renders the student master of powerful agencies, which he is encouraged to use only for his own selfish ends.

After all, an education which should absolutely neglect the moral nature, in its cultivation of the intellect, is an impossibility. Theological instruction, which is a purely intellectual matter, may and must be left out of our scheme : moral education, which is life and influence, cannot be absent from any living system of education. If it is absent in any case — if the processes of education do not exert a positively elevating and ennobling influence upon the pupils — they must be positively debasing and demoralizing. Moral education is in truth but another side of intellectual : a side without which the intellectual is incomplete and inefficient. Not only must any judicious and well-administered system of intellectual training react upon the moral nature, and serve to stimulate it, but unless it so reacts, it will itself fail of its highest possibilities. The indispensable foundation of that thoroughness in study and execution which has been our principal theme thus far is that virtue which embraces a larger share of human duties within its definition than any other — faithfulness. Thoroughness is impossible without faithfulness ;

for the moment any motive comes into play, except that of performing one's whole duty — the moment the thought of advantage to self is permitted to intrude, the moment reputation, gain, or even intellectual satisfaction takes the lead in our intellectual work — that moment the thoroughness of the work is necessarily impaired. Our standard is no longer genuine excellence ; some hidden flaw in the structure, some want of finish in less conspicuous parts, some specious argument or unworthy appeal, designed to gain victory rather than to elicit truth, takes the place of the solid work that will last for generations or the solid reasoning that will last forever.

Faithfulness is the highest and noblest of all human qualities ; for with it all other excellences are sure to spring up, and without it no other virtue is possible. Nor is its scope confined to human relations only. Spiritual devotion is but one of its manifestations ; and not without logical discernment have the devotees of one or another religious creed branded as "faithless" — *infidel* — those who have accepted another set of beliefs than their own, even if this has often been done at the expense of humanity and charity, and by the sacrifice of essential qualities to mere forms and dogmas.

And this crown of virtues is the peculiar virtue of the school-room. There is no system of training so well calculated to bring out this merit and develop it to consummate excellence as the regular daily work of a well-ordered school : where the pupils themselves see in their teacher a model of never-tiring faithfulness ; where the work assigned is such as to appeal to their best intellectual tastes ; where the standard of execution is no external, factitious display, but intrinsic excellence ; where the reward of success is the consciousness of well-doing and the approbation of the instructors — not the *ignis fatuus* of rank or the gross incentives of prizes. I do not think that there is any one thing so destructive of the spirit of faithfulness in our colleges as the custom of assigning marks to the exercises of the students as a basis of class rank.

We would not establish too high and unattainable a standard either of motive or of performance. We would recognize the fact that students are amenable to the motives and subject to the same short-comings as men in active life. Why not then, it may be said, take these motives and short-comings as fully into account with them as we do in the affairs of the world? In these we find prizes and rank among the most effective of the inducements to action : why exclude these from education? For the simple reason that we are not dealing with everyday affairs of the world. We are engaged in *educating.* We are dealing with a body — not of adults in the heat and ardor of life's struggle, not of common youths, as they walk our streets and meet in our parlors — but with choice material, destined for exalted ends. Every village and almost every farm-house picks out its most promising member — the one that shows most aptitude for scholarship, that promises to exert most influence in the world — and sends him to us, to train him, not for the ordinary work of life, but for its best work. The young men and women who are placed in our hands are to take the lead in the next generation. Why should the State incur the enormous expense of educating them if not to use their trained powers in its best service? They are of right, therefore, not to be subjected to the average standard of the world's morality, and to be credited with its average motives of action. Our code of morality should be that of the saints and heroes of the world, not of its Fisks and Tweeds.

But in the next place, while we reject the low standards of the world, we need not deny that the motives to real faithfulness which are found most effective in political and commercial circles will be also most effective in our little world. Of these the most powerful is the sense of responsibility. I think it is not stating the case too strongly to say that the lack of an effective responsibility is the chief immediate cause of the growth of corruption and crime among us. It does not create the criminal disposition, but gives it opportunity. It is no derogation to the merits of the purest and most single-minded of men to say that even they feel surer of themselves, better equipped for action, more able to meet temptation, if they feel themselves to be under a constant obligation to render an account of themselves. It is here that religion touches morality, in assuring a responsibility of the most personal and unceasing nature. But for the needs of mankind in their ordinary transactions this sanction is too distant and unperceived, unless supplemented by a very direct and visible responsibility to men. The certainty that our actions will be scrutinized by those who have the authority to do this — that our short-comings will be censured and our transgressions punished, is not only the surest means of holding the wicked in check, it is the strongest support and encouragement to the good.

In our public affairs this feeling of responsibility has for many years been becoming less and less. It is one of the disastrous results of that fatal preference of party to country which has revolutionized the whole spirit of our government that offences against the public are easily condoned, while insubordination, or, as it is the fashion to call it, treason to the party, is never forgiven. The whole influence of every administration — the whole influence of each party organization, is exerted, not to prevent crime in men of high position, but to prevent its discovery and punishment, because these would weaken the party and endanger its hold upon power. And public opinion, whose function it is to afford an additional agency for responsibility, is debauched as well. We, the public, have our share in the guilt of this lamentable state of things; it was our business to guard the guardians. But in that excessive and criminal good nature, which is a leading characteristic of the American people, we have shrunk from severity of judgment, or punishment adequate to the offence, until the wrong-doers have come to feel that their only fault was want of audacity or secrecy.

It is one of the compensations of an aristocratic government that it secures a genuine public opinion, and a real responsibility resting upon it. With us the party has become of more importance than the nation, and no public sentiment, except within party lines, is found to exercise any substantial control. In an aristocratic structure of society the class occupies the position which the party does with us. The sentiment of the ruling classes in England is a real power; and being divided between the parties, and exercised in behalf of what is to all intents and purposes the national interests, it maintains a sound and wholesome standard of public morality. It behooves us, while maintaining our party organizations for ends of public policy, to re-establish a public sentiment as an engine of responsibility — a public sentiment which shall rest upon all the soundest elements in the whole nation — not in a mere portion of it, whether a faction as at present with us, or a class as in England.

Now, the feeling of responsibility, the only effective means for the maintenance of a high standard of action in the affairs of the world, is equally so in education. Rank, prizes, special privileges, are only occasional rewards in real life, and their influence is only restricted and spasmodic: responsibility is — or should be — felt everywhere. So in schools: a watchful and ever-present responsibility is the only sure guaranty for faithful performance. Extrinsic rewards may stimulate a few, and for a limited time; but they discourage a larger number than they stimulate, and the good habits they may possibly induce in some cases are more than counterbalanced

by the reaction which is sure to come in most cases when
the special occasion is past. But responsibility reaches all
alike — the best and the worst, the highest and the lowest, the quick and the dull, the faithful and the dishonest.

Through an effective responsibility we shall be enabled
to establish and maintain that high sentiment of honor
which is one of the most precious possessions of any
community. As the consciousness of responsibility does
not supersede, but fortifies and stimulates, the virtue of
faithfulness, so a noble sense of honor is the helpful ally
of a clear sense of right. And, in truth, they cannot be
separated even in thought. Honor is the sentiment of
what is becoming; and, while whatever is right is becoming, it is equally true that nothing is becoming but what
is right.

Why, then, call for a feeling of honor apart from a judgment of right? Why appeal to a lower motive instead of
the highest? Just as in the case of responsibility, because of its practical efficiency; because it is a concrete
and always intelligible idea, while that of right is abstract
and often puzzling. There are a few choice souls which
require no other standard than that of absolute right,
whose faithfulness and purity are ingrained. Most of us,
however, are materially helped by the perception that
what is right is also becoming; and we find it easier to
gauge our conduct by the standard of what is becoming
than by the more difficult standard of right; or, rather, the
perception of what is becoming gives us a serviceable clue,
both to determine what is right and to decide promptly
when we are called upon to act.

Right or wrong, honor always has been, and always
will be, a leading motive of human action. And it is
especially strong and effective in classes or limited associations of men. The public sentiment just spoken of as
so powerful in its influence upon government and party
action in England is at bottom a sentiment of honor —

what is becoming to the classes in possession of the
government. So with the slave-holding aristocracy of
our Southern States before the war : it was distinguished
by its sensitive feeling of honor — what was becoming to
them as gentlemen ; a sentiment which spread also to
a secondary aristocracy — that of the so-called "poor
whites," who felt themselves also set apart from the
colored population, and maintained a code of honor closely
copied after that of the slave-holders. In this way is
explained the peculiar strength of the feeling of honor
among college students : forming a community singularly
devoid of recognized classes and inequalities of station,
they are a little world by themselves, with their own
interests, their own pursuits, their own modes of action,
and, as a natural result, their own standards of right.
This isolation is quite peculiar to this epoch of their life.
Their point of view during these four years is wholly one-
sided, and their sympathies very narrow. Under these
circumstances there often grows up among them an ina-
bility to appreciate any point of view but their own, an
obtuseness to principles of conduct which are otherwise
universally recognized. And this false standard of conduct, when once set up, is almost impossible to eradicate,
because of the tenacity with which small communities
cling to their cherished customs and prejudices, and because the structure of college society rests upon a regular
and constant influx and efflux, so that with all change the
society still continues the same.

Now, as I have already remarked, the sentiment of
honor is but the reflection upon one's personal dignity of
the sentiment of right : it is necessarily and properly
identical with the judgment of right. If, therefore, there
is in college society a false and demoralizing sense of
honor, this means simply that there is a false and incomplete notion of right and wrong ; that students regard
actions as right in their own case which they would recog-

nize as wrong in anybody else. To correct this sentiment of honor, we must therefore begin at the bottom by establishing correct notions of right and justice. It has been my effort, in all that I have said, to show that this, the highest aim of education, is adequately accomplished by a wise system of secular instruction.

Intellectual honesty is conditioned upon moral honesty. Thoroughness of work is impossible without uprightness of motive. Faithfulness is essential to all real success. And from all these excellences of mind and spirit there may spring, as the vital and inspiring characteristic of college society, a noble sense of honor, quick to detect unworthiness, chivalrous in its maintenance of right, ambitious to attain the best — not, as we see such codes, quick only in taking offence, chivalrous in defence of abuses, and ambitious for personal ends.

The fruits of education which I have attempted to describe are, in the highest sense of the word, practical. Even in the lowest and narrowest meaning of the word, they do not fail us, as your chancellor so well showed last night. Whoever wishes for worldly success will most surely attain it by honest work and faithful service. I am a firm believer in the old maxim, so often scoffed at nowadays, that honesty is the best policy. But it must be honesty, not the show of it. All these virtues which go to make up righteousness must be genuine virtues, growing up in a harmonious character, not planted artificially and laboriously cultivated with a view primarily to the rewards. As fame does not come to those who seek it, but is the reward of laborious service in a good cause; as happiness is not the prize of seeking after pleasure, but of patient endeavoring to do the duty which lies next to one, so worldly success is in the long run enjoyed by those who steadily and without discouragement keep on in the doing of honest and faithful work. If they see cheats and charlatans rolling in wealth, they need not say to themselves, " Honesty is not the best policy." They may con-

sider that it is the ability of these cheats and charlatans —
not their dishonesty — that gains them success ; that,
if genuine integrity were possible to them, their success
would be as sure, and of a higher and more permanent
kind — just as many a college student displays an amount
of talent and industry in cheating his way to a degree
which, if honorably employed, would result in real scholarship; that they should look, not at the brilliant display of
the present, but at the collapse that is almost sure to follow ; and that at any rate, for one who by dishonesty
reaches wealth and station, ten bring up in the jail or the
almshouse.

The present is a good time for considerations like these.
The whole nation is aghast at the depth of corruption and
misgovernment which has been brought to light. We
know very well that such weeds as these do not spring up
of themselves, neither will they flourish and crowd out all
wholesome growth unless we suffer them to do so. There
are causes for all these abuses ; causes that can be ascertained and removed — this gives us good ground for hope ;
causes that must be removed, if we would not sink into
infamy — this warns us that our hope must be mingled
with fear and with a serious sense of responsibility. In
this work of purification and renovation, fittingly begun
at this solemn epoch in our nation's existence, every class
and every man must be ready to take a due share — none
more than we, who owe peculiar obligations to the State
which gave us our work to do, and whose work — education — is in its nature second to none as an agency for
future good. By faithfulness in season and out of season,
by thoroughness of acquirement and of performance, by
living under and inculcating a constant sense of responsibility to God and man, we may do something towards
quickening that sentiment of Christian honor in our own
little community, and so, by healthy and expansive influence, in our beloved country, which alone can save the
commonwealth at such a crisis as this.

THE UTILITY OF CLASSICAL STUDIES AS A MEANS OF MENTAL DISCIPLINE.*

By this topic I understand to be intended not a general defence of the disciplinary value of classical studies, but rather a definition and analysis of this value; that is to say, an examination of the kind of benefit derived from them, and the class of students to whom they are best adapted. With this view, I will lay down the proposition that, in a course of study the primary object of which is discipline, there is a certain stage at which the ancient classics form the very best basis of instruction; and, as a corollary to this, that in any course of study, so far as the object is discipline, the ancient classics are likely to prove the best feature to introduce at a certain stage.

This definition excludes, in the first place, all purely professional courses of study. If the classical languages find a place in these, as, *e.g.*, Latin in a medical course and Greek in a theological course, it is for their practical usefulness, not for their disciplinary power. It excludes, in the second place, all the lower grades of common school studies. The great majority of persons leave school at so early an age that their studies must necessarily be such as will be of immediately practical use to them — the common English branches, which every person must have, and which are well enough adapted to the mental discipline required in their case. Our consideration is therefore confined to what we may call the High School Course and the College Course: in both of these courses discipline is the main thing, and practical utility a secondary one. The proportion of persons who have at once the opportunity and the taste to pursue such a

---

* Paper read before the Wisconsin Teachers' Association, December 30, 1873.

course is small in any community; but the experience of our seats of learning shows that, to make this "opportunity," money is far from being the essential. Our most brilliant and successful scholars are often those whose "opportunities" were simply "brains" and "will."

I think that the discussions of the last few years have resulted in two important conclusions in regard to College Courses; and I think I shall be supported in bringing High School Courses under the same category. These are: first, that their primary object is discipline, as I have just assumed; second, that discipline is only the primary, and not the sole object, and must be combined with practical usefulness. That is to say, the problem is to decide what studies combine the highest degree of mental discipline with some degree at least of practical usefulness in the work of life. It may very well be that there are, for example, some developments of theoretical mathematics, some complicated applications of the rules of logic, some details of natural history, which have no conceivable use except in training the reasoning faculties or exhibiting the principles of classification, but that their serviceableness in these respects is so great as to warrant their introduction into a course of study. There may very well be a certain proportion of mere mental gymnastics such as these; but a course made up exclusively, or in any large proportion, of such studies can find no place in our present schemes of education. Life is too short, and there is too much hard work to be done in it, to allow much of it to be spent in *mere* preparation; especially since it may be maintained that in general the studies that give us the best training, at the same time give us the best tools.

I should not be justified, therefore, in arguing for the introduction of the classical languages into a course which is essentially disciplinary, if it could not be proved that the knowledge of these languages will be serviceable in after life. This point I will not stop to prove, partly because it is not a part of my subject, partly because it has been proved a great many times already. It will be enough to say that there is probably no person who has a fair knowledge of Latin who is not glad of it, and few persons of culture who are devoid of it who would not be glad to have it.

My proposition is, then, that at a certain stage in the High School and College Course the ancient classics form the best means of discipline, and therefore may be pronounced an essential part of such course. To define further what this stage is, it will be necessary to enter into one or two preliminary inquiries, which will at once show their usefulness as a means of discipline, and at the same time define the point in question, the age, or grade, at which they will be found most advantageous.

Leaving out of view the moral and æsthetic nature, education must be mainly directed to the development and training of three faculties — Observation, Memory, and Reason. This is their natural order : we first observe, then remember, then reflect. The first two are devoted to the acquisition of knowledge, the third to its application. Following out this division, we come again to a proposition which has been generally agreed to by educators, and which, therefore, I will not stop to argue — that the education of the child ought to follow this natural order; that observation and memory should come first, and reasoning afterwards. Not that the three can or should at any time be entirely separated. The weak and immature reasoning powers of the child can receive a healthy exercise and development at every step in the acquisition of facts; and it is in this that the skill of the teacher mainly consists. Those teachers are equally at fault who make the entire instruction of the child a matter purely of memory, and those who on the other hand task their reasoning powers too severely by lessons above their comprehension. These views are supported by the almost unanimous judgment of experienced writers and thinkers upon education, who are constantly urging the introduction of Natural History into the lower grades of schools, and the relegation of the technicalities of English Grammar to the upper classes, where they belong.

At the age, say, of ten years, when the reasoning faculties should begin to receive a moderate exercise on their own account, no longer incidentally as in the earlier stages of education, probably the best selection of a study that could be made for this purpose is that which has been made in practice — Mental Arithmetic. Arithmetic, and the other branches of mathematics, continued steadily and moderately — not in the exorbitant degree which is common in our schools — should form the staple of *intellectual* education for some time after this period.

The lower mathematics, however, develop the reasoning faculties only on one side, that of exact proof; for this they are indispensable, and this is one indispensable side of education. But most demonstration is not exact, but only probable; and, to train the reasoning faculties in the direction of probable proof, another class of studies is required. That is to say, to train the mind for its principal work, that of judging of evidence, when the evidence is conflicting or incomplete, when it is possible to come to only a provisional and uncertain decision, a mathematical training is inadequate. And, as this is the character of most of the labor which the intellect has to perform in life, it follows that the main object of a disciplinary education should be to prepare the student to form judgments upon uncertain and conflicting evidence.

For this end a large number of studies are well adapted, none better than, for example, Geology, Physics, and Political Economy, which are studies of the highest educational order. But these are studies which require as a foundation an amount of previous acquirement, in the way of subsidiary sciences, or of observation of facts, which make them come full early enough, if they are placed in the senior year, at the very end of a long course of study. The same thing is true in a degree of scientific and moral subjects as a whole : in proportion as they are highly educational, they are difficult and complicated ; in proportion as they are simple and easy, they are unsuited to this, the main end of education, for the reason that they appeal chiefly to the eye and memory rather than the reasoning faculties. The question is, What branch of studies will best fill the gap? will best develop in the youthful mind the capacity of reasoning upon doubtful and conflicting evidence? will form the best introduction to those higher sciences — physical and moral — which task the highest powers of the mind?

For this object there is nothing so good as the concrete study of language; that is, not the abstractions of grammar, but the practical dealing with words and sentences. The abstract study of language, whether in the philosophy of grammar or the details of linguistic science, belongs further on, with the higher range of subjects which come in best at a more advanced stage. At the period in question, say from twelve to sixteen years of age, the work of translation from one language into another — handling its concrete forms — calls into active and healthy exercise all the intellectual powers which need to be exercised at this stage. The memory plays a large part, especially in learning words and forms; but the translating itself is essentially a process of reasoning. The rules of inflection, indeed, may be so largely generalized as to make the learning of paradigms principally a matter of classification ; and the study of the derivation and relationship of words takes away its purely mnemonic character from the acquisition of a vocabulary. But, when it comes to constructions, the memory has very little to do with it : the pupil is obliged from the very first to work logically — the forms must be determined accurately, and the power of each form must be understood, so that each step in translating shall be not a hap-hazard effort to make the words mean something, but an intelligent analysis of the elements present, so as to ascertain what they must and actually do mean.

It is not necessary to enter more minutely into this argument, because this, too, is a point well agreed to by educators. Every disciplinary course of study intended for the classes in question — High School pupils and the lower College classes — is as a matter of fact made to consist very largely of the two branches, Mathematics and Language. The only point with regard to which there is any difference of opinion is what languages are best suited to this end. The old system made use of the ancient languages : the present tendency is to institute the modern languages ; and I will admit frankly that, if there is room but for one language, in a course which, while mainly disciplinary, is still intended to finish the pupil's formal education, the claims of some modern tongue could hardly be resisted. Any language can be made highly disciplinary ; and every course must have an eye to practical profit as well as to discipline. Our concern is with courses that admit of more than one language.

My proposition is that, apart from practical considerations, the Latin and Greek languages are intrinsically the best for the purposes of discipline ; so much the best that, if a course were exclusively disciplinary, there should be no hesitation, and, in any course that admits of even but two languages, one of these should be one of the two.

The most obvious, although not the weightiest reason is the very fact of the remoteness and strangeness of the language. It is a mistake, at the age in question, to try to make the work too easy for superficial labor. Real work, but not too much of it, is the right principle. The

English language, for example, is as deserving of minute study and as favorable to mental discipline as any; but this study must consist in a considerable degree of abstractions, or of recondite points of scholarship, for the reason that the work that first engages the student of a foreign language, and which gives him the mental exertion I have described, is impossible here. The boy knows what the sentence means, to start with; and, if he is told to study its meaning more intently, he is set to a work of subtle and delicate order, unsuited to his rough style of mental labor. For this reason English affords material for only a term or two of severe study adapted to this stage. And what is true of English is true in a degree of the modern languages cognate to English. The pupil finds nearly the same order of words and rules of construction as in his own language, so that he makes use very much more of mere memory, and less of the reasoning powers.

This brings us to the second and most important argument — the character of the languages themselves. The reason that translating from French or German is much more a matter of the memory than from Latin or Greek is that their difficulties consist, in so much greater degree, in idioms rather than constructions — a natural result of their analytical character, or use of auxiliaries and prepositions instead of inflections. There is of course a difference in this respect. German is far less idiomatic than either French or English, and is for this reason the best adapted for purposes of mental discipline. Greek, on the other hand, is more idiomatic than Latin, and for this reason less adapted for purposes of mental discipline. It is in the language, as in the institutions of Rome, that the pupil comes most completely under the dominion of law.

Now, the analysis of idioms is a most useful and interesting practice at a more advanced stage; but for beginners they are a matter of pure memory, while laws of construction belong exclusively to the domain of reason. A regular construction may be readily analyzed by the comparatively young pupil, and studied in its principles and application ; and these laws of construction, in their varied uses and complicated relations, present precisely the kind of mental exertion which the pupil needs. In proportion, therefore, as a language is syntactical rather than idiomatic, it is adapted to the purposes of mental discipline; and, while German and Greek possess this character in a high degree, the Latin possesses it in the highest degree. No language, therefore — no one, that is, of the languages commonly studied — can compare with Latin for this purpose. It should at the same time be remarked that, in arguing for a classical language, it does not necessarily follow that it should be Latin. Many persons are in favor of beginning Greek first ; and, if our text-books were adapted to this order, there would be no conclusive objection to this course. And, if but one ancient language is to be studied, it might very well be that the superiority of Greek literature might outweigh the superior disciplinary advantages of the Latin language.

As our subject is the disciplinary power of the ancient languages, the discussion might end here : their disciplinary value consists essentially in the two features just indicated — the rigorous application of laws, and the unfamiliar character of the constructions, which enables them to be studied from a more independent and objective point of view. This does not by any means exhaust the benefits of classical study, but the other benefits come under a somewhat different head. The philosophy and institutions of the ancients, for example, indispensable as they are to any student of philosophy or of political science, may — for this purpose — be as well studied through translations and modern commentaries and treatises as from the original writers. There is, however, one large class of benefits which may very properly come in here, although they have reference rather to the æsthetic than the intellectual nature; that is, the literary excellence of the ancients. The style, although primarily a matter of taste, is largely also dependent upon the reason; and from this point of view we find the study of the ancient *authors* as serviceable as that of the ancient *languages* is in the point of view already considered. This is an advantage that can be obtained only from the study of the original, not of translations; for the very essence of a good translation is that it should not preserve the idioms and stylistic peculiarities of the language from which the translation is made, but should transfer the thoughts and statements of the original into the idioms and forms of expression which belong to the language into which the translation is made.

The qualities of style in which the ancient writers far surpass the moderns are symmetry, precision, and compactness; and these qualities arise chiefly from that same inflectional character which is the source of their syntactical perfection. The genius of the modern languages tempts to a loose, inexact, and irregular style, so much so that, if a modern writer makes it his direct aim to reproduce these distinguishing qualities of the classical writers, the result is almost sure to be something at once obscure and ungraceful. I can hardly think of any English writer, except Lord Bacon, and perhaps Milton and Ralph Waldo Emerson, who have developed a style as elegant and perspicuous, and at the same time as terse, exact, and vigorous as the ancients. Now, it is of no use for a modern writer to *imitate* these qualities of the ancients; but it is of the greatest use to study them, to be familiar with them, to have the mind imbued with them, and then, unconsciously, when he is simply doing his best to write correct, idiomatic English, some traces perhaps of their fine qualities will find their way to his pen.

The course of study, therefore, which I favor for those who have the opportunity and taste for a thorough disciplinary training, is to begin in childhood with those branches that train the eye and exercise the memory — drawing, coloring, natural history, the elements of geometry, simple applications of numbers, stories from history, and the descriptions of foreign countries. All of these, in a greater or less degree, admit of some exercise of the reasoning powers ; and, as these powers become more vigorous and mature, their exercise should occupy a larger and longer share of time, until at some period, between twelve and fourteen, or even later, the pupil may to the best advantage take up the study of the ancient languages, with a view to regular and systematic intellectual discipline.

It has been necessary for me, in presenting my views as to the place of the ancient languages in an educational scheme, to touch somewhat upon the province of others, so far as to assign their respective places to other studies. All parts of an educational scheme hang so closely together that one cannot be adjusted without reference to the others. No apology therefore is due for thus transgressing.

THE CREED AS A BASIS OF CHURCH ORGANIZATION.*

ORGANIZATION in social concerns is systematized co-operation. We all know how essential co-operation is in all our undertakings. Without it, every man would be reduced to his own unaided resources ; and this means that society would go back to the condition of savage life. Division of labor, service, exchange — all these are forms of co-operation, devices by which every man's efforts are made to assist the labors of other men, and every man's labor is thereby rendered many-fold more effective. Now, it is readily seen that, if this co-operation, by nature voluntary, fitful, irregular, is made regular and certain, its efficacy is vastly increased. This is organization, the value of which has been recognized by mankind at every stage of progress. Government is a very complicated organization ; all great industrial enterprises are highly organized ; it may be said that all the routine work of society depends chiefly for its success upon organization; that is, upon mutual aid rendered with regularity and certainty.

Notice the limitation : all *routine* work. Work that is not mechanical, but spontaneous — the productions of genius, the exercise of affection and pity — may sometimes be aided by organization, and almost always by co-operation : but in these the organized action is never the principal thing. When, in activities of this kind, organization is allowed to take the leading place, and spontaneity is subordinated to it, either, as in the As-

* Paper read before the Wisconsin Unitarian Conference, at Milwaukee, Wis., November 6, 1885.

sociated Charities, it is because the individual exercise of charity towards strangers is attended with mischiefs which can be prevented only by converting such charity into a matter of routine; or, on the other hand, the spontaneous and sympathetic qualities of the mind will be deadened. The system of Associated Charities — that is, the organization of charity — is desirable only where there is not scope for the play of personal sympathies. It is far better, where practicable, to have charity the act of individual, unorganized beneficence, blessing the giver as much as the receiver. But in most cases this is not practicable, because the amount of poverty, the great distances to be traversed, and the blank wall of separation which divides the well-to-do from the destitute render impossible the personal acquaintance and the personal interest which are indispensable to the exercise of charity of the highest order.

Religion is a thing in which, more perhaps than in any other human interest, organization would seem to be unnecessary and even harmful. It is personal, individual, purely a matter of feeling ; and, although it is worthless unless it manifests itself outwardly in a good life, its true sphere is the most interior of all, the spiritual nature of man. It would seem as if here even mutual helps were impossible, except in the way of personal influence — the inspiration exerted upon the soul of an individual by contact with a nobler and purer character. It would seem that here, if anywhere, we could dispense with system and order ; that organization would be sure to blunt the finer feelings, and make the religious life a thing of routine and outward show and perfunctory morality. And all experience supports this conclusion. No organizations are so hopelessly given over to formalism as those of religion, whether Christian or heathen ; no life, I suppose, has ever been more irreligious than that of those organized bodies of men and women which, in the Middle

Ages, assumed, by way of pre-eminence, the distinctive name "religious."

But organization in religion has even worse results than formalism and hypocrisy — worse, that is, in immediate relation to the happiness of society. Organization means effectiveness for action; that is, power. Organizations, by a law of their being, are seldom satisfied with increased efficiency within their sphere. One organization comes in contact with another, and a struggle for power ensues between them. They eagerly strive to bring more and more individuals or communities within their lines, often quite as much in order to increase their own power as to advance the spiritual welfare of the new associates. Towards their own members they are hard taskmasters, subordinating their individual good to the interests of the body. Rivalries, jealousies, the iron rule of a spiritual despotism, persecutions, religious wars — we do not need to go to past eras to find the saddest chapters of history those which deal with religious organizations. Even in the present day, where these organizations have become relatively so weak, we can discern these same dangers and evils wherever the prosperity of a church or a sect is regarded as so paramount as to warrant questionable means for its furtherance — wherever the church is made anything more than an instrument for building up a religious life.

Nevertheless, in spite of all this, we see that religion has at all times been pre-eminently the subject of organized action. Organized religions are perhaps the most conspicuous institutions in history and in modern society, and they are distinguished above all others by splendor and elaborate display. We have no right to attribute this, as is often done, to the scheming ambition of priests. The scheming ambition of priests has had much to do with the development of the organizations, their acquisition of power, and the enormous abuses that have at-

tended its exercise; but how did the priesthood themselves come into existence? No organization of religion
would have been possible if it had not been found to bring
some advantages with it; and the universality of such
organizations proves the universal feeling of their
necessity.

It is easy to see that there are real and positive benefits that accompany the organization of religion, not connected with the primary nature of religion, which is private, personal, and a matter of sentiment, but with its regular and necessary workings in relation to society. The
religious sentiment is, it is true, private, personal, and
individual; but it is a sentiment which needs for its perfection, even for its perfection in the individual, to pass
outside of the individual, and bear fruit in the outward
life. Unless religion ceases to be purely individual, and
becomes relative, or altruistic, it is morbid and barren.
This is the case with a large proportion of what is distinctively called the religious life, especially in non-
Christian countries and in the Eastern branch of the
Christian Church. The intensely practical character of
the peoples of western Europe has in most cases prevented
the monastic life among them from degenerating into
utter isolation and selfishness, and has, indeed, at several
epochs made it the chief agency for the promotion of
intellectual and industrial progress.

Religion, therefore, while it must not cease to be essentially personal, must at the same time become co-opera-
tive, must ally itself with human action and develop into
morality. Here, therefore, is the justification of religious
organizations. Organization is, as I have said, a chief
means of effectiveness for action. Just so far, therefore,
as religion passes into action, it will be assisted by organization. We all recognize, in spite of the temptations to
formalism and hypocrisy, to jealousy and despotism, the
noble work which is done by the organized charities of

the present day in every department of human necessity. The good far outweighs the evil. But it is our business not merely to let the evil be overbalanced by good, but to remove the evil so far as possible, and make our religious organizations wholly an instrument for good. The man who, in his insistence upon individuality, refuses to associate himself with any religious organization, is in danger of missing the best fruits even of personal religion.

The first and most fundamental question, therefore, in the relation of the church to society, is with regard to its basis of organization. We have seen that religion, like all the other interests of life, having practical and social bearings, becomes organized, in obedience to a universal tendency, which we have found to be also necessary and salutary. We have seen on the other hand, both from the nature of things and from historical experience, that serious temptations and dangers accompany this process. The problem before us is to secure the benefits of organization, in the way of vigor, unity, and efficiency of action, while escaping the lowering of motive and the loss of spiritual earnestness that have commonly resulted from the organization of religious work. In considering this question in relation to the practical needs of the American people, we need not concern ourselves about the special dangers and evils that have beset religious organizations in ancient times, in the Middle Ages, or among the heathen nations of our own day. Each of these has its own sins to answer for: our concern is with the American Church of the present day, whose worst enemy, I do not hesitate to say, is the creed as a basis of organization.

Church organizations, as they exist, are almost without exception founded upon a creed; that is, upon a formal and authoritative statement of belief, acceptance of which is required as a condition of fellowship. In the Protestant body the creed is the starting-point. Most of the

Protestant sects are built upon some point of doctrinal belief which distinguishes their creed more or less broadly from that of others. In the church of the Middle Ages the procedure was just the opposite of this : the church, claiming absolute and universal authority in matters of belief, formulated its creed by deliberate act, and imposed it rigorously on all. And both alike, the unity of the mediæval church, enforced by sword and stake, by inquisition and crusade, and the diversity of Protestantism, eternally wrangling upon questions of secondary import, and frittering away its strength in endless divisions, are a scandal to Christianity. But so completely has this false notion, that a creed is the only possible basis of a church, taken possession of men's minds that the first question asked, when a new religious body comes to one's notice, is, What do they believe? and a church without a creed is to this day a matter of surprise and bewilderment to the majority of people.

This is not to be wondered at. The moment that the Christian Church ceased to be a private association of the followers of Jesus, and was raised by Constantine to the dignity of a State religion, unity of belief rather than integrity of life became its principal aim, to be enforced by all the authority of the State. Œcumenical councils sat under imperial auspices, and in them bishops kicked and pounded each other, sometimes even to death — all to determine shades of doctrinal differences too delicate to be stated in any language but Greek. And, when in any case the controversy was settled, the victorious opinions were triumphantly installed as those of united Christendom, the defeated creed languishing for a while in out-of-the-way corners, as the tenets of some obscure sect of heretics. The great schism of East and West rested mainly upon the insertion or omission of the conjunction "and " in the creed. The string had been drawn too tight, and snapped. In the Protestant schism of the sixteenth century it snapped again, and this time beyond repair. But, although unity was gone, the despotism of creed remained. At first every native, then every group of like-minded persons, claimed the right to make their own creed; and, if they could not force everybody to accept it, they could at any rate comfort themselves by denying the Christian name and the possibility of salvation to all that rejected it. From this followed the numberless sects of Protestantism, the legitimate result of the dogmatic and unnatural unity of Catholicism.

As a vindication of the right of private judgment, this deserves all sympathy. Nor do I see very well by what right these diversities can be censured from the point of view of the Catholic Church, which had for centuries taught and enforced the principle that correctness of belief is all-important; that the creed is the essential thing in a church. Mankind had been taught this so thoroughly that, when they once came into the enjoyment of intellectual freedom, nothing seemed to them so fatal as diversity of belief. Hence disputes as endless, and upon points as unessential, as the Homoöusian and Homoiousian controversy: only that now the defeated party in any controversy did not strike its colors and surrender its cherished dogma, as in earlier times, but seceded, organized a new church of its own, of which this dogma was the central article, and thus added another to the long list of Protestant sects. In all this there is nothing to be wondered at, seeing for how many centuries unity of belief had been considered the most vital thing in the life of the church. But when we reflect that all these hostile bodies profess absolutely the same purpose — to promote morality and spiritual life, and to advance the kingdom of God in the world — it is hard to realize how large a share of their energies has been wasted upon questions of secondary import.

In this I do not mean to say that questions of belief

are unimportant.   Far from it.   Next to right living,
right thinking is the most essential thing to all of us ; and
it is a matter of no slight importance that our opinions
upon religious questions should be clear and logical; and,
more than this, that they should ripen into convictions
for which a man is willing to labor unweariedly, suffer, and
even die.   The indifference in matters of belief which
passes itself off so frequently for liberality is not a credi-
table or encouraging characteristic of the religious life of
to-day.   But creeds will not help this.   They are at best
somebody's else statement of what I believe : the earnest
consideration which we desire is not as a matter of fact
the fruit of the creed itself, but of the allegiance to the
church authority which makes its votary willing to accept
its creed ; and in nine cases out of ten it would be precisely the same if the creed contained a totally different
formula.   At any rate, this conviction is personal, not collective, belongs to that private and individual side of
religion   which   organization   harms   rather   than   helps.
Enforced assent to a creed often offensive, generally ill
understood, and always the expression of another person's
reasonings and opinions, is one of the worst results of the
tyranny of organization of which I have spoken.   But,
while the statement of belief is personal and theoretical,
the church is public and practical : opinions are not the
object for which it is primarily founded.   Creeds can
noways help, and may seriously hinder, the principal work
of the church, in contending with the great crushing needs
of poverty, sin, and suffering.

I would not, therefore, underrate the importance of correct thinking in questions of religion ; nor would I deny
that a general agreement upon these questions is a natural
and perhaps indispensable foundation of religious fellowship.   But it should be a general agreement merely, not
the enforced acceptance of a special formula.   Nor indeed
would I deny the value of special formulas in special

cases. A statement of belief by an individual or a body of individuals may serve a valuable purpose. Only it should be purely a *statement of belief*, not crystallized into a creed; that is, not become formal, final, and authoritative. I am willing to state what I believe to-day, but I would not promise to believe it to-morrow; nor would I make agreement with it a condition of co-operation with me in religious work.

The world is fast learning that it has been wrong all through these centuries, and creeds are every day losing their hold. But there are few who have the courage to throw them away entirely: it is thought that by amending them, by omitting this objectionable phrase and modifying that, the creed can be brought into harmony with the thought of the day. And so it can, no doubt, be made to express the average religious opinion of to-day; but it is still a dead and unelastic thing, incapable of being adjusted to future changed conditions of belief. As we alter it to-day, to make it agree with what we believe, the next generation will alter it in its turn, to make it agree with what will then be the average of religious opinion. And what a satire it is upon the very definition of a creed, as the statement of absolute truth, that each generation shall tear to pieces the work of its predecessor, and substitute a new formula — equally authoritative, equally a statement of absolute truth! No; what is wanted is not a series of creeds, each more attenuated than the last, but courage to reject the very idea of a creed. It needs to be recognized that any statement of belief upon so vast and obscure a subject must necessarily be incomplete, partial, and colored by the individuality of its authors, so that it cannot possibly be acceptable to any other age, or to any body of men differently educated or differently circumstanced; and that, even if it were possible to draw up a creed which should be a perfect and unchangeable expression of truth, even then it would be a mistake to found an association for religious co-operation on a statement of intellectual belief.

A far greater evil attending the system of creeds than the necessity of adjusting them to changed conditions of belief is found in the constant temptation either to adjust individual belief to the creed or to accept the creed with a mental reservation or a private understanding. I have no blame for the man who, having in good faith bound himself by a creed which he really believed, has moved away from it by insensible degrees, and finds himself at last wholly out of sympathy with his professed opinions. I can understand very well that a man so situated may regard his work as more essential than the form of belief, and may satisfy his conscience with ignoring what he cannot accept and emphasizing what is vital in his eyes. It is not an honest or an heroic attitude, but it is not consciously dishonest. But to persuade one's self to believe a creed, not because it seems true, but because it affords admittance to a particular organization, is to stultify one's self; and outwardly to profess belief in a creed which one does not believe is treachery to one's moral nature. The loss of moral earnestness which must accompany any such act of insincerity will far outweigh all that is gained by the co-operation either given or received.

Would I not, then, have any doctrinal test whatever, any *minimum* of theological belief, as a basis of church organization and a condition of church fellowship? I can see nothing but harm in any such doctrinal test. As a statement of religious truth, it must by necessity be incomplete and inelastic, making no provision for growth in thought, and, by its exclusive formulation of one phase of opinion, arousing a combative and controversial temper; in many cases either stifling independent thought or inviting a hollow and insincere conformity.

A distinction may, however, properly be made between

a formal statement of belief, which, when made a condition of fellowship, we call a Creed, and the incidental assertion of belief in the statement of a common purpose. Such a statement of purpose may, in its terms, take for granted what it would not be wise to formulate dogmatically. The excellent bond of fellowship drawn up by Mr. C. G. Ames, and adopted by many of our churches, declares the object of the association to be "the worship of God and the service of Man." To this there can be no objection. What can a church be but an organization for worship and mutual helpfulness? It is in this feature of worship that the *church* differs from the philosophical club or the society for ethical culture ; and, as long as we associate ourselves into churches, such a phrase, implying theistic belief, is wholly proper. But if we should undertake to follow up this statement of a common purpose, in which we all agree, in which our very associated life consists, with a statement of common belief, even one identical in its purport with what we here implicitly affirm, we at once open the door for disagreement and controversy. Suppose we say, " I believe in God": immediately there arises the necessity for definition. Believe in what God? The God of Calvin or the God of Channing? The "magnified non-natural man" of Matthew Arnold or the pure abstraction of pantheism? Many a person will agree to labor for the service of God, who will seriously hesitate to set his name to any statement of belief in God, because it is impossible to make any such statement which shall command assent and agreement.

Even if we could draw up a statement of belief the terms and definitions of which would be immediately acceptable, it would, like all statements of belief, lose its vitality directly, would be outgrown by the progress of thought, and would require restatement in a very short time. Why, moreover, should we shut out from co-operation with us those who are willing to help in our work, but cannot subscribe to our formulas? If any man is willing to join with me in advancing the kingdom of God, I do not see why I should refuse to accept his help unless he agrees with me as to precisely what the kingdom of God is, or just how to define God.   He may say he is an atheist, for aught I care.   If he has no formal *belief* in God, but his deeds show that he has *faith* in God's government, that is enough for me.   For, although *belief* is unessential, *faith* is not — an earnest sense of the distinction between right and wrong, a recognition of the mighty power of truth, and a reverent submission to that moral government of the universe which we call the law of God.   No man can define the Supreme Being or form any conception of the future life which any other thoughtful man would be willing to accept; but, although a man may refuse to give his assent even to a belief in the existence of God or in immortality, he may have a religious faith as deep, and as ready to manifest itself in good works, as the most devoted adherent of a creed.

I am not insensible to certain intellectual advantages which are connected with creeds.   There have been two great systems of religious thought in the Christian world: those of Thomas Aquinas and of John Calvin, which may almost be said even to this day to divide the Christian world between them.   In these two systems of thought gigantic intellects have been trained: there is a cogency, a coherency, a logical power in them, which makes profound study and hearty acceptance of them an educational work of the highest value.   But there is no education, no intellectual activity, no merit of any sort, in blindly accepting the formal propositions of either of these great thinkers on the authority of somebody else.   And this is what is meant by signing a creed.   Not one in a hundred of those who accept these systems does it from any intellectual conviction: it is purely a moral act — a submission of the intellect to the authority of the church to which they think it their duty to belong. Whatever intellectual benefit might be derived from the study of an elaborated system of thought is precluded by the blind acceptance of the formulas in which its results are stated.

Neither would I argue that the church, any more than the individual, should be indifferent to matters of belief. As I have said, right thinking stands next in importance to right living — indeed, forms a part of right living. For although we would not say, with Socrates, that sin is only the outcome of ignorance, we must all admit that our conduct is largely influenced by our opinions, and that at any rate nothing is a more integral part of ourselves than our conceptions and our reasonings. But this does not lead us to the acceptance of creeds : on the other hand, it makes their harmfulness more emphatic. It is the function of the church to be a leader of thought as well as a guide of conduct : and it is because I desire the church to be a leader of thought, that I would not have it limit its range of thought, and fetter itself with the trammels of a creed. It is one part, and that not the least important, of the work of the church, to investigate and teach spiritual truth ; but the imposition of a creed would estop this investigation wherever it conflicts with its formulas. Religious faith rests upon the conviction that all God's truth is precious and welcome: it sins against itself when it submits itself to formulas of human invention.

In place of the creed, therefore, the false basis devised in a corrupt age, the church of the nineteenth century should substitute *an intellectual attitude* — a receptivity of mind, inspired by a living faith, and welcoming all truth in the devout conviction that no truth can be indifferent or harmful. This is nothing more nor less than the adoption of the scientific method in religious inquiry. There are questions with which even the scientific method is incapable of dealing, such as the existence and nature of God, and the assurance of the future life. But the dogmatic method is even more out of place here; for this asserts without proof what must always be a matter of reverent faith alone — it requires collective assent to what is the concern only of the individual, and of each individual in a degree varying with the liveliness of his faith and the reverence of his spirit. But the largest part of religious discussion is upon questions which are to be determined by evidence and argument; and in these it is the duty of the church as well as of the individual frankly to accept and courageously to assert whatever is proved by science or scholarship. The church that is bound by a creed does not do this.

I have spoken at what may seem a disproportionate length upon the subject of Creeds, because it is in these that we find the distinguishing characteristics of the several churches of the present day. Each denomination is built upon its peculiar article of belief, and every new divergence in belief calls into existence a new denomination. A church, therefore, like ours, which has no creed, which has instead an intellectual attitude of free but reverent inquiry, has this very feature for its distinguishing mark, and stands by virtue of it not among the churches that rest upon creeds, but apart from them — not necessarily hostile, but following a method utterly at variance with theirs. Any other basis of church organization is, as things now stand, wholly secondary to the intellectual one. All alike aim to cultivate holiness of life in their members, and all alike engage actively in works of social beneficence: their differences are intellectual, either in details of doctrine or in method of inquiry. This has therefore with propriety formed the principal topic, in treating of the basis of the church organization.

We are sometimes told, partly by way of wish, partly

by way of prophecy, that Unitarians will some day have a creed like the rest. If they do this, they will be false to their traditions. It is true the very name *Unitarian* expresses a theological doctrine — the unity of the godhead, as opposed to the generally accepted trinity. But it does it impliedly, not in the way of formal statement or definition. Just as the word *church* implies belief in God, so does the word "Unitarian" imply a certain conception of God. But, dogmatically, it is a negative term: it means simply that we have turned our back upon the old theology, and are moving in an opposite direction. Just what point we have reached in this direction it is for each person to determine for himself, in accordance with our fundamental principle of free rational inquiry. Let us lay our foundations as broad and deep as possible in a positive religious faith, in the devout recognition of the fatherhood of God and the spiritual leadership of Jesus. Let us enlarge as far as possible the sphere of our activities. So far, in the field of faith and of ethics, we are on sure ground. But as soon as we undertake, in the intellectual field, to fetter our faith with a formula of words, we shall depart from the original and distinctive principle of our denomination, and give up all hope of doing our part in the evangelization of the world.

MONOGRAPHS.

THE LEX CURIATA DE IMPERIO.*

IT is well known that the Roman magistrates, after entering upon their offices, procured the passage of a law defining their powers with precision. In the case of the censors this law was passed in the *comitia centuriata;* in the case of all the other patrician magistrates, in the *comitia curiata*, an assembly which existed in the later centuries of the Republic for hardly any other purposes than this, and which accordingly sank into a purely formal assemblage, in which the several curies were represented by an equal number of beadles, *lictors*. Nevertheless, this purely formal act was regularly insisted upon down to the close of the Republic. The law was of the same general character, whether passed by curies or centuries, and whether dealing with the *imperium* or not. Nevertheless, as it is best known in connection with the *imperium* of the consuls, prætors, and dictators, it has come to be known by the inexact title of *lex curiata de imperio*. The phrase *de imperio* is not properly a part of the title, but simply describes the scope of the law in reference to this particular group of magistrates. In the case of the ædiles and quæstors, as well as of the censors, it would necessarily be *de potestate*. Nevertheless, it is only with regard to the *imperium* that the question can have any practical importance. Upon assuming office, all magistrates entered without delay upon the exercise of the administrative and purely civil functions of their office ; and the neglect to pass this law, or its failure through intercession of the tribunes, can have worked no practical reduction of their powers. The *imperium*, on the other hand, carrying with it the right to command troops and to inflict the death

* From Transactions of the American Philological Association for 1888, vol. 19, p. 5.

penalty, was too formidable a power to be exercised by any one who had not been formally invested with it. Consequently, while the law in question was, in relation to other offices, so pure a formality that it is known to us only as a piece of antiquarianism, the law *de imperio* is an act frequently mentioned, and possessing a real historical importance.

Here it is to be noticed that in the period after Sulla the consuls and prætors within their year of office possessed only the civil *imperium ;* that is, general executive and administrative power within the limits of Italy. For them, therefore, it made no difference whether they se-cured the passage of this law or not, until the time came for them to go to the government of a province in the fol-lowing year. This the possession of the *imperium*, which did not require to be renewed, enabled them to do with-out interruption. There is no doubt that the law, being now a mere formality, was often neglected. Cicero says (*Leg. Agr.* ii. 12, 30), *consulibus legem curiatam ferentibus a tribunis plebis sæpe est intercessum.* In this case no embarrassment would result until it came to acts which rested distinctly upon the military *imperium*, such as holding the *comitia centuriata* (which power was, of course, contained in the limited *imperium* of this period) and taking the government of a province. Since our dis-cussion, therefore, is exclusively confined to the right to exercise these powers, we will speak of the law in ques-tion by its familiar, if inexact, title, as *lex curiata de im-perio.*

It has usually been held that this law actually conferred upon the magistrate the powers of his magistracy, the elec-tion and inauguration in the office being only inchoate and incomplete acts. Mommsen, however, in his "Rö-misches Staatsrecht" (i. p. 52, first edition), takes the ground that it is not to be looked upon as an act of legis-lation, but rather as an obligatory act, which the citizens cannot refuse to a magistrate who has already entered upon his office (*Als eigentlicher Volksbeschluss darf er nicht aufgefasst werden, sondern vielmehr als eine Verpflichtung, die die Bürgerschaft dem verfassungsmässig ins Amt gelangten Beamten nicht verweigern kann*), and that it in strictness of speech gives the magistrate no right which he does not already possess (*Auch giebt der Act streng genommen dem Beamten kein Recht, das er nicht bereits hat*). It is with diffidence that one differs from a scholar of Mommsen's authority; but as it is upon a question of interpretation rather than of fact and as it is a frequent charge against this great man that he is prone to push his preconceived theories beyond what is warranted by the evidence, I will venture to present the grounds upon which I conclude that the *lex curiata de imperio*, even if it had become a mere formality, was nevertheless a necessary act, and did really confer the *imperium;* that without it the authority of the magistrate was incomplete.

Mommsen admits indeed that his proposition does not admit of positive proof (*geradezu beweisen lässt dieser Satz sich nicht*): he maintains, nevertheless, that it follows by necessity from the nature of things, and is supported by the evidence of several well-established instances. If the city should be attacked before this law had been carried, it is not to be supposed that its defence would be omitted for the lack of a person qualified to take command. As to this it can only be said, *Salus populi suprema lex*. The case is quite analogous to that of a province left by the sudden death of its governor without any legitimate commander: in such a case, as Mommsen has himself shown (p. 179), there must of necessity have been some way of temporarily filling the vacancy. We may compare also the formula *videant consules ne quid res publica detrimenti capiat*, by which the Senate bestowed the military *imperium* upon the consuls, in great emergencies, during the period after Sulla, when these magistrates possessed only the civil *imperium*. It may be assumed that, if the magistrates lacked the formal power to command troops, the Senate would have bestowed upon them this extraordinary authority.

The first example which Mommsen adduces to support his view is that of Caius Flaminius, consul B.C. 217, who entered upon his office at Ariminum, and who, consequently, could not have carried the *lex curiata* for himself, as was certainly usual and as is assumed to have been requisite. But this assumed necessity is by no means proved. In the case of the inferior magistrates, who had not the power to convene the assembly, the law must of course have been presented for them by one of the consuls; and it is hard to see why the same cannot have been done by a consul for his colleague, as indeed had been Mommsen's opinion previously. The objection that the senatorial faction would not have been inclined to overlook an irregularity in the case of so obnoxious a person as Flaminius cannot have much weight in regard to a body inspired by so lofty a sense of patriotism as that which the Roman Senate displayed the next year towards a still more obnoxious consul, Varro. It is to be noticed that in the irregularities charged against Flaminius by the senatorial leaders (Livy, xxii. 1, 5) — *quod illi iustum imperium . . . esse?*—there is no mention of the want of the *lex curiata*. The objections are purely formal : *magistratus id* [i.e., *auspicium*] *a domo, publicis privatisque penatibus Latinis feriis actis, sacrificio in monte perfecto, votis rite in Capitolio nuncupatis secum ferre ; nec privatum auspicia sequi, nec sine auspiciis profectum in externo ea solo nova atque integra concipere posse.*

Another instance is that of the consuls of B.C. 49, Lentulus and Marcellus, who continued to exercise authority during the following year as proconsuls, notwithstanding that they had neglected to procure the *lex curiata* before leaving Rome at the beginning of their term of office. But this case tells on the other side. The senatorial government at Thessalonica abstained from organizing for the year 48, by the election of new magistrates, for the reason that the failure to procure the *lex curiata* made it impossible for them to hold the *comitia centuriata* (ὅτι τὸν νόμον οἱ ὕπατοι τὸν φρατριατικὸν οὐκ ἐσενηνόχεσαν, Dio Cassius, 41, 43). The lack of this law had not, it is true, prevented them from exercising military authority during the year 49 : as has already been said, the military emergency required the assumption of power, and this may have been done by the authority of the Senate. But when it came to the specific formal act of holding the centuriate assembly, which, as being the army, could only be held in virtue of the military *imperium*, the consuls shrank from such a transgression of the law, and preferred to continue the informal exercise of the *imperium* which they already held. The case of Camillus, in his dictatorship, the only other case referred to, can be met by analogy with either of the two cases considered : as Mommsen says, he must either have foregone the *lex curiata* or it must have been procured for him by some other magistrate.

A more puzzling case is that of Appius Claudius, consul B.C. 54, which is cited in another note. The circumstances in this case are peculiar, and can be understood only in connection with the succession of events during this summer, which are known to us pretty completely through Cicero's correspondence.* When the elections of July approached, rumors began to be rife of a corrupt bargain (the notorious *coitio Memmiana*) between the consuls Claudius and Domitius Ahenobarbus on the one hand and the consular candidates Memmius and Domitius

---

* His letters to his brother Quintus (ii. 15 and 16, and iii.), nearly all dated, enable us to construct the chronology with approximate accuracy. Those to Atticus (iv. 15 to 18) are in great confusion; *e.g.*, No. 16 has the date October 1 (§ 7); but § 5 belongs to July 3–5 (cf. 15, 4), while §§ 9–12 come after October 24. The edition of Baiter and Kayser has rearranged these sections so as to correspond to the chronology of the letters to Quintus.

Calvinus on the other (*ad Q. fr.* ii. 15, b. 4; *ad Att.* iv. 15, 7), but the terms of the bargain do not seem to have been known. It was probably these rumors that caused the election to be put off until September (*ad Q. fr.* ii. 16, 3). Towards the end of September, the two consular candidates having quarrelled, Memmius divulged the terms of the bargain in the Senate (*ad Q. fr.* iii. 1, 16), placing indeed written evidence in the hands of the consuls. The contract was to the effect that the consuls should secure the election to these two men, and that they for their part should produce fraudulent testimony to the passage of the *lex curiata de imperio* and of a *senatus consultum* making appropriations for the government of their provinces. Cicero's words are: *ipse et suus competitor Domitius Calvinus . . . HS quadragena consulibus darent, si essent ipsi consules facti, nisi tres augures dedissent, qui se adfuisse dicerent, cum lex curiata ferretur, quæ lata non esset, et duo consulares, qui se dicerent in ornandis provinciis consularibus scribendo adfuisse, cum omnino ne senatus quidem fuisset* (*ad Att.* iv. 18, 2).

It would seem that the *lex curiata*, which was regularly passed in March, in which month the military *imperium* commenced, had not been passed this year; and, as the year drew to a close, the consuls, to whom provinces had been assigned by the Senate, were anxious to secure the authority to enter upon their government. Of course the whole compact came to naught, when once divulged. Both candidates were at once indicted for bribery, as well as their competitors, Messala and Scaurus, and the consuls must seek for other authority to take their provinces. Appius declared promptly that he would go to his province without the law, and pay his own expenses (*ad Q. fr.* iii. 2, 3; *ad Att.* iv. 16, 12). This was in October. The fullest statement of his plans is given in a letter (*ad Fam.* i. 9, 25) to Lentulus Spinther, the then governor of Cilicia, to which there is no date, but which must have been written at this time: *Appius in sermonibus antea dictitabat, postea dixit etiam in senatu palam, sese, si licitum esset legem curiatam ferre, sortiturum esse cum collega provinciam: si curiata lex non esset, se paraturum cum collega tibique successurum: legem curiatam consuli ferri opus esse, necesse non esse: se, quoniam ex senatus consulto provinciam haberet, lege Cornelia imperium habiturum, quoad in urbem introisset.* Here is a positive assertion by Claudius, upon which Mommsen relies in his argument, that, although the consul was under obligation (*opus*) to bring the law before the *comitia*, the passage of the law was not indispensable (*necesse*) to his possession of the *imperium;* and that, if he is prevented (by tribunician intercession) from taking his province by regular procedure, he will do it by a simple agreement with his colleague. Cicero adds that there is a difference of opinion as to the legal question, and that he himself does not feel quite certain — *mihi non tam de iure certum est* — *quamquam ne id quidem dubium est*, etc.; the last phrase apparently meaning that he is pretty certain that it is bad law. As a matter of fact, Appius went to his province and returned with the expectation of a triumph; but whether he had procured the *lex curiata* is uncertain. The year at any rate ended with an interregnum.

It will be noted that what Appius claimed was the right *de facto* to exercise the *imperium* in the province: the province had been assigned by the Senate, and, by the Cornelian Law (of Sulla), he could continue his command until he returned to the city. This seems to point to an exercise of military command by authority of the Senate, similar to that granted by the phrase *videant consules ne quid respublica detrimenti capiat;* but, instead of resting his case simply upon the necessity of keeping the governmental machinery in operation, he undertook to defend his position by a legal quibble — that the law was *opus*, but not *necesse.*

That this assertion of Claudius was not a recognized principle of constitutional law, but a theory got up for the occasion, is made probable by the character of the man and his family. This Appius Claudius, elder brother of the demagogue Publius Clodius, was the head of that Claudian gens which Mommsen has shown to have been distinguished, not for conservatism and patrician arrogance, as is usually assumed, but for a revolutionary and innovating spirit. His consulship (b.c. 54) affords another illustration of his reckless interpretations of law. The Pupian Law forbade the Senate to meet on *dies comitiales:* the Gabinian Law set apart the sessions of the Senate in the month of February, to be devoted to foreign affairs — receiving embassies and making provision for the provincial governments. When Appius reached the day of the Quirinalia (February 17) in his consulship, he appears to have found that the consideration of foreign affairs had not made so much headway as was desirable. The remainder of the month of February being chiefly made up of *dies comitiales*, he declared that he would use these for meetings of the Senate in spite of the Pupian Law: *Comitialibus diebus, qui Quirinalia sequuntur, Appius interpretatur non impediri se lege Pupia, quominus habeat senatum, et, quod Gabinia sanctum sit, etiam cogi ex Kal. Feb. usque ad Kal. Mart. legatis senatum quotidie dari* (Cic. *ad Q. fr.* ii. 13, 3). In his view the Gabinian Law superseded and set aside the operation of the Pupian Law. Nor was Appius the only lawless interpreter of laws in these lawless times. Two years before (b.c. 56), we find a tribune of the plebs claiming precedence over the consuls in the right to put questions to vote in the Senate: *Lupus, trib. pl. . . . intendere cœpit ante se oportere discessionem facere quam consules* (Cic. *ad Fam.* i. 2, 2) — a claim which Cicero justly characterizes as *et iniqua et nova*. In the year of Appius's consulship (b.c. 54), we have a proprætor, Pomptinius, demanding a triumph, which is opposed for the lack of the law under discussion: *negant latum de imperio, et est latum insulse* (Cic. *ad Att.* iv. 16, 12). Cicero adds, in amazement at Appius's hardihood: *Appius sine lege, suo sumptu, in Ciliciam cogitat.*

One is tempted to suspect that the embarrassment of the consuls of B.C. 54 was similar to that of B.C. 49 — the incompetency to hold the *comitia centuriata* without the formal grant of the *imperium.* It is certain that this was the difficulty with the consuls at Thessalonica. Dio says (41, 43) that they had consuls and a Senate of two hundred members, and a place consecrated for the auspices (*templum*), so that they might be reckoned to have the people and the city there, but for the lack of the *lex curiata* they could elect no magistrates. It is easy to see a distinction between the two acts — the exercise of military command and the holding of the assembly for elections. The one was an absolute necessity in an emergency, such as might arise at any time, and could not be anticipated. If an enemy attacked the city before the *imperium* had been formally conferred upon the magistrates; if by any accident or disaster an army in a province was left without a legally qualified commander — in neither of these cases could it be supposed that the safety of the State would be allowed to depend upon such a mere formality as the passage of this law had now come to be. The *comitia,* on the other hand, was part of the organic law, a necessary part of the constitutional machinery, not dependent in any way upon accident or emergency: it might therefore be held strictly to all the formal requirements of the law for its validity. It is easy to understand, therefore, that the military *imperium* might be exercised merely by the authority of the Senate, or by no formal authority at all; while the *comitia* could not be summoned unless all the formal conditions had been observed. There is no indication in the record that this consideration had any weight with Appius Claudius; but our information is very imperfect, and, as it was clearly the governing consideration with the consuls of B.C. 49, it may very well have had weight at this time. The object of Memmius and Calvinus may have been, not merely to obtain the influence of the consuls in their behalf, but to secure for the consuls the formal right to hold the election.

Turning now from special cases to the question of legal obligation, we find the most positive statement of the absolute necessity of the act for the exercise of military authority in all its forms. Livy (v. 52, 15) uses the expression *comitia curiata, quæ rem militarem continet*. Cicero's expression is even stronger: *consuli, si legem curiatam non habet, attingere rem militarem non licet* (*De Leg. Agr.* ii. 12, 30). In relation to this same agrarian law, which provides for ten commissioners, whose authority should be granted by a *lex curiata*, he says: *sine lege curiata nihil agi per decemviros posse* (11, 28), and adds that the law provides for the contingency of the *lex curiata* not being passed: *si ea* [*lex*] *lata non erit* ... *tum ii decemviri eodem iure sint quo qui optima lege.* That is, the law creating the office, while conferring the *imperium* upon the commissioners (in the regular form by a *lex curiata*), makes provision against a formal defect, which would nullify the purposes of the law, by giving their actions entire validity even in that case. It follows that without this provision the failure to carry the law would make their action invalid. Again, in the year B.C. 56, the demagogue Clodius, being himself curule ædile, and engaged in prosecuting Milo, the champion of the Senate, contrived (no doubt through some tribune) to prevent the passage of the *lex curiata: πρὶν γὰρ ἐκεῖνοντεθῆναι*, says Dio (39, 19), *οὔτ' ἄλλο τι τῶν σπουδαίων ἐν τῷ κοινῷ πραχθῆναι, οὔτε δίκην οὐδεμίαν ἐσαχθῆναι ἐξῆν.* The purpose of Clodius, says Dio, was to keep up the confusion, *ὅπως ἐπὶ πλεῖον ἀπορoίη.* What is significant for our argument is Dio's statement of the legal effects of the failure to pass the law.

But, although the formal grant of the *imperium* was regarded as necessary for the exercise of military authority, it is a significant fact that under several circumstances it was regularly made, not by the *comitia curiata*, but by some other organ of the government. It may be questioned whether this was ever the case with the power to hold the centuriate *comitia;* but, with the power to command the army, especially in the case of proconsuls, there are numerous single instances, and even classes of instances, in which this was the case. For example, in regard to the proconsul Quintus Fulvius, B.C. 211, the Senate voted: *cui ne minueretur imperium si in urbem venisset, decernit Senatus ut Q. Fulvio par cum consulibus imperium esset* (Liv. xxvi. 9, 10). Here the *imperium* was not granted, but the already existing *imperium* was elevated in rank. A better known case is that of Cæsar Octavianus, to whom the Senate gave the *imperium* early in the year 43 : *demus igitur imperium Cæsari, sine quo res militaris administrari, teneri exercitus, bellum geri non potest* (Cic. *Phil.* v. 16, 45). But even the plebeian assembly of the tribes regularly granted the *imperium* on two occasions: first, to enable a victorious commander to retain the authority over his army within the city on the day of his triumph (Liv. xxvi. 21, 5. See Becker, "Alterthümer," ii. 2, 66) ; secondly, in the more important case of a proconsul or proprætor who entered upon the government of a province after an interval of time since the expiring of his magistracy — *e.g.*, Cicero's proconsulship in Cilicia, B.C. 51. In both these cases the *imperium* was conferred by a *plebiscitum* (Mommsen, "Rechtsfrage zwischen Cæsar und dem Senat," p. 45, note). These cases prove not that no formal grant of the *imperium* was necessary, but that it might be made by some other authority than the *comitia curiata;* not, however, it would seem for the purpose of holding the *comitia centuriata.*

The reason given by Cicero for the requirement of the law shows that it was regarded as, in its origin, not a bare and unessential formality, but a substantial grant of power. He says that its object was to give the people an opportunity to reconsider their action in the election of magistrates, implying that, if they had elected an unfit person, they could, at any rate, by refusing to pass this law, limit his power of doing mischief. *Maiores de singulis magistratibus bis vos sententiam ferre voluerunt. Nam cum centuriata lex censoribus ferebatur, cum curiata cæteris patriciis magistratibus, tum iterum de eisdem indicabatur, ut esset reprehendendi potestas, si populum beneficii sui pæniteret* (*Leg. Agr.* ii. 11, 26).

This view is supported by the account which he gives of the first historical example of the law in the succession of Numa Pompilius to the kingly authority: *quamquam populus curiatis cum comitiis regem esse iusserat, tamen ipse de suo imperio curiatam legem tulit* (*De Rep.* ii. 13, 25). The same action is ascribed to Tullus Hostilius (17, 31), Ancus Marcius (18, 33), and Tarquinius Priscus (20, 35).

Why this twofold action of the people was required (*cum maiores binis comitiis voluerint vos de singulis magistratibus indicare*, Cic. *de Leg. Agr.* ii. 11, 27) can be best understood if we look a little more closely at the fundamental institutions of the Roman State. King, Senate, and Popular Assembly are the three integral institutions naturally evolved in the progress of early society; but they are not always developed in the same degree or on the same lines. In Greece, the king was the preponderant power, having an hereditary authority somewhat approaching that of Oriental monarchs. Among the Germans, sovereignty, if we may use a modern term, resided in the popular assembly. The early Roman constitution, on the other hand, was essentially aristocratic, the Senate being the controlling element.* This resulted from the peculiar structure of

*This point was first established by Rubino, in his " Untersuchungen über römische Verfassung und Geschichte."

Roman society, in which the patriarchal authority of the father of the family, the *patria potestas*, was strained to a greater degree of rigor than in any other known society. I will not discuss the question whether, as Sir Henry Maine held, this Roman *patria potestas* was the original type, or, as the late Professor Ernest Young argued, it was an exceptional form peculiar to the Romans. I will only say that Professor Young's arguments seem to me unanswerable. According to this *patria potestas*, however derived, the Roman *paterfamilias* was the only member of the family who had any status before the law; he was its absolute ruler and its sole proprietor. The assembly of these heads of family, the *patres*, was, in a legal point of view, the Roman people. This assembly, therefore, known as the Senate, or council of old men, was, in this stage of society, regarded as in absolute possession of the auspices, or the religious sanction upon which the State rested. This point of view was never lost out of sight through the whole period of the Republic. Under all constitutional charges, and in spite of the ever-increasing disintegration of the patriciate, the patrician senators continued to be the source of all government, the body to whom all authority reverted whenever there was an interruption of the regular action of the governmental machinery. When this machinery *ran down*, as we may say, from a failure to elect the new magistrates in season, or from any other cause, as it did several times in the course of the last century of the Republic, the patrician senators were the only authority competent to wind it up again. On the occurrence of an interregnum, the *interrex* was invariably a senator of patrician family.

Now, with this fundamental principle of the Roman polity, by which the sovereignty belonged to the patrician Senate — an essentially aristocratic principle — the Romans associated two other principles of great practical importance, the one of a monarchical, the other of a

democratic character.   The first was the Roman practice
of lodging in the hands of their magistrates for the time
being the greatest fulness of executive authority of which
we have record in any free state.   The auspices belonged
to the Senate, it is true; but their temporary possession,
except in the case of an interregnum, was with the magistrates, and its exercise was practically unlimited during the
term of office.   The other principle, democratic in character, was that by which, in the duties and privileges of citizenship, the son *in potestate* was the full equal of the *paterfamilias*.   The assembly of the people, the popular branch
of the constitution, was composed of every man of fighting
age — it was the army, convened for purposes of government.   Thus, while the ultimate authority rested with the
Senate, composed only of *patres*, or persons who were *sui
iuris*, in the assembly the son had equal authority with his
father, and was equally entitled to hold a magistracy.

If we put these three principles of the Roman constitution together — the original sovereignty of the Senate
as the impersonation of the people, the concentration
of authority in the hands of the magistrates, and the
equality of all citizens of fighting age in political relations — we shall see the purport of the *lex curiata de
imperio*.   The magistrate was first designated by the
assembly, but the Senate, by its *patrum auctoritas*, had
the right to refuse its sanction to the action of the people:
next, the elected magistrate was inaugurated, and thus
placed in possession of the auspices.   The possession
of the auspices made him for the time being the representative of the Senate as the impersonation of the State,
and gave him authority to convene the Senate and the
assembly of the curies.   But the complete authority of
the magistrate, the *imperium*, by virtue of which he
could command the armies and condemn to death without appeal — this authority he must receive by a special
act : it must be formally conferred upon him, by the

army which he was to command, the citizens over whom he was to have the power of life and death.

The question naturally occurs, if the *imperium* was granted by the army in its political capacity, why this function did not, along with the rest of the functions of the *comitia curiata*, devolve upon the *comitia centuriata*, when this assembly became the principal assembly of the Republic; for the *comitia centuriata* was primarily and distinctively a military organization. The reason is probably to be sought in the fact that the centuriate organization did not all at once supersede the curiate, but served for some time as the basis of the army before it was turned to political purposes. The centuriate organization, as established by Servius Tullius, served as a schedule for the military levy; but the citizens still continued to vote by curies, and of course to grant the *imperium* by a *lex curiata*. Then when, on the establishment of the Republic, the *comitia centuriata* was made the regular organ of popular action, this special formality had become so completely associated with the *comitia curiata* that it seemed necessary to retain that assembly for the sole purpose of its exercise. Or it may have been that the patricians, when they surrendered the right to elect magistrates to an assembly composed of both orders, kept in their own hands the power of conferring the *imperium*, by the exclusively patrician *comitia curiata*. Mommsen has proved, it is true, that the plebeians were admitted to the curies at some time, and suggests that this was done at the establishment of the Republic, as one provision of the compromise then made between the orders. But this is only a suggestion, as there are no data that prove the admission of the plebeians to the *comitia curiata* until a considerably later time. It does not follow that membership of the curies necessarily carried with it at once the right to vote in their assembly. The curies, it should be noted, were not merely divisions of the patrician citizens : they were also divisions of the territory. The Italian peoples appear to have entered Italy with a tribal organization, consisting of *gentes*, or family groups. As is regularly the case with settlements made by nations at this social stage, these *gentes* settled by themselves, each in a district of its own : the *gentes*, originally purely personal divisions, thus became localized. As the curies were groups of *gentes*, and the tribes were divided into curies, it follows that these divisions were also localized.* We have positive evidence of each of these facts. Of the local tribes, established by Servius Tullius, every one of the twenty earliest (with the exception of four city tribes) bore the name of a patrician *gens* — a fact which is taken by Mommsen to prove that it received the name of the most prominent *gens* within its territorial limits. Of the curies and the tribes we have more explicit testimony. Of the curies, Dionysius Halicarnasensis says (ii. 17) : διελὼ`ν τὴν γῆν εἰς τριάκοντα κλήρους ἴσους, ἑκάστῃ φράτρᾳ κλῆρον ἀπέδωκεν ἕνα. Of the three patrician tribes Varro says (*L. L.* v. 55) : *ager Romanus primum divisus in parteis tris, a quo tribus appellata Tatiensium, Ramnium, Lucerum.* These passages prove at least that, according to tradition, both tribes and curies occupied definite territorial areas. The plebeians were therefore by necessity residents of the districts which were associated with the several curies, and they appear to have made use of this organization for the election of their tribunes during the first years after the establishment of that office, until that more serviceable organization by tribes was established through the Publilian Law, B.C. 471.

To conclude, it appears that the *lex curiata de imperio* was regarded by the Romans as a substantial bestowal of power, designed in its origin to establish an effective check upon popular election, by reserving the highest executive function for a special grant, which in the

* See Mommsen, " Römisches Staatsrecht," iii. 94.

Republic was conferred by an assembly organized upon a different principle from that which made the election; in this respect having a certain analogy with our modern bi-cameral legislatures. Further, that, even when it sank to a mere formality, it never came to be considered an unessential formality, but was looked upon as an act which must be secured in some way : that, therefore, in cases where the power was not conferred by this special act, some equivalent action (of Senate or Tribal Assembly) was nevertheless required; while for the assembling of the centuriate *comitia*, an integral organic act of the constitution, there is reason to believe that this specific act was indispensable.

THE MONETARY CRISIS IN ROME, A.D. 33.*

DURING the retreat of the Emperor Tiberius at Ca-
preæ, A.D. 33, Rome was visited by a crisis in the money
market so severe and obstinate that credit was at last restored only by the direct intervention of the emperor, who
advanced one hundred million sesterces (about four million dollars) from the treasury, in the shape of loans without interest to individual debtors—an occurrence which
calls to mind the purchase of bonds by our Treasury
department, for the purpose of relieving the money market during the panic of 1873. A tolerably full account of
this affair is given by Tacitus (*Ann.* vi. 16, 17); and it
is also mentioned briefly and incidentally by Suetonius
(*Tib.* 48) and Dio Cassius (58, 21). The account given
by Tacitus is in many points difficult to understand, by
reason of his characteristic compression of style and habit
of omitting details, which perhaps seemed unessential
from his point of view, but are needed by us for a full
comprehension of the circumstances. With the assistance of these other writers, we find the account given by
Tacitus consistent, and, no doubt, substantially correct,
while still presenting some obscurities where it may be
supposed that his statements were perfectly intelligible
to his contemporaries. I will give a free translation of
his account of the affair, accompanied with such comments and illustrations as may seem called for.

"At this time the accusers burst with great violence
upon those who made a profession of loaning money at
interest, in violation of the law of the Dictator Cæsar,
which regulates loans and landed property in Italy—a

* From Transactions of the American Philological Association for 1887, vol. 18, p. 5.

law which had fallen into desuetude, because the public welfare is less regarded than private gain."

The law in question was probably passed by Cæsar in his first dictatorship, B.C. 49, after his return from Spain and Massilia. We learn at this time of two laws designed to remedy the economical embarrassments of society. One, temporary in nature, cancelled existing debts by the surrender of real and personal property (*possessionum et rerum*) according to the valuation which it had before the war, the disturbed condition of affairs having now, of course, lowered values (Cæs. *B. C.* iii. 1 ; Suet. *Jul.* 42 ; Dio Cass. 41, 37 ; App. *B. C.* ii. 48). This law, called by Plutarch (*Cæsar*, 37) σεισάχθεια, *a shaking off of burdens*, cannot properly be called a law to regulate loans and landed property, and cannot therefore be identified with Tacitus's law *de modo credendi possidendique*. Besides that, it was a merely remedial and temporary measure, while the one here referred to must have been a permanent measure of policy. The other law is mentioned by Dio Cassius (41, 38) as the re-enactment of an old statute, forbidding any person to possess, κεκτῆσθαι, more than 15,000 drachmas (*denarii*) (about $2,400) in gold or silver. This statement is evidently incomplete, and probably inaccurate. It may nevertheless contain in a distorted form some provisions of the law in question. If no person could have in his possession more than a certain fixed maximum of cash, the rest of his money he must invest or loan. Dio suggests indeed that the object of the law was to facilitate loaning ; while the phrase used by Tacitus, *credendi possidendique*, may properly be applied to loans or purchases of land made with the balance above the prescribed maximum. We may therefore assume that this is the law of Cæsar referred to in the passage before us.

This second law, therefore, may be assumed to have been of a permanent character, and to have defined

Cæsar's policy in regard to the economical condition of Italy. As to its provisions, we are left in the dark, except for the general assertion of Tacitus that it regulated loans and real estate, the unintelligible statement of Dio that it prohibited the keeping on hand of more than a certain sum of money, and another from the same author (58, 21), that it related to contracts. Perhaps we have a right to infer from these provisions, taken in connection with the events of the present year, that, as Mommsen says (iv. p. 626), it "fixed a maximum amount of the loans at interest to be allowed in the case of the individual capitalist, which appears to have been proportioned to the Italian landed estate belonging to each, and perhaps amounted to half its value." [*] Whatever the provisions of the law, it had become a dead letter; and the pecuniary embarrassments of the present year were caused by an ill-timed and badly-arranged attempt suddenly to put it in execution.

The next passage to be considered is one of great historical importance, which is, in spite of its brevity, a principal source of our knowledge of the Roman usury laws, but of which it is hard to see the bearing upon the occurrences in question.

"The curse of usury is in truth of long standing in the city, and it has been a most fertile cause of seditions, for which reason it was held in check even in ancient times, when morals were less corrupt. For at first the laws of the twelve tables forbade any higher rate of interest than ten per cent., the rate having before this been at the pleasure of the lender; then by a tribunician law it was reduced to five per cent., and finally loaning at interest was forbidden."

Two phrases in this passage require special discussion — *unciario fænore* and *vetita versura*.

That *unciario fænore* is one-twelfth of the principal for

---

[*] Mommsen makes no citations or references in support of this statement, and I am unable to find any foundation for it except the provisions of this law, as given above. His words, however, seem to me more positive than the evidence warrants.

the original year of ten months — that is, 8⅓ per cent. for the year of ten months, and ten per cent. for the year of twelve months — is the now generally accepted view of Niebuhr: it would make no difference in the question before us if we took it to refer primarily to the twelve-month year, in which case it would give a rate of twelve per cent. The fixing of this rate, ascribed by Tacitus to the Decemvirs, is placed by Livy one hundred years later, B.C. 356, and the reduction by one-half to the year 346. The attempt to suppress the trade of usury belongs to the year 342, by the so-called Genucian Law, *ne fænerare liceret* (Liv. vii. 42).

The word *versura* has caused some unnecessary trouble. It is sometimes explained as "compound interest"; *i.e.* to balance the account and then turn over the page (*vertere*), and open a new account where no interest had been paid, would be compound interest, and this is some-times the meaning of the word. Its regular use, however, in classical Latin is explained by Festus (p. 37) as equivalent to *loan: versuram facere mutuam pecuniam sumere ex eo dictum est, quod initio qui mutuabantur ab aliis, non ut domum ferrent, sed ut aliis solverent, velet verterent creditorem.* This is illustrated by numerous examples in Cicero (*e.g., Att.* xvi. 2, 2): *non modo versura, sed etiam venditione, si ita res coget, nos vindicabis; id.* vii. 18, 4, *cum tale tempus sit ut . . . nec hoc tempore aut domi numos Quintus habeat, aut exigere ab Egnatio aut versuram usquam facere possit.* So v. 1, 2; v. 21, 12, etc. *Vetita versura,* "loans on interest were forbidden," is therefore precisely equivalent in meaning to *ne fænerare liceret;* that is, it was not interest as such, *usura,* or even exorbi-tant interest, what we understood by "usury," that was prohibited, but the trade of money-lending. So far as the language of these writers goes, it might have been still law-ful to collect interest on debts; but to borrow money to pay a debt was forbidden, and thus the trade of money-lend-

ing — in that condition of society a fertile source of mischief — was made unlawful.   It is not at all unlikely that
the law went further than this, and — as so many crude
reformers at all ages have desired — undertook to prohibit
not only the trade in money, *versura*, but interest altogether, *usura*.   But this we have no right to infer ; and,
if the law was passed, it was never enforced.

We shall better understand the question if we consider
the radical difference between the business of money-lending in ancient times and in modern society.   At the present day the legitimate business of bankers and other
money-lenders consists in advancing funds to be employed
in productive operations.   The banker, when his business
is carried on in a legitimate way, forms a necessary and
useful intermediary between persons who have money
which they do not understand how to use productively
and those who are engaged in industrial occupations in
which they can use advantageously more capital than they
themselves possess.   Loans at interest, therefore, when
credit is not strained to excess, are a necessary and
useful part of the complicated industrial system of our
time.   It was quite otherwise in antiquity.   There was no
such thing as productive industry on any large scale.
When money was borrowed, it was not to assist production, but for purposes of consumption, or, still worse,
to pay for past consumption.   Money was borrowed in
order to pay debts ; one debt incurred in order to cancel
another ; precisely what is expressed by the word *versura*.

There is no more fundamental contrast between ancient
and modern society than in the place which industry takes
in the minds of men and their relations to one another.
The most striking feature of the organization of modern
society is the co-operation of the resources of all classes
and interests, for the furtherance of industry.   This is
done by means of banks and other monetary associations,
through the instrumentality of which every industrial en-

terprise is able to make use of all the means which it can
employ to advantage, and the accumulated wealth of generations is placed at the disposal of those who are engaged
in creating more wealth.   In the ancient world industry
was held in no honor, and occupied no such commanding
position.   The few commodities which were required by
the simple habits of society were manufactured by the
slaves of the household ; commerce consisted in hardly
more than bringing to the imperial city the forced contributions of the provinces ; agriculture, the only branch of
industry deemed worthy of a freeman, fell more and more
into the hands of slaves.

The trade of the money-lender, *fœnerator*, therefore, was
deservedly in disrepute, because he rendered to society no
service at all corresponding to the gains he derived from
society.   All his profits were of course drawn from the
proceeds of industry, because all wealth is created by industry ; but industry received nothing from him in return.
We have a similar class in modern society — we are all
familiar with it from the pages of " Pendennis " — and we
know that this class, an excrescence upon society, is not
to be ranked with that which stores up the unused masses
of capital, and holds them in readiness for productive use.
From this point of view it is easy to see why interest
upon money was regarded by the ancients as fundamentally wrong.   The explanation which they gave themselves, that money was by nature barren, and could not
produce money as offspring — a notion which found expression in the figurative use of the word τόκος to designate interest — may seem fanciful at first sight.   But it
proceeded from a profound comprehension of its nature,
as it existed in their day.   No such argument against
usury would be possible at the present time ; for our loans
at interest are really productive, and interest may properly be described as τόκος.   But with the ancients money
was borrowed only to relieve distress or to provide means

for debauchery ; and for neither of these purposes did it seem to them right that interest should be paid. The historian goes on : —

"And many *plebiscita* were passed to put a stop to the devices by which the law was evaded ; but, repress them as often as they might, they sprang up again in astonishing forms."

Of course the law was found impossible to execute. It probably undertook more than any legislature can accomplish, and at any rate economical forces and the selfish interests of men were too strong for it. Twenty years after its passage, B.C. 326, the authority over the debtor given by the old harsh laws of debt was exercised so outrageously by one *fænerator* that the laws of debt were as a consequence radically changed, so as to deprive the creditor of his power over the body of the debtor (Liv. vii. 28). Shortly after the Second Punic War, B.C. 193, Livy (xxxv. 7) still says that the State suffered from usury, *fænore laborabat,* and that, although there had been many usury laws, *fænebribus legibus,* they had been successfully evaded, *via fraudis inita erat.* The method of fraud on this occasion was to advance the loan in the name of some *socius,* or citizen of an allied State ; and the remedy was to extend the provisions of the civil law to this class. In the last century of the Republic it became the custom to charge the interest monthly, and, by adding it to the principal, to obtain a very high compound interest. A certain check was placed upon the senatorial class, by public opinion ; but this was a weak restraint, and the unblushing eagerness for gain of even the best among them is illustrated by the well-known case of Brutus, who, having, in the name of other parties, made a loan to the city of Salamis in Cyprus, where the legal rate was twelve per cent., with compound interest annually, demanded four times that rate, and called upon Cicero, the governor of the province, to assist in its collection (Cic. *ad Att.* v. 21, 10–13).

One of the chief obscurities in this passage of Tacitus is the difficulty of understanding the relation between this legislation and the law of Cæsar, revived by Tiberius. As we have seen, the Genucian Law prohibited, if not the taking of interest under any circumstances, the making loans at interest, the trade of money-lending. Cæsar's law, on the other hand, *de modo credendi possidendique*, περὶ τῶν συμβολαίων, although described by Dio as an old law revived, πρότερόν ποτε ἐσενεχθέντα ἀνανεούμενος, clearly had a different scope, aiming not to prohibit, but to regulate, the trade in money. That there was no attempt, either by Cæsar or Tiberius, to *prohibit* the taking of interest, appears from the fact that the 100,000,000 sesterces advanced by Tiberius upon this occasion were for the purpose of loans without interest, *sine usura* — a circumstance which would not have been noted if interest had been altogether forbidden by law.

It appears that the proceedings to enforce the law emanated from the emperor himself. This is not stated either by Tacitus or Suetonius; but Dio Cassius says, in the passage just cited (58, 21), that "he revived the laws concerning contracts imposed by Cæsar"— τοὺς νομοὺς τοὺς περὶ τῶν συμβολαίων ὑπὸ τοῦ Καίσαρος τεθέντας . . . ἀνενοήσατο; mentioning it in connection with the death of Nerva, father of the emperor of that name, who, he says, committed suicide because he foresaw the troubles, ἀπιστία καὶ ταραχή, that would result from an enforcement of the law.* The Emperor Tiberius, with all his faults a profound statesman, and a man who had a keen insight into the causes of the economical decay of his country, appears to have conceived the idea of remedying these economical evils by enforcing Cæsar's law. In a remarkable letter addressed to the Senate eleven years before (*Ann.* iii. 53, 54), after touching upon the pettiness and inadequacy of the sumptuary measures proposed by that body, he goes on:

---

* It should be mentioned that Tacitus (*Ann.* vi. 26) does not mention this as having anything to do with the suicide of Nerva.

"None of you see that Italy requires assistance from abroad, that the life of the Roman people is daily risked on the uncertainties of the sea and the tempests. And unless the resources of the provinces came to the rescue of masters, slaves and fields, we should have little reason to expect that our parks and country seats would support us." He does not speak here of free men or free labor : he means that Italy is wholly taken up with pleasure grounds and slave plantations, and that by neither of these can its population be supported. These words of Tiberius are a significant commentary upon the famous expression of Pliny — *latifundis perdidere Italiam.** Feeling as he did about the economical condition of Italy, and seeing, too, as we can have no doubt that he did, the pernicious effects of the money traffic, it is not to be wondered at that the emperor undertook the enforcement of a law by means of which, in Mommsen's words, "every Italian man of business would be compelled to become at the same time an Italian land-holder, and the class of capitalists subsisting merely on their interest would disappear wholly from Italy." The experiment seemed worth trying.

"But now the prætor Gracchus, who presided over this court, influenced by the multitude of those upon whom the penalties of the law would be visited, laid the matter before the Senate ; and the Senate, in great apprehension (for hardly any one was free from fault in the matter), begged the prince for indulgence, and by his consent a year and a half were allowed, within which time each person should adjust his business relations in accordance with the requirements of the law. From this there resulted a stringency in the money market, all debts being called in at the same time, and great amounts of cash being locked up in the treasury, by reason of the number of condemnations and confiscations."

* It is shown by Mommsen in an article in *Hermes* (vol. xi.) that Pliny's expression is much exaggerated.

In "from this there resulted a stringency" we must understand not the circumstance just mentioned — the extension of the time to eighteen months — but the original necessity of settling the accounts. Although eighteen months were now allowed for this, each person, as was natural, hastened to settle his own affairs as speedily as possible. But the ancients were not acquainted with the use of credit as furnishing a circulating medium : they were confined to the use of coin, and the coin could not be got at by reason of the recent confiscations. This is the historian's explanation, but it is quite inadequate. The amount of confiscation — even at the height of the reign of terror after the fall of Sejanus — could not have caused any such deficiency ; and, in fact, even if there had been any way of employing credit in effecting exchanges, the panic could not have been prevented. No doubt under this reign of terror there was much hoarding, and much coin was thus withdrawn from circulation ; but the stringency was really created by the enforcement of the law, which caused a general disturbance of contracts, and set a great number of creditors to call in their debts all at once.

"To meet this difficulty, the Senate had ordered that every money-lender should invest two-thirds of his principal in lands in Italy."

In this difficult passage we must first consider the meaning of certain words and phrases. The phrase with which it opens, *ad hoc*, usually means "besides." If that is the meaning in this case, it follows that the measure here described was a part of the original law, the enforcement of which had caused the trouble. In that case, this requirement of the Senate would be an additional cause of embarrassment, over and above the requirement to settle within eighteen months. If, on the other hand, with most editors, we take it as meaning *in this view, for this purpose*, it is to be taken as a remedial measure, to help relieve the scarcity. But it is hard to see how the obligation to invest two-thirds of the debt in land could afford any relief. The very difficulty in the case was that the debtors could not get the money to pay their debts : how then could the creditors invest money which they could not get into their hands? Or, if they could, how would this help the matter? The thing needed was to enable the debtors to pay their debts, not to direct the creditors how to invest their funds.

In both these points we are helped out of the difficulty by Suetonius (*Tib.* 48), whose brief statement proves that it was a remedial measure, not a part of the original law; and that, therefore, *ad hoc* must be rendered "to meet this emergency"; and shows further how it was that it was intended to help solve the difficulty. His words, *cum per senatus consultum sanxisset,* "when he had required by a *senatus consultum,*" show that the measure proceeded originally from the emperor, not from the Senate, and that it is likely therefore to have been a device for the emergency, not a part of the old law. And what is made probable by these words is made nearly certain by the closing words, after the description of the provisions of the measure, *nec expediretur,* "but the difficulties were not resolved." We shall see presently, moreover, that this measure was essentially identical with Cæsar's remedial measure of B.C. 49, and appears to be of a temporary and remedial character rather than a persistent policy.

Even more important is a provision of the *senatus consultum,* omitted by Tacitus, but given by Suetonius, by which alone we are in a position to understand it. His words are "that the money-lenders should invest two-thirds of their estate in land, and the debtors should pay at once the same proportion of their debt"—*ut fœneratores duas patrimonii partes in solo collocarent, debitores totidem æris alieni statim solverent.* This second provision, about the debtors, is not contained in Tacitus's account : perhaps it has dropped out of his manuscript (to which it is restored by Nipperdey) ; more likely it was in his mind, but omitted in writing, because the matter seemed to him intelligible without it—a not unusual thing with him. In the first proposition Suetonius uses the word *patrimonii,* "estate," where Tacitus says *fænoris,* "principal" (a well-established use of the word in classical Latin, as in the phrase *fænus et impendium,* "principal and interest," Cic. *ad Att.* vi. 1, 4). Tacitus is evidently right, as the context shows : the statement of Suetonius may come from a confusion with the provisions of Cæsar's law.*

The relief measure in question, therefore, consisted in the requirement that the debtor should pay two-thirds down, and the creditor invest this two-thirds in land. As the problem to be solved was the difficulty of paying cash down, this can only be a clumsy and roundabout way of saying that two-thirds of the debt might be paid in land, the balance remaining for the eighteen months. Of course this could apply only to those who had land, and, in all probability, only to those who had hypothecated their land when obtaining their loan. It was, in a sense, a general foreclosure of mortgages, but differed from a true foreclosure in being summary, without legal process, and no doubt at a price for the land which was to be ascertained, not by public auction, but by the assessment lists, perhaps of the previous year. In all these respects it corresponded closely to Cæsar's law, only that that law applied to the whole debt, and allowed personal property, as well as real, to be taken in payment. Such as it was, it was a σεισάχθεια, or shaking off of burdens, a measure for the relief of debtors; and it naturally aroused the opposition of the creditors.

---

* It is an interesting fact, as showing the permanent policy of the Empire, that the Emperor Trajan made a similar requirement, only making one-third of the estate the proportion to be invested in land: *eosdem patrimonii tertiam partem conferre jussit in ea quæ solo continerentur* (Plin. *Epp.* vi. 18, 4). Suetonius's use of the word *patrimonium* may have been borrowed from this nearly contemporary measure.

" But the creditors demanded payment in full, and those upon whom the demand was made could not, without losing credit, fail to meet their obligations. So they ran hither and thither with entreaties [*i.e.*, as Furneaux says, for money or time], then the prætor's tribunal resounded [*i.e.*, with demands, entreaties, and notices of legal proceedings]; and the purchase and sale of property, resorted to as a remedy, worked just to the contrary, because the money-lenders had laid aside all their money for the purchase of land, while the land offered for sale was in such quantities that it fell in price ; the more heavily burdened any one was with debt, the harder he found it to dispose of his property in small lots, and many were ruined in their fortunes."

We must understand by this that the object of the money-lenders was to purchase entire estates, for which reason they refused to buy in small lots, as we shall see in the next passage. The demand made by the creditors for payment in full at once was, of course, in violation of the *senatus consultum*, and might have been legally refused by the debtors. But business men could not afford to take advantage of a mode of settlement which would give a temporary relief, but destroy their business credit. To the creditors the proposition must have seemed wholly unjust. By waiting until their notes should fall due, and the inevitable collapse in the value of real estate should have come, in the mean time hoarding up such sums as should be paid on account, they would be enabled to buy large estates at a bargain ; and such was the stoppage of trade and the glutting of the market that even small lots could find no purchaser. The debtors did not dare to insist upon their legal rights, and the σεισάχθεια was a failure. There now remained but one resource — the direct interposition of the government.

I have changed the punctuation in one place in this passage. In all the editions with which I am acquainted,

there is a full stop after *condiderant* — "The money-lenders had laid aside all their money for the purchase of
land" — and the passages which follow are joined with
the sentence which tells of the emperor's intervention.   I
propose to put a full stop after *provolvebantur*, and associate the intervening line with what precedes, as following
quia.   It has been said, "The purchase and sale of property, resorted to as a remedy, worked just to the contrary,
because —."   To say "because the money-lenders had
laid aside all their money for the purchase of land" is no
explanation.   That they had hoarded their money in
order to buy land could not, taken by itself, prevent the
purchase and sale of land from working as a remedy, but
rather the opposite.   If money was hoarded up for the
purchase of land, that was just the condition of things
needed for a solution of the difficulties by the sale of land.

But the circumstances taken in their connection — that
the money-lenders had laid aside their money to buy land,
and that so much land was offered that it fell greatly in
price, with the significant fact, not mentioned directly,
but implied in *distrahebant*, that their purpose was to buy
up large estates when prices should touch bottom, and
that for this reason they refused to buy the portions of
estates which the debtors desired to dispose of — in these
circumstances we find a sufficient reason for the failure of
the scheme.   Two clauses, therefore, instead of only one,
must be taken to follow *quia*.

"Dignity and reputation went to crash with the loss of
fortune, until Cæsar came to the rescue, and deposited
100,000,000 sesterces in banks, the debtors having the
privilege of borrowing for three years, without interest, on
giving landed security to the State for twice the amount
of the loan.   Thus credit was restored, and gradually it
was found possible to borrow from private persons also.
But the purchase of land was not carried out according to
the prescriptions of the *senatus consultum ;* for, as is usual

in such matters, what was begun with vigor ended with remissness."

It should be noted that the banks referred to in the phrase *per mensas* were not private banking establishments, but that the money, as Dio Cassius tells us (58, 21), was placed in the hands of certain senators, ὑπ' ἀνδρῶν βουλευτῶν, who appear to have acted as the emperor's agents in making the loans.

Thus the plan of the emperor for averting the economical ruin of Italy, by taking up the reforms of Cæsar, came to naught. Probably the mischief was incapable of remedy, for any economical system which rests upon slave labor contains in itself the seeds of decay. Probably, too, the plan itself, of the details of which we really know nothing, was insufficient and untimely ; for the sagacious Nerva foresaw its failure. And, when it had once failed, Tiberius — always characterized by a certain self-distrust and infirmity of purpose, and now old, broken in mind and body, and, we may suppose, thoroughly scared at the commotion his well-meaning action had excited — never had the heart to make another attempt.

THE PRIMITIVE DEMOCRACY OF THE GERMANS.*

THE political institutions of the ancient Germans, as described by Tacitus, are of an essentially democratic character. Some of their nations have kings, but royalty is not a necessary part of their constitution; for many nations have no king, and, where there is but one, he is not invested with any very positive or absolute powers.† Nobles are frequently mentioned, but special privileges or powers are never ascribed to the nobility: and, so far as appears from the information in our possession, it was a social rather than a political aristocracy. There are serfs, but we are absolutely without information as to their origin or their relative numbers — whether they are Germans, who have sunk from a condition of freedom, or the remnants of a conquered race; whether they are few or many. We cannot, of course, expect to find organized government of the modern type, or any precise definition of powers; but, so far as we are warranted in any positive conclusion upon the subject, we may say that the sovereign power was in the hands of the whole people, acting collectively, meeting in a general assembly at stated intervals. (Tac. *Germ.* 11, 12.) The people in their family organizations also compose the army. ‡ From a compar-

---

* This paper is composed of two papers: one, upon the village community system, read at the meeting of the Wisconsin Academy in 1881; the other at the meeting in 1883. Being properly supplementary to one another, they were united by the author and the discussion of both papers brought down to the date of publication (1886) in Transactions of the Wisconsin Academy of Sciences, Arts, and Letters, vol. 6, p. 28.

† Nec regibus libera aut infinita potestas. Tac. *Germ.* 7.

‡ Non casus nec fortuita conglobatio turmam aut cuneum facit, sed familiæ et propinquitates. Tac. *Germ.* 7.

ison of Tacitus with Cæsar,* an earlier writer, we have a right to infer that these same family organizations live in common occupation of independent districts of land. There are magistrates, holding their office, it would seem, for life, elected by the people in their national assembly, and acting as a board of administration in the intervals between the meetings of assembly,† but also having each his own district where he presides over the administration of justice. ‡ From other authorities we know that in this district administration of justice the magistrates only preside; the verdict is rendered by the people of the district in an assembly of the district.

This is a thoroughly republican constitution of society, and this sketch, which rests in every detail upon positive statements of Tacitus, supplemented in only two instances by evidence from other but equally unimpeachable authority, justifies us in the statement that the political institutions of the primitive Germans were essentially democratic. This is also the conclusion at which we should arrive by the analogy of other primitive peoples, especially those of the Indo-European family. Most of them established a kingly office, most of them had slaves, or serfs, or imperfectly qualified citizens to whom they stood in the relation of a ruling aristocracy ; but, as a rule, all authority is regarded as emanating from the body of the citizens.

There was, however, an institution of the Germans, not inconsistent in its original character with the democratic theory of their institutions, which, nevertheless, must have interfered materially with the democratic working of these institutions, and which in the end effected a complete revolution in them of a strongly aristocratic

* Magistratus ac principes in annos singulos gentibus cognationibusque hominum quantum et quo loco visum est agri attribuunt. *B. G.* vi. 22.

† De minoribus rebus principes consultant, de majoribus omnes. Tac. *Germ.* 11.

‡ Principes qui jura per pagos vicosque reddunt. *Id.* 12.—Principes regionum atque pagorum inter suos jus dicunt controversiasque minuunt. Cæs. *B. G.* vi. 23.

character. This was the so-called *comitatus*, the body of personal followers. It appears to have been of relatively recent origin; for, as Cæsar describes it,* it was quite imperfectly developed, consisting simply in the custom of voluntary leaders in times of war, around whom gathered a group of voluntary followers, the relation apparently continuing only for the period of the war. In the time of Tacitus, one hundred and fifty years later, it has been converted from a *custom* into an *institution:* the relation is a permanent one. The followers live at the expense of their chief in peace as well as war.† There are grades in dignity among them, and the several chiefs emulously rival one another in the number and prowess of their followers.‡

Both Cæsar and Tacitus use the word *princeps*, "chief," to designate the leader of the *comitatus;* and this is the same word which is used by both writers to designate also the permanent magistrates who have been already described. The question has naturally arisen, and has been debated with considerable warmth, whether the right of entertaining a *comitatus* was confined to the magistrates or chiefs of the State. Some have held that any person who chose might gather about him a body of followers: others, on the other hand, have taken *principes* in this relation to mean "nobles," and have regarded the right as a privilege of nobility. I have already said that neither Cæsar nor Tacitus ascribes any political privileges to the nobility, which appears, therefore, to have been a purely social distinction; and this statement is correct, if we take only the terms *nobiles* or *proceres* to mean "nobles," they being the words regularly used in this sense. The

* Ubi quis ex principibus in concilio dixit se ducem fore, qui sequi velint profiteantur, consurgunt ii, etc. Cæs. *B. G.* vi. 23.

† Epulæ et quamquam incompti largi tamen apparatus pro stipendiis cedunt. Tac. *Germ.* 14.

‡ Gradus quin etiam et ipse comitatus habet judicio ejus quem sectantur; magnaque et comitum æmulatio, quibus primus apud principem suum locus, et principum cui plurimi et acerrimi comites. *Id.* 13.

word *principes*, on the other hand, does not properly mean "nobles," but "chiefs" — individuals invested with certain governmental powers. It is purely begging the question to assume that, in relation to the *comitatus*, it is used in a different sense from its usual one. But the connection in which the word is used is conclusive upon this point. Both the writers in question speak of the *principes* as magistrates before speaking of them as leaders of the *comitatus;* and in Tacitus the passages follow close upon one another, with no interruption. He passes directly from the election and the judicial functions of the *principes* to the description of the *comitatus:* the conclusion is irresistible that the *principes* who maintain the *comitatus* are the same as those who administer the government of the State and preside over the judicial assemblies of the districts.

It will be readily seen that an institution like this, which, as Tacitus says, had a direct interest in war,* must have had a powerful influence in converting a peaceful community of peasants into the turbulent and quarrelsome nation of warriors who invaded and overthrew the Roman Empire. But our immediate connection is with the constitutional change which it effected. We see a body of elected magistrates (to use a modern term) holding their office for life, and, therefore, virtually irresponsible, administering the government in the intervals between the assemblies, having the administration of justice wholly under their direction and gathering about them a body of armed retainers, whom they support in peace as well as in war, but whose interests are wholly in war. The elected magistrates are to all intents and purposes converted into barons, holding their fellow-countrymen in control by armed force. Moreover, although there is no indication and no likelihood that nobility of birth was a necessary qualification for the office of *princeps*, it was natural that an office of so much power

---

* Magnum comitatum non nisi vi belloque tueare. *Germ.* 14.

would be filled almost exclusively from the wealthy and distinguished members of the nobility. The *principes* were not nobles as a class, or by any necessity; but, as individuals, they must in almost every instance have been of noble birth.

We are able, in the light of this condition of things, to interpret the single passage which has appeared to identify the *principes* with the nobles : Tacitus, Annals, i. 55, where it is said that Segestes, the friend of the Romans, urged the Roman general Varus, in view of the impending revolt of his countrymen, to put in custody both himself, his rival Arminius, and the rest of the nobles — the common people would venture upon no movement when they had lost their chiefs.*

The *principes* and the *proceres*, in their origin wholly different — the one elected magistrates, the other a social aristocracy — became identified with each other : the office of *princeps* would tend to become hereditary, and the social aristocracy was gradually converted into a political aristocracy.

The primitive and fundamental democracy of the Germans was, therefore, in the time of Tacitus, confronted by a wealthy and powerful official aristocracy, the forerunner of the feudal nobility. By the side of the national army, the organic divisions of which were formed by groups of kindred, there appeared the bands of military followers, fighting under the leadership of their personal chief, who at the same time, in his official capacity, must have commanded also the national host. By the side of the primitive communities of free tribesmen, also composed of family groups, there appeared the baronial residences of the chiefs, like feudal castles among the villages of peasants. Both of these systems, the democratic and the aristocratic, are clearly described in the *Germania* of Tacitus, the work in which he treats of their institutions from an antiquarian

---

* Ut se et Arminium et ceteros proceres vinciret : nihil ausuram plebem principibus amotis.

point of view. In his historical works, where the Germans are introduced, we see clearly the aristocracy as the preponderating force. The same appears also in native pictures of Germanic life, like the poem of Beowulf and the Icelandic sagas.

In two books published within the past year, by Mr. Frederic Seebohm,* an eminent English writer, and Mr. D. W. Ross,† of Cambridge, Mass., these baronial—or, as Mr. Seebohm prefers to call them, manorial—features of the primitive Germanic constitution are sketched with great learning and cogency. Other writers have emphasized the aristocratic features of this constitution; but to Mr. Seebohm, approaching the subject from an economic rather than an historical point of view, belongs the credit of having first pointed out that the German institutions were working themselves out upon "manorial lines." But, just as the generally accepted democratic theory undervalues the aristocratic elements of German society, so Mr. Seebohm appears to undervalue its democratic elements. To him the German institutions appear to have been fundamentally aristocratic, while the sketch given above represents the aristocratic features as a relatively late outgrowth.

The argument of Mr. Seebohm and Mr. Ross is founded principally upon a passage in the *Germania* of Tacitus (chap. 16), which we will now proceed to consider. It is as follows: "They dwell separate and scattered, as a fountain, a plain, or a grove catches their fancy. They build their villages, not like ours, with houses touching one another, but each house has a space about it."‡ Here are two modes of habitation described—that of villages and that of isolated homesteads. The passage, like most passages in ancient works, has been variously interpreted;

---

* English Village Communities. London. Longmans & Co.

† Early History of Land-holding among the Germans. Boston. Soule & Bugbee.

‡ Colunt discreti ac diversi, ut fons, ut campus, ut nemus placuit. Vicos locant non in nostrum morem conexis et cohærentibus ædificiis : suam quisque domum spatio circumdat.

the interpretation of Mr. Seebohm and Mr. Ross is, that the method first described is that followed by the free tribesmen, and that the villages are of their serfs. This very ingenious theory leaves the democratic features of the German institutions wholly out of account. It represents the free tribesmen as petty barons, each with his village of serfs, and of necessity assumes the free tribesmen to have been a relatively small number of nobles ruling over a large conquered or subject population. It explains half the facts in the case, but leaves the other half unaccounted for — and this not only in the antiquarian statements of the *Germania*, but also in the incidental mention in the historians, poets, and writers of sagas. For, while, as has been already remarked, the aristocratic character appears very strongly in these works, it is no less apparent that the free tribesmen are a numerous, homogeneous body, inferior in wealth and influence, but equally qualified members of the State.

Again, the language of Tacitus does not warrant any so broad contrast between the dwellers in the isolated homesteads and those in the villages. Mr. Seebohm remarks (p. 339) that "it is obvious that the Germans who chose to live scattered about the country sides, as spring, plain, or grove attracted them, were not the villagers who had spaces round their houses." This we may admit; but, when he adds, "We are left to conclude that the first class were the chiefs and the free tribesmen, . . . while the latter, the villagers, must chiefly have been their servile dependents," the inference is not so clear. It would seem that if Tacitus had meant to distinguish not individuals, but classes, and especially if he had meant that the one class were chiefs and the other their servile dependents, he would have said so in plain terms. The two kinds of residence are so coupled together that the only natural inference is that they were alike the residences of the free Germans of whom he is speaking. They are his subject throughout the early part of his work : it is not until he is nearly through with speaking of them, in the twenty-fifth chapter — eight chapters later than the passage under discussion — that he mentions the serfs.

We must conclude, therefore, that the free tribesmen lived in villages as well as in isolated homesteads ; and this conclusion is supported by the incidental mention of villages in other relations : for example, in the first book of the Annals, chap. 56, in an invasion of the German territory by Germanicus, Tacitus says that the Germans scattered into the woods, leaving their districts and villages — *amissis pagis vicisque.* If, then, some of the free Germans inhabited villages, while others inhabited isolated homesteads ; if, further, some of the free Germans fought in companies by family groups, while others followed personal chieftains ; and if these personal chieftains were at the same time really noblemen and public officers, it seems probable that it was these chieftains who lived in isolated homesteads, surrounded by their free retainers and their serfs — just as is assumed by Mr. Seebohm and Mr. Ross — while the common freemen, a class ignored by their theory, lived in other villages.

Assuming, then, that the common freemen of the Germans lived in villages, the question arises, What kind of villages were they, and what was the nature of their occupation ? In other words, are we warranted in assuming the existence of free village communities among the Germans of Cæsar and Tacitus, as is done by many modern writers ? The evidence as to this point is very scanty, being confined to a few isolated statements of these writers, but it is, I think, sufficient to warrant a positive conclusion, partly affirmative, partly negative.

We must begin by defining our terms. The village community is a group of persons occupying a tract of land, which they own and cultivate in common. For the purpose of this common cultivation they must have their residences near together, in a village, from which the arable lands, the meadows, pasture and wood land, will be equally accessible to all. The view of the German writers, von Maurer, Thudichum, and others, who have worked up the theory of village communities, is that some communities, *Markgenossenschaften*, had such villages, and others not. It is only those that had them that formed *Dorfgenossenschaften*, or village communities proper; and they hold that this was the prevalent form of the occupation of land in the countries occupied by Germanic nations in the early Middle Ages. The land being owned in common, all members of the community were, originally at least, equal partners: a democratic structure of society is, therefore, necessarily taken for granted by the theory.

As time went on, individual property in land came into existence. The lands were divided up — the lots occupied by individual marksmen became their property: first the house-lot, then the strip of arable land, became the subject of individual ownership; and, when this had taken place, the entire aggregate belonging to one member of the community — house-lot, share of arable land, and right to the pasture, forest, etc.— was called in English, *hide*. Every member, therefore, of the primitive democracy, had an equal property at the outset. The irregularities in wealth and station were the outgrowth of the natural workings of competitive relations in the more advanced state of society.

The question of village communities is essentially a question of the occupation of land, and its theory stands in the closest connection with the history of the origin of the feudal tenure of land. It necessarily involves, moreover, the discussion of another subject which may be treated independently in other historical epochs, but which, in the early history of institutions, is inextricably connected with that of land — the structure of society.

The reason of this is that, whereas in modern society the State or political organization starts with a given territory, and embraces all occupants of that territory, in ancient society it was exactly the reverse. The tribe or nation was the starting-point, a given body of persons; and the State — if we may use this expression for this period — comprised whatever territory was occupied by these persons. We see survivals of this primitive condition of things in the tribal organization of our North American Indians. Although occupants of part of the territory comprised within the limits of the United States, they are, nevertheless, not recognized as belonging to that nation, for the reason that they keep up their tribal organization, with a *quasi*-authority over the lands assigned to them by the national government.

The structure of society forms, therefore, the first subject of inquiry in the history of early institutions. And here we notice a still more fundamental contrast with modern society. Modern society, at least here in the United States, has no structure at all beyond the loose institution of the *family*. Apart from these petty communities, our society is composed simply of individuals with no organic connection with one another, except such as grows out of political relations or private association. But all early societies are highly organized and closely coherent. The man does not exist except as a member of an organization. Any person who stands outside of the organization is, in the strictest sense of the term, an outlaw. The structure of society must, therefore, be sought first, and the land system will necessarily be an outgrowth of that.

I will first examine the earliest writer, Cæsar, by himself, then see how far the statements of Tacitus agree with those of Cæsar, and what system of society and land tenure may be assumed for both periods.

It has become a commonplace of political history that

early society was founded upon the family ; or, if we go back to the rudest beginnings where the family as an institution did not exist, upon kinship. That this was the case among the ancient Germans, and that the occupation of the land was based upon the family, is testified to in the most positive manner by Cæsar (*B. G.* vi. 22), where he says that the lands are assigned by the magistrates to the several clans and kindreds of men (*gentibus cognationibusque hominum*). This assignment, he adds, is made for a year at a time (*in annos singulos*), and that it is made at a public gathering appears to follow from the words *qui una coierunt,* "who have assembled together," where the relative must refer to *hominum,* "men." Among the reasons mentioned for this custom of annual division is the significant one that thus they are able to maintain an equality of possessions (*cum suas quisque opes cum potentissimis æquari videat,* "each one of the community seeing his own possessions equal to those of the most powerful"). This fact is further emphasized by the statement that no one has land of his own (*neque quisquam agri modum certum aut fines habet proprios*) ; and he adds that this annual shifting is imperative and under the direction of the government (*anno post alio transire cogunt*). These last statements are found also in the description of the Suevi (iv. 1) : *privati ac separati agri apud eos nihil est, neque longius anno remanere uno in loco incolendi causa licet.* "There is among them no private and individual land, nor are they allowed to remain longer than a year in one place for the purpose of habitation."

In these few clear and positive statements Cæsar gives us the materials for determining precisely the stage of social progress reached by the Germans of his time. They were still in the patriarchal stage, in which kinship rather than territory formed the basis of their organization ; but they had passed beyond the stage of nomadic life. The individual had no permanent home, neither had the family ;

but the nation had. More than this, it would appear that
there were already certain fixed and determinate territorial divisions of the territory of the nation, for the assignments of land are made with absolute authority by the
magistrates, who assign lands and compel the annual
changes ; and these magistrates, as we learn from chap.
23, have authority over territorial districts (*principes regionum atque pagorum*). From this we may infer that the
shiftings of occupation were made rigidly under the direction of the magistrates, and within the limits of definite
territorial districts. Thus Horace (*Od.* iii. 24, 12) says of
the Getæ, a Germanic people : —

> " Immetata quibus jugera liberas
> Fruges et Cererem ferunt.
> Nec cultura placet longior annua
> Defunctumque laboribus
> Æquali recreat sorte vicarius."

Here are clearly indicated the shifting annual occupation, and the lack of any permanent boundaries to the
cultivated fields — no ownership, but temporary occupation
and use ; perhaps also the alternation of agriculture and
service in the field, described by Cæsar, *B. G.* iv. 1 : *Sin-
gula millia armatorum bellandi causa ex finibus educunt.
Reliqui qui domi manserunt se atque illos alunt. Hi rur-
sus in vicem anno post in armis sunt, illi domi remanent.*

Passing now to the account given by Tacitus, who lived
about one hundred and fifty years later, we find that his
description partly confirms and partly supplements that of
Cæsar ; that it nowhere contradicts it, but in some points
shows the changes which might reasonably be expected
to take place in the course of a century and a half,
among a semi-barbarous but vigorous and intelligent people, in direct contact and constant intercourse with a
highly civilized nation.

As to the structure of society, Tacitus testifies, just as
Cæsar does, to the persistence of the family principle,

only he mentions it in connection with the military organization instead of the occupation of land (*Germ.* chap. 7): *non casus nec fortuita conglobatio turmam aut cuneum facit, sed familiæ et propinquitates,* "Their divisions of cavalry and infantry are not made up by chance or accidental assembling, but by families and neighborhoods"—the same patriarchal groups, no doubt, which are described by Cæsar's *gentibus cognationibusque.* The two statements naturally form the complement to each other: if patriarchal groups lived together, as Cæsar says, they naturally formed military divisions together, as Tacitus says.

Tacitus does not tell us that the patriarchal groups lived together; but it may be inferred that this was the case, from the fact that they fought side by side. When he takes up the subject of the occupation of land (chap. 26), he merely speaks of the land being occupied by communities, *ab universis.* The passage is so important and so difficult to interpret that I will cite it at length: *Agri pro numero cultorum ab universis in vices occupantur, quos mox inter se secundum dignationem partiuntur: facilitatem partiundi camporum spatia præstant. Arva per annos mutant, et superest ager.* "It is their practice to have their lands taken into possession by communities, turn by turn, in amounts proportioned to the numbers of their members, and afterwards to share these out among the members according to rank: the wide extent of the tracts occupied makes this division easy. They change the fields in cultivation every year, and there is land left over."

Here we have, just as in Cæsar's description, a periodical shifting of occupation; and this is the only feature of the two descriptions which we identify positively. For the reasons already given, we may infer that these communities, like those of Cæsar's time, were patriarchal, at least prevailingly so; but the distribution was probably no longer a yearly one. It will be noticed that two distinct procedures are described — the shifting occupation (*agri . . . occupantur*) and the shifting cultivation (*arva per annos mutant*). It is hardly possible that there could have been any shifting cultivation — that is, rotation of crops — unless the occupation was for more than one year. I think, therefore, that, although not explicitly stated, it is distinctly implied, that the assignment of lands was made for a period of years, as is the case with the Russian *Mir* and the Hebrew seven years' period. This points to a marked progress of society in the period between Cæsar and Tacitus.

In another point this progress is more positively asserted. We have seen that in Cæsar's time there was not only no private property in land, but no disparity in property or in occupation. Tacitus, on the other hand, states with equal positiveness that the lands were assigned according to rank — *secundum dignationem ;* that is, there was still no private property in land, but the amount of land temporarily assigned to individuals varied according to their rank. This disparity probably had reference only to the nobles and magistrates : the most of the common freemen in all likelihood received equal lots. And when, at the end of the period, the community was transferred to another tract of land, the process was begun over again. There could therefore be no aggregations of landed property; but there was a condition of things out of which such aggregations might easily grow, as soon as the occupation of a definite tract of land by a particular community should become permanent.

We find from this analysis that in the first century after Christ the Germans were grouped in family communities, not yet established in permanent homes, but probably changing their residences at intervals of some years, although always within a definite territorial district. This district was, as we learn from the same authority, a permanent political institution. It follows as a matter of course that at this period there was not only no private property in land, but no common property in land; that is, no property in land at all. Neither the community nor the family *owned* the land or occupied it personally, any more than the individual. It might perhaps be urged that the district owned the territory within which the shifting occupation took place, but it may be doubted whether even this would be a correct statement of the facts. Property in land was probably a conception which lay wholly outside of their imagination as well as their experience. The land, like the air, was a free gift of nature, to be used in common, but with no thought of ownership.

As the theory of the village community implies not merely permanent occupation, but ownership of the land, on the part of the group of occupants, our conclusion must be that the village community did not exist in the time of Tacitus. Nevertheless, it must be admitted, on the other hand, that the condition of things here described is one out of which the village community could very easily have arisen. In the fact that the distribution was periodical instead of annual, we see a movement towards permanence of occupation, and therefore towards ownership, on the part of the community. The time would very soon come, in the progress of society, when the community would have accumulated so much fixed wealth in the course of its occupation that it would be a hardship and an injustice to force it to change its habitation. The next change therefore — hardly a greater change than that from annual to periodical redistribution — would be to convert the temporary occupancy into permanent occupancy, which means property. If this stage was reached, and it is hard to conceive of its not being reached, at least as a temporary condition of things, there resulted the village community; that is, the ownership in common of a definite tract of land by a group of persons who were in their origin an enlarged family.

By the side of the movement towards permanency of occupation, we saw another, towards inequality of possession. The important testimony of Tacitus shows that already in his time there was, not individual property in land or inequality of ownership, but inequality of station and of temporary occupation. Out of this would speedily be developed the inequality of property which the theory of village communities recognizes as one of the causes of the dissolution of the institution. And thus we find confirmed, from the point of view of the occupation of land, the conclusion drawn from the evidence of political and military institutions, of the development of an aristocracy of a baronial type; or, in Mr. Seebohm's words, of development on manorial lines.

PRIMITIVE COMMUNITIES.*

DURING the year 1883 three books were published which were of so great importance in the early history of institutions that it seems worth while to examine them with some care in their relation to one another, in order to determine the precise extent and value of their contribution to this study. These books are Sir Henry Maine's "Early Law and Custom," Mr. Frederic Seebohm's "English Village Communities," and Mr. D. W. Ross's "Early History of Land-holding among the Germans." Sir Henry Maine's book, being a collection of essays of a considerable range of discussion, will be touched upon only incidentally : the other two, those of Mr. Ross and Mr. Seebohm, being in the same general line of investigation and arriving at essentially the same results, deserve careful study by themselves.

The principal object of these two books, so far as they are controversial in character, is to disprove the accepted theory of village communities. The existence of village communities as a feature of serfdom they readily accept; and Mr. Ross even recognizes certain *quasi*-communities of freemen, of a comparatively late date and of subordinate importance. But the agricultural community of free peasants, purely democratic in its structure, as a regular and necessary phase in the history of Germanic society, they either deny altogether or accept as a merely transient and unimportant phenomenon.

It may be noted here that neither of these treatises aims to cover the entire ground of the inquiry. Mr. Seebohm's investigations are, for the most part, confined to the English people — an intruding people, settled by

* From *Science*, vol. 3, p. 786 (June 27, 1884).

conquest upon a soil to which they were foreign. Here he appears to have completely established his thesis by a series of inductions of remarkable fulness and cogency, and to have shown that the evidence before us does not warrant us in going back of the *servile* community which we know to have existed in the Middle Ages. But, when he passes from England to the original home of the English, he contents himself with the discussion of two or three points, of considerable interest and importance, it is true, but which do not go to the bottom of the matter. Mr. Ross pursues his inquiries by a precisely opposite method. Instead of working back inductively from the present to the past, he begins with the first settlement of the Germans in their permanent homes, and traces their landed institutions step by step down to fully historical times. Like all deductive processes, his reasoning depends for its force upon our acceptance of the proposition with which he starts.

This proposition is (p. 1) that "the freemen settled neither in villages nor in towns, but apart from one another, in isolated farmsteads." Of the evidence for this proposition, derived from chap. 16 of the *Germania* of Tacitus, I spoke some months ago (see *Science*, No. 45), in a review of Mr. Ross's book. My object now is not to repeat what I said then, or to examine the proposition itself, but to bring it into relation with other connected branches of inquiry. Mr. Ross has given us an invaluable treatise upon early German land-holding; but landed institutions are only one of a group of institutions, and, however fundamental their importance, they cannot be fully understood except in connection with the social organization and the political institutions of the people in question. Moreover, however fundamental the landed institutions are at the stage of civilization in which the Germans were at the time of the migrations, in the earlier stages of society they are of only secondary importance, and, indeed, only come into existence at a relatively late epoch in the life of any community.

Primitive communities stand in no relation to the land except that of occupation. Land is to them a free gift of nature, just like air; and individual ownership, or even permanent individual occupation, is inconceivable to them. For primitive communities, the most fundamental consideration is that of the social organization — the structure of society : the relation to the land does not come into consideration until the people has passed through savage life and the lower stages of barbarism, and has settled down to permanent occupation and systematic agriculture. Then, upon the passage from the personal to the territorial basis of organization, the land becomes the subject of the first consequence. It is readily seen, therefore, that Mr. Ross, starting with individual property in land, leaves out of sight — as he has a right to do — all the earlier phases of landed relations, as well as the entire question of social structure. We cannot, however, fully understand the landed institutions themselves, or fully appreciate the bearing of Mr. Ross's researches, without bringing them into relation with these cognate branches of inquiry.

It will be well to diverge here for a moment to Sir Henry Maine's book, which raises a question similar to that under consideration. In chap. vii., "Theories of Primitive Society," he pronounces in favor of the "patriarchal theory of society"—that is, "the theory of its origin in separate families, held together by the authority and protection of the eldest valid male ascendant"—against the view presented by Morgan and McLennan, of its origin in the horde. That this was the history of society as we are in condition to trace it, especially in the Indo-European family of nations, there is no doubt; but the patriarchal family, like individual ownership of land, requires something back of it to account for its origin. It is not primitive, but must itself be the outcome of ages of gradual advancement.

The theory of the patriarchal family, as defined by Sir Henry Maine, lends itself readily to Mr. Ross's theory of landed relations. The German warrior, upon the settlement of his tribe in a new region, may be supposed to have taken a tract of land and settled upon it with his sons and daughters, his slaves and serfs. From this beginning the sketch of landed relations presented by Mr. Ross possesses unity and consistency. To accept it in full, however, as an exhaustive theory of the subject, we must not only agree to the interpretation of Tacitus, by which he establishes his premise, but must also bring his theory into harmony with what we know of the primitive social organization of the Germans.

It is generally agreed that the Germans, in the time of Cæsar — and these remarks apply also, in the main, to the time of Tacitus, a hundred and fifty years later — were in what is sometimes called the semi-nomadic stage, but what we may perhaps better describe as the end of a series of migrations. There is good evidence that the intruding Germans had displaced Celts in some parts of Germany at a relatively recent date; and the great invasion of the Teutones and Cimbri at just the time of Cæsar's birth was, no doubt, a part of this general migration. This erratic movement of the Cimbri and Teutones was checked by the Romans with considerable difficulty; but an effective barrier was placed against the slow westward advance of the Germans by Cæsar's defeat of Ariovistus, the later campaigns of Drusus and Tiberius, and, finally, by the *limes*, or line of fortified posts, constructed from the Rhine across to the Danube in the second century.* The Germans, at the time of Cæsar, cultivated the ground to a certain extent — a form of industry not inconsistent with the slow migration, occupying perhaps several centuries, by which they passed from their original home to Central Europe. Once this migratory movement stopped,

---

* For the historical importance of this *limes*, see Arnold, " Deutsche Urzeit," Book I, chap. iii.

no longer finding scope for expansion, the Germans appear to have settled quietly within their now established boundaries, and to have passed with great rapidity into a settled condition of society with permanent occupation of land, and a regular system of cultivating it.

At this point there is an absolute blank in our knowledge for a period of nearly three hundred years, after which time, in the weakness and disruption of the Roman Empire, the Germans burst over the barriers which had held them stationary, and began a new series of migrations of a very different type. These years, as I have said, are a complete blank except so far as we are enabled to infer what happened during the interval from what appears at its close. In the time of Cæsar, and probably in that of Tacitus, when the *limes* was in process of construction, the Germans appear to have been still in the stage of temporary occupation of land by groups of kinsmen. What was the nature and organization of these family groups, it is impossible to tell : only we have every reason to conclude that they were of far less importance in their system than in that of either Greeks, Romans, Slavs, or Celts. Like the Romans, the Germans advanced to the territorial or political stage at a relatively very early period ; but, while the Romans continued even under their highly developed political system to retain their gentile organization unimpaired — although only as a branch of private law — the corresponding institutions among the Germans were rapidly outgrown, and have left very slight traces in their later institutions. The larger subdivisions, which may very likely have been *gentes* in their origin, appear in the time of Cæsar and Tacitus to have become purely territorial districts, in which, so far as our information extends, there is absolutely no feature of the family principle. They are administered not by an hereditary or *quasi*-hereditary chief, representing the original patriarch, as among the Slavs and Celts, but by elected magistrates (*principes*), in which no trace of the patriarchal origin is discernible; and so strongly developed are the political habits of the people that these magistrates are elected by the entire nation in their public assembly, and assigned to the several districts.* Within these districts the family groups still continue, and receive annual assignments of land at the discretion of the magistrates. This is in the time of Cæsar. In the time of Tacitus, even these lesser family groups appear to have lost much of their original character; for he does not mention it as a feature of their constitution. When we reach the settlement of the Angles and Saxons in England, we find that the *mægth*, or legal kin, was not a precisely defined group, like the Roman *agnatio*, but was irregular and fluctuating in the highest degree.† The same fact, the inferior importance of the kin as compared with all the other European branches of the Aryan race, is shown distinctly in the popular literature. In the story of "Burnt Njal," for example, the patriarch lives surrounded by his sons and daughters; but so far is he from possessing the Roman *patria potestas* that he has no power even to withhold his sons from the perpetration of a gross crime.

When the Germans come under our observation again, at the time of the migrations in the fourth and fifth centuries, we find, in place of the system of shifting occupation of land, a fully developed system of individual ownership. This Mr. Ross appears to have completely proved. That the ownership was not yet complete for the purposes of alienation and devise does not affect the main question. It was precisely so among the ancient Romans, who possessed the most vigorous and logical conception of individual property (*dominium*) in land which any people has ever had : nevertheless, the *paterfamilias* held this property in trust, as it were, for his heirs, without power

---

* This subject I have discussed more fully in a paper in vol. 6 of the Transactions of the Wisconsin Academy of Sciences, Arts, and Letters.

† See Professor Young's essay upon Anglo-Saxon Family Law.

either of alienation or devise. Here comes in the importance of the distinction made by Mr. Ross between *common* and *undivided* property. The land belonged to the
freeman and his heirs, not to the community ; and, when
divided, was divided *per stirpes :* it was, therefore, not
common, but undivided.

The question now arises, What connection was there
between the system of shifting occupation described by
Cæsar and Tacitus and that of individual ownership
which existed at the time of the migrations ? To answer
this question, we have absolutely no positive data, but
may arrive at certain inferences by following deductively
the tendencies at work in the earlier period or by detect-
ing in the later period survivals of perished institutions.

It may be said that the natural course of events would
be something like this. The family group, which in the
time of Cæsar received an assignment of land for a year
at a time, appears in the time of Tacitus to have held it
for a series of years, its family character being, perhaps,
at the same time modified. This is what we should naturally expect, and it is the most probable explanation of
the much disputed passage in the twenty-sixth chapter
of the *Germania.* This shifting occupation, the natural
accompaniment of semi-nomadic or migratory life, would
cease by the force of circumstances when this form of life
came to an end. The German nations being confined
within definite territories, divided into permanent districts,
the lesser groups would likewise become fixed. The
habits of settled agriculture, the attachment to lands and
residences once occupied, would very soon transform the
shifting occupation into a permanent occupation ; and with
permanent occupation comes in at once the idea of ownership. Ownership of land is the outcome of a settlement in
permanent homes, and the adoption of a regular system
of agriculture. This ownership would be of the group, the
universi of Tacitus, and must be *common* ownership in

the strictest sense of the word ; for the shifting occupation of individuals or households (*quos mox inter se secundum dignationem partiuntur*) would continue for a while after that of the larger groups (*agri ab universis in vices occupantur*) had ceased, and in this interval there would be real ownership, because permanency of occupation, on the part of these larger groups (*universi*), originally themselves family groups in nature, and probably still so in their prevailing character. At last the same causes which had called into existence the common ownership of the larger group would create, in turn, the individual ownership of the household. This would probably be a very rapid process. Such as it is here described, as a probable result of known causes, it is precisely what Mr. Seebohm appears to have in mind (p. 367) when he says, " It is certainly possible that during a short period . . . tribal households may have expanded into free village communities." If it took place at all, it must have been in this period of blank between the construction of the *limes* and the migrations of the fifth century.

The free village community is therefore a natural and probable connecting link between what we know to have existed in the first century and what we know to have existed in the fifth century. That it actually existed among the Germans during this epoch we have no direct and positive evidence; but there are numerous features of the later system, in the community of cultivation, the rights of pre-emption, and the traces of occasional redistribution, which are easiest explained as survivals of the village community. For a description of these, I need only refer to Sir Henry Maine's " Village Communities," and similar works.

Of actual cases of village communities, indeed, in any country, it is surprising how few we have knowledge of, considering the large part they have played, of late years, in treatises upon early institutions. The villages of India are composed of independent families, joint or individual; those of the South Slavonians are groups of house communities; the Celts never appear to have had any institution of this nature; the Greeks and Romans afford no traces of them; the German villages, as Mr. Ross has proved, were communities of independent proprietors, although bound together by ties which seem to indicate a previous condition of collective ownership; Russia alone affords unquestionable examples of the village community of the theory. What is common to all of these, and may be fairly pronounced a universal institution of the Indo-European race, if not of the human race, in its early stages, is the family group with collective occupation of land. The nature and organization of the group, and the later history of its relation to the land, are questions into which we have not space to enter.

The obscurity and vagueness in the prevailing ideas upon the subject result from not attending to the fundamental character of the transition, in early society, from the personal structure of society (based upon the family relation) to the political organization (based upon territory). In the earlier stage we have family groups occupying a definite territory: in the later stage we may have a definite territory — the *mark* or village circumscription — occupied and owned in common by a group of proprietors. These proprietors may be the family group of the earlier stage or they may have taken in members of different origin: in any case, the point of view has shifted, and is now territorial instead of personal. This condition of things, if it ever existed, is the free village community.

THE VILLAGE COMMUNITY AND SERFDOM IN ENGLAND.*

THE existence of village communities with collective ownership of land, in England, is a fact of comparatively recent discovery. Long after von Maurer and the writers of his school had submitted the subject to an exhaustive investigation, in relation to the Teutonic countries of the continent, it was believed that England afforded no examples of the system. The eye of the American traveller upon the continent is constantly struck by the ribbon-like strips, which almost everywhere testify to a system of occupation and cultivation of land differing widely from that of his own country; while in England the fields, of irregular size and shape — although enclosed with hedges instead of stone walls and rail fences — are precisely what he is familiar with at home. It was only after the inquiry was, so to speak, completed for the continent, that a German scholar, Professor E. Nasse, of Bonn, took it up in relation to England, and showed that here, too, the system of village communities, with an open-field system of husbandry, was the prevailing one during the Middle Ages.†

The line of inquiry entered upon by Professor Nasse in the work referred to was shortly after followed out by Sir Henry Maine in his "Village Communities" (1871.); and more recently Mr. Frederic Seebohm, in his "English Village Communities" (1883), has given a description and analysis of this institution which could not be surpassed

* From Transactions of the Wisconsin Academy of Sciences, Arts, and Letters (1884), vol. 7, p. 130.

† See his treatise, translated and published by the Cobden Club, "The Agricultural Community of the Middle Ages, and Inclosures of the Sixteenth Century in England." London: Williams & Norgate. 1872.

in thoroughness and lucidity. Since the publication of this work, in 1883, there has no longer been any room for difference of opinion as to the existence of village communities in England, or, indeed, as to their organization in almost the smallest detail. A new controversy has, however, been suggested by his work. Mr. Seebohm holds that these village communities were not, in their origin, groups of free peasant proprietors, reduced by gradual steps to a condition of serfdom, as the accepted theory maintains, but that serfdom was their original condition, there having been no essential change in this respect from the first settlement of England down through the feudal period. This view is closely connected with Mr. Seebohm's theory of the primitive aristocracy of the Germanic nations, which I discussed in a former paper.* Holding that serfdom was the original condition of the mass of the German people, he naturally holds that the same was true of the English settlers. And it must be conceded that, if his theory is true for Germany, it must perforce be true for England; while the converse does not hold. To prove the primitive democracy of the Germans does not prove a primitive democracy for the English, for the reason that their migration and conquest of a foreign land may have worked a fundamental change in their social institutions.

The question to be considered is, it will be seen, not whether the village community existed or not — that has been placed beyond controversy by Messrs. Nasse and Seebohm: it is whether it was a free or a serf community; and the question resolves itself at once into a larger one, as to the origin of serfdom in England. This will form the subject of the present paper.

It has generally been held that serfdom in England was, in part at least, the result of a gradual deterioration in the condition of an originally free peasantry — that, while no doubt some serfs were in their origin emancipated slaves, and others conquered Britons, while others again were

---

* See Transactions of the Wisconsin Academy of Sciences, Arts, and Letters, vol. 6.

brought over as serfs by the English conquerors, never-theless the largest portion of them were the descendants of the conquerors themselves, the rank and file of the invading armies, who had sunk by degrees to a condition not much above that of the native Britons. This view is disputed by Mr. Seebohm. According to him there was no large body of free Germans, but the invading armies were composed of chieftains with servile followers, whom they settled at once as serfs upon their estates. The manorial system of the Middle Ages, therefore, existed from the first. The free Angle or Saxon was the lord of the manor, or thegn : the serfs whom he brought with him or found already upon the soil were the same body as the villeins of the feudal period.

His line of argument is as follows : Finding serfdom to be the condition of the peasantry in the Middle Ages, in association with the village community, he traces both institutions back, by an inductive process of remarkable ingenuity and cogency, to the reign of Alfred, at the beginning of the tenth century, at which point of time he shows that the condition of the peasantry did not differ essentially from what it was in the reign of Edward I., four hundred years later. Further back than this he is not able to go with the same thoroughness of detail, for the want of documentary evidence. He finds, however, passages in the laws of the seventh century which appear to support his view, and maintains that, if we find no change in tracing the institution back six hundred years to the time of these laws, we should not be likely to find any change if we could trace it back still further, for the much shorter period of two hundred years or so, to the first settlement of the Angles and Saxons in Britain. This argument is still further strengthened by the assertion that serfdom not merely existed in the tenth century (and probably in the eighth) as well as in the thirteenth, but that it was more complete and harsh at the earlier date than at the latter. If these conclusions are correct, if the agricultural population of England was in a condition of serfdom uninterruptedly from the eighth century to the thirteenth, and if its early form was more severe than its later, he must be admitted to have made out his case.

As to the first point, it should be noted that he has *proved* the existence of serfdom only as far back as the tenth century: its existence at an earlier date is only an inference, partly from analogy, partly from evidence which, as will be shown further on, proves the existence of the open-field system of husbandry, but not of serfdom. The positive evidence goes no further back than the time of Alfred. Now, the interval between Alfred and the original settlement of the Anglo-Saxons in Britain is just about as long (four hundred years) as that between Alfred and Edward I. Moreover, it is an important considera-tion that the years directly following the conquest would be likely to witness far more rapid and radical changes than the later period.

The second point in his argument, that serfdom is found to be more harsh in its type as we trace it further back in time, requires a careful examination, being op-posed to the accepted view, and resting upon evidence of a rather doubtful character. We have numerous docu-ments belonging to various points of time from the tenth to the thirteenth century, which contain a detailed enu-meration of the duties and obligations of serfs, as well as the amount of land they held. Now, the obligations, so far as they are specifically enumerated, are much more numerous and burdensome at the later period than at the earlier; but, at the earlier date, we find, in addition to the specific obligations, such general and indefinite ones as " to work as the work requires," and "every week do what work they are bid." In such general and unlimited obli-gations as these, he says, consists the essence of servi-tude.

This argument requires that the obligations, beginning in the tenth century with unlimited liability to labor, should go on regularly lessening in amount and becoming easier through the feudal period. The contrary is, however, the case. Leaving out of account for the present the indefinite expressions just cited, to which we shall return presently, we find the precisely enumerated obligations to be less in the tenth century than in the twelfth, and in the twelfth century again to be less than in the thirteenth. That is, while there is an uninterrupted continuity through these four hundred years in the organization of the peasantry and the general character of their obligations, these obligations, as specified in detail, appear to have been steadily increasing during this period. Even the example given by Mr. Seebohm (p. 157), of the manor of Tidenham at the two periods, sustains this view, except for the phrase, " work as the work requires," at the earlier period ; and a comparison of the duties specified in the *Rectitudines singularum personarum* with the numerous descriptions in the *Rotuli hundredorum* or the Cartularies in the reign of Edward I. shows a much larger amount of required labor at the later period.*

In one instance, we have positive evidence in detail of this increase in burdens. The residents of Weston, in Bedfordshire, made a complaint to the officers of Edward I. that, in the reign of his grandfather, King John, they were accustomed to labor in autumn only for three harvest days, on which days they were provided with food at their lord's table, one day of fish and two of meat. But William de Bokland, to whom King John granted the estate, increased the aforesaid service by one additional

---

* Compare, for the earlier period, the *Rectitudines singularum personarum*, the *Codex Diplomaticus*, No. 977, and the illustration given by Mr. Seebohm, p. 157 ; for the twelfth century, the Domesday of St. Paul, and the Abingdon Cartulary, vol. ii. p. 301 ; for the close of the thirteenth century the documents are very abundant, the most numerous examples being in the *Rotuli hundredorum* and the Gloucester Cartulary, vol. iii.

day at the lord's table. Afterwards the aforesaid manor came to John Tregoz, who augmented the service to such a degree that now they perform ten days' work in autumn at their own providing, and one day besides.* Here we have on record an actual example of an abuse of power by the feudal lord, in increasing the burdens of his serfs, such as we must suppose to have been common in those evil days. It is a significant point that the extortions here described were not the work of one man, but of three successive proprietors.

As to the phrase in question — to do "every week what work they are bid" — it is best explained as a general authority to call upon them when there was need, with an understanding that no unreasonable demands should be imposed upon them. In this respect this obligation resembles the feudal aids and tallages, which also were levied at discretion, but were understood to be only occasional, and implied nothing servile in the relation. Feudal aids and tallages were nevertheless liable to abuses and extortion by reason of their indefiniteness, and were at last defined by law. So in like manner the indefinite obligations in question gave opportunity for arbitrary exactions, like those in the manor of Weston, described above. It may have been the case, too, that such obligations as these were not universal, but peculiar to such and such an estate. The tenth century document, *Rectitudines singularum personarum*, says distinctly that the obligations vary, being lighter here and heavier there; but what it describes as the usual ones are much less in amount than what was common in the thirteenth

---

* In tempore Regum Henrici et Johannis dicti homines non consueverunt operari in autumno nisi tantum tres messes in quibus diebus debebant exhiberi in cibis et potibus ad mensam domini una die in esu piscium et aliis duabus in esu carnium. Postmodum Willelmus de Boclond augmentavit dictum servicium et per ipsum crevit per unam diem messis ad mensam domini. Postmodum Hamo le Crevequer tenuit dictum manerium in eodem statu toto tempore. . . . Item deinde venit dictum manerium ad manus Johannis Tregoz qui prædictum servicium augmentavit in tantum quod modo fiunt decem operaciones in autumpno ad mensam suam. Item præter istam operacionem exigitur ab hominibus prædictis una water-bederipe et fit. Et tunc bibunt aquam, et hoc crevit primo per dictum Hamon, etc. *Rotuli hundredorum*, i. 6.

century. It should be noted also that the *Rectitudines* speaks distinctly of the tenants in question as freemen.*

I cannot, therefore, concede to this part of Mr. Seebohm's argument the weight which he claims for it. He does not seem to me to have proved that the obligations were less in the thirteenth century than in the tenth: on the other hand, the evidence seems to me to lean strongly the other way. But he has proved, and it is a fact of great importance, that the character of the obligations, and the status of the peasantry, did not, so far as our information goes, differ essentially in the tenth century from what we find in the thirteenth. It is, therefore, perfectly legitimate on his part to infer that this condition of the peasantry, found alike in the thirteenth and in the tenth century, probably existed in the earlier centuries also. The inference is, however, only a probable one, in the absence of direct evidence; and direct evidence is wanting. For the period before the time of Alfred, he is obliged to have recourse to indirect evidence, in the assumption that serfdom and the "open-field husbandry" went together.

Up to this point he has traced the open-field system and serfdom step by step, accompanying each other hand in hand. Beyond this point he is not able to trace serfdom; but the open-field system is traced back at least two centuries further, and he says that, as it has always carried serfdom with it in the later period, it may fairly be assumed to do the same thing in the earlier. "The community in villeinage," he says (p. 105), "fitted into the open-field system as a snail fits into a shell." But it is by no means clear that a free community might not have fitted into this shell equally well, as, indeed, the prevailing theory holds. The only argument to prove that the community could not have been a free one is (p. 177) that the Teutonic custom of dividing estates equally among heirs would have led to endless and intricate subdivisions of

---

* Sicut omnis liber facere debet.

land. But this is exactly what we find to have been the case. The virgate, or "yard-land," which he assumes to have been the regular peasant's holding, and which as a matter of fact was the usual one in the thirteenth century, was the fourth part of a hide; and it is generally held that the hide, not the virgate, was the original holding. And at any rate, in the thirteenth century, we find tenures of half and quarter virgates, and even smaller aliquot parts, by the side of the regular tenure of the virgate; * exactly the condition of things which Mr. Seebohm says would have come about.

To carry back, therefore, the open-field system to the seventh and sixth centuries, as Mr. Seebohm does by almost certain inference, is a valuable contribution to our knowledge; but that serfdom went back with it is an unwarranted inference. The question of freedom or serfdom is the fundamental one, that of land tenure or husbandry being really but secondary. To this fundamental question of status, therefore, we will now apply ourselves, leaving that of land occupation aside for the present.

At this point it must be conceded, as I have said before, that the existence of a large body of free peasants in the Germanic nations of the continent, which I consider to be fully proved, does not necessarily prove the existence of the same class in England. The Angles and Saxons settled forcibly and very slowly in Britain; and it is not in itself impossible that the whole body of the conquerors became a landed aristocracy in their new home, establishing such a system of manors, with a population of serfs upon them, as we find in later centuries. This is Mr. Seebohm's view. But the probability is the other way.

---

*For example, in the manor of Broctrope (Gloucester Cartulary, iii. p. 140) I find among the freeholders two tenants holding entire virgates, and five holding half-virgates; and among the customary tenants one with a virgate, nine with half-virgates, two with quarter-virgates, and five with an amount of land equal to a sixteenth of a virgate, these differences evidently coming from the subdivision of the original hide. For other examples, see my paper on "Rural Classes in the Thirteenth Century," *post ;* that the socage freeholds were originally servile holdings is shown in my paper on the "Origin of the Freeholders," *post.*

The Angles and Saxons did not enter Britain as the Normans did afterwards, as a handful of conquerors, ruling over a subject people. They came *as a people*, bringing their wives and children with them, not *as an army;* and with regard to the Angles we are expressly told * that they left vacant the country which they had formerly occupied, the entire people having migrated. Moreover, the native inhabitants were *as a people* exterminated. In the eastern parts of the island their language, their religion, and, so far as we can judge, their institutions and customs disappeared. If the invaders established a system of serfdom in Britain, they must have brought the serfs with them : otherwise, the servile population would have had the preponderance of numbers, and the resulting community would have been, as in the case of the Normans and the Franks, the native population with an admixture of the conquerors, instead of — as the language shows to have been the case — the conquering population with an admixture of natives. Now, the Germans had in their native land a class of serfs called *lidi*, or *lazzi;* and the Anglo-Saxon laws mention a similar class called *laet*, whom we must suppose to have been the serfs (*lidi*) brought with them by the invaders. These *laet*, the serfs of the Anglo-Saxon period, Mr. Seebohm suggests (p. 175), may have been identical with the *villani*, who were the serfs of the later Middle Ages. This cannot, however, be the case, as the *villani* are invariably identified with a quite different class, the *ceorls*.

This brings us to the most fundamental question in the subject under consideration : Were the *ceorls* of the early period a free or a servile class ? Two things are entirely certain : first, that the Anglo-Saxon *ceorls* were the *villani* of the Latin documents ; secondly, that the *villani* of the later Middle Ages were serfs. The point at issue is

* De illa patria quæ Angulus dicitur, et ab eo tempore usque hodie desertus inter provincias Jutorum et Saxonum perhibitur. Beda, *Hist. Eccl.* i. 15.

whether these *ceorls* were originally serfs, as Mr. Seebohm's theory would require, or became serfs by a gradual process of deterioration, as the common theory
holds. I shall endeavor to show : first, that the *ceorls* of
the early Anglo-Saxon period were freemen ; secondly,
that the *villani* of the later period were not always serfs,
there being found some survivals of their original free
condition.

The first thing to be noted is that, as has been already
pointed out, there was in the early Anglo-Saxon period a
class known by the name of *laet,* who were undoubtedly
serfs, the *lidi* of the continent. They had below them
the slaves, *esne* and *theow,* and above them the *ceorls.*
Now, as the *ceorls* certainly ranked above this servile class,
it may be assumed that they were themselves probably
free. This probability is made stronger by the consideration that the Saxons of the continent had a class of common freemen intermediate between the *lidi,* or serfs, and
the *edelingi,* or nobles, a class which has no representatives
among the Anglo-Saxons unless in the *ceorls,* the class
under consideration. This class upon the continent was
called *frilingi ;* and in Anglo-Saxon also we meet the *fri-
man* (freeman),* although this term is for the most part
superseded in the early Jutish laws by the Scandinavian
word *ceorls.*

The probability is, therefore, that the *ceorls* were a free
class. We will proceed, however, to examine the actual
uses of the word, in order to determine whether this
probability is sustained by facts. First, we will take up
the poem of Beowulf, a work which, whatever its date
and place of composition, unquestionably presents the
most ancient picture in existence of the institutions, condition, and manners and customs of the Anglo-Saxons.
In this poem I find the word *ceorl* six times. In none of

* *Leg. Æth.* 24, 27, 29, 31.

these is it applied to a servile class, or even used in a disparaging sense. Twice (vv. 416 and 2972) it is used of princes, in three cases (vv. 202, 908, 1591) of the people in general, and in the sixth case (v. 2444) of a man of the people. If it has one meaning that could apply to all these cases, it is perhaps *man*.*

We pass next to the Anglo Saxon codes of law. In the earliest of these laws, those of Ethelbert of Kent (about 600), *ceorl* is several times used as equivalent to *man* or even *husband*. It is also used to designate a legal class below the king and *eorl* (officer). The king's *mundbyrd* is placed at 50 shillings, the eorl's at 12, the ceorl's at 6. The ceorl was, therefore, a man of standing. He even had other men under his protection. Section 16 speaks of his cup-bearer, *birele;* section 25 of his *hlaf-aeta*, "loaf-eater," or dependent — the correlative of *hlaford* (lord), or "loaf-giver." The ceorl could therefore be the lord of another man. Section 17, following directly upon the mention of the ceorl's *mundbyrd* and *birele*, speaks of a *man's tun*, or estate, as it has before spoken of the king's and the ceorl's *tun*. Evidently, the *man* here is the *ceorl:* the ceorl could therefore have an estate of land.

The later laws of Kent contain nothing that adds to the evidence here given. The next stage in the inquiry is the Laws of Ine of Wessex, about 700; that is, about 100 years after those of Ethelbert, and 200 years after the first settlement of Wessex. In these laws we find clear recognition of the ceorls as a free class, inferior to the noble class of *sithcundmen*. The ceorl's fine for neglecting military duty is 30 shillings, that of the *sithcund man* being 60 or 120, according as he had land or not (§ 51). Now, by Germanic law none but freemen could

---

* It should be noticed that in the Rigsmal, the allegorical poem which treats of the origin of the Scandinavian classes, *Karl (Ceorl)* is the common freeman, "the red-haired and ruddy-cheeked lad with piercing eyes," whose sons were "Freeman and Braveman, Hold, Thane and Smith, Broadshoulders and Bonde [*Peasant*]," etc. The corresponding German word *Kerl* has a somewhat disparaging signification, while the English word *churl* is significant of the degradation which the class sustained in England.

render military service. Therefore, the ceorl was a free-man. Again, in accusations of homicide, he is placed in regard to compurgation on precisely the same footing with the *sithcundman* (§ 54). On the other hand, a certain degradation is clearly visible in the penalty of amputation of hand or foot, inflicted for certain offences (§§ 18, 37). It would appear also that the ceorl was already required, or at least expected, as he certainly was afterwards required, to have a lord: sections 37, 38, and 40 treat of the ceorl, and between them comes section 39, referring to "any one" running away from his lord — which would certainly seem to mean "any ceorl."

There is another passage of the Laws of Ine (§ 67) brought up by Mr. Seebohm as a proof of the existence of serfdom at this period, but which rather shows that it was in the process of introduction than that it was already existent. I give his translation: " If a man agrees for a yard-land or more at a fixed gafol (rent) and plough it, if the lord desire to raise the land to him *to work and to gafol* he need not take it upon him if the lord do not give him a dwelling." This statute testifies to the practice of exaction and encroachment by which tenants were converted into serfs, a process well attested at this very period in the Frank monarchy. It is clear that the peasants (assuming them to have been originally free) had already in large part been reduced from proprietors to tenants, the lands were rapidly being absorbed into large manorial estates, and by the same process their proprietors were becoming tenants: the next step was to convert them from free tenants into serfs.

At about this period — the close of the seventh century — belong the earliest (except three or four) of the charters and land grants, which exist in great abundance, and afford the most valuable material for the study of early English social and economical relations. In them we find that the grants consist regularly of estates with their tenants; * and the size of the estates is regularly estimated by tenants — *cassati, manentes, tributarii,* sometimes *mansa* and *hida,* all these terms being used as equivalent.† This shows that the peasants were at this time largely tenants upon the estates of others: it does not show that they were originally so, or that they were serfs. That they were still personally free, although upon the point of losing their freedom, is, I think, proved by the evidence which I have brought up: it is a fair inference, from the analogy of other Germanic nations, that their land was also originally their own; and this seems also to follow from the mention of the "mannes tun" (*Æth.* 17), when speaking of the ceorls.

After Ine's laws, of about the year 700, there is a gap of nearly two hundred years, until the time of Alfred, in which reign the series of statutes begins again, and continues in an unbroken succession until the conquest. The most important change noted in the new series of laws after this interval is the uniformity and reiteration with which it is required that every man must have a lord, and the rights of the lord are maintained against the caprice

---

*The charters in question begin in the reign of Ethelbert of Kent, the first Christian king, in the year 605. In all his charters the grants are merely of land: *aliquantulum telluris mei* (a little bit of my land), Thorpe's *Codex Diplomaticus,* No. 1; *aliquam partem terræ juris mei* (a certain part of the land under my jurisdiction), No. 2; *villam nomine Sturigao* (an estate named Sturigaw), No. 4. A charter of his son Eadbald (No. 5) says *quandam partem terræ regni mei, xxx aratrorum* (a certain part of the land of my kingdom, 30 plough-lands). It is not until the close of the century that the land is defined as of so many occupants: the first is (670) No. 7, *unum cassatum* (one cottager). From this time this is the universal method; but there are several expressions which show that it is still the land, reckoned in peasants' holdings, rather than the peasants themselves, that is conveyed by the grant. No. 8 (575) says *quandam terram . . . id est, decem manentes* (a certain piece of land . . . that is to say, ten tenants); No. 10, *terram . . . xviii manentes continentem* (land containing eighteen tenants); No. 12, *centum manentes qui adjacent civitati* (a hundred tenants adjoining the city); No. 33 (691), *terram . . . quadraginta quatuor cassatorum capacem* (land containing forty-four cottagers); No. 40, *quadraginta terræ illius manentes* (forty tenants of that land); and, especially, No. 20, *terra super verticem montis . . . est sub estimatione sex manentium* ('and on top of the mountain reckoned to be of six tenants). In all these cases it is clear that measurements of land are in question, and in the last instance it is apparently unoccupied land, roughly estimated in terms of peasant holdings.

† " . . . *terram septies quinos tributariorum jugera continentem. Est autem rus prædictum in quatuor villulis separatum . . . quinque manentium . . . decem cassatorum . . . decem mansionum . . . decem manentium.* Cod. Dipl. cxi.

of the man or the rivalry of other lords. *Omnis homo habeat advocatum suum* (every man shall have his surety), Edward, 1 : *non recipiat aliquis hominem alterius sine licentia illius* (no person shall receive the man of another without his permission), *id.* 7 — are regulations repeated in substance in nearly every body of laws. But, notwithstanding the rigid requirement of this submission to a lord, it appears that there still survived a certain freedom of choice in the act : *ne dominus libero homini hlafordsoknam interdicat* (let not the lord prohibit the free man to choose a lord). Here the free status of the man is clearly implied ; and in the laws of Alfred we have a number of provisions testifying to the law-worthiness and, therefore, original freedom of the peasants. *Si quis in ceorlisces mannes flet gefeohte,* i.e., *in rusticani hominis domus area pugnet* (if any one fights in the court of a ceorl). Section 40: *ceorli eodorbrece,* i.e., *rustici sepis fractio* (trespasses upon the enclosure of a ceorl), where the ceorl is placed on the same footing as the king, the bishop, the alderman, etc. Section 10 places the ceorl on the same legal footing with the twelfhynd and sexhynd men, who were thegns. Section 25 speaks of *ceorles mennen = ceorles mancipium* (the slave of a ceorl). Sections 11 and 35 are peculiarly significant, as they aim to protect the ceorl and his wife against personal violence, showing that, while they were still free in law, they were, nevertheless, on the road to serfdom, and were especially subject to abuse by the powerful.

We have thus followed the word *ceorl* and the class which it designates (the peasants) from the earliest times down to the time of Alfred, exactly the point of time which Mr. Seebohm reached, from the opposite direction. As he traced the manorial organization and a servile peasantry, step by step, from the time of Edward I. back to that of Alfred, so we have traced a class of free peasants from the time of the original conquest down to the reign

of Alfred, and have found it gradually subjected to re-
strictions and obligations which have converted it into a
servile or semi-servile class. Mr. Seebohm's serfs were
known as *villani*, the free peasants of the early period
were known as *ceorls*, and there is the most indisputable
evidence that these are the Latin and the Anglo-Saxon
names respectively for the same class. This class was
the peasantry, who by this evidence appear to have been
at first freemen, and afterwards serfs.

Undoubtedly there were manorial estates with serfdom,
in the earliest times, existing by the side of the townships
of free peasants, and following the same system of open
field husbandry. On the other hand, it appears clearly
that the entire class of peasants, or ceorls, was not reduced to servitude. We could not be surprised if no free
villani or free townships (*villæ*) were met with in the
records; for it was only the proprietary townships, or
manors (especially those belonging to ecclesiastical proprietors), which had a sufficiently systematic administration, and exercised sufficient care in the preservation of
documents, to afford adequate evidence as to their existence and condition. But, as a matter of fact, there is
clear evidence of free peasants and even of free townships
in the feudal period. For example, Alvarstoke in Hamp-
shire, at the time of Domesday Book (i. 41, b.), was held
by its own *villani* (*ceorls*), tenants of the convent of St.
Swithin, of Winchester. The number of *villani* was forty-
eight; and there were no slaves, or tenants of a lower
grade (*bordarii*). Two hundred years later their charter
was confirmed by the prior of Winchester, to the effect
"that they and their posterity (*sequela*) should be forever
free and quit from tallages, salt-rent, cherset of hens and
eggs and pannage of hogs; should be at liberty to make
wills and dispose of their children and avers [*averia* =
beasts]; ... all pleas except pleas of the crown should,
by consent of both parties, be pleaded and tried without

delay in the court of Alwarstoke, in the presence of the prior and his seneschal, according to the law and customs of England, and the usage of the free tenants of the country." This document is fortified by the seal of the community, given by Sir Frederic Madden in the Winchester volume of the Archæological Proceedings as : *Sigill: comune : hominum : prioris : Sci Swithuni : de Alwarestoke.* In 1841, an inquisition declares "that there are no traders in Alverstoke, and that all live by agriculture and hand labor." Melebroc (Millbrook) in the same county the Domesday record (i. 41, b.) gives as being held by *villani.* Of Ibthorpe we are told, "The people of Ibthorpe are lords of their own manor, and to this day exercise their manorial rights."* It is hard to explain these cases except as original village communities of free peasants, who, in losing the ownership of their land and becoming tenants, did not lose their freedom or their rights as a community.

I have shown that the Anglo-Saxon *ceorls,* or peasants, were in the sixth and seventh centuries — that is, the period directly following their migration to England — not serfs, but freemen, possessing houses, lands, serfs and slaves of their own; that at the end of the seventh century, the period of the Laws of Ine, they are still distinctly recognized as freemen, but as subject to certain exactions and encroachments on the part of the more powerful classes, which were reducing them to a semi-servile condition, in particular encouraging the practice of *commendation,* or placing themselves under the protection of a lord, and becoming his "men"; and that in the time of Alfred this practice of commendation had become universal and obligatory, and their servile condition distinctly recognized.

In short, the history of the English peasantry in the Anglo-Saxon period corresponds very closely to that of the same class upon the continent in the same period. In both England and Germany the free peasants appear

* *"Antiquary,* February, 1888.

to have been forced, by the disorders and distresses of society, to *commend* themselves, or seek the protection of men higher in station than themselves. The protection was not granted without some equivalent — service, following, surrender of land to be given back again as tenure, requirements of labor, becoming more and more onerous as the relation became more and more fixed, until at last they were stripped not only of their possessions, but even of personal freedom, and reduced to the state of complete serfdom — not so complete, however, in the case of the English peasants, but that the memory of their original freedom was preserved in the principle that it was only in relation to their lords that they were serfs, and that towards all others they were freemen, having well-defined rights before the law and a recognized place in the constitution.

VILLAGE COMMUNITY AND FEUDAL MANOR.*

THE problem to be solved is the conversion of the free village community into the feudal manor. The accepted theory says that this was accomplished by "encroachment on the part of some overgrown ceorl." Mr. Seebohm contends that there never was a free village community at all, but that the manors existed from the first, essentially as they were in feudal times. Mr. Earle accepts the free village community, but by its side, or in connection with it, the manorial system, as "part of the first plantation," and says that this theory ought to approve itself by "the luminous effect which new truth generally has in lighting up places that were dark." It is certainly so. Mr. Seebohm taught us to recognize the manorial feature which the accepted theory ignored ; but, on the other hand, he ignored the free elements of society. Mr. Earle has developed a theory which, in its general character, seems to reconcile perfectly the two contradictory systems.

The starting-point in this theory is Mr. Kemble's words : "There can be no doubt that some kind of military organization preceded the peaceful settlement, and in many respects determined its mode and character." The people of England, like the primitive Germans, were, on their first settlement, organized in military divisions, and the territorial areas which they occupied were based upon and determined by these military divisions : the territorial hundred was simply the district occupied by the numerical hundred. "Upon this military principle," Mr. Earle goes

* Extract from a review of Earle's " Hand-book to the Land-charters and other Saxonic Documents," in *The Nation*, vol. 47, p. 523 (December 27, 1888).

on (p. lv), "I conceive the English settlements were originally founded, that each several settlement was under a military leader, and this military leader is the ancestor of the lord of the manor"—the *tiane* of the later Anglo-Saxon period being the connecting link between the two. "The military officer, settled with a suitable provision by the side of his company, is the lord by the side of the free owners" (p. lxii). This theory commends itself as well by its simplicity as by the completeness with which it explains the evolution of the manor. But when we carry the inquiry further into detail, and ask with what Anglo-Saxon class we are to identify these military leaders, the question becomes more complicated and the answer more uncertain. Mr. Earle's suggestion may be the right one: it has much in its favor, but, on the other hand, leaves some difficulties to be explained. This theory is that the *gesithas* of the early Anglo-Saxon laws, the *comites* of Tacitus, were the officers of the invading army, and that they, settling "with a suitable provision" of land by the side of their free companions, became a kind of "local police officer. In the Laws of Ine it is assumed and implied that there is in every township a gesith. This is a universal institution: the local administration of public order rests everywhere upon the gesithas" (p. lxviii).

This assertion is more positive than the evidence will warrant. The Laws of Ine do not say a word about townships in connection with the gesithas; nor do they in any explicit or certain way attribute to them any police powers. One of the three passages cited (Ine, 50), must certainly be omitted, as the word *inhiwan*, rendered "community," is in the Latin translation *familia*, and in Schmidt's Glossary *der Familie angehörig*. The passage (23, 1) which gives the gesith a share of the fines need not necessarily imply "a magisterial privilege," but may mean that the king shares the fines with his followers. The obligation upon the gesith (30) to pay his wergeld is most naturally explained, as not for the misdemeanor of the ceorl, but for a similar misdemeanor on his own part. This is, at any rate, the only passage which can with any probability be made to support Mr. Earle's view, and this is too obscure to be relied upon with any confidence. On the other hand, the gesithas are distinctly mentioned (Withred, 5; Ine, 50, 63, 68) as a class of dependent followers.

Again, the *comites* of Tacitus — with whom these gesithas should unquestionably be identified, as Mr. Earle, following Kemble, holds — do not appear to correspond to the officers of an army, but to the suite or personal retinue of the chief. This is not by itself a conclusive objection, as such members of a staff, as we may call them, might easily have been assigned to duty as division commanders; but there is no indication that this was the case. They lived in the household of the chief, and served in his company as horsemen, being apparently the cavalry described in the sixth chapter of the *Germania*. But the infantry of the Germans, as is shown in this and the following chapter, was made up of family groups, and, it is natural to suppose, was commanded by the heads of these family groups. This was the German people in arms: the chief and his followers were an excrescence. We should say that Mr. Earle's military leaders, the ancestors of the lords of the manor, were more likely to be these heads of families than the personal followers of the king or chief. It may be observed, further, that this theory of the police functions of the gesith conflicts with the generally accepted doctrine of the mutual responsibility of the *mægth*, or kindred, while this mutual responsibility would be naturally and easily associated with the heads of the family groups.

If there was any class of officers over the free tribesmen other than the heads of their families, we should incline to think that it was the *eorls*, a class which Mr.

Earle, like almost every recent writer, regards as "nobles," but, as we think, without sufficient reason. It is surprising how slight is the ground for this now accepted view. Mr. Earle confesses (p. lxviii), "I do not know that a clear instance of EORL in this original sense can be found after the Laws of Æthelbert, though there are many passages where it might seem so to the unwary reader." If there are no passages after the Laws of Æthelberht, there are certainly none in these laws ; for they mention the eorls only twice (chaps. 13 and 14), in speaking of an eorl's *tun* (town or farmstead), and *birele* (handmaid), in a connection which might quite as well mean an officer as a noble. This word is found in no laws before the tenth century (where it is admitted to have had a different meaning), except the laws of Kent. Now, the settlers of Kent were Jutes (that is, akin to the Scandinavians) ; and the Earls of Kent must of course have been the same as the Scandinavian Jarls, who were appointed officers, not an hereditary nobility. Indeed, a speech of Withred of Kent, in the Saxon Chronicle, says that the king appointed his *corlas*.

We are inclined to think, therefore, that Mr. Earle is mistaken in making the gesithas to have been township officers. Their relation to their chief makes it improbable ; the Laws of Ine do not clearly support it ; and it is much more likely that the officers of the infantry were the heads of their own families, or, if appointed, were the eorls. Mr. Earle is himself embarrassed (p. lxxx) by the mention in the Laws of Ine (chap. 51) of two classes of gesith — the one land-owners, the other having no land. He understands "by the latter such gesithas as had no family estate, whether ethel or bookland, but were provided for in the common field." A much more natural interpretation is to compare them with the two classes of *vassi* mentioned in a capitulary of 825 : one, *qui in nostro palatio serviunt ;* the other, *qui beneficia nostra habent.*

Whether Mr. Earle is right or wrong in this particular point, it must be admitted that his theory gives a perfect explanation of the origin of the class of thanes, or country gentlemen, as derived out of these natural heads of the village communities. Not that there was any absolute uniformity in the matter. The common theory admits that there may have been manorial estates (eorls' tuns?) intermixed with the free communities; and Mr. Earle admits (p. lxxvi) that there were, at least afterwards, lord-less free communities. And it should be noted that his theory requires on the part of the head of the community a process of encroachment such as that usually ascribed to the "overgrown ceorl," by which he was converted into the lord of the manor. We must not forget, too, that we have distinct testimony to the latter process in the provisions of "Peoples' Ranks and Law," by which it is said a ceorl might become a thane; and of "Wer-gelds," where it is said that he may become "of gesith-cund race."

We think Mr. Earle is mistaken (p. 63) in making the Court Baron "the original court of the free settlers under a president." The Court Baron had no president of its own, but was necessarily presided over by the lord of the manor or his steward. It is true that Sir Henry Maine, Professor Freeman, and Bishop Stubbs make the Court Baron to have been "the ancient gemot of the township"; but this is because they considered the free tenants of the feudal period to have been the survivors of the free proprietors of the early period, while, in fact, they seem only to have made their appearance after Domesday Book, and to have been an integral part of the feudal institution of the manor. The Court Leet, an absolutely democratic institution, and, according to Ritson and Elton, the most ancient court in the land, may probably be identified with the original assembly of the free township — the prototype of the New England town meeting. Neither can we accept Mr. Earle's distinction between *township* and *vill.* *Vill* — a mere abbreviation of *villata* — is the Latin equivalent of *township*, and is regularly so used in mediæval documents.

While, however, we cannot — at least, with our present light — agree with Mr. Earle in regarding the *gesithas* as the antecedents of the lords of manors, we gladly recognize that he has put us on the right track. He has given us the key to the problem, even if he has not himself solved it.

TOWN, TOWNSHIP, AND TITHING.*

THE town is in many respects the most characteristic institution of the political system of the Northern States of the American Union, and of the primitive constitution of the English people. It may be defined as a territorial district, the inhabitants of which compose a body politic, small enough to allow the immediate participation of all its citizens in the government of its local concerns, and forming an organic part of the structure of the State. Its powers of local self-government are not original and inherent, but derived from the larger body of which it forms a part. They are, nevertheless, substantial and permanent, in this respect differing from those of the school districts or wards into which the town or city is divided. The city under our system is only a larger and specially organized town : the incorporated village of New York and the West is a peculiar addition to the town system, not forming structurally a part of it.

The town, as thus defined, is peculiar to England and

* From Transactions of the Wisconsin Academy of Sciences, Arts, and Letters (1885), vol. 7, p. 141.

Professor Allen first brought to the attention of the American people the significance of Nasse's treatise, showing the existence of the village community in England; and offered the fruitful suggestion that many points in the land tenure of New England indicated a similar condition of land community to that described by Nasse. In this note (*The Nation*, September 22, 1870) he also said, "It would be worth while to examine how far the early settlers in this country were influenced by the traditions and surviving remnants of this system, and how far, on the other hand, similar causes led to similar results." Sir Henry Maine called attention to these American forms of collective ownership in his work on "Village Communities," which appeared the following year.

In *The Nation* of January 10, 1878, Professor Allen presented a study of land community still existing upon the island of Nantucket, at the same time pointing out, with his characteristic caution, that "the Massachusetts community system may have been merely the natural outgrowth of the circumstances, and not even an involuntary copying of the institutions of Old England." He added a characteristic illustration drawn from his own experience by saying that "an interesting example of a community in cultivation, which might possibly have developed into community of ownership, was afforded by the freedmen of the Sea Islands of South Carolina during the war." This article is republished as the last article in the present volume.— EDS.

the United States, and, in its complete development, to the New England States. In all the other Germanic countries the territorial division corresponding to the town stopped short of an independent political life, being, from the point of view of the State, nothing but a private corporation for economical purposes, with only inchoate functions as a body politic. In all these countries the hundred was the smallest district of a public character, just as in our Southern States the county is the agent of local self-government. But the county and the hundred are too large to allow the immediate participation of all the citizens in the transaction of public business. The communities in which these large districts are the only agent of local self-government are necessarily aristocratic in their political character. It was the growth of feudalism, or the establishment of centralized monarchies, in the Germanic countries of the continent, that checked the development of an institution corresponding to the English town. In England the growth of a landed aristocracy and of a centralized monarchical power was not early or rapid enough to kill the germs of local self-government, although they seriously interfered with its development.

The political functions of the English towns were so largely obscured during the Middle Ages by the manorial or feudal organizations to which they were subjected that there have arisen some doubts as to their extent, and even their existence. Bishop Stubbs, in his "Constitutional History of England" (vol. i. p. 82), asserts that (in Anglo-Saxon times) "the unit of the constitutional machinery is the township, the *villata* or *vicus.*" This is the view which I have already presented; but a review of Stubbs' work in the *North American Review* (July, 1874), understood to be by the then editor of the *Review,* Professor Henry Adams, takes exception to the assertion, saying that the township has no constitutional functions "of any kind, sort, or description"; that the unit of the constitutional machinery in England, as on the continent, was the hundred. "The one permanent Germanic institution," he says, "was the hundred. The one code of Germanic law was Hundred law, much of which is now the common law of England. The Hundred and its law survived all the storms which wrecked dynasties and Witan. It was the foundation of the judicial constitution under the conqueror as it had been under Cnut and Alfred." The same view is repeated in Professor Adams' "Essays on Anglo-Saxon Law," p. 32.

That the hundred was the lowest political division in Germany, as Professor Adams asserts, admits of no doubt. This fundamental fact, together with the non-political character of the lower territorial divisions, is perhaps best formulated by Sohm,* who points out that the local governments in Germany were purely private corporations, having no public character or functions. But it does not follow that what was true of Germany was necessarily true of England. England, although a Germanic country, received in many respects a different development from Germany; and it is the essence of Bishop Stubbs' position that this was the case with the territorial organization below the hundred. As the word "town" (*tun, tunscip*) is peculiar to England, so, it may be, is the thing designated by it. This distinction is supported by von Maurer, the writer of highest authority upon the genesis of local institutions, who, in his "Einleitung zur Geschichte der Mark, Hof, Dorf, und Stadtverfassung" (§ 145, p. 332), asserts that the English institutions differed fundamen-

---

*The following passage expresses Sohm's theory with great fulness: "Zum grossen Nachtheil der Gesammtauffassung nicht blos der Verhältnisse des fränkischen Reiches, sondern der gesammten mittel-alterlichen Entwickelung wird die Thatsache in der Regel übersehen, dass, der Reichsverfassung der fränkischen wie der deutschen, eine Ortsgemeindeverfassung unbekannt ist. Die Reichsverfassung kennt keine weiteren Zwecke ausser denjenigen, deren Realisirung in Gau und Hundertschaft vor sich geht. . . . Die Ortsgemeindeverfassung ist aus keinem anderen Grunde local für jede Ortsgemeinde verschieden, als weil die Ortsgemeindeverfassung aus der autonomen Entwickelung der einzelnen Gemeinden hervorgegangen ist. Die Ortsgemeindeverfassung ist Verfassung nur kraft Corporationsrechts, nicht kraft Reichsrechts."—*Sohm, Altdeutsche Reichs und Gerichtsverfassung,* i. p. 231.

tally from the German in this respect. When, therefore
Professor Adams says that such an institution as the one
in question "would be quite at variance with all that we
know of German law," he appears to stretch the argument
from analogy further than is warranted. The very question
at issue is whether the development of English institutions
did not upon this point depart from German analogy.

I shall speak first of the territorial character of the
English towns, and then of their political character ; and
shall try to show that we are to seek for analogies with
them, not so much in the institutions of Germany, from
which those of England were in a sense derived, as in
those of New England, which are simply a continuation
of those of England.

That the towns in England formed a complete territorial system as subdivisions of the hundreds needs no
argument, as it is amply attested by mediæval writers
and documents. It is a familiar fact that they were regularly represented in the courts of the hundred and the
shire. I will also cite the authority of Chief Justice
Fortescue, in his *De Laudibus Legum Angliæ*, who says that
the Shires or Counties were divided into Hundreds, and
the Hundreds into Towns or Vills (chap. xxiv.). *Hundreda
vero dividuntur per villas.* This language indicates clearly
that "towns" were, in the middle of the fifteenth century,
territorial divisions of the hundreds ; that is, that the
entire area of the hundred, and therefore of the county,
was divided up into the areas of the several towns composing the hundred. And this is still further shown by
his going on to say that under the appellation of towns
"the cities and boroughs are included. For the boundaries of these vills are not ascertained by walls, buildings,
or streets, but by a compass of fields, large districts of
land, some hamlets, and divers other limits, as rivers,
watercourses, woodlands, and wastes of commons." It is
evidently the intention of the writer in these words to

contrast the English towns with some other towns the
bounds of which are determined not by natural objects,
but by artificial ones ; and this object of comparison can
be only the walled towns and cities of the continent,
especially of France, the country with which Fortescue
constantly compares England. Attention is here drawn
to the important fact that, whereas upon the continent the
municipal system was sporadic, the open country having
no institutions of local self-government proper, the English
municipal system was continuous, embracing the entire
territory of the country. The borough was, as Bishop
Stubbs says (vol. i. p. 92), "simply a more strictly organized
form of the township," and the city a bishop's seat, with
borough organization. And both borough and city made,
as Chief Justice Fortescue says, a part of the town system.

This town system was brought over to this country by
our ancestors, and put in operation in all the northern
colonies. The town system of New England, as a system
of territorial areas, is the town system of mediæval England ; and, when the people of New England had outgrown
the town system in its primitive form, they developed a
new form of organization on precisely the same lines as
the English. The New England "city" (and so the Penn-
sylvania "borough") is simply a specially organized town,
and forms a part of the town system, just as is the case
with the boroughs and cities of Chief Justice Fortescue's
definition. A city is territorially a town. And here, as in
the case of so many so-called Americanisms, we have preserved the old English usage, which has disappeared in
England itself. The town, in its ecclesiastical organization, was a "parish"; and in the sixteenth century the
parish organization began to supersede the co-ordinate
town organization for purposes of local self-government.*
It would seem that in the seventeenth century, when this

---

* See Gneist's "History of the English Constitution," vol. ii. p. 196. As this great
writer is wont to depreciate the popular elements in the English constitution, it is not surprising that he does not recognize the town, *villata*, as a regular part of the machinery of government in the Middle Ages.

country was settled, this process had not been completed. The colonists brought with them both institutions, and — as all New Englanders know — the parish and the town were, as a rule, identical in New England as in Old England. But while in New England the ecclesiastical organization became quite secondary, and has now practically disappeared, in Old England the reverse was the case. The parish organization has crowded out that of the town. As an English correspondent writes me: "With us town = market town" — a specially privileged, and I suppose specially organized, class of towns. The towns of the open country are known as parishes; and the functions of local self-government, so far as they continue to be kept up, are administered by the vestry, or parish assembly. Still, even now we find a survival of the old usage. The same correspondent writes: "I am talking with the squire. The church bell sounds, and I ask him if he knows why. He replies, 'For a parish meeting, I suppose.' Again, in a conversation with a laborer, to the same question he will reply, 'For a town meeting, I suppose, sir.'" Here the primitive term has lingered among the peasantry, while it has been dropped by the aristocracy.

The transition from town to parish, and the equivalency of the terms, as well as the fact of local self-government, to be considered further on, are illustrated by local documents. For example, in the reign of Edward VI., under the influence, I suppose, of the radical reformation of the Church favored by that monarch, we have a record of a large amount of church plate and other property sold in the eastern counties, by the authority, as it is stated, sometimes of the town, and sometimes of the parish, showing that the two terms are employed as identical. For example: "Barkinge. Certifficat of Church wardens there. We present that we have solde by the consente of thole paryshe a crosse parcell gylte, etc. . . . to Robert Knappe and Roger Hylle of the same towne." "Beccles

. . . solde anno primo Edwardi sexti Regis etc, by the Townshype and Churchewardens so moch plate as amounteth to the some of xll." *East Anglian*, May, 1885. "Churchwardens of Martillesham. . . . goods sold by the said churche Revies and other the hoole Inhitants of the said towne." *Id.*, March, 1887. This last instance appears to show an identity of the church wardens with the mediæval reeve. At a later date we find the village of Exning (Suffolk), which at the close of the sixteenth century "appears," says the correspondent who mentions it, "to have been dignified with the title of 'Town,' namely:—

"1590.

"'Item. pd the xx daye of Aprill for a quarter of wyne for the TOWN xij. d. etc.'" *Id.*, March, 1888.

It will be noticed that in these extracts the words "town" and "township" are used interchangeably. This was the case also in the early history of New England. For example, in the Massachusetts Body of Liberties (1641) we find "town" in Articles 16, 50, 51, 57, 62, and 85; "township" in Articles 66, 68, and 84, used with no apparent distinction of meaning. Article 74 couples them together — "the freemen of every town or township." We can perhaps trace a disposition to use the word "town" when speaking of the corporate body, and "township" for territory; *e.g.*, Article 78, where it is forbidden to expend "any town treasure but by the freemen of that township." At present I believe the word "township" is not in use in New England, except occasionally to designate the town from the point of view of the territorial area; never as a body politic. Curiously enough, it is this word, fastened upon by De Tocqueville, that is regularly used by foreign writers to describe the New England *town* system. The term "*township* system" is properly used in this country only for the six-mile square divisions of the public lands, laid out by the government surveys. The States erected out of these public lands have a *town* system of their own, parallel with the national *township* system, and generally coinciding with it in respect to division lines, but not always. For example, the town of Trempealeau, Wis., contains the whole of Township 19, N., Range 9, W., and parts of Townships 17 and 18, Range 9, and 18 and 19, Range 10. In the primitive Anglo-Saxon usage the word " township," *tunscip*, appears to have been regularly used to designate the town as a municipality ; while " town," *tun*, was the settled portion — what in New England is called the " village," or the " middle of the town."

This distinction is quite in accordance with the etymology of the word. It is well known that " town," *tun*, is the same word with the German *zaun*, hedge or fence. But, while the Germans never used the word *zaun* to designate the enclosed (fenced in) area, the Anglo-Saxons, on the other hand, never used the word *tun* except to designate this enclosed area, the primitive meaning of *enclosing body* having been entirely lost. Now, the thing fenced in was the village, or group of houses, which was accordingly the *tun ;* and the *tunscip*, or township, was the area of land which belonged with the village as a municipal organization. As a consequence, the word *tun* was popularly applied to any place of collective residence ; as where the Saxon Chronicle (Land Ms. An. 584) says : *Ceawlin manige tunas genam* — " Ceawlin took many towns." In the course of time the word *town* appears to have crowded out the more strictly correct word *township*, in the sense of designating the territorial area as a municipality ; and in this sense the word was brought to New England by the colonists of the seventeenth century. In this country the meaning of the word is precisely that of Fortescue's time. In England, on the other hand, the modern use appears to be a survival of the loose and popular early usage, as applying to any place of collective residence, being limited in England at the present day to large places.

In limiting the signification of the word *tun*, to designate, not the object which encloses (its primitive meaning), but the space enclosed, the Anglo-Saxon agrees with the Scandinavian language, as is the case with so many words and institutions of the early Anglo-Saxon period. The definition of the Icelandic *tun*, as given by Vigfussen, is: "a hedged or fenced plot, enclosure within which a house is built; then the farm-house with its buildings, the homestead." This is precisely the meaning which the word has in the earliest Anglo-Saxon laws, those of Æthelbert of Kent: it will be recollected that the settlers of Kent were Jutes (that is, Scandinavians) rather than Saxons, like the rest of the migratory tribes. In these laws we read of a king's *tun* (chap. 5), an eorl's *tun* (chap. 13), and a "*mannes tun*" (chap. 17), in all which cases *tun* is clearly the hedged enclosure, the homestead.* From the fenced enclosure of an individual homestead or field to that of a village, as in the later laws, is an easy step; or, rather, the two uses are alike easy transitions from the original signification of the enclosing fence or hedge.

This further extension of the word, however, does not appear to have been made by the Scandinavians of the continent any more than by the Germans. None of the Teutonic nations of the continent appear to have had any territorial subdivision of the hundred, of a substantial, individual, public character. With them the hundred was the unit of the constitutional machinery, and any lesser subdivisions stood to the hundred very much as our school districts or wards do to our towns or cities — as mere shifting administrative districts, having no substantial powers and not forming a body politic. Scholars are now agreed, as I have already said, that the *Dorfschaft* was a division of a purely secondary character, for agricultural and economical purposes. Nevertheless, it corresponded

---

* This signification appears to have survived in Scotland; as, in Scott's "Redgauntlet," Letter XI., where Darsie Latimer expresses a doubt whether he ought to go to Redgauntlet's "town" in disguise, the context showing that it is only his house that is meant.

closely in its origin to the English *township*, and might, except for the early feudalization of Germany, have attained an equal degree of independence. *Dorf*, village, is the exact equivalent in meaning (not in etymology) of the English *tun*, and the affix *schaft* is the English *scip*, so that "township" is in meaning precisely the German *Dorfschaft.**

From the territorial character of the English township, we pass to the consideration of its political character, as "the unit of the constitutional machinery." Direct evidence for this is not very abundant, but seems to be entirely sufficient. I have already spoken of Chief Justice Fortescue's mention of town (*villa*) as an integral part of the hundred, just as the hundred was an integral part of the shire. It is important also to note the well-known fact that the town (*villata*) was throughout the mediæval period the unit of representation †—and that not as a mere representative district, but as a body politic; for at this period representation was never of artificial divisions, but of corporate bodies. This is clearly a political or constitutional function. Such phrases as "by the consent of the saide Township" and "with the consent of the hole Towne," in the sales of church property mentioned above, imply organized and collective action — an assembly or "town meeting" of some sort.

That the township lacked the higher judicial powers is admitted by Bishop Stubbs, who says (p. 90): "Their assemblies are rather gemots, or meetings, than proper courts; for any contentious proceedings amongst men so closely connected and so few in number must have been carried immediately to the hundred court." That the township did have a gemot, or meeting, is proved by the

---

* The German city of the Middle Ages was created not like the English borough, by giving higher powers to an aready existing organism, but by cutting out a section of territory and bestowing upon it public functions of a municipal character. See articles by Von Below, *Historische Zeitschrift*, 1888.

† *Per quatuor legaliores homines de qualibet villata* (Assize of Clarendon, 1).

mention of a *tunscipesmot* in a charter of Richard I., and
that this meeting had certain definite powers of self-government, apart from its function as a unit of representation, is shown, for example, by the Costomary of Tetten-
hall Regis ("English Gilds," p. 432), a body of regulations
or "bye-laws" made by the tenants of the manor at their
Leet, or Law-day. This Costomary is a complete body of
laws for the government of the community; and in the
body of these laws the word "town" is twice used to
designate the manor in its public relations.

"Art. 19. No man shall make yates or gapes in the
common field, upon the corne or grasse of his neighbors,
but by the consent of [the] comonty; and, if he do, he
shall give to the lord 2s., and to the comonty of the
towne 2s."

"Art. 21. No man of oure towne shall enter upon the
stubble of any other towne while the corne is upon the
ground, except it is upon his own land, and by the good
will of all his neighbors, under payne of iijs. to the lord."

In the passages just cited we have "town" used as
equivalent to "manor," just as in those previously cited
it was used as equivalent to "parish." The manor was
the feudalized township; that is, the township converted
into a fief, as the parish was the township regarded as an
ecclesiastical organization. And just as in the sixteenth
century the parish, or ecclesiastical organization, superseded the township, so in the Middle Ages the manorial or
feudal organization superseded, or at any rate obscured,
the township, the original municipal division. This process of feudalization, or converting a free township into a
seignorial estate, began very early in the Anglo-Saxon
period. Indeed, even on the assumption that England
was colonized by free peasants, organizing in free townships, we must at the same time admit the probability of
a considerable proportion of seignorial townships, or manorial estates, side by side with the free communities, and

intermixed with them. And, whatever may have been the original status, it is certain that long before the Norman conquest there remained very few self-governing townships, composed of free peasants.* I do not consider the king's, eorl's, and man's *tun* of Æthelbert's Laws to have been feudalized townships, at least not always or necessarily: they appear rather to have been farmsteads. But fifty years later the charters of the *Codex Diplomaticus* afford ample evidence of towns which were the private property of the king or powerful noblemen, the peasants, or *ceorls*, being their tenants and fast becoming their serfs, as I showed in my paper of last year.

The twofold process here described, of converting the free townships into manorial estates and the free peasants into servile tenants upon those estates, was consummated in the complete feudalization of England, which followed the Norman conquest. Nevertheless, the town organization was not obliterated, but only obscured. We have seen that it continued to serve as a basis for representation; and we have frequent mention of the town, *villa*, as the equivalent of the manor. The word *villa* is used about a dozen times in Domesday Book, at least three of these times as equivalent to manor; *e.g.* (i. f. 199 b.): "Wluuin the thane held this manor. In the same town Reginald holds half a hide of Alberic." (So ii. 31 and 31 b.) The Exeter Domesday and the Ely Inquest, documents which appear to be the rough draft from which the great record was made up, often use the word *villa* where the Exchequer Domesday says *manerium*, "manor." † But the two words are not used as equivalent, but rather as describing the same territorial area from different points of view. There might have been two manors in the same vill, or lands in the vill which were independent of the manor. Indeed, it would naturally be the case that the

---

* For example, see paper upon Village Communities and Serfdom in England, *ante*.

† The Ely Inquest rests upon the evidence, among others, of *sex villani uniuscujusque villæ*.

manor would often vary from the town in respect to metes and bounds, while the parish, or ecclesiastical organization, would, like the town itself, be an unchangeable district. The manor, being a piece of private property, would be subject to the laws of private property, and would be divided, added to, or diminished, through the processes of purchase, sale, inheritance, and intermarriage. So greatly have these processes changed the boundaries of manors that it is stated that in East Kent there is only one manor coextensive with the parish. (*Academy*, No. 167.) We find, however, instances of this identification of manor and town as late as the sixteenth and seventeenth centuries. In the "Certificates of Church Goods in Suffolk," in the reign of Edward VI., is mentioned "Mr. Sakford, lorde and patron of the Towne," evidently lord of the manor. In the time of the Civil Wars (1648), the Memoirs of Colonel Hutchinson speak of Cromwell having "a design, by insinuating himself into Colonel Saunders, to flatter him into the sale of a town of his called Ireton" (ii. 137).

When the town was feudalized and became a manor, its *gemot*, or meeting, seems to have become that branch of the manorial court known as the Court Leet. The Court Leet, found also in the hundred and the borough, was, as is shown by the example given above, an assembly for the passing of by-laws and administering the affairs of the town, the precise prototype of the New England town meeting. It also had a limited police jurisdiction, held to be derived from that of the Sheriff's Tourn or Leet of the hundred. It was not a necessary part of the feudal or manorial organization, but "was created by special grants from the crown to certain lords of manor, in order that they might administer justice to their tenants at home." Quoted by Elton, "Custom and Tenant Right" (1882), p. 89. It was a thoroughly democratic institution, "being regarded as the court of the residents within the district, not of the tenants of the manor"; and "so far is this carried that a stranger passing by may be compelled to serve on the leet jury. The fact of his being found within the district is deemed sufficient evidence." Digby, Int. to the Law of Real Property, p. 45. The Leet, as a popular court, is also found in Iceland during the Middle Ages. The antiquity and primitive character of this court is attested by Elton, who says (on Copyholds, p. 240), it "is, in all probability, older than the manorial system itself"; and by Ritson, "The Jurisdiction of the Court Leet," who says (p. 6), " The Leet is the most ancient court in the land." This court elected the constable, and, in some boroughs, the mayor (*id.* p. 10).

It is not surprising, considering their early and almost universal conversion into manorial estates, that we find so few traces of free townships in England. From their absence, Mr. Seebohm has attempted to establish the thesis that the townships of England were regularly manorial estates, and the peasants serfs, from the earliest settlement of the Anglo-Saxons in the country. "The evidence of the earliest Saxon and Jutish laws," he says, "thus leaves us with a strong presumption, if not actual certainty, that the Saxon *ham* or *tun* was the estate of a lord, and not of a free village community." ("English Village Communities," p. 175.) I attempted in my paper, read a year ago, to show that, with regard to the peasantry, his evidence was inadequate, and that we have good ground for affirming the existence of a large class of free peasants in the earliest time. My object in the present paper has been to continue the argument, and show that there is good reason to believe that there were free townships as well as a free peasantry in the earliest English period. In arguing, however, that the township was a body politic, and "the unit of the constitutional machinery," I would not be understood to claim for it original and self-existent autonomy, even in the period of the earliest evolution of institutions. Assuming that the

Germanic peoples passed from a community of occupation based upon kinship to one based upon territorial relations, it was the hundred, not the township, that formed the earliest territorial community, or *Markgenossenschaft*. The township, or *Dorfschaft*, is shown by Thudichum to have been formed out of the hundred by a process of subdivision ; and in this process the German district thus formed succeeded to no integral share of the powers of the original organization, but stood to it as ward to a city. The English district corresponding to it, on the other hand, became an autonomous community, with substantial and important, if not original, powers.

The English town has, therefore, no counterpart in any other Germanic nation ; for in all the other Germanic nations the unit of the constitutional machinery is the hundred, a district too large to allow of this immediate and detailed exercise of local self-government which we find in the New England towns, and, as has been made to appear, in those of England. Much less has it any counterpart in the Celtic and Slavonic nations, which never advanced unassisted to the territorial principle of government ; nor in the Romance nations, whose government, derived from that of the later Roman Empire, was wholly summary and authoritative. On the other hand, the ancient Greeks and Italians — the only branches of the Aryan race which possessed an equally strong political sense with the Germanic — developed a territorial system which has a strong analogy with the English.

The City (*civitas*, πόλις) is the political type of the Greeks and Italians, as the Town is of the English ; and, while the two institutions diverged greatly in their development, they were essentially identical in their origin and structure. The Greeks, Italians, and Germans alike passed from the social stage of institutions, based upon personal relations, to the political, based upon territory, at a very early period. In all of these we find the territory divided

up into autonomous districts, small enough in extent to
permit the direct participation of all the citizens in the
work of government. The Greek City was thus identical
with the German Hundred. But the development of all
the Germanic nations, except the English, was arrested by
the creation of great centralized monarchies. Even in
England the more perfectly organized district, the Town,
was shortly checked in its development by the establishment of the manorial system ; and even where a higher
municipal type was developed, in the boroughs, it was
sporadic, and thus incomplete.

The Greeks and Italians, on the other hand, concentrated and intensified their political life by what is known
as *Synoikismos* — the establishment in the middle of the
territory of each city of an *oppidum*, or *urbs*, a place of
collective residence, surrounded by walls, in which were
erected their public buildings, and where they transacted
all public and private business. This higher organization
was applied to *all* cities, not merely to some here and
there, like the English boroughs. These nations became
urban in their life, while the English remained rural.
But, in becoming urban, in building a city surrounded
with walls for residence, trade, worship, and social life,
they did not shift the basis of their political organization.
The city continued, as it had always done, to comprise
the rural districts as well as the walled town ; citizenship,
indeed, was based upon ownership of land outside the
walls equally with residence or property within the walls ;
the distinction between *rus* and *urbs* was purely social, in
no sense political Now, the *oppidum*, enclosed within
its walls, is very much the same thing as the *tun*, enclosed with a hedge — a higher development upon the
same general lines. But there was one point of contrast
of vital moment. The Greek or Italian city, even if of no
greater extent and population than an English town, was
a sovereign state : the English town, however large and

populous, was only a municipality, a part of a larger organism.

The word that is used in the Latin documents of the Middle Ages as meaning "town" is *villa* (or *villata*) — a word that has had a curious and interesting history. In classical Latin it means a country house — whether a farm-house, *villa rustica*, or a gentleman's country seat, *villa urbana*, in which sense it corresponds precisely to our modern word, *villa*. From meaning "house" it came, by a not long or difficult transition, to mean the "estate" surrounding the house; and in this sense we find the word used in the later Roman Empire. This was a period of great landed properties; but these properties, at least in Gaul, were not "plantations," *latifundia*, or vast and indefinite stretches of land, like the Dalrymple farm. Each great property was made up of a number of *villas*, not necessarily contiguous, each of these *villas* being a compact, organized estate of a moderate size. The small peasants' estates had, for the most part, disappeared; and Gaul at this epoch may be described as divided up into seignorial or domanial estates, corresponding roughly to the *communes*, or smallest territorial divisions of modern France. These *villas* agreed, in many important particulars, with the English manors, being, perhaps, of about the same extent, and being ruled autocratically by their owners.

The important fact to be noted here is the change in the significance of the word *villa*. From meaning a gentleman's country house, it has come to mean the estate depending upon that house; that is to say, it has acquired the meaning of a territorial district. And, although the district thus designated in Gaul is a seignorial estate, it is easy, when the word has once become associated with the idea of an area of land, to extend its use to other districts of similar extent and grade. Thus we find it applied even on the continent to the *Dorfschaft*, or village mark; * and in England it is used to designate the town-

* Van der Kindere, *Notice sur l'Origine des Magistrats Communaux.*

ship, whether free or seignorial. But that it is the township that is thus designated as a territorial area, and not the seignorial estate into which the township has been converted, is proved by the important fact, already noticed, that the manor and the township (*villa*) are not always identical. No argument, therefore, for the originally servile character of the English *tun* can be drawn from the fact that *tun* is in Latin *villa;* for, although in Gaul a *villa* was a seignorial estate, in England it was not the estate as such, but an area of land often identical with the manor, but often containing two or more manors, or parts of manors, or isolated pieces of land.

Thus the word *villa*, having acquired the signification of a territorial area, was used in England as the Latin equivalent of *tunscip*. And as *villa* was " *town*," whether free or seignorial, so the cognate word *villanus* was "townsman," whether free or serf. It is used regularly as the Latin equivalent of " ceorl," the free peasant of the early period, the semi-servile peasant of the later period, and the *villein* of the feudal period. When the ceorls lost their ownership of land and their free status, their name sinking from the designation of a free yeoman to the opprobrious term "churl": so the equivalent word *villanus* sank likewise, until it too, from meaning a free townsman, a member of the body politic, came to mean one who lived upon the land of another man who was his master, paying for it by obligatory labor. And, as "ceorl" has sunk to "churl," so the honorable term *villanus* has sunk to the opprobrious term *villain*.

A few words in conclusion, upon a subject more obscure in itself and of more purely antiquarian interest — the connection of *tithing* and *township*. The word *tithing* is used as equivalent to *township* in some of the southern counties of England at the present day * ; and it has been a matter of some controversy what is the origin of this

* Stubbs, Const. Hist. i. 85.

territorial signification of the word, and how far back in time it dates. For the discussion of this question I will refer to Prof. H. B. Adams' excellent paper in the Johns Hopkins Studies, vol. i., No. 4. It is admitted that there is no positive evidence of any but the numerical use of the word *tithing* in Anglo-Saxon times, as designating a group of ten men — *tenmanne tale* (Edv. Conf. xx.) — formed for the purpose of enforcing mutual responsibility, as the fundamental principle of the system of the time for the preservation of the peace. The groups would seem at this period to have been strictly organized by tens. But after the Norman conquest, under the more efficient *frith-borg* system then established, the numerical value appears to have become a secondary consideration; and we very soon find a tendency towards localizing the term. Of course the original tithings were in a sense local; that is, each voluntary group of ten must have been composed of neighbors, and each township would naturally contain a number of such groups, none of them extending their membership beyond the bounds of the township. But in the thirteenth century (1284) we find, in the *Liber Niger* of the monastery of Peterborough, a list of townships each of which consists of a fixed number of tithings, varying, no doubt, according to the population. Of the town of Bartona we read (p. 109) : *tota villata debet presentari per sex capitales decennarios* — the *capitales decennarii* being the " headboroughs " or " tithingmen." Other towns range from six of these officers to one, and we see the local character of the office in the fact that they are the regular representatives of the town in the great court of the hundred : (p. 113) *omnes libere tenentes et omnes capitales decennarii de predictis villis et fœdis a tempore cujus non extat memoria, sc. ante tempus Willemi Regis Conquistoris . . . solebant venire bis in anno ad duas magnas curias que appellantur Turna vicecomitis*, etc. Now, it is evident that in the small townships which had only one tithing it would be very natural and easy to identify the two terms, and thus localize the word *tithing*. Of this we see further evidence in the Cartulary of the monastery of Gloucester. Vol. iii., No. 966, gives the items in the view of frankpledge in the Court Leet of the manor, among which we read: *de hiis qui sunt xii annorum, et non sunt in tœthinga.* From this passage the tithing might appear to be a purely numerical group; but in No. 1011 we read: *sunt tenentes in tethynga de Chirchesdona,* where the word tithing seems to have a clearly local value.

The passage from the numerical to the territorial significant cation is an easy one, and is illustrated by these passages. We see from the passage above cited that all boys of twelve were enrolled, not merely heads of families, as is sometimes assumed; and the same rule was observed in Anglo-Saxon times, as is shown by the law of Canute (ii. 20, *ofcr xii wintra*). With the growth and order of good government, so large a number of groups as this came to be no longer necessary. Two centuries after the conquest, we find small towns containing but one tithing, and the largest only six, which may perhaps have been divisions of its territory into wards or districts. From this condition of things the purely territorial meaning of the word in some parts of the country may easily have been derived.

My object in this paper has been partly to trace the origin and powers of the English town, partly to help to an understanding of its connection with the New England town. New England being colonized at just about the time that the parish organization was superseding that of the town in the mother country, it would seem, as I have already said, that the colonists, breaking away from the English ecclesiastical system, held to the town organization, making the parish purely secondary. The powers of the New England towns do not differ very widely from those of the English towns. We find, for example, in Russhemer, the "Implyments" of the money obtained by the sale of church goods to have been enumerated as follows : —

towards the reparacioning of our churche	.	. .	xl s.
ffurther to makyng of a pulpett & a lectern	.	. .	xxiij s. iiij d.
also to the makying of a grett chest with locks .	.	.	iij s. iiij d.
Item to the pore peple of the parysshe	.	. . .	xx s.
Also to the mendyng of the high weyes	.	. . .	xxiij s. iiij d.

East Anglian, July, 1887.

In other cases we find : "for ssyendyng fforthe of v Souldeors to the Kyngs Majesties warrs"; "in the wallyng of their marssh, in costs & chargs upon the havyn, And upon ther bulwerks of Gunnys. powder, & shotte for the defense & safegard of the town"; "to mainteyne a ffree scoole," etc

These examples are taken from what I suppose to be small country villages, the prototypes of the New England towns. It may reasonably be supposed, however, that the boroughs, or higher class of towns, would give the example for the larger powers exercised by our more independent towns; and I find in the East Anglian (1886–88) a series of extracts from the records of the important town of Ipswich, as late as the time of the Commonwealth, which remind one, by the variety and the minuteness of their functions, of those of the New England towns : for example, the hiring of preachers and teachers, as well as the care of roads, the supervision of markets, etc. The "Great Court" of Ipswich, consisting of "all the freemen, Portmen, Aldermen, and Bailiffs," corresponds very closely to the New England town meeting. The most characteristic feature of the New England town meeting is, however, wanting — the requirement that the magistrates assume no control of the assembly, but retire into a private station, as it were, for the occasion; the meeting electing its own chairman, and exercising authority as a self-governing democracy. In most popular assemblies the magistrates are the presiding officers : in the English "vestry," or parish meeting, it is the parson ; in the Great Court of Ipswich, one of the bailiffs. This feature of the New England town meeting, which, with others, it shares with the higher parliamentary bodies, may perhaps be claimed as another instance of the survival in America of usages or institutions which have become extinct in the mother country. Gneist says (p. 202) : " The meeting was summoned by the churchwardens ; the chair was regularly taken by the parson, as the landlord of the vestry, and the first member of the ecclesiastical parish, as a matter of courtesy, but a positive right of presiding could be established neither by precedent nor by analogy. In analogy with the tax-granting commoners, the meeting was rather regarded as its own master, in respect to the appointment of a chairman, as well as in respect to its adjournment. The voting was conducted with equal rights for each individual, after the manner of the old courts leet, the parliamentary elections, and the parliamentary resolutions. The mode of giving the vote was, as a rule, by show of hands, but in difficult and doubtful cases by a poll."

My thesis, that the English towns of the Middle Ages were an integral part of the constitutional machinery, and not mere corporations, like the corresponding bodies of Germany, I have attempted to prove by showing : first, their territorial character, as conterminous areas of land, embracing the entire country ; secondly, their practice of self-government in local concerns and their organic relation to the larger representative bodies. We have seen that in the sixteenth century, at which time the parish became the organ of local self-government, the terms *town* and *parish* were used indifferently for the same institutions ; and that in the seventeenth century, when the American colonies were planted, the colonists carried with them a *town system* essentially the same as the *parish system* which continued in England. The analogy with German institutions is misleading. The English people developed the institution of the "town" upon their own soil; and it is to be compared, not with the imperfect creation of the continental Germans, from which it was perhaps derived, but with the matured institution of New England, to which it gave birth.

PEASANT COMMUNITIES IN FRANCE.*

THE investigations into the system of collective property in land, which have recently thrown so much light upon the early history of institutions, have been for the most part confined to the Teutonic and Slavonic nations of Europe. Among these nations collective property in land has been found to have been nearly universal in early times, and in many of these clear traces of it exist to the present day. In regard to the nations of Southern Europe, the field has hardly been explored at all. Mr. Maine, in his last work, "The Early History of Institutions," says, in relation to France, that "this darkness has recently given signs of lifting" (p. 5), and that " M. Le Play and others have come upon plain traces of such communities in several parts of France." Bonnemère, in his "Histoire des Paysans," devotes a chapter to these communities; La Chavanne, in his " Histoire des Classes Agricoles," discusses them at some length ; and Laveleye, in his "Primitive Property," describes them in two or three very interesting chapters. Nevertheless, there has been no systematic and exhaustive examination of this subject for France, such as the works of von Maurer and Thudichum for Germany, and of Nasse for England.

Some light may perhaps be thrown upon this inquiry by an examination of such registers of seignorial estates as are accessible, to ascertain whether any traces are discernible in them of a systematic organization of the peasantry, such as is manifest to the most superficial glance in England. I have, in former years, read to this society the results of an examination of such English

* From Transactions of the Wisconsin Academy of Sciences, Arts, and Letters (1877), vol. 4, p. 5.

documents of this class as I had within reach, from which it appeared that the peasantry, down to the fourteenth century, fell into regular organized classes, holding their lands in a precise manner and in uniform parcels. As a modest contribution to the investigation, I propose to present the results of a similar examination into such French documents as have come within my reach.

It should be remarked at the outset that the probabilities are against any such uniformity, whether in France or in any other of the countries occupied by the so-called Latin nations. The Teutonic and Slavonic nations are on the whole homogeneous in race, and as a rule have occupied the territories where they are now found from the very beginning of our historical knowledge of them. The population of France, on the other hand, is not only mixed, but has been subjected at several times to violent and sweeping revolutions. It was, no doubt, practically a homogeneous people when conquered by the Romans 2,000 years ago. The Gauls, a Celtic nation cognate to the Gaels of Scotland, are found in clans somewhat similar to those of Scotland — clans which appear to rest upon a common origin, either real or assumed, like the original subdivisions of most primitive peoples. But this primitive and homogeneous people, with its primitive and uniform institutions, has been at different times subdued by at least two great conquests — first by the Romans, then by the German tribes. It has changed its language, its religion, and its customs ; and it is fair to assume that it has modified its internal organization and its mode of holding land as well. Assuming, as we are perhaps entitled to do, that the Gallic tribes in Cæsar's time held their land in common, it is still probable : first, that this tenure of land was not held in village communities, like the Germans and Slavonians, but in clans, like the Celts of Britain ; and, secondly, that even this degree of community of tenure was broken up in a large degree by the

shock of successive conquests.   Wherever on the soil of
France we find a Germanic colonization on a large scale,
we may expect to find village communities : elsewhere, we
may expect an irregular and unorganized peasantry, the
result of disturbing influences from without — precisely
as similar cases have now at length brought about a similar irregularity and unorganized tenure of the soil in Germanic countries.   It confirms this expectation that the
greater part of the village communities described by
Bonnemère and La Chavanne as existing in France are
found in the essentially Teutonic portions of France, like
Franche Comté ; but it would not militate with this view
if such communities were found sporadically in every part
of France, because there were, as a matter of fact, extensive settlements of Germans scattered all over France.

The documents which I have been able to examine in
this investigation belong entirely to the ninth, tenth, and
eleventh centuries ; to a period, that is, before the full
establishment of feudalism, and in which, therefore, we
may expect, if anywhere, to find the primitive organization of the community.

Of these documents the first is the most important and
instructive for my point of view.   It is the Polyptichum
of the Abbot Irmino — a register of the estates belonging
to the abbey of St. Germain des Prés in the time of
Charlemagne.   In the fulness and minuteness of this
survey we are reminded of the greatest mediæval work of
this character, the Domesday Book of William the Conqueror ; but this Polyptichum is confined to only a small
part of France, all within forty leagues of Paris.   Moreover, Domesday Book is a public document, drawn up for
the use of the government, while this is a private register
of the estates belonging to a religious corporation.

The first point that strikes one on examining this register is that the estates are not enumerated according to
public divisions of the territory, but are grouped into what

are called *fiscs* : in this grouping there is the greatest irregularity,* bits of land scattered here and there in different villages, being combined merely for purposes of administration. Now, in English documents of this nature we find the public divisions uniformly observed, even in reference to private estates. What is of even more importance is that tenures of land in England are always given in hides or aliquot parts of the hide — the hide being the part of land falling to a full member of an organized community : in the French documents, on the other hand, estates are given by their dimensions, which vary very greatly.

For example,† Erlenteus and his wife Hildegarde hold one *mansus* (peasant's holding) containing six *bunuaria* (about five acres) of arable land, three *aripenni* (thirty-six rods) of vineyard, and two and one-half of meadow. Besides this, he has of allodial property three *bunuaria* of arable land and one *aripennus* of meadow. And so throughout : land is held not in uniform and equal portions, but always in specified and varying amounts. In ten holdings, for example, in *Theodaxium*,‡ the *bunuaria* of arable land range from two to twelve, the *aripenni* of vineyard from two and one-half to four and one-half, the *aripenni* of meadow from one and one-half to two and one-half.

Nearly contemporary with this document in date is the Polyptichum of the abbey of St. Remi, at Rheims. In this register we find a totally different system. Each estate is given under the term *mansus*, and the size of the *mansus* is not described. It is a natural inference, therefore, that *mansi* were of uniform extent, corresponding, therefore, to the English *hide*. Now, these lands, being in the neighborhood of Rheims, at a considerable distance to the east of Paris, may very easily have been settled under a different system. Moreover, being near the German frontier, there was in all likelihood

---

* Prolegomena, p. 30.   † Book xxv. 8.   ‡ Book xiv.

a larger proportion of German population than in the neighborhood of Paris. However this may be, we find in the dissimilarity of these nearly contemporaneous records a confirmation of the *a priori* probability that the tenure of land in France would be irregular or heterogeneous.

Appended to the Polyptichum of St. Remi are fragments of a rather later date, of the description of some estates in the neighborhood of Trèves, still further east, and in a country of nearly pure German population. Here, as might be expected, we find a complete uniformity in the tenures, so far as the incompleteness of the documents permits us to form a judgment. The *mansi* are spoken of as being themselves definite and uniform quantities of land, like the English *hide;* and their extent, in acres, *bunuaria* or *aripenni*, is not alluded to.

There remain two documents, considerably later and far less complete in this respect than the two Polypticha, but which completely support the view already taken, that there is not likely to be found any near approach to uniformity in the peasants' holdings. In the Cartulary of the abbey of St. Père de Chartres there is a complete lack of uniformity. Grants of land are, to be sure, usually stated in *mansi;* but *mansus* has not necessarily, like *hide*, the meaning of a definite share in a village community, but means a peasant's property of whatever extent. And, when we come to the detailed description of estates, there is hardly a vestige of uniformity as between the several estates. This description is very meagre in amount, and is copied into the Cartulary from some old papers, the copyist himself professing himself unable wholly to understand them. The date of these documents is assigned by the learned editor, Guèrard, to some time before A.D. 1000.

In one or two of the estates there are, to be sure, some indications of uniformity in the condition of the peasants of the same estate; *e.g.*, in Cavanuis Villa (p. 37) are given the names of twenty-one peasants (*agricolæ*), all of whom paid the same dues to the convent: nothing is said as to the size of their holdings. In Cipedum there are ten peasants, all paying the same dues. But next follows Comonis Villa, with four peasants, two holding five *bunuaria* and paying three measures of corn, two holding six *bunuaria* and paying four measures. On the next page Abbonis Villa has thirty-three peasants: twenty-one of these paid one shilling, and the rest sums varying from sixpence to three shillings. On page 40 begins the enumeration of seventeen holdings, paying ten different sums, varying from sixpence to fifteen shillings. Only two of these, to be sure, are called *mansi;* but these two pay respectively two and five shillings, and one *mansellus* three shillings.

There remains the Cartulary of the monastery of St. Bertin at St. Omer, in the extreme north of France, therefore in a territory largely settled by Germans. The date of these registers is about the middle of the ninth century. Here we find, as might be expected, a uniformity almost as great as in England. The estates are regularly stated in some such manner as this: "*Mansa XV per bunaria XII, et ille dimidius per bunaria VI*"—"fifteen *mansi* of twelve *bunuaria* each, and a half one of six *bunuaria*." The size of the *mansus* varies exactly as that of the virgate in English manors;* that is, it is generally uniform in the same villa, but ranges in the different villas from ten to twenty-four *bunuaria*, with sometimes, however, two or three different standards in the same villa. For example, in Pupurninga there are ten *mansi* of twenty-four *bunuaria*, ten of twenty, ten of fifteen, seventeen of thirteen, and one-half *mansus* of eight. We find also a large number of peasants with independent holdings, not given as *mansa*, and very irregular in amount, like the freeholders of England.

* See Transactions of the Wisconsin Academy of Sciences, Arts, and Letters, vol. 2, p. 223.

The result of this inquiry, which embraces all the documents relating to France which I have been able to examine, is completely to confirm the expectations which appeared probable on general grounds. We find here and there, especially in those provinces which had a considerable German element in the population, decided indications of uniformity in single villages or estates, sometimes even on a larger scale. But, as a whole, uniformity is not the rule, but the exception: the communities, if they were such, appear to have been isolated and scattered amid a population which was prevailingly irregular and heterogeneous.

RANKS AND CLASSES AMONG THE ANGLO-SAXONS.*

THE accepted doctrine as to the original classification among the Anglo-Saxons is that the entire population fell into two distinct classes, *eorls* and *ceorls*, terms which have been corrupted into the modern *earl* and *churl*, but which originally implied nothing more than a certain ill-defined hereditary distinction in rank, hardly so strong as that of *noble* and *freeman*. This view, which is held by Lingard, Palgrave, Kemble, Hallam, and Stubbs, is nowhere better expressed than by Mr. Freeman.† "In the primary meaning of the words, *eorl* and *ceorl* — words whose happy jingle causes them to be constantly opposed to each other — form an exhaustive division of the free members of the state. The distinction in modern language is most nearly expressed by the words *Gentle* and *Simple*. The ceorl is the simple freeman, the mere unit in the army and the assembly, whom no distinction of birth or office marks out from his fellows." This is, as I have said, the prevailing view at present, and, so far as the word *ceorl* is concerned, there is no question as to its correctness; but, with regard to *eorl*, I am inclined to go back to the earlier opinion, held by Thorpe ‡ and Lappenberg, § and to take the ground that it never desig-

---

* From Transactions of the Wisconsin Academy of Sciences, Arts, and Letters (1874), vol. 2, p. 334.

† Norman Conquest, i. p. 37.   ‡ Glossary to "Ancient Laws and Institutes of England."

§ Vol. ii. p. 313.   Compare also Waitz, "Deutsche Verfassungsgeschichte," i. p. 76. Waitz remarks, as a matter of course, that the Anglo-Saxons, like the Franks, had no hereditary nobility. To explain this departure from the prevailing institutions of the Germanic nations, we must consider, in the first place, that the German nobility was very limited in numbers — among all the Saxons, there were only about twenty-five noble families; and, in the next place, that they migrated, not under kings, but chiefs — *heretoga* — and that these chiefs undoubtedly included whatever nobles chose to join in the enterprise. It is hard to see, therefore, what can have been the origin of the eorls as an hereditary class.

nates an hereditary rank, but always a personal office or relation. It is admitted that this was the case in the eleventh and partially in the tenth century. It appears to me that the weight of evidence is as to having always been so — that it never essentially changed its meaning until after the Norman conquest, when, in its modern form, *earl*, it became an hereditary title of nobility.

The passages in which the word *eorl* occurs may, for our purposes, be classified into three groups — the early Kentish laws of the seventh century, the laws of Alfred and his successors, and the Saxon Chronicle and other works of literature. Between the two groups of laws there is an interval of about 200 years; and it is to be noticed that the arguments for " the distributive character of the words " *eorl* and *ceorl* — *i.e.*, as, with the meanings " nobleman " and " freeman," making up the entire free population — are derived wholly from two or three passages in the later laws. Taken by themselves, neither the early laws nor the scattered passages in the Saxon Chronicle and other documents would suggest any such meaning. Now, it may fairly be urged that the use of the words in the seventh century, if explicit enough, is sufficient by itself to establish their original signification.

First, however, it will be proper to compare the English *eorl* with the Danish *jarl*, which is of course the same word, and may fairly be presumed to have the same original meaning. The settlers of Kent, it will be remembered, in which kingdom we first meet the term as a legal one, were neither Angles nor Saxons, but Jutes, or natives of the peninsula of Denmark. That is, while the English as a whole are more nearly related to the Scandinavians than to the Germans, the Kentishmen stand in a peculiarly near relation to the Scandinavians. It may be assumed, therefore, that the Eorls of Kent were identical with the Jarls of Denmark and Norway. Now, the Scandinavian Jarls were not an hereditary class of noblemen, but were officers or magistrates appointed for life or pleasure.* It is significant, too, that the late well-established use of Earl, as the governor of a province, is attributed to Danish influence.

In the laws of Kent its use is never inconsistent with this. *Ceorl* is used, as it always is, for the common freeman — "peasant," if we choose to employ this term, but not by any means a low order of peasant; the *ceorls* are represented as land-owners and even slave-owners, and may perhaps be best described by the term "yeoman." The legal standing of the *corl*, as represented by the *bot*, or composition, is double or triple that of the *ceorl;* but this is by no means a proof of difference in hereditary rank, but may equally well indicate a personal authority or a special relation to the king.

Turning to the Saxon Chronicle for this early period, we find this conclusion strengthened. In a speech of King Withred of Kent, A.D. 692, we read: "Kings shall appoint Earls and Ealdormen, Shire-reeves and Judges" (eorlas and ealdermen, scire-revan and domesmenn). From this it appears clearly that the *eorls* were not an hereditary, but an appointed class. In the same document, A.D. 657, we read (of the King of Mercia): "to all his thegns, to the archbishop, to the bishops, to his earls." Note the word "his," showing a personal rather than an hereditary relation. Again, A.D. 675 (in Mercia): "neither king, nor bishop, nor earl, nor no man." This, although not so explicit as the others, certainly implies no hereditary rank. The above are all the instances of the use of the word *corl* which I have been able to find before the time of Alfred except in works of poetry. I think it will be admitted that they clearly support the view that the

* Dahlmann, *Gesch. Dänemarks*, ii. pp. 88 and 305. The same view is taken by the latest Norwegian historians, Munch and Keyser, as I am informed (being myself ignorant of Norwegian) by Mr. R. B. Anderson, Instructor in the Scandinavian Languages in the University of Wisconsin [later Professor in the University of Wisconsin, and afterward U. S. Minister Resident at Copenhagen.— EDS.].

English *eorls* were, like the Danish *jarls*, appointed officers or magistrates, not hereditary noblemen.

Let us now pass to the later group of laws, those of
Alfred and his successors. Here we find four passages in
which the words *earl* and *ceorl* are coupled in what appears to be a distributive use. These are: Laws of Alfred,
4: "all degrees, whether earl or ceorl"; *Judicia Civitatis
Lundoniæ*, Intr. : "as well eorlish as ceorlish"; Laws of
Ethelred, vii. 21 : "We know that through God's grace a
thrall has become a thane, and a ceorl has become an
eorl"; "Of Peoples' Ranks and Laws": "each according
to his condition, eorl and ceorl, thegen and theoden."
These four are, I believe, all the instances of the so-called
distributive use of the terms *eorl* and *ceorl*. Upon these,
therefore, the prevailing theory is exclusively founded.

It may be observed, in the first place, that in the Latin
translation of these documents, dating probably from the
twelfth century, Earl is uniformly rendered by *comes*, a
word which has more than one use, but which certainly
never has the general meaning of gentleman or nobleman,
but always that of some special rank or office, as follower,
magistrate, or, in later times, count or earl. I do not rest
much upon this argument, for the reason that this translation was made at a time when *earl* had a fixed meaning
in English, as designating particular grades of nobility, so
that it is very easy to suppose that the translator con-
founded the meaning of the word in his own day with that
which it had in the original document. It is more to the
purpose to remark that we have an equal number of cases,
in genuine Latin laws of the tenth century,* in which
comes and *villanus* are used precisely as these same words
are used in the translation just referred to, and as *earl* and
ceorl are used in their originals. If, therefore, *earl* and
ceorl are distributive, we have a right to infer that *comes*
and *villanus* were so; that is, that all persons who were

---

* *Æth. Decr. Episc.* 6; *Decr. Sap. Ang.* 3 and 6; *Eadm. Conc. Cul.* vii.

not ceorls or peasants (the accepted meaning of *villanus*) were *comites* — a use of *comes* which is certainly inconsistent with any accepted meaning of this word. It is still more to the purpose to note that *thegn* is joined with *ceorl* in precisely this same way (Ord. resp. the Dun-sætas, 5) ; and the inadequacy of the argument is proved by noticing that in Ethelred's Law *thrall* and *thegn* are joined, exactly as *ceorl* and *earl* are. Now, a thrall was a slave; and it certainly was not true that all who were not slaves were thegns. The coupling of *earl* and *ceorl* is easiest explained by the jingle, as that of *thrall* and *thegn* is by the alliteration. It may be noticed, too, that the Norsemen made use of precisely the same jingle — *jarlar ok karlar.* As to the explicit statement (Eth. vii. 2) that a ceorl might become an earl, Mr. Freeman is obliged, in consistency with his view of the strictly hereditary rank of the earl, to question the correctness of the statement: "I may remark that the jingle of beginnings and endings has carried the lawgiver a little too far. In strictness, the Ceorl could not become an Earl (in the older sense of the word)." *

When we leave these four passages, we find that the use of the word *earl* in the ninth and tenth centuries is perfectly consistent with what we find in the sixth. It is usually assumed that the later use of *earl* as a governor of several counties was introduced by Cnut ; and it is certain that Cnut did reorganize the kingdom and establish a new grade of governor with this title. It is no less certain, however, that even before his time the word was frequently used to designate magistrates, as equivalent to *ealdorman* (see Bosworth, Anglo-Saxon Dictionary, s. v.), and that this use occurs even in legal documents. In the Laws of Edward and Guthram (12), we find, "If any man wrong an ecclesiastic or a foreigner, then shall the king, or the earl there in the land, and the bishop of the people, be unto him in the place of a kinsman and of a protector."

* Norm. Conq. i. p. 95, n. 1.

Again, in the Saxon Chronicle (A.D. 963), "neither king, nor bishop, nor earl, nor shire-reeve." In these two passages the earls are certainly not an hereditary class, but persons invested with power and authority. This view is supported by the fact that in the Saxon Chronicle this word is regularly used for the Danish jarls.*

The use of the word in poetry is not inconsistent with the view here presented. In Beowulf,† for example, the earliest Anglo-Saxon poem, it is translated by Mr. Thorpe twenty times by *warrior*, thirteen times by *earl*, seven times by *man*, *hero* once, and *noble* once: where it is translated *noble* (v. 4488), either of the other terms would have made equally good sense. Indeed, if one always rendered it "man," using the word with the same latitude that we do in English (*e.g.*, as in the expressions, "this was a man," "a company of so many men," "he was such a one's man"), it would answer fairly enough. In several verses (3458, 4272, and 6327) we find *eorlscipe* translated "bravery"—*virtus*. (Noble is regularly *ætheling*. See vv. 1968, 2592.) This is consistent likewise with the song of the Battle of Brunanburh (Sax. Chron. A.D. 937), where Athelstan is called "Eorla Dryhten" (lord of earls). Again (A.D. 957), we read of Edgar "thaet cyningas and eorlas georne to him bugon" (that kings and earls willingly submitted to him). In Christian poetry Christ is called "Eorla hleo," refuge of men.

There is, however, one poem of very great antiquity, the Rigsmal, which certainly appears to support the view that the Danish jarls were originally an hereditary class. It is cited by Munch and Keyser to show that this was the mythical or prehistoric meaning, although they hold without any question that its historical meaning was that here presented. In this poem the three classes, of nobles, commons, and slaves, are represented as descended from

* *E.g.*, A.D. 871, 915.

† Most of these references to Beowulf were furnished to me by my friend, Mr. Thomas Davidson, of St. Louis.

three brothers, Jarl, Karl, and Thrall. Inasmuch as my concern is simply with the historical value of the term *eorl*, as applied to the Anglo-Saxon classes, its mythical or prehistoric value makes no difference to my argument. I will only mention, to show how little consistency there is in this mythical genealogy, that among the sons, not of Jarl, but of Karl, are, besides Smidr (Smith) and Bondi (peasant), Thegn, which is the title of the later nobility in England, and which even as early as Beowulf (v. 3293, ealdor Thegna, *prince of Thegns*) indicated a vassal of rank, and Hauldr, the designation, according to Dahlmann,* of "a genuine primitive nobility," and which we find also among the Danish invaders of England,† and afterwards as the highest nobility in the Danish parts of England.‡

We are warranted, therefore, in the conclusion that, although there are a few expressions a little hard to explain, there is nothing really inconsistent with the view supported by the great weight of evidence — that *carl* originally designated some purely personal rank or position, one to which even a peasant, *ceorl*, could rise. It must have been the title either of a class of officers or magistrates, or of the personal followers of the king.

* *Gesch. Dänemarks*, ii. p. 304.   † Sax. Chron., A.D. 905, 911, 915.
‡ Of Wergelds, North County Laws, 4.

THE ENGLISH COTTAGERS OF THE MIDDLE AGES.*

In the statute entitled *Extenta Manerii*, enacted in the fourth year of Edward I. (1276), three classes of tenants of the manor are enumerated : the *libere tenentes*, or freeholders ; the *custumarii*, or customary tenants ; and the *coterelli*, or cottagers. In former papers I have inquired into the origin of the first two of these classes, and attempted to show that the customary tenants were representatives of the primitive village community, and that the freeholders were of feudal origin. In the present paper I propose to consider the third class, the cottagers.

The class who in this document are called *coterelli* are known by several other names — *cotagii, cotmanni, cotarii, coterii, cotlandarii*. The several manors enumerated in the Gloucester Cartulary use these terms indifferently; while the Domesday of St. Paul's, in a passage corresponding to that in the *Extenta Manerii*, uses the word *cotagii* instead of *coterelli*. The Exchequer Domesday has *coterii* and *cotmanni*, as well as a new variation, *cosceti* or *coscez ;* and the laws of Henry I. also mention *cotseti*. Lastly, the *Rectitudines singularum personarum*, of the period before the Norman conquest, has *cotsetlan*, a form which is repeated in the *cosctl'* of the Abingdon Cartulary, in the latter half of the twelfth century.

Here are ten forms of the same word, evidently having the same derivation, and apparently the same meaning. Nor is there any difference discernible in their tenures and services. They generally hold a messuage and curti-

* From Transactions of the Wisconsin Academy of Sciences, Arts, and Letters, vol. 5, p. 1.

lage ; that is, a cottage with a yard, or an acre or two of land, and render therefor some trifling services. Still, they occasionally are found with estates of considerable size ; as, an entire virgate,* twelve acres,† ten, nine, and so on. ‡ Neither are we entitled to assume an absolute identity in the several terms, inasmuch as *cotarii* and *cosceti* are occasionally found in the same manor.§ To add to the perplexity, Domesday Book regularly uses a word of entirely different etymology, *bordarii*, for the class of cottagers, the terms *cotarii*, *cotmanni*, and *cosceti* being only occasionally used, and then being often found on the same estate with *bordarii*.

The differences here indicated were no doubt slight and unessential, and, at any rate, it would be a hopeless task to attempt at the present day to trace them in detail. Let us return to the threefold classification made by the *Extenta Manerii :* this classification evidently indicates broad and intelligible distinctions. We will inquire first into the position of the cottagers of the thirteenth century, and then proceed to trace the origin of the class. We are here at the start upon firm standing-ground. The cottagers of the thirteenth century are sufficiently well understood. In order, however, to make their condition intelligible, a brief review of the previous history of the peasantry will be necessary.

The peasantry of the Germanic nations were, in the earliest times, divided into small communities, each occupying a definite tract of land, called *mark*, which they owned and cultivated in common. When they reached a more advanced stage of progress, which required the ownership of land in severalty, each member of the community received an equal portion of land, consisting of house-lot and arable land, with rights of user in the meadows, pasture, and forest, which he held as his own, subject, however, to the methods of cultivation followed by the

* Domesday of St. Paul's, p. 5.   † Boldon Book, p. 566.
‡ Exchequer Domesday, i. f. 128.   § *E.g.*, Carletone in Wiltshire. *Id.*, p. 67.

community. This share was called in England *hide*, on the continent *mansus*. At first the proprietor of the hide held it as it were in trust for his family : he could not alienate it, but must transmit it to his heirs. Soon, however — at a very early time in England — he acquired the right of alienation ; and, as a matter of course, the primitive equality of ownership was speedily succeeded by great inequality. A few became rich, others were forced to dispose of a part or even the whole of their land. We have, therefore, rich peasants, poor peasants, and landless peasants.*

The name given to the village mark in Latin — the language almost universally used for public documents in the Middle Ages — was *villa*, and its inhabitants were *villani*. Now, in the changes in landed property, so long as a man kept his hold upon his share (hide), or even upon any aliquot portion of it, he was by right a *villanus*, a "townsman," and entitled to all the political and economical privileges which belonged to the community. Thus the manor of Sandun † gives first of this class those who held half a virgate (*i.e.*, one-eighth of a hide, the regular share having been reduced to this amount by successive subdivision), then the *operarii* of ten acres, and then those of five. These three classes were the *villani* proper, or, as they were now called, the *custumarii*, or customary tenants. They were the higher order of serfs, bound to labor by an hereditary obligation from which they could not escape, but having an interest in the soil, also hereditary, of which they could not be deprived. Above them were the freeholders, *libere tenentes*, also having an interest in the soil, and held to labor, but an interest and an obligation resting upon definite and personal contract. But there was a class below the customary tenants — serfs, like them held to labor by an obligation which they did not themselves enter into and from

* See, on this point, Thudichum, " Gau und Markverfassung," p. 211.

† Domesday of St. Paul's, p. 13.

which they could not escape, but having no interest in the soil to compensate for it. They might hold land, even in considerable amount; but it was purely at the will of the lord. These were the cottagers. If the customary tenants may be called *villeins regardant* (prædial serfs), the cottagers may be called *villeins in gross* (personal serfs), with a status hardly better than that of slaves proper. Both classes held their lands nominally "at will," but with the customary tenants the prescriptive rights of the tenant were effective against the bare legal right of the lord.

It will be noted that there were no slaves in England at this time (the close of the thirteenth century). There had been at an earlier time; but they had been gradually emancipated, and were, of course, one element of the class of cottagers. Another element was the poorer or more shiftless members of the village community. However low they might sink, so long as they retained by prescriptive right a share in the mark, they were *villani*, or customary tenants: if they lost this, and were dependent upon the lord for grants of land, they were cottagers, tenants at will.

Personal status and tenure of land are two points of view from which every class of persons in the Middle Ages must be regarded. In treating of the changes in landed property, I have partly anticipated the companion topic of personal status. While the hide was subdivided, and while many members of the community were losing their share altogether, a parallel process was going on, by which the entire body of free villagers, *villani*, were transformed into serfs. And side by side with this was a process familiar to all students of social history — the converse process, by which the slaves were elevated in position and became personally free, while still held to obligatory labor. The common freemen, by a process of degradation, and the slaves, by a process of elevation, met on the common ground of serfdom, and were distinguished from one another, not by any difference in personal status, but by their relation to the land. The common freemen, the *villani,* were now villeins regardant : the landless freemen and the slaves were villeins in gross, or serfs proper. For it should be noted that the distinction made by modern law-writers between villeins regardant and villeins in gross is not recognized by the law-writers of the time, and must be considered as not at all a difference in personal rights, but in right to the land. *Quicumque servus est,* says Fleta,* *ita est servus sicut alius, nec plus nec minus.* The higher class were attached to the soil simply because they had a prescriptive and inalienable right to the soil : the lower class could be transferred from hand to hand or estate to estate, like slaves, simply because their obligation to labor was not joined with a permanent right to a definite estate of land.

Therefore, we have a clew to start with — the twofold origin of the cottagers. We must look to the slaves as well as to the landless freemen for their source.

For assistance in this inquiry we must have recourse chiefly to two documents of the eleventh century : the *Rectitudines singularum personarum,* which gives the obligations of three classes of free peasants shortly before the Norman conquest; and the great or Exchequer Domesday Book, which gives the numbers, on every estate, of two principal classes, only in a few cases stating the extent of their tenure and their obligations. Both documents mention also slaves ; but it must be understood that the "slave" of this period was rather a serf than a chattel slave. It will be noted that the passage from Fleta, just cited, uses the word *servus* at a time (about A.D. 1300) when chattel slavery had been long abolished.

Our three principal documents, therefore, give us the following classification; the *Rectitudines singularum per-*

sonarum, three classes, *Geneat, Cotsetel,* and *Geburs;* Domesday Book, two classes, *Villani* and *Bordarii;* the *Extenta Manerii,* three classes again, *Libere Tenentes, Custumarii,* and *Coterelli.* Our problem is to reconcile these differences.

In the first place, it should be remarked that the *Libere Tenentes,* or freeholders, having come into existence since the time of Domesday Book, do not correspond to any one of the earlier classes, and may therefore be left out of account. In the next place, it is perfectly well established that the *Geneat* of the *Rectitudines,* the *Villani* of Domesday Book, and the *Custumarii* of the *Extenta Manerii* are the same class. We have, therefore, only to determine the relation of the *Coterelli* to the others of these earlier classes, and especially to explain how it is that Domesday Book has only one principal class, the *Bordarii,* where a few years earlier there were two, the *Cotsetel* and the *Geburs.*

Here I must call to mind the fact to which I directed attention a short time ago, that the class of *Coterelli* had its origin in two sources — the slaves and the landless freemen. The slaves, therefore, of the eleventh century were certainly one source of the cottagers of the thirteenth century; and so, in all probability, were a part at least of the classes intermediate between the slaves and the *Villani* — that is, the *Bordarii* of Domesday Book and the *Cotsetel* and *Geburs* of the *Rectitudines.* Let us proceed to examine these three classes.

The essential features of the *Kotsetlan-riht,* according to the *Rectitudines,* are the following : The *Cotsetel* is explicitly spoken of as a freeman, but as not paying a land tax, like the *Geneat* or *Villanus.* His holding is generally five acres, and his regular obligations are one day's labor a week. His free status associates him with the *Villanus,* but his obligations, labor instead of money or produce, appear to show that his tenure is not one of prescription, like that of the full member of the community, but is at the lord's will.   These features all point to this class as that of which we are in search — freemen who have lost their hold upon the land, and who have received from their lords small and precarious grants.   The obligation to labor one day in the week seems to have been a very common one in England.   In analyzing some years ago the tenants of some English manors at the period of the *Extenta Manerii*, I found a class intermediate between the *Custumarii* and the *Cotcrelli*, which it was difficult to attach positively to either of these classes.   These are the *Lundinarii*, or "Mondaysmen," who had holdings ranging from two to six acres, and labored one day a week throughout the year.   I pointed out this feature which they had in common with the *Cotsetel*, but did not attempt at the time to pursue the subject further.

The *Geburs* are described, in the same document, in terms which show that they were not a free class, and were in a rather harsh condition of serfdom.   Their ordinary obligation was two days a week (besides numerous occasional services), their holdings averaged larger than those of the *Cotsetel*, and they received stock and seed; but at their death everything they had was the property of the lord.   This last is the clearest mark of serfdom, and is called *mainmorte*.

We pass now to Domesday Book.   The names of both the classes above described are found in Domesday Book, but in very small number: there are enumerated in all England 1,749 *cosceti* (all in the west of England), 5,054 *cotarii*, mostly in the south, a few *cotmanni*, and 64 *geburs*, also in the south.   Of course it is impossible that this handful should represent the cottagers as a class. The class of cottagers are the *bordarii*, 82,119 in number, distributed in due proportion in every part of England, and constantly associated with the *villani*, 108,407 in number.   Here we have evidently the customary tenants and the cottagers. Unfortunately, Domesday Book rarely gives any information as to the obligations of the several classes. We have, however, a few items of information. In the first place, the *bordarii* are regularly associated with the *villani*,* from which it appears that they occupied the village, and not the lord's demesne. In one case, their labor is put at one day in the week.† And although, as a rule, the holdings are not given, yet in several manors of the county of Middlesex they are given in detail ; and here we find the *bordarii* holding five and six acres apiece ; also holdings in common — 6 *bordarii* of 30 acres, 16 of 2 hides (acres not given), 36 of 3 hides, 4 of 40 acres, and 8 of 1 virgate (or one-fourth of a hide). From these data it follows with certainty that the *bordarii* were an outgrowth of the village community ; that they were originally villagers, like the *villani.* They would appear also to have held their lands by prescription, and not at will ; but this is not a positive inference, and on other accounts seems hardly probable.

With regard to the *cotarii,* we learn just about as much as with regard to the *bordarii.* We find these, too, associated with the *villani,*‡ and find them holding four and five acres apiece, or mere gardens for a shilling each,§ or in common, 3 with 9 acres, 2 with 4 acres, 22 with half a hide, and 46 with a whole hide. These facts prove that the *cotarii* likewise were an outgrowth of the village community, and belonged properly to the class of *villani.* But the *cotarii* and *cosceti* are so few in number and so scattered that we can infer very little in regard to them.

The name *bordarius* used in this document and in a

---

*Vol. i. f. 4, a. Leminges in Kent: centum et unus villanus cum xvi bordariis habentes lv carucas.—f. 284, c. Colingeham in Nottinghamshire : vii villani et xx bordarii habentes xiv carucas.—f. 350. Tatenai in Lincolnshire: v villani et ii bordarii arantes v bobus.

† Vol. i. f. 186. Ewies in Herefordshire : xii bordarii operantes una die ebdomada.

‡ Vol. i. f. 9, a. Wichehame in Kent: xxxvi villani cum xxxii cotariis habent ix carucas.

§ Vol. i. f. 128. Westminster in Middlesex.

few other occasional cases may assist us to a conclusion. It is a French term, used by the French officials of William the Conqueror instead of the native English term. In France, the *bordarius* was the tenant of a *bordaria*, a smaller estate attached to a *mansus*, or hide, upon the outskirts of which it was situated.* The *bordarius*, therefore, although not a full member of the community, was an outgrowth of the community, and belonged by origin to the class of *villani*. He was a cottager, but a cottager of free origin.

The French *bordarius*, therefore, the occupant of a cottage upon the estate of another peasant, belonged by his origin to the class of *villani*, but did not hold his land by prescriptive right, like the *villani* proper, but by special grant, like the serfs. He was a cottager, but a cottager of free, not servile, origin. It does not follow, of course, that the compilers of Domesday Book used the term strictly in this sense. In all probability it meant to them simply *cottager*, and they applied it without discrimination to all those English peasants whom this term could properly describe. It is not surprising that they classed together, under this name, the *cotsetel*, or free cottagers, and the *geburs*, or serfs, seeing that these classes agreed in occupying cottages with a few acres attached. It must be remembered that Domesday Book does not, as a rule, record *tenures*, but classes of men. It was no object to distinguish between the different classes of cottagers, whether as to tenure or as to status. And, if in a few instances we have *cotarii* or *cosceti* by the side of *bordarii*, all we are entitled to infer is that the officials who drew up the report of this particular manor noted distinctions which other officials passed over as insignificant; that the distinctions existed generally, but were not generally put on record. It was not even necessary that the *bordarius* should hold any land at all. Domesday

* Lamprecht, *Beiträge zur Geschichte des französischen Wirthschaftslebens*, p. 38.

Book mentions one *bordarius* who, on account of poverty, had nothing,* and ten who had no land of their own.

We are therefore entitled to conclude that under the French name *bordarius* Domesday Book includes the two Anglo-Saxon classes of *cotsetel* and *geburs*, two classes which were both, probably, of free origin, but one of which had sunk into genuine serfdom, while the other might still be described as free peasantry. Two hundred years later, the class of cottagers included also the now emancipated slaves, all being equally serfs in status, and equally lacking any interest in the land beyond that of a tenure at will.

But the cottagers of free and of servile origin, although agreeing in status and in tenure, were, nevertheless, not wholly identical. They appear to have differed in the locality of their residence and tenure. It has been already said that the cottagers of free origin in the eleventh century, so far as can be traced, being sprung from the class of villagers, had their residence in the village † among the tenants of higher class. This is certainly the case with the French *bordarii*, and it may be inferred to have been the case in England. But the slaves, being the personal property of their lord, had their residence not in the village on the tenement lands or *utland* of the manor, but on the lord's personal estate, the demesne or *inland;* just as on our Southern plantations the negro quarters were in the neighborhood of the " big house." When the slaves were emancipated, it was natural that they should continue to live upon the demesne, occupying cottages and petty holdings, just as the older class of cottagers did upon the tenement lands.‡ Or, if new lands were cleared upon the waste, they might receive patches of this. At any rate,

---

* Vol. i. f. 177, b. Hatete in Worcestershire. Vol. ii. f. 290. Gepeswiz in Suffolk.

† See, for the residence of cottagers in the villages of Germany, von Maurer, *Geschichte der Fronhöfe*, vol. iii. p. 198.

‡ Von Maurer, *id.*, p. 311, speaks of *coloni* upon the *Hofländereien* (or demesnes).

they would not be in the village with the customary tenants and their companions.

This probability is converted into a certainty by a few isolated facts which we meet with in the period between Domesday Book and the *Extenta Manerii.* The rent-rolls of the end of the thirteenth century, the period of the *Extenta Manerii*, class all the cottagers together. The status and the tenures had now reached their fully developed form. But in the earlier rent-rolls we find these classes clearly distinguished. Thus the Abingdon Cartulary,* after enumerating the freeholders and customary tenants of the manor, adds (manor of Boxole): *In eodem hamel sunt* xv *cotsetl' ad opus*, etc. ; and then goes on : *Hi extracti sunt a dominio*, giving the names of twenty-six petty tenants. A few years later (1222) is the Domesday of St. Paul's, edited with learning and judgment by Archdeacon Hale. This contains the rent-rolls of twenty-two manors, and in nearly every case the roll begins with *Isti tenent de dominico*, to which follows a list of petty holdings upon the demesne ; then come the freeholders and other tenants. *Cotarii*, when there are any, are put after the freeholders and customary tenants ; that is, upon the tenement lands. I cannot find any direct evidence to support the view, in itself shown to be probable, that these tenants in the demesne were the descendants of slaves. It is noticeable, however, that the handicraftsmen are generally found here ; † and upon the continent it is an established fact that the handicraftsmen were of unfree origin. Whether it was so as a rule in England or not, I cannot say.

The same document enables us to make a comparison between the tenants of the same manor at two different periods, which, so far as it goes, confirms the view here taken. It must be observed that the period between

---

* Vol. ii. p. 301.

† Thus, in the manor of Beauchamp, p. 33, I find *textor* (tailor), *pelliparius* (tanner), *faber* (smith), *carpentarius* (carpenter), and *pictor* (painter). So in the manor of Boxole, given above, there were a tanner and a miller upon the demesne.

Domesday Book (1086) and the Domesday of St. Paul's (1222) was full of convulsions, social as well as political. During this time the class of freeholders came into existence, and the class of slaves went out of existence. It is difficult, therefore, to trace any clear connection between the classes of the peasantry in the two documents. The following will serve as examples. The manor of Sandun in Middlesex had, according to Domesday Book,* 24 *villani*, 12 *bordarii*, 16 *cotarii*, and 11 *servi*. In 1222 there are 24 *operarii* (corresponding exactly to the 24 *villani*), only 8 *cotarii*, 23 *libere tenentes*, and 24 tenants of the demesne, a considerable number of whom are also reckoned in the other classes. This would appear to show that the freeholders originated in cottagers as well as in *villani*.

In the little manor of Norton in Essex † there were only two *bordarii*. In 1222 there were six tenants holding from five to ten acres apiece. Here it would appear that the *bordarii* were petty tenants with no special rank.

The conclusion which we seem entitled to draw is that the *cotsetel* of the *Rectitudines*, lumped together with other cottagers in Domesday Book, were nevertheless a quite permanent class, reappearing in feudal times, under the name of *Lundinarii*, or "Mondaysmen," as a kind of aristocracy among the cottagers; that the *geburs* were, like the *cotsetel*, of free origin, but lower in condition, and that they were the principal source of the cottagers upon the tenement lands; while the cottagers of the demesne and the cleared lands were in great part the descendants of the slaves of the eleventh century.

* Vol. i. f. 136.   † Vol. ii. f. 12.

THE ORIGIN OF THE FREEHOLDERS.*

THE accepted view at present as to the origin of the class of freeholders is that they represented the old village community, and that their Court, the Court Baron, represented the old village assembly. Sir Henry Maine says (Village Communities, p. 137) : " We cannot doubt that the freeholders of the Tenemental lands correspond in the main to the free heads of households composing the old village community." Professor Stubbs speaks (Constitutional History, vol. i. p. 399) of the "court baron, the ancient gemot of the township." And Mr. Digby says (Introduction to the History of the Law of Real Property, p. 38) : "There can be little doubt that tenure in socage [that is, freehold] is the successor of the allodial proprietorship of early times." And again (p. 43) : "The manor court is the successor of the ancient assembly of the village or township."

In opposition to this view, I undertook to show in a previous paper † that the so-called customary tenants, who were as a rule serfs, were the representatives of the old village community, and suggested that the tenants in socage, or freeholders, were "specially privileged *villani*." I propose at present to develop this last point further, and show that free socage was in its nature a feudal tenure, and that the freeholders, as a class, had a feudal origin.

First, it should be noted that free tenure was of two kinds — by chivalry, or knights' service, and by socage, or

* From Transactions of the Wisconsin Academy of Sciences, Arts, and Letters (1877), vol. 4, p. 19.

† See Transactions of the Wisconsin Academy of Sciences, Arts, and Letters, vol. 2, p. 220.

agricultural service — and that the two classes of tenants, although differing widely in the form of their services and in social position, formed nevertheless legally one class. The lists of free tenants, *libere tenentes*, always begin, as is natural, with the most honorable class, the tenants by knights' service, and then continue without a break with the tenants by socage. And all the freeholders, *omnes libere tenentes*, composed the Court Baron of the manor, and owed suit to the court of the hundred and the shire. Now, as the two categories of freeholders composed but one class in law, it is natural to suppose that they had the same origin. The tenants by chivalry were of course a purely feudal class, holding their estates by the strictly feudal tenure of military service. The tenants by socage, it is natural to suppose, may have had a similar origin.

As a matter of fact, the two classes came into existence at the same time. Tenure by chivalry was, as a matter of course, introduced when the feudal system was introduced. The precise time and manner of this is still a matter of uncertainty. What is certain is that feudalism, in its complete form, did not exist in England at the time of the Norman conquest (1066), but that it is found completely developed at the accession of the House of Anjou (Henry II.), in 1154. Now, this interval of about a hundred years is precisely the time in which the tenure by free socage and the class of tenants by socage made their appearance.

Even as late as Domesday Book (1086) there was no freehold (except by military tenure), and no class of rural freeholders. But the Boldon Book (1183), and the Abingdon Cartulary, of about the same time, contain lists of freeholders of both the military and the agricultural class, and standing above the mass of servile tenants. It is therefore *a priori* probable that the tenure by free socage and the class of free socagers came into existence in connection with the establishment of feudalism, and as a part of this process. It is true, as I pointed out in a former paper,* that there is a large class of *sochemanni* enumerated in Domesday Book; but, first, this class is confined to a few counties in the east of England, and, secondly, it appears to have been a class of persons, not a category of tenure — there were *sochemanni*, but no *socagium*. There was likewise found in the eastern counties a class of freemen, *liberi homines;* but they appear to have been allodial proprietors, not free *tenants*.† Whatever, therefore, the origin and status of these two classes may have been, they could have had no *historical* connection with the later freeholders. Even the county of Kent, where villenage in its proper form is said never to have existed, had neither *liberi homines* nor *sochemanni* in Domesday Book.

I will now take up in succession the several features in which the free socagers stood related to the manor and its lord.

First, their tenure was in its form strictly feudal. They were formally enfeoffed with their lands, by "livery of seisin," were subject to most of the feudal incidents, and were regarded as having a definite legal interest; while the serfs or customary tenants held their lands by prescriptive title, and were in strictness of law only tenants at will, not being "regarded as having any legal interest in the land at all." Their estates, as I have shown on another occasion, were exceedingly variable in size and nature; but often they were regular portions of the customary lands, which they held upon the performance of the customary services, or a part of them.‡ It was not

---

* Transactions, vol. i, p. 167.

† " It is characteristic of the growth of tenure that in Domesday (if the index is correct) we hear of different classes of tenants, but not of different *species* of tenure: of *liberi homines*, but not of *liberum tenementum* ; of *milites*, but not of tenure *per militiam* ; of *sochemanni*, but not of *socagium* ; of *villani*, but not of *villenagium*." — Digby, p. 40, n. 1.

‡ " The tenure of a certain number of these fields is freehold." — Maine, *Vill. Comm.*, p. 137.

uncommon for one of the customary tenants to have also a freehold.*

Next to the tenure of land comes the manorial court, in which the jurisdiction of the manor was exercised. This was known as the Court Baron; and its judges were the free tenants of the manor, whether by chivalry or by soc-age. The constitution of the court was strictly feudal.† Every feudal lord had his feudal court, composed of his immediate vassals — those, that is, who were peers of one another. The feudal court required, for its maintenance, a minimum of tenants. Now, the Court Baron of the English manor fell, if there were not at least two free-holders to take part in it. It followed, moreover, the feudal rule, that the judgment, both as to law and to fact, was given by the tenants, the suitors or peers of the court, the lord or his steward only presiding. The name, moreover, Court Baron, is hard to explain by English etymology; but, as the French manorial court was called *Cour de Baronnie*, it is easy to suppose that the name was introduced along with the feudal system itself. On the other hand, the customary tenants, the compact and or-ganic body of the peasantry, had no function in this court, except that of lookers-on. They had their own court — the Customary Court — whose powers were "administra-tive rather than judicial," ‡ in which, therefore, they had no real power, such as the freeholders had in the Court Baron, being hardly more than witnesses.

This was, in short, such an assembly as that of the members of a corporation might be expected to be after the corporation had lost its effective powers. We may, therefore, consider it to represent the assembly of the mark or village community, reduced to a servile status.

---

* In the manor of Ledene, out of nine customary tenants, each holding a virgate, of fifty acres, six also had freeholds, varying from one to thirteen acres. Gloucester Cartulary, iii. 126.

† The *liberi homines* are almost confined to Norfolk and Suffolk; the *sochemanni*, to these counties and Nottingham, Northampton, Leicester, and Lincoln.

‡ Digby, p. 216.

The freeholders, it should be remarked, "are not, generally speaking, suitors at the Customary Court," from which it follows, almost of necessity, that they did not, as *freeholders*, have any share in the administration of the community, but only in so far as they held customary lands.

In the next place, the rights of the two classes in the waste differed. Each had the right of common appendant to his arable land ; but that of the copyholder or customary tenant was by the custom of the manor, while that of the freeholder was by "virtue of his individual grant, and as incident thereto." * This would show that here, too, the customary tenants represented immemorial antiquity, the freeholders a special and recent grant.

It remains to supplement these general arguments by special examples of the genesis of freehold. This is not easy to do, inasmuch as the period of the development of this class, the century following the Norman conquest, is very barren in documents of the required character. When we begin to meet with rent-rolls and other records of the manors, the freeholders are already a large and recognized class. There are, nevertheless, a few statistics which appear fully to prove the point in question.

The manor of Beauchamp in Essex was the property of the Chapter of St. Paul. At the time of the Exchequer Domesday (1086), it contained 24 *villani*, 10 *bordarii*, and 5 *servi*, no freeholders. In 1222, in the document known as the Domesday of St. Paul's, there were 34 *libere tenentes*. This class, therefore, had come into existence in this interval. Now, it so happens that for this manor we have the fragment of a record, of the year 1181, known as the Domesday of Ralph of Diceto. Its importance can be judged from the fact that this is the only manor I have been able to find of which there is a rent-roll in existence at two different periods. By means of this we are able to compare the condition of the

---

* Digby, p. 215. Williams, Law of Real Property, 467 ; compare 483.

manor at an interval of forty-one years. Unfortunately, the list of the *operarii* (as the customary tenants are here called) is incomplete : the *libere tenentes* are eighteen in number. From this it appears that the class of free-holders was not merely a new class, originating in the century after the Norman conquest, but that it was a class that was steadily added to, having more than doubled its numbers in less than fifty years. Nor was this wholly by dividing the estates, for the lands held by them were during this period increased from 667 acres to 744.

The continuousness of the tenures is shown very clearly by these lists. More than half of the estates of both classes can be traced from father to son or other relative, even after the long space of forty-one years. In only one case is the same tenant found. Robert, son of Wlurun, a customary tenant, held in 1181 an entire virgate of land. In 1222, he appears as holding only a half-virgate of customary land; but his name stands also in the list of new freeholders, as holding another half-virgate. Evi-dently being one of the richest and most prominent of the serfs, he had been converted into a freeman and a free-holder by being enfëoffed with half of his customary estate, the other half remaining in villenage. Lambert Gross in 1181 held two half-virgates of customary land. In 1222, his widow Alice held one half-virgate by the same tenure, and his son William the other half, as a freehold. Here are two clear cases of the conversion of serfs into freemen, and of customary tenure into freehold.

It would appear, therefore, to be proved that the free-holders, or tenants by free socage, were, as a class, the creation of feudalism; that the feudalization of England was accompanied, or rather accomplished in detail, by the creation of a body of immediate tenants to the lords of the manors, who without these would have had no com-plete jurisdiction. The tenure itself would appear to be simply the French *censive* or agricultural fief, which is in its nature and form wholly analogous with the fief proper. It may also have had some analogy to the tenure by which the *sochemanni* of the eastern counties held their land, and from this to have received the name *socagium*. If this view is correct, it would follow that the feudalization of the township, its conversion into the manor, consisted in the introduction of this new class of tenants, holding by a new tenure. For this purpose, leading villeins would naturally be selected; and the cases of Robert, son of Wlurun, and Lambert Gross show very clearly the process. That this class, new and of foreign and feudal origin, became the most valuable and characteristic of the English institutions, is due to the strong vitality and power of assimilation of the English constitution, whose trial by jury was also of foreign origin, and which even turned an exceptionally despotic royalty into an instrument of freedom.

THE RURAL POPULATION OF ENGLAND,

·AS CLASSIFIED IN DOMESDAY BOOK.*

DOMESDAY BOOK is the record of a survey of the landed property of England made by William the Conqueror, when he had been about twenty years on the throne: it was completed in 1086. It contains a nearly complete census of the rural population and property of the whole country, with the exception of a few of the northern counties, which were in too disorderly a condition to be reported in detail. For some parts of the country there remain also the preliminary memoranda, which are considerably more detailed than the final report: these are the "Exeter Domesday," for the western counties, and the "Ely Inquest," for the estates depending upon the abbey of St. Ethelred of Ely. For the counties of Norfolk, Suffolk, and Essex, this preliminary register is all that is extant.

These documents give us a more exact and detailed knowledge of the condition of England at this early date than we possess for any other country of Europe. And, nevertheless, such are the inherent difficulties in the way of understanding the social condition of a period so far removed from our own, and so meagre is our collateral knowledge of the matters treated, that there are many questions raised by an examination of these documents, which have never been satisfactorily answered. Among these is the precise status of the different classes of population enumerated.

* From Transactions of the Wisconsin Academy of Sciences, Arts, and Letters (1872), vol. 1, p. 167.

The whole population recorded in Domesday Book is 283,242 — the heads of families only, it will be remembered, and, in the main, only of the rural parts of England. These are enumerated in several different classes, to the four largest of which our attention will be chiefly confined. These are: the *villani*, numbering 108,407; the *bordarii*, 82,119; the *sochemanni*, 23,072; the *liberi homines* (free men), 12,138. There are also 25,156 slaves; but these do not come within the scope of our inquiry.

[The pages which discuss the *villani*, *bordarii*, and *liberi homines* will be omitted, except the summary which follows of the general results of the inquiry.]

1. The *villani* appear to have been in the main the body of the *ceorls*, or common freemen; the representative of the primitive village communities (see Maine, Vill. Comm., p. 82). "From all that we can gather on the subject, it seems that they were situated on the outside of the demesne land, and in 'common field' culture." Larking's "Domesday Book of Kent," App., p. 30.

2. The *bordarii* were those who, through misfortune or improvidence, had lost their little estates, and been reduced to the condition of common laborers, together with emancipated slaves and such others as floated to the several localities from one place or another. These had cottages (*bord*), not in the "village" proper, but on the lord's demesne, or "in-land": they became the villains in gross of feudal times, and their holdings were in time transformed into copyholds (see again Larking).

3. The *liberi homines* were independent freeholders, disconnected with the regular village or manorial organization of the peasantry. The large numbers of them that we find in Norfolk, Suffolk, and Essex, are to be explained by supposing them to be the descendants of the Danes of Guthorm (see Lappenberg's "Norman Kings of England," p. 202).

4. We come next to the *sochemanni*, who present, undoubtedly, the most puzzling problem connected with these inquiries. It seems to me, however, that the difficulty has arisen chiefly from the attempt to identify them with the socage tenants of later times, to whom also the term *sochemanni* was applied; and from the further attempt to explain the word by *socagium*, socage, which is itself a derived word, rather than by *soc* or *socha*, from which both of these must have been derived. It is easy to see how inadequate this method is. The tenants in "free and common socage" made up the body of the freehold tenants in all parts of England; but the *sochemanni* of Domesday Book are found only in certain counties in the east of England, so that the theory in question makes no provision for the socagers of Wessex and western Mercia. Further, it has been shown [in the pages omitted] that the *villani* held their lands by a tenure which was to all intents and purposes free and common socage; that is, a tenure "by any certain and determined service."* The *villani*, therefore, who are found in all counties of England, must be, in part at least, the representatives of the later socagers. Consequently, the *sochemanni* must have had something to distinguish them besides this tenure.

We must, then, leave the late and derived word *socagium*, and have recourse to the primitive *soc* or *socha*, and determine from this, on etymological grounds, the probable meaning of *sochemannus*. Etymology is a very unsafe guide to the actual meaning of a word at any given time; but it gives a certain clew to what must have been its meaning at one time — to one of the phases of meaning through which it must have passed. Thus the derivation of *socage* has been greatly disputed, and, whatever this may have been, it is not at all a safe indication to the meaning of *socman;* for, although the two words may have been and probably were derived from the same source,

* Blackstone.

yet there is no likelihood that either was derived from the other. Now, it is probable that *socagium* (socage) was derived from the Anglo-Saxon *sôc;* but it is almost certain that *sochcmannus* was so derived. From the meaning of *sôc*, therefore, we can deduce not what was the meaning of *sochcmannus* at any particular epoch, whether at the time of the conquest or two hundred years later, but what must have been its meaning when the word was first formed.

Sôc, in Latin *socha*, is the territory of the jurisdiction of a thegn. As the village community was transformed into a manor, its territory came to be regarded as the property of the thegn, or country gentleman, the "lord of the manor" of feudal times. More than this: as the development of feudal institutions went on, he became, "not only a proprietor, but a prince," and the villagers not only his tenants, but his subjects. This was a gradual process. The rights of jurisdiction were at first granted to individual thegns, as a special privilege, or *franchise*, as it was called. Some received them, others did not. A law of Edward the Confessor* contrasts "*barones qui curias suas habent de hominibus suis*" with "*barones qui judicia non habent.*" Again, the franchise was not always in the same degree. Full powers of jurisdiction, civil and criminal, were comprised under the terms, "sac, sôc, toll, team, and infangthef." A lesser degree, relating only to civil cases and petty offences, was "sac and sôc," or, very frequently, simply *soc*. Domesday Book gives the names of thirty-five persons, thegns and persons of high rank — among them Queen Edith and the Bishop of Durham — who had "sac, sôc, toll, and team" in Lincolnshire; but in the city of Lincoln alone there were twelve who had "sac and sôc," one of them being mentioned specially as having also "Toll and Theim." After the Norman conquest, when the feudal institutions had become fully developed, and the powers of jurisdiction had been parcelled out among the feudal tenants, they were an essential adjunct to every manor; but at the time of the conquest, as we must constantly bear in mind, the system was still in process of development, and various stages of it were in existence side by side.

Sôc, then, is the territory within which a thegn possessed jurisdiction; and it is often put for the jurisdiction itself, which was more properly expressed by *sac*. Illustrations of this use of the word are common in all parts of Domesday Book; but they are most common in Lincolnshire and the adjoining counties, in which the socmen are principally found. A peculiarity of these counties is that nearly every manor has enumerated as *Soca* a list of small detached tracts in other manors. For example (I take a very simple case), the manor of Tuxfarne in Nottinghamshire has 32 *villani* and 2 *bordarii*. As *Soca* belong: 1, in Schidrinton and Walesbi, 2 hides of land with 6 *sochemanni* and 1 *bordarius*; 2, in Agemuntone, 1½ hides with 1 *sochemannus* and 3 *villani*. Agemuntone has a manor of its own; and in Tuxfarne itself is a *soca* of Westmarcham, containing 3 carucates of land with 3 *sochemanni* and 5 *villani*. Lincolnshire and Nottinghamshire, and, to some extent, other counties in the neighborhood, are in this way cut up in a remarkable degree into small pieces of detached jurisdiction. It should be remarked that the *sôc* varies very much: it appears sometimes to belong to a person, sometimes to a manor.

Now, the term *sôc* was not properly applied to the *demesne* land, of which the lord of the manor was *proprietor*, but to the tenement lands, as they were called, of which he was the *prince*. The lands of a manor were strictly divided into two parts, both of which were essential to its existence. The *demesne* land, or "inland," as it was called in Anglo-Saxon times, was the private estate or farm of the lord, where he had his manor house, or castle, and lived surrounded by his retainers and serfs. This land was cultivated by slaves, or serfs hardly better off than slaves; and these serfs I have shown to be, probably, the *bordarii* of Domesday Book. The "utland" (*out*-land, contrasted to *in*-land), or *upland*, as it is generally called, was that of which the lord was recognized as proprietor, but only to the extent of receiving certain dues and services, and exercising a certain degree of jurisdiction. Its inhabitants were freehold tenants, and it therefore came to be known as the *tenement lands:* these, I have shown, were probably the *villani* of Domesday Book. The upland, or tenement lands, were also called the *foreign* * lands, as being in a certain sense free and independent of the lord of the manor. Over the *demesne* he was *master:* over the tenement lands he was only *lord.* The inhabitants of the inland, or *demesne*, were, so to speak, members of his household: those of the upland, or tenement lands, came under his authority only in certain specified points.

Now, it was to the upland, not to the inland, that the term *sôc* † was applied; that is, to the legal and special jurisdiction over freemen, not the irresponsible mastership over serfs and slaves. But I have shown that the inhabitants of the upland, or tenement lands, were the *villani* of Domesday Book ; these were, therefore, within the sôc of the thegn, and were strictly *socmen.* I will go a step further, and anticipate a point which does not properly fall within the limits of this paper, by saying that because they lived within the sôc they were called *socage* tenants.

It appears, then, from the etymology of the word, that the *sochemanni* must have been people living within the sôc, or jurisdiction, of individual thegns, as contrasted with

* *Extenta Manerii*, 4 Edw. 1.

† In dominio aulæ sunt x bovata de hac terra. Reliqua est soca. *f.* 283 *a.*

the slaves and cottagers upon their demesne lands. It follows that the *villani*, if they were, as I think is proved, the inhabitants of the uplands, members of organized village communities, were properly socmen, *provided their thegn possessed the franchise of sac and soc.* Under the fully developed manorial system all lords of manors possessed these franchises, and all inhabitants of the tenement lands became socmen, or, as the terms were then identical, socagers. But, when the system was still in process of development, only those *villani* would be socmen whose thegns had obtained these franchises by special grant; and, on the other hand, there might be tenants living within the jurisdiction of a thegn, and thus properly socmen, who were not members of the organized village communities. There were therefore *villani* who were not socmen, and there might be socmen who were not *villani*. In a register like Domesday Book it would be natural to enumerate a great class like the *villani*, which was found throughout England, under this its special name, and that whether they were strictly socmen or not; while the term *socmen* would be reserved for those who were not *villani*, and yet who stood like these under the sôc of a lord or a manor.

It appears probable, therefore, that the *sochemanni* of Domesday Book were persons holding tracts of land independent of the organized village communities, but coming, like the villagers, under the jurisdiction of the thegn. We might therefore expect them to be a comparatively scattered and occasional class; and the record shows that, as a matter of fact, there was a great disparity in their position and protection. We find 2 *sochemanni* of 24 acres of arable land, and 4 of meadow; 14 of 9 acres; 12 of 40 acres; 5 of 20 acres; 1 of ½ hide; 3 of ½ hide, etc. Their position in the record varies also. Sometimes they are enumerated with the other classes (2 *sochemanni*, 1 *villanus*, and 1 *bordarius* — 25 *sochemanni* and 15 *villani*), very rarely standing last. Sometimes they are put by themselves (5 *sochemanni* of 3 hides, and 35 *villani* and 20 *bordarii*). A very common expression is, "There belonged to this manor so many *sochemanni.*" Occasionally, a socman seems to rank almost as a thegn; as, "in Nortun, 1 *sochemannus* with 81 acres of land, and 1 acre of meadow, and 1 *villanus* and 7 *bordarii;* and he was of a free man of Roger Bigod." Here we have *villani* and *bordarii* under a socman, himself under a "free man," who was the vassal of the great lord Roger Bigod. Again, "7 *sochemanni* having 12 *villani* and 6 *bordarii.*" Also, *sochemanni* holding lands "in demesne," like lords of the manor. Again, the introduction to the Ely Inquest proposes to ascertain how many *villani*, how many *cotarii*, how many slaves — then "how many free men, how many socmen."

The following is a fuller example of socmen from Cambridgeshire, a manor held by one Guido : —

(In the time of King Edward) "sixteen sochemanni held this land. Of these, 10 had 2 hides and ½ virgate * of the soca of St. Ethelred of Ely, of whom one could not sell his land, the other nine could sell to whom they wished, but the sôc of all remained to the church; and 6 others held one hide and 2 virgates of Count Algar, and could give or sell."

Of 24 socmen, "1 held under Edith the fair — all the others were socmen of King Edward."

We have thus ascertained the probable meaning of *sochemannus*, from its etymology, and found this to be supported by the facts as recorded in the survey. Both etymology and evidence go to show that this was a class in nearly the same social position with the *villani*, but not, like them, members of the village organizations; that they were an occasional and scattered body, and that they differed very widely from one another in wealth and posi-

---

* The virgate was 8 acres; the hide, 4 virgates.

tion. This theory finds a strong support in a provision of the Laws of Edward the Confessor,* by which in the Danalagu the "manbote" of the *sochemannus* and of the *villanus* is the same, while that of the "free man" is twice as much. A class like this, equal in rank to the members of the native organizations, but occasional, scattered, and differing very widely in standing and wealth, can be best explained by supposing an intrusion or an invasion and occupation by the side of the old inhabitants.

Having considered the probable meaning of the term, and the way in which it is used in Domesday Book, let us consider the geographical argument, the one which led Lappenberg to so fruitful results in the case of the "free men." In what counties of England do we find socmen? and is there anything that distinguishes these counties from other parts of England?

1. With very trifling exceptions, the socmen are found exclusively to the north and east of Watling Street.

2. They are most numerous in Lincolnshire, and next to this in the counties adjoining — Nottinghamshire, Leicestershire, and Norfolk. In the counties next to these they are in much smaller numbers. That is, they may be said to spread out from Lincolnshire south and west, over the other counties of the Danalagu.

3. In Lincolnshire, and, in a less degree in the adjoining counties, we find that the *sochen*, or detached places under the jurisdiction of the lord of the manor, are very numerous.

We might expect from this that the socmen would be found exclusively in these *sochen*; but,

4. Although these *sochen* almost always contain socmen, they do not always contain these, and, on the other hand, socmen are found in the manors themselves. This I shall attempt to explain presently. So far as it goes, it is

*Chap. xii.

a fact of some importance that socmen *prevail* in these *sochen*, even if they are not found in them universally and exclusively.

The facts here given lead of themselves to the theory which seems to me probable. Just as the *liberi homines* are found in the counties occupied by the Danes of Guthorm, so the counties in which the *sochemanni* most abound are precisely those in which the later settlements of Danes were principally made. We find the socmen most numerous exactly where we know that these Danes were most numerous. I can hardly resist the conclusion that the socmen were the descendants of these Danes. When they conquered the country, they did not disturb the organized village communities of the English, but there being plenty of unoccupied land — partly public land, partly the waste of the several manors — assigned tracts to their followers from this. The leaders became thegns, and under their *soc* were two classes, equal in rank, the native *villani* and the *sochemanni*, the rank and file of their own army. This will explain the irregularity and disparity in the condition of the socmen.*

The theory that the socmen were the descendants of Danish settlers finds confirmation in a law of King Cnut, which fixes the *heriot;* that is, "the military equipment of a vassal, which on his death reverted to the lord" (Stubbs). After giving that of the three grades of nobility, the earl, the king's thegn, and the medial thegn, it goes on, "and the heriot of a king's thegn among the Danes, who has his soken, four pounds." † Now, we have found *soken* — that is, detached places under the jurisdiction of a thegn or manor — to be very abundant in the counties where the Danes were found; and the passage

---

* When the Danish counties were recovered by the English kings, the Danish thegns were not displaced, and, says Palgrave, "as late as the reign of Ethelred, we can trace their existence as a privileged community, distinct from the kingdom in which they were included." A. S., p. 97.

† Stubbs, Select Charters, p. 73.

just quoted proves some peculiar and special relation of these soken to Danish thegns.

I have now shown : 1. From the meaning of the word *soc* and its use as contrasted with the "inland," or demesne, that the *sochemanni* were probably a somewhat scattered and irregular class, under the jurisdiction of the several thegns. 2. From the records of Domesday Book, that they were actually a scattered and irregular class, under the authority of individual thegns, nobles, and great persons. 3. From the Laws of Edward the Confessor, that their rank was the same as that of the *villani*, who were the native English peasantry, and were likewise under the jurisdiction of their several thegns. 4. That the existence of such a local and exceptional class as the socmen can be best explained by supposing an intrusion from some foreign country, which introduced an irregular body by the side of the compact and organized one. 5. That we know as a fact that there was such an intrusion of Danes, and that the intruders had their centre and seat precisely in those counties where we find the socmen. 6. That the Danish origin of the socmen is further supported by the passage in the laws of King Cnut, which speak of Danish thegns who have their *soken*, as well as the law of Edward the Confessor, which speaks of *sokemanni* in the Danalagu, as contrasted with the rest of England.

It does not follow from these arguments that all the *sochemanni* registered in Domesday Book were of Danish origin, or that all of Danish origin were *sochemanni*, or *liberi homines*. The point to be explained is the existence of these two great classes in a certain group of counties, by the side of the classes of *villani* and *bordarii*, which are found everywhere. This circumstance is easiest explained by supposing a prevailingly Danish origin. But the time when Domesday Book was compiled was a time of rapid and sweeping changes. The conquest must have acted powerfully in breaking up the old organizations and mixing together the several classes of population. After this time we find no mention of *bordarii*. The term *villanus* gradually lost its dignity, and became equivalent to "serf," while *sochemanni* were no longer confined to the Danish counties, but the name came in time to be applied to the body of the free peasantry in all parts of England.

THE RURAL CLASSES OF ENGLAND IN THE THIRTEENTH CENTURY.*

AT the last annual meeting of the Academy, I had the honor to read a paper upon the rural population of England in the eleventh century, a part of which has been printed in the Transactions of the Academy. I propose, to-day, to follow up the line of inquiry there suggested, and examine the changes in the social relations of the English peasantry during the two centuries that followed. I take two centuries rather than one, simply for the reason that the materials within my reach for the twelfth century are so meagre as, by themselves, to afford no certain results, while for the thirteenth century the materials are relatively abundant and instructive. On the other hand, I go down no later than the thirteenth century, because at this epoch the social institutions of the Middle Ages had reached their complete development, while after this they were subjected to rapid and fundamental changes. In the thirteenth century the abuses of feudalism had reached their height, and remedies began to be provided. In the thirteenth century jurisprudence began to be studied, and usages that had grown up in the confusion of the preceding century were reduced to a system, formulated, and, so to speak, codified. The thirteenth century was the century of Magna Charta, of the " Establishments " of St. Louis, of the " Customs of Beauvoisis," of the treatises of Bracton and Britton, of the legislation of Edward I., the " English Justinian." In the fourteenth century, on the other hand, the feudal ties were loosened, and the system essentially undermined ;

* From Transactions of the Wisconsin Academy of Sciences, Arts, and Letters (1873), vol. 2, p. 220.

commerce and industry began to assume a leading place in society. In the fourteenth century serfdom was abolished. At the accession of Edward I., in 1272, English villenage was at its height : at the death of Edward III., in 1377 (just about a century later), villenage no longer existed. The commencement of the reign of Edward I. is therefore the time which one would choose, of all others, to study the full development of feudal institutions.

It so happens that this is precisely the time at which our materials are most abundant — those materials, at all events, to which I have had access. If anything is lacking to the full understanding of them, it is not so much in the actual existence and workings of the institutions as in their history and formation.

Edward I., the greatest king who sat upon the throne of England between William I. and William III., has left the marks of his legislative activity in every department of English law. From him, as is natural, we derive our first clew to the solution of the problem before us. In the fourth year of his reign, 1276, a document was issued, entitled *Extenta Manerii*, which prescribes the several points to be reported upon in what we may call the census of the manors — their extent, population, and value. In this document we find three classes of tenantry specified — the *liberi tenentes* (free tenants), *custumarii* (customary tenants), and *coterelli* (cottagers), the free tenants being again divided into those who held by military service, those who held by socage, and those who held in any other manner (*alio modo*). There is no mention by name of *villeins*, which we know from other sources to have been at this time the appellation of the great mass of the tenantry. Here we have a general classification of the English peasantry, to which we may expect the census of the several manors to conform.

The Cartulary of the abbey of St. Peter of Gloucester [*] contains the register of twenty-seven manors belonging to this abbey, dating from the years 1265 and 6. This was a few years before the statute *Extenta Manerii;* and, as would be expected, the reports do not precisely follow the rules laid down in that instrument. They follow them, however, in the main; that is to say, they contain most of the points of information there specified, although sometimes in a different order and with some variation in names. For example, for the second class, instead of *Custumarii* they give *Consuetudinarii* — an equivalent Latin form in place of the Latinized form of an English word. In like manner, for the third class, besides *Coterelli,*[*] we find *Coterii,*[†] *Cottagii,*[‡] and *Cotlandarii,*[§] forms which are obviously the same at bottom, and which appear precisely equivalent in meaning. We have thus the three classes defined in the *Extenta Manerii;* but, besides these, we find other classes not there mentioned — *Honilond, Ferendelli,* and *Lundinarii,* besides a few occasional ones, described by terms which appear to be a variety of expression for one of these others. It is obvious that, however many shades of servile tenure there may have been, and however many local usages and expressions, all these must have been reducible, in the judgment of the authors of the statute *Extenta Manerii,* to three general classes — free tenants, customary tenants, and cottagers.

On examination of the documents, we find it possible to assign at least two of these additional classes to one of these principal ones. In order to do this, let us take up the several classes in their order.

The register of each manor begins with the names of the tenants and estates of the first class. These differ very widely from each other in the amount of land held, varying from a *hide* of 160 acres (or even larger estate) down to a mere messuage and lot of land. They differ

---

[*] *Extenta de Churchehamme,* p. 139. [†] *Extenta Berthonæ Abbatis,* p. 164.
[‡] *Extenta de Broctrope.* The obligations of these are somewhat higher than the rest.
[§] *Extenta de Hynehamme,* p. 119.

also in the terms on which these estates are held — some by military service, some by the payment of a fixed sum of money, some by a personal service of an honorable nature; as, for instance, holding * the towel while the Lord Abbot is washing on the day of St. Peter and Paul. These three forms of tenure would appear to be, respectively, knight service, free socage, and the "*alio modo*" referred to in the statute. In a few cases there is agricultural labor in addition to the money payment; but this labor is of the highest class of agricultural operations, and is always moderate and fixed in amount — as, "he shall gather and carry hay for four days." † The tenure likewise varies in form and degree : some hold by deed, some by ancient tenure, some for life, some at the will of the lord. What they all agree in is in the services being free and honorable in character, and, except the military, fixed in amount and time. The number of this class differs widely in the different manors — in some there are only one or two, in others a considerable number.

In a few manors there come next to the free tenants the tenants of *Honilond* — that is, " Honey-land " — whose estates are small, and whose rent is a certain amount of honey; *e.g.*, one gallon to each acre.‡ This is, of course, an equally free and certain service — equally *socage* — with those before described. The tenants of Honilond fall, therefore, in the class of free tenants, as their position in the register would indicate.

Next come the *Consuetudinarii*, the largest, and, in a sense, the most important class. In this class, instead of the irregularity of the free tenants, we find the greatest possible regularity and uniformity : all (with very slight exceptions) hold an equal amount of land (or, at least, an amount proportionate in quantity) and are subject to the same services. The customary land, *terra*

---

* *Extenta de Hynetone*, p. 55.   † *Extenta de Clifforde*, p. 51.
‡ *Extenta de Ledene*, p. 128.

consuetudinaria, is invariably given by *virgates*, and the *virgata* varies very widely in extent.* I find ten different values given to it, ranging from eighteen to eighty acres, but almost without exception the same in all estates of the same manor. The customary tenants hold either a virgate apiece or half a virgate apiece, or a virgate in common between two. For this they render a very great variety of services, prescribed with the greatest minuteness, hardly varying at all in the same manor, and not varying much in different manors. The enumeration of these occupies in each case from a page to a page and a half in the book ; and, when they have been enumerated for one tenant, the register goes on merely to give a list of the names of those holding the same estate, adding to each *et facit in omnibus sicut prædictus Robertus*, or whatever the name may be.

The *Consuetudinarii* are the one class, besides the free tenants, who are found in every manor : the classes that follow are quite variable. The *Ferendelli* come next, when they are mentioned at all, and their tenures and services are precisely analogous to those of the *Consuetudinarii*, and are given in the same uniform style. Their estate is always one-fourth of the virgate; that is, twelve acres where the virgate is forty-eight, sixteen acres where the virgate is sixty-four. The *Ferendellus* is the Latinized form of *ferding*, a form equivalent to *farthing*, and meaning a fourth part. As the farthing is one-fourth of the penny, the ferding is one-fourth of the virgate. The name *ferdingi* occurs in some documents of the twelfth century.† In one manor ‡ we find this estate called *quarterium*, and the tenants have no special name. The services also vary in about the same proportion to those of the *virgatarii*, as the holders of a full virgate are sometimes called. It is clear that the *Ferendelli* are properly classed with

---

* It is always one-fourth of a hide, the hide being a variable quantity.

† *Leges Henrici Primi*, xxix.   ‡ *Extenta de Berthona Regis*, p. 69.

the *Consuetudinarii,* as holding one-fourth of a virgate. Indeed, sometimes they are enumerated under the same head with them,* just as the holders of a half-virgate are regularly.

The *Coterii, Coterelli, Cotlandarii,* and *Cotagii,* all agree in holding *cottagium* or "*messuagium cum curtilagio*"; that is, a cottage with a small lot of ground, for which they pay in services similar to those before described, but less in amount. They are the lowest class of laborers, and have no farms, nothing but cottage lots. The *Lundinarii,* "Mondaysmen," are less easy to classify. Their place in the list is after the *Ferendelli,* and before the *Coterii;* but they occur oftener than either of these classes. Their estates vary in different manors, but do not appear to have any relation to the virgate. The "*lundinarius,*" or estate of this class, is defined as "*messuagium cum curtilagio*"—thus associating them with the cottagers — and, in addition, so many acres of land, generally two, four, or six; that is, small farms besides their cottage lots.

The distinguishing characteristic of their tenure, implied in their name, is that of laboring one day in the week throughout the year; but this does not exclude other services. It would seem likely therefore that they were a specially privileged class of cottagers; and I feel inclined, although with some hesitation, to place them with this third category of the *Extenta Manerii.* It is true we meet the expression "*lundinaria consuetudinaria,*" † and the introduction to the Cartulary ‡ quotes an expression, "*duo crofta, cum duabus lundinariis terræ, vocata* Mundais land *de custumariis terris manerii.*" Still, in the strict sense of the word, all below the free tenants hold by customary services — that is, defined amounts of agricultural labor; and in one case, in fact, we find all of them grouped as *Consuetudinarii majores* and *minores,*§

---

* *E.g.,* Manor of Bertonestret, p. 160.   † *Extenta de Culne Rogeri,* p. 207.

‡ p. cvi.   § *Extenta de Culne Sancti Alywini,* p. 203.

several times as *Consuetudinarii* simply. I am inclined, therefore, in spite of this expression, to consider these as cottagers who had received additional allotments of land on the tenure of certain customary services rather than as customary tenants proper, of an inferior grade — as privileged cottagers rather than as inferior customary tenants. In one case * they are, in fact, classed with the *Coterelli.* It may be remarked that the services of the *Lundinarii* agree very nearly with those of the *Cotsetlan,* the second, or intermediate, class of peasants of the *Rectitudines.* The importance of this distinction will appear further on.

It will be observed that in this Cartulary, as in the statute *Extenta Manerii,* we hear nothing of *villeins* as a class. I have met in it with the word *villani* once and *villenagium* twice, as will be shown presently.

The result of an examination of these registers is fully to confirm the classification of the statute *Extenta Manerii.* We find that the three classes there enumerated are distinctly mentioned here, under names essentially the same; and we find that every other class can be easily reduced to one of these three, with the single exception of the *Lundinarii,* who agree in certain points with one class, and in certain points with another. Probably what puzzles us now was perfectly plain to the men of that time. Further, the result of this examination is to develop the fact that the class of *consuetudinarii,* or customary tenants, ranking between the other two, was distinguished by a remarkable regularity and uniformity, both of estate and of services; while the free tenants, the class highest in rank, are exceedingly variable and irregular, and the cottagers, the third in the list, are uniform, it is true, but wholly insignificant. The customary tenants enjoy a relatively very respectable standing; and their estate — the virgate, usually of 36 to 60 acres — is a very comfortable farm, especially when it is considered that this was exclusively arable land, and that they had be-

Extenta de Ledene, p. 131.

sides the use of the common pasture, woodland, etc.
For this farm they paid in a great multiplicity of prædial
services, burdensome no doubt, but determined in amount
and time. Including the *ferendelli*, this class far out-
numbers all the others taken together. The *consuetudinarii* may therefore be pronounced the main body of the
peasantry, and the uniformity of their estate and services
shows them to have been a compact, organized body.

It remains to trace, so far as possible, the origin of
these three classes. In this our starting-point must
be Domesday Book. According to this there existed
throughout England in the eleventh century (besides certain local and occasional classes) two great classes of
peasantry — the *villani*, or villagers, and the *bordarii*, or
cottagers. Both these classes are found in every county,
and in nearly every manor.

In the paper that I read last year, I attempted to prove
that the *villani*, who are generally recognized to have
been the Anglo-Saxon *ceorls*, were the representatives of
the primitive village communities, which recent investigations of Nasse, Maine, and others have shown to have
existed in early times in England, as in other Germanic
countries. The argument may be briefly summed up as
follows: 1. The word *villanus* means villager etymologically, and we find no trace in the eleventh century of
the servitude or degradation which is associated with the
villeins of the thirteenth century. 2. The *villani* are,
in the document entitled *Rectitudines singularum personarum*, identified with the Anglo-Saxon *geneat*, as the
highest class of the peasantry; and their services are
described as more moderate and of a higher order than
those of the other classes. 3. In the Exeter Domesday the *villani* are regularly spoken of as landholders,
as distinguished from the *bordarii* on the one hand, and
from the lord's demesne on the other. 5. The Laws of
King Edgar * contrast the thegn's "inland," or demesne,

with the "geneat-land"; and we have just seen that the *geneat* were the *villani.*

Thus far we have proved only that the *villani* were the occupants of the "*utland*," or "tenement lands," of the manor, that the land held by them was of a very considerable amount, and that they held these lands on the tenure of a moderate and determinate amount of agricultural labor. But nothing so far shows in what manner these lands were distributed among these tenants. So many *villani* hold so many *hides*, or *bovatæ*, of land; but, from all that appears, their estates may have been variable, like those of the *liberi tenentes* of the Gloucester Cartulary, or uniform, like those of the *consuetudinarii.* Fortunately, we are able to supply the required proof, and to show that the *villani* held their lands in equal estates, from which we may infer with certainty that they were identical with the *consuetudinarii*, only with changed name.

The first link in the argument is supplied by the Boldon Book, a register of the property of the see of Durham, A.D. 1183, just about 100 years after Domesday Book, and 100 years before the Gloucester Cartulary. This document describes the services of the *villani*, very much as those of the *consuetudinarii* are described a century later; and, what is of more importance, the *villani* are described as holding uniform estates of two *bovatæ* each, amounting to 32 acres. Below the *villani* is a class of *cotmanni*, or cottagers; and there are also a number of *firmarii*, who hold similar estates to those of the *villani*, but on a privileged tenure. Here the *villani*, from the description of the services, appear to have sunk below the position which they enjoyed when the *Rectitudines* was compiled, although the services are less burdensome than those of the *consuetudinarii* of the following century.

Nearly contemporary with the Boldon Book, we have the rent-roll of a few manors of the abbey of Abingdon in Berkshire.* This gives three classes of tenants, precisely corresponding to the three classes of the *Extenta Manerii*, except in name. First come a few free tenants, holding estates of various sizes, by very varying tenures. Next follow the *neti*, the most numerous class, who hold equal estates of one or two virgates, and pay for them in an equal amount of specified services, similar to those of the *consuetudinarii*, but far less burdensome. Lastly, the *cotsetcl*, who appear to correspond with the *coterii* of the thirteenth century. Now, the word *neti* is evidently the Latinized form of *geneat*, which we have found to be the Anglo-Saxon equivalent for *villani*. This class, therefore, forms another link between the *villani* and the *consuctudinarii*.

We have now seen: 1. That the *villani* of the eleventh century are identified with Anglo-Saxon *geneat*, and that the term is applied to the highest class of peasantry, the body of the Anglo-Saxon *ceorls*, who held considerable amounts of land by the tenure of prædial services of a respectable character, moderate and fixed in amount. There is nothing to show the size of their individual estates at this period. 2. That in the twelfth century the *villani*, and in the south of England the *neti*, whose name is obviously the Latinized form of *geneat* (*villanus*), held equal estates of a very respectable size on the tenure of prædial services of a respectable character, moderate and fixed in amount. But they are no longer the highest class of peasantry. There is, above the *neti*, a body of free tenants, whose estates are irregular in amount, often quite inconsiderable, although under a privileged tenure. 3. In the thirteenth century, that there was a class of *consuetudinarii*, who, in like manner, held equal amounts of land in respectable quantities, but on the tenure of prædial services of a very multitudinous and burdensome character. There is above these two a body of free tenants, precisely corresponding to those of

* *Chronicon Monaster ii de Abingdon*, ii. p. 302.

the twelfth century. Each of these classes appears to embrace the main body of the peasantry at their respective epochs, and to have been a compact and organized body.

We find, then, that the class which makes up the substance of the peasantry is called by different names at these three epochs — *villani, neti,* and *consuetudinarii.* Further, we find that its position has deteriorated in two respects: first, by the development of another class above them ; second, by the increase in number and degradation in character of the services by which they hold their lands. In other respects the classes are identical in character, and we may fairly infer that the *neti* of the twelfth century and the *consuetudinarii* of the thirteenth are the same as the *villani* of Domesday Book. This view is supported by the fact that the term *villenagium* is twice applied, in the Cartulary of Gloucester,* to the tenure of these *consuetudinarii.*

The question next arises, What was the origin of the *liberi tenentes,* a class that has come into existence since the time of Domesday Book ? For the *liberi homines* of Domesday Book are almost exclusively confined to two or three counties (Norfolk, Suffolk, and Essex) ; and that document gives only *villani* and *bordarii,* in manors where, two centuries later, we find *liberi tenentes.* An examination of the lists of *liberi tenentes* will show, as has been already remarked, that there was a very great disparity in their condition. The *Extenta Manerii* distinguishes those who hold by knight's service and those who hold by socage. Those who hold by knight's service need no explanation. They were members of the aristocracy, who had received grants of land in the manors, but were broadly separated from the other tenants. The tenants in socage, on the other hand, appear to have been specially privileged *villani.* In the manor of Ledene, for example, nearly all the free tenants appear also as customary ten-

---

* *Extenta de Lutlethone,* p. 37; *Linkeholte,* p. 42.

ants ; that is, they held two estates at a time (not at all an uncommon thing), and these two estates were of different rank — the one free, the other servile.   In some cases, again, the freehold is precisely the virgate or half-virgate of the customary estate ; and the freeholder would appear to have received the special privilege of setting apart his strip of land from the strips of the rest of the villagers, fencing it off, cultivating it after his own system, and paying for it in money instead of in services.   In other cases, the freehold is nothing but a cottage or a messuage with a garden lot.   It is testified by Britton * that a villain may be enfëoffed by his lord, "et par tel fëffement est le vileyn fraunc."   It is a strong confirmation of this view that, in the only place in which the word *villani* occurs in this Gloucester Cartulary, it is used of the tenants in free socage.†

The free tenants in socage appear, therefore, to have been members of the class of *villani*, and to have been either advanced by way of privilege to a more favored condition or were exempted from the burdens gradually imposed upon the rest of the class, and thus remained more nearly in their original freedom ; for there seems no doubt that the villagers, as a class, had sunk between the eleventh century and the thirteenth — the *villani* had become *villeins*, serfs.   Probably the correct view is between the two.   The *villani* held by prædial services in the eleventh century, as is shown by the *Rectitudines*. The free tenants were, therefore, actually privileged by having these services commuted for money payments, while at the same time the services of the class from which they were raised were made more base and burdensome. This view agrees with that of Mr. Finlason, editor of Reeve's History of English Law,‡ that "our common freehold estates arose out of villenage."   It is also supported . by the rent-roll of the manor of Addington in Kent, dating 1257–71, where we find a similar irregular and quite insignificant class of freeholders, while the mass of the tenants hold by prædial services.*

As regards the position of this class which I have called the body of the peasantry — the *villani* of the eleventh century and the *consuetudinarii* of the thirteenth — I have attempted above to identify them with the members of the primitive village communities, which have lately been shown to have continued in existence down through the Middle Ages, and even in some cases to the present day. There are many indications that the land held by the *consuetudinarii* of these manors was subject to certain of the obligations of the community. The equal size of the estates — the virgate or half or quarter virgate — is a proof of something organized and regular in the assignment of the estates. In one case, the estate is a virgate, "*in utroque campo*" † — another indication of regularity and organization, and undoubtedly a reference to the custom of having the arable lands in two or three fields, which were alternately cultivated and fallow. There are still clearer indications of this "three-field culture" in other manors.‡

In saying that the *consuetudinarii* were the representatives of the village communities, I would not be understood to imply that they all had their origin in such communities, or that all such communities had kept up their compact organization down to the thirteenth century. As Mr. Maine says : § "It cannot be supposed that each of the new Manorial groups takes the place of a village group which at some time or other consisted of free allodial proprietors. Still, we may accept the belief of the best authorities, that over a great part of England there has been a true succession of one group to the other." And, at any rate, the "compact and organically complete assemblage of men, occupying a definite area of

* Larking's Domesday Book of Kent, App. p. xxi.

† *Extenta de Duntesburne*, p. 194.

‡ *Extenta de Lutlethone*, p. 36; *Linkeholte*, p. 42.   § Village Communities, p. 135.

land," * can be identified with nothing but the *villani* of the eleventh century and the *consuetudinarii* of the thirteenth.

My object in this paper has been to trace one of the steps in the social history of the English peasantry. Several questions have presented themselves, in the course of this inquiry, which I have not been able to answer. I think, however, that the facts and arguments here brought forward are sufficient to establish the essential identity of the most important class of the peasantry during the period between the Norman conquest and the accession of Edward I. At this time the process of deterioration in their social condition had reached its lowest point, and the free villager had become a servile villein, bound to the soil, and almost a slave. After this time the history of the class is one of progress and amelioration, no longer of degradation.

NOTE.— Since writing the above paper, I have succeeded in procuring a copy of Nasse's important work, "The Agricultural Community of the Middle Ages," which I tried in vain to secure while preparing it. Professor Nasse's attention is given rather to the organization of the community than to the classification of the peasantry: he gives a few pages, however, to the latter; and his views are, in the main, the same as those here presented. Especially, he takes the same ground as to the identity of the *consuetudinarii* with the *villani* (p. 39), and as to the *Lundinarii* being "a peculiar kind of 'cotarii'" (p. 42). It may be remarked that his authorities, for the thirteenth century, are entirely different from mine. He makes no reference to the Gloucester Cartulary; and, on the other hand, I have not had access to the documents to which he refers. I need not say that I have been on my guard against drawing conclusions broader than the facts will warrant. I have made use, for this period, of only a small group of manors in the west of England, and, what is of more importance, the property of an ecclesiastical corporation, where we might expect to find peculiar usages, and perhaps a more liberal order of things. It is gratifying, therefore, to find my conclusions supported by researches based upon such a mass of evidence as that used by Professor Nasse.

* Village Communities, p. 133.

A SURVIVAL OF LAND COMMUNITY IN NEW ENGLAND.*

IT is only a very few years since the attention of English-speaking people was directed to the fact that all
ownership in land was collective in early times, and that
remnants of this collective ownership have survived in
some countries, and in secluded districts of most countries, down to the present day. We pointed out at the
time, in a paragraph (see *Nation*, No. 273) which Sir
Henry Maine did us the honor to cite in his "Village
Communities" (p. 201), that the early settlement of New
England was made upon the plan of collective ownership,
and that remnants of this survived down to the period of
the Revolution. We have since been informed by the
Hon. J. H. Trumbull of some very curious instances of
the same thing in Connecticut, even within the present
generation ; and we propose now to describe a very remarkable system of land community which still exists
upon the island of Nantucket.

In the first place, however, it should be noted — as a
Western correspondent pointed out at the time of our
former paragraph (see *Nation*, No. 275) — that community of property need not by any means have had the
same origin in all cases ; and, as we ourselves suggested,
the Massachusetts community system may have been
merely the natural outgrowth of the circumstances, and
not even an involuntary copying of the institutions of Old
England. An interesting example of a community in cultivation, which might possibly have developed into community of ownership, was afforded by the freedmen of the
Sea Islands of South Carolina during the war.

* From *The Nation*, vol. 26, p. 22 (January 10, 1878).

The plantations were the unit at the South; and, except in cases of extreme cruelty and misgovernment, the state of society was, in a certain sense, patriarchal. When, therefore, the masters departed and the slaves were left to themselves, they did not at once scatter: the plantation with its semi-patriarchal character still remained the organic unit, even in the absence of the proprietor — the Northern superintendent serving as a bond of union in his stead. The system of cultivation was that of two fields. (In the village communities of Europe, the three-field system was the common one.) The two great fields into which each plantation was divided were alternately planted with cotton or corn and left fallow. The freedmen in a dim way conceived that the plantation belonged to them collectively, and each year a fresh assignment of land was made to each of them of the field in cultivation. Here there was no fixed proportion, or *hide :* each head of a family took as much land as he chose to cultivate — so many *tasks*, a term quite analogous to *jugerum*, *morgen*, or *ox-gang*. Neither was the cultivation for themselves, but for the proprietor or lessee. But it is easy to conceive that a plantation might have been bid in by its own occupants at a sale of confiscated property (as was done in some cases), and, instead of being divided up, carried on upon this system on their own account. They would have elected their old driver, or some other leader of their own number as *starosta*, and a system have grown up quite like that prevailing in the Danubian principalities.

To return to Nantucket. This island was originally granted to a company of men, like other New England towns : only, instead of speedily dividing it up, they developed a most complicated system of community, both of ownership and of cultivation, which still exists in all its integrity, although confined now to a very small number of people, and a very small portion of the island. There are at the present day something less than a dozen persons who possess perfect rights in the common land of the island; but there is only one man living, Mr. Alfred Swain, who understands the system and knows what these rights are.

Nantucket was settled in 1662, by the method usual in New England towns. A company of twenty-seven proprietors owned all the land of the island, except *Quaise*, a patch of about 130 acres, retained by a former proprietor. Each proprietor had a right to take up 45 acres as a house-lot; and this was done from time to time, according to convenience or caprice. Only a few years ago a claim of 10 acres was made on this account. Until 1717 the company of proprietors were the town: in that year each organization was made distinct, and thenceforward the proprietors, or commoners, were a sort of aristocracy, distinct from the body of townspeople. They have their own records, and continue to have proprietors' meetings, distinct from the town meetings.

In all this, Nantucket differs from other old New England towns only in the late date to which the distinction of commoners was preserved. The development in other respects has been very different. In the other towns they proceeded at once to set off land in full property to the different townsmen — a bit here and a bit there, according as they severally desired meadow, woodland, bog-land, etc.— until the whole was taken up. In Nantucket, however, as in the village communities of the Old World, the house-lots were the only pieces of land owned by individuals, and other tracts set off for agricultural purposes were still held and cultivated in common. The first tract thus set off was *Shammo* (120 acres), about 1717. The method now adopted appears to have been followed in all subsequent divisions. The 27 shares were measured off and staked off permanently, but without the privilege of fencing off. But subdivisions of shares, which had now become the rule, were not recognized at all, except by the coparceners among themselves, by private agreement. From time to time other districts were set off in the same way, of various extent: *Warehouse Lots*, containing only 64 rods; *Swamps*, 534 acres and 119 rods; and so on — *Fish Lots, Beach Lots, Squam, South-east Quarter*, etc. In this last division, and perhaps in others, each share consisted of two separate lots, the object being to balance bad land by good. In this division each share (divided and staked off) contains about 90 acres, so that each of the later subdivisions of *sheep's commons*, to be described presently, contained about one-sixth of an acre in this part of the island, held in undivided severalty with the other proprietors of the share.

Meantime the shares were divided and subdivided, until in 1778 a new arrangement was made. Each of the 27 shares was now divided into 720 "*sheep's commons*," 19,440 in all. From this time, therefore, the *sheep's common* is the unit of proprietary rights, but it is only an ideal division. The shares, 27 in each district, have been actually surveyed and set off, and are easily known by their numbers: the sheep's commons have never been set off, but the proprietors — be they many or few — of the 720 (or 636) sheep's commons in any share are the proprietors in common of that share. The proprietor of any single sheep's common, therefore, only knows that his proprietary rights are in share No. 12 or 13, and so on, in every district on the island.

The ownership is as complicated as possible. In 1820 there were 322 proprietors, some owning entire shares or even more, and others varying amounts, such as 5, $101\frac{6}{12}$, $179\frac{8}{12}$ sheep's commons (a cow's common, by the way, was reckoned equal to 8 sheep's commons); and the owner of a sheep's common was proprietor of one undivided nineteen thousand four hundred and fortieth part of each one of some twenty divisions — including such as the 64 rods of *Warehouse Lots* and about 2,500 acres of *South-*

east Quarter, besides general proprietary rights over the undivided parts of the island.

In 1813 another complication was added. A number of proprietors desired to have their shares in severalty, and obtained a decree from the Supreme Court to that effect. The district known as *Plainfield* was therefore set off to these parties as the equivalent of their rights in the undivided parts of the island : they still retained their rights in the divided parts, such as Squam, Shammo, and South-east Quarter. But in the subsequent divisions, made in 1820 and 1821 — *Middle Pastures, North Pastures, Smooth Hummocks, Head of Plains, Woods and Lower Plains, Trot's Hill*, and *Maddequet* and *Great Neck* — the shares were divided into 636 instead of 720 sheep's commons each. In these seven districts, therefore, a sheep's common is $\frac{1}{17173}$ of the whole. A full proprietor of a sheep's common at the present day (worth about $2.50 in the market) owns, besides whatever land he may have in severalty, this fraction of these seven districts and $\frac{1}{15155}$ of the twenty (or thereabouts) older districts, besides numerous other scattered and ill-defined rights. Most proprietors have, however, divested themselves of some portion of their proprietary rights. Since Plainfield was set off, the community has been rapidly dissolving.

The cultivation of these tracts was determined from year to year by vote of the proprietors. In the year 1724–25, 13th day of the eleventh month, the records say : —

"Voted and agreed that the propriety will lay out a general field for planting this year. It is voted and agreed that Mattakit shall be the general planting field for ye year insuing.

"Voted that John Barnard, John Coffin, and Jethro Starbuck shall lay out the said Mattekit into shares, and to order where ye fence to enclose ye same shall stand."

It will be seen that this division was merely temporary.

Maddequet was not permanently set off until 1821. In 1726 the North Pasture was set off "for the space and term of tenn years"; in 1821 it was laid out permanently. January 24, 1746:—

"Voted that Squam land be laid out for mowing for six years, to be mowed but once a year."

Squam was permanently divided in 1778. January 16, 1754:—

"Voted that Squam be stocked this year."

The same year two acres to a share were planted with turnips.

In the early part of this century it appears to have become a practice to plant one of the seven great divisions each year, by turn, with corn, and the next year with oats, letting it then remain fallow for five years. After these districts were permanently divided, however, in 1820–21, this system went out of use, and a rage for sheep-raising set in. The land, indeed, had been ruined for agricultural purposes already, because, under the system of community, it was no man's interest to manure his land or seed it down, and the ocean winds sweeping over the dry stubble blew all the soil into the sea. Sheep-raising, too, was a failure, because of a conflict that soon set in between the owners of sheep and the owners of sheep's commons; and for some years these once fertile fields have been bare stretches of scrubby grass.

BIBLIOGRAPHY.

BIBLIOGRAPHY.

It is believed that the following list contains every published writing of importance that came from Professor Allen's pen. A star (*) following the title signifies a book. A dagger (†) signifies a monograph, or article. Reviews are unmarked. **Full-faced type** indicates that the paper is to be found in the present volume.

PRIMITIVE SOCIETY.

Bourke's Snake Dance of the Moquis of Arizona. *Dial*, vol. v. p. 242, January, 1885. -

Keary's Dawn of History. *Nation*, vol. xxvii. p. 101, August, 1878.

Maine's Ancient Law. *Nation*, vol. xi. p. 192, September, 1870.

Maine's Early Law and Custom. *Science*, vol. iii. p. 786, June, 1884.

Morgan's Ancient Society. *Penn Monthly*, vol. x. p. 115, February, 1879.

Morgan's Origin of the Classificatory System of Relationship. *Nation*, vol. vii. p. 395, November, 1868; *Penn Monthly*, vol. xi. p. 487, 1880.

Perkins's Collection of Copper Implements. *Nation*, vol. xxii. p. 29, January, 1876.

Primitive Communities. *Science*, vol. iii. p. 786.

Rawlinson's Origin of Nations. *Nation*, vol. xxxiii. p. 118, August, 1881.

Schröder's Laws of Marriage. *Nation*, vol. xviii. p. 333, May, 1874.

Tylor's Primitive Culture. *Nation*, vol. xviii. p. 161, March, 1874.

Williams and Calvert's Fiji and the Fijians. *Christian Examiner*, vol. lxviii. p. 145, January, 1860.

THE ORIENT.

Bonvalot's Through the Heart of Asia. *Dial*, vol. x. p. 32, June, 1889.

Cooke's China. *Christian Examiner*, vol. lxvi. p. 145, January, 1859.

Lenormant's Oriental History. *Old and New*, vol. ii. p. 96, July, 1870.

Rawlinson's History of Parthia. *Nation*, vol. xvi. p. 339, May, 1873.

Sayce's Ancient Empires of the East. *Nation*, vol. xl. p. 165, February, 1885.

Towle's Marco Polo. *Nation*, vol. xxxi. p. 364, November, 1880.

Wright's Ancient Cities. *Nation*, vol. xliv. p. 63, January, 1887.

GENERAL HISTORY.

Archer's Decisive Events in History. *Nation*, vol. xxviii. p. 325, May, 1879.

Buckle's Miscellaneous Works. *North American Review*, vol. cxvii. p. 224, July, 1873.

Collier's Great Events of History. *Nation*, vol. xvi. p. 203, March, 1873.

Dean's History of Civilization. *Nation*, vol. viii. p. 112, February, 1869; *Christian Examiner*, vol. lxxxvi. p. 241, February, 1869.

Fisher's Universal History. *Nation*, vol. xlii. p. 155, February, 1886.

Freeman's American Lectures. *Nation*, vol. xxxvi. p. 40, January, 1883.

Freeman's Chief Periods of European History. *Nation*, vol. xlv. p. 196, September, 1887.

Freeman's Historical Essays. *Old and New*, vol. vi. p. 607, November, 1872; *Nation*, vol. xxx. p. 331, April, 1880.

Freeman's Outlines of History. *Nation*, vol. xvi. p. 80, January, 1873.

History Topics for High Schools and Colleges. Boston, 1888, 12mo. pp. 121.*

Johnson's Normans in Europe. *Nation*, vol. xxviii. p. 221, March, 1879.

Labberton's Outlines of History. *Nation*, vol. xii. p. 453, June, 1871.

Lorenz's Die bürgerliche und die naturwissenschaftliche Geschichte. *Nation*, vol. xxvii. p. 213, October, 1878.

Mombert's Great Lives. *Nation*, vol. xliii. p. 201, September, 1886.

Myers's General History. *Nation*, vol. xlix. p. 434, November, 1889.

Nichol's Tables of European History. *Nation*, vol. xxxviii. p. 328, April, 1884.

Rawlinson's Universal History. *Nation*, vol. xlvi. p. 350, April, 1888.

Thalheimer's General History. *Nation*, vol. xxvi. p. 362, May, 1878.

Thompson's American Comments on European Questions. *Nation*, vol. xl. p. 62, January, 1885.

Wheeler's Course of Empire. *Nation*, vol. xxxvii. p. 496, December, 1883.

Wikoff's Four Civilizations of the World. *Nation*, vol. xix., p. 94, August, 1874.

Willard's Synopsis of History. *Nation*, vol. xxvii. p. 245, October, 1878.

Wilson's Studies of Modern Mind and Character. *Nation*, vol. xxxiv. p. 486, June, 1882.

ANCIENT HISTORY.

Barnes's History of Ancient Peoples. *Nation*, vol. xxxiii. p. 123, August, 1881.

Ducoudray's History of Ancient Civilization. *Nation*, vol. xlix. p. 137, August, 1889.

Myers's Outlines of Ancient History. *Nation*, vol. xxxv. p. 317, October, 1882; *Dial*, vol. iii. p. 114, October, 1882.

Rawlinson's Ancient History. *Nation*, vol. xi. p. 47, July, 1870.

GREEK HISTORY AND PHILOLOGY.

Abbott's History of Greece. *Nation*, vol. xlix. p. 216, September, 1889.

August Boeckh. *Christian Examiner*, vol. lxxxiii. p. 388, November, 1867.

Benjamin's Troy. *Nation*, vol. xxxii. p. 193, March, 1881.

Bikólas's Griechen des Mittelalters. *Nation*, vol. xxx. p. 370, May, 1880.

Boises's First Lessons in Greek. *Nation*, vol. xiii. p. 95, August, 1871.

Butcher's Demosthenes. *Nation*, vol. xxxv. p. 119, August, 1882.

Cox's Athenian Empire. *Nation*, vol. xxv. p. 108, August, 1877.

Cox's General History of Greece. *Nation*, vol. xxii. p. 339, May, 1876.

Cox's Lives of Greek Statesmen. *Nation*, vol. xliii. p. 221, September, 1886.

Curteis's Macedonian Empire. *Nation*, vol. xxxii. p. 156, March, 1881.

Curtius's History of Greece. *Christian Examiner*, vol. lxiv. p. 452, May, 1858; vol. lxxii. p. 131, January, 1862; vol. lxxxv. p. 109, July, 1868; *Independent*, April 20, 1871.

Droysen's Alexander. *Nation*, vol. xxxi. p. 206, September, 1880.

Felton's Clouds and Birds of Aristophanes. *Christian Examiner*, vol. lxxi. p. 444, November, 1861.

Felton's Greece, Ancient and Modern. *Nation*, vol. iv. p. 185, March, 1867.

Fyffe's History of Greece. *Nation*, vol. xxi. p. 16, July, 1875.

Gilbert's Griechische Staatsalterthümer. *Nation*, vol. xli. p. 447, November, 1885.

Gladstone's Juventus Mundi. *Nation*, vol. ix. p. 254, September, 1869.

Harrison's Story of Greece. *Nation*, vol. xli. p. 361, October, 1885.

Hartung's Religion und Mythologie der Griechen. *Christian Examiner*, vol. lxxxii. p. 118, January, 1867.

Historical Introduction to Ginn's Plutarch. Boston, 1886. 12mo. pp. 9.*

Leighton's Greek Lessons. *Nation*, vol. xiii. p. 95, August, 1871.

Lenormant on Schliemann. *Nation*, vol. xviii. p. 316, May, 1874.

Mahaffy's Alexander's Empire. *Nation*, vol. xlv. p. 179, September, 1887.

Moberly's Alexander in the Punjaub. *Nation*, vol. xx. p. 367, May, 1875.

Newman's Homeric Translations. *Christian Examiner*, September, 1865.

Pervanoglu's Culturbilder aus Griechenland. *Nation*, vol. xxxi. p. 136, August, 1880.

Rawlinson's Herodotus. *Christian Examiner*, vol. lxvi. p. 183, March, 1859 †; vol. lxix. p. 149, July, 1860.

Sankey's Spartan and Theban Supremacies. *Nation*, vol. xlii. p. 433, May, 1886.

Schliemann's Excavations at Troy. *Nation*, vol. xvii. p. 387, December, 1873; vol. xx. p. 348, May, 1875.

Shilleto's Pausanias's Description of Greece. *Nation*, vol. xliv. p. 344, April, 1887.

Stewart's Tale of Troy. *Nation*, vol. xliii. p. 505, December, 1886.

Timayensis's History of Greece. *Nation*, vol. xxxii. p. 339, May, 1881.

Tyler's Theology of Greek Poets. *Nation*, p. 291, No. 119, 1867.

Wilkinson's Greek Course in English. *Nation*, vol. xxxix. p. 222, September, 1884.

Wilkinson's Preparatory Greek Course in English. *Nation*, vol. xxxv. p. 451, November, 1882.

Wilson's Mosaics of Grecian History. *Nation*, vol. xxxviii. p. 198, February, 1884.

ROMAN HISTORY AND LATIN PHILOLOGY.

Annals of Tacitus, Books I.–IV. Boston, 1890. 12mo. pp. xi, 444.*

Arnold's Roman Provinces. *Nation*, vol. xxix. p. 231, October, 1879.

Arnold's Second Punic War. *Nation*, vol. xliii. p. 220, September, 1886.

August Boeckh. *Christian Examiner*, November, 1867.

Beesly's Catiline, Clodius, etc. *Nation*, vol. xxvii. p. 133, August, 1878.

Beesly's The Gracchi. *Nation*, vol. xxx. p. 179, March, 1880.

Beloch's Italian Confederacy. *Nation*, vol. xxxviii. p. 280, March, 1884.

Bender's Rom und römisches Leben. *Nation*, vol. xxxvii. p. 77, July, 1883.

Bender's Roman Literature. *Nation*, vol. xxx. p. 314, April, 1880.

Bernhardy's Roman Literature. *Christian Examiner*, September, 1859.

Boissier's La Religion Romaine. *North American Review*, vol. cxxi. p. 206, July, 1875.

Cæsar's Gallic War. Edited with J. H. Allen and J. B. Greenough. Boston, 1885. 8vo. pp. 149.*

Capes's Age of the Antonines. *Nation*, vol. xxix. p. 13, July, 1879.

Capes's Early Roman Empire. *Nation*, vol. xxiv. p. 386, June, 1877.

Church's Story of Carthage. *Nation*, vol. xliii. p. 484, December, 1886.

Cicero de Senectute. Edited with J. H. Allen and J. B. Greenough. Boston, 1875. 12mo. pp. 57.*

Coulanges's Landed Property in the Roman Empire. *Nation*, vol. xvii. p. 369, December, 1873.

Crowell's Latin Poets. *Nation*, vol. xxxv. p. 228, September, 1882.

Curteis's History of the Roman Empire. *Nation*, vol. xxi. p. 266, October, 1875.

Davis's Carthage and her Remains. *Christian Examiner*, vol. lxxi. p. 447, November, 1861.

Day with a Roman Gentleman, A. *Hours at Home*, vol. x. p. 389, March, 1870.

Dietrich's Beiträge zur Kenntniss des römischen Staatspächtersystem. *Nation*, vol. xxviii. p. 302, May, 1879.

Duruy's Histoire des Romains. *Nation*, vol. xxvii. p. 70, August, 1878.

Dyer's Kings of Rome. *Christian Examiner*, vol. lxxxv. p. 47, July, 1868; *Nation*, vol. vi. p. 433, May, 1868.

Dyer's Pompeii. *Christian Examiner*, vol. lxxxvii. p. 228, September, 1869.

Erbe's Cornelius Nepos. *Nation*, vol. xliv. p. 34, January, 1887.

Fröhlich's Cæsar-Literatur. *Nation*, vol. xxviii. p. 232, April, 1879.

Froude's Cæsar. *Nation*, vol. xxix. p. 161, September, 1879.

Gardner's Latin School Series. *Nation*, vol. xvi. p. 47, January, 1873.

Geffroy's Germania of Tacitus. *Nation*, vol. xix. p. 9, July, 1874.

Gentz's Das patricische Rom. *Nation*, vol. xxviii. p. 302, May, 1879.

Gerlach und Bachofen's Die Geschichte der Römer. *North American Review,* vol. lxxxiv. p. 226, January, 1857.

Germania and Agricola of Tacitus. Boston, 1880. 8vo. pp. 68.*

Guiraud's Comitia Centuriata *Nation,* vol. xxxiii. p. 494, December, 1881.

Hardy's Letters of Pliny and Trajan. *Nation,* vol. xlix. p. 260, September, 1889.

Hartung's Religion der Römer. *Christian Examiner,* January, 1867.

Heisterbergk's Jus Italicum. *Nation,* vol. xliii. p. 12, July, 1886.

Herty's Young Carthaginian. *Nation,* vol. xliii. p. 459, December, 1886.

Hirschfeld's Untersuchungen auf dem Gebiete der römischen Verwaltungsgeschichte. *Nation,* vol. xxviii. p. 302, May, 1879.

Hodgkin's Letters of Cassiodorus. *Nation,* vol. xliv. p. 279, March, 1887.

Holzapfel's De Transitione ad Plebem. *Nation,* vol. xxviii. p. 302, May, 1879.

How the Roman spent his Year. *Lippincott,* vol. xxxiii. p. 345, April, 1884.†

Ihne's Early Rome. *Nation,* vol. xxvii. p. 249, October, 1878.

Ihne's History of Rome. *Nation,* vol. ix. p. 319, October, 1869; *North American Review,* vol. cxii. p. 424, April, 1871; *Nation,* vol. xxxii. p. 151, March, 1881.

Inge's Society in Rome. *Nation,* vol. xlvi. p. 456, May, 1888.

Jordan's Die Könige im alten Italien. *Nation,* vol. xlvii. p. 34, July, 1888.

Jordan's Topographie der Stadt Rom. *Nation,* vol. xlii. p. 194, March, 1886.

Judson's Cæsar's Army. *Nation,* vol. xlvii. p. 237, September, 1888.

Knoke's Kriegszüge des Germanicus in Deutschland. *Nation,* vol. xlv. p. 461, December, 1887.

Kuhn's Verfassung des römischen Reichs. *International Review,* vol. vi. p. 479, April, 1879.

Laing's Seven Kings of the Seven Hills. *Nation,* vol. xv. p. 409, December, 1872.

Lanciani's Ancient Rome. *Dial,* vol. ix. p. 238, January, 1889.

Lange's Römische Alterthümer, *North American Review,* vol. cxv. p. 464, October, 1872.

Latin Composition. Boston, 1877. 12mo. pp. 40.*

Latin Lessons. Edited with J. H. Allen. Boston, 1870. 12mo. pp. 134.*

Latin Reader. Edited with J. H. Allen. Boston, 1869. 12mo. pp. 205.*

Latin Selections. Edited with J. H. Allen and J. B. Greenough. Boston, 1873. 12mo. pp. 64.*

Leighton's History of Rome. *Nation,* vol. xxx. p. 757, January, 1880.

Lex Curiata de Imperio. *Proceedings of the American Philological Association,* July, 1888.†

Locality of the Saltus Teutoburgiensis. *Proceedings of the American Philological Association,* July, 1888.†

Long's Decline of the Roman Republic. *Nation,* vol. xi. p. 208, September, 1870; *North American Review,* vol. cxv. p. 467, October, 1872; *Nation,* vol. xix. p. 352, November, 1874.

Madvig's Roman Antiquities. *Nation,* vol. xxxiv. p. 146, February, 1882.

Manual Latin Grammar. With J. H. Allen. Boston, 1870. 12mo. pp. 145.*

Marquardt's Roman Antiquities. *Christian Examiner,* vol. lxiv. p. 137, January, 1858; vol. lxxxii. p. 120, January, 1867; *North American Review,* vol. cxix. p. 428, October, 1874.

Marquardt's Staatsverwaltung. *Nation,* vol. xviii. p. 333, May, 1874; vol. xxiv. p. 281, May, 1877.

Merivale's Fall of the Roman Republic. *Nation*, vol. iv. p. 451, 1867; *Christian Examiner*, vol. lxxxiii. p. 386, November, 1867.

Merivale's General History of Rome. *Nation*, vol. xxii. p. 31, January, 1876.

Merivale's History of the Romans under the Empire. *Christian Examiner*, vol. lxxx. p. 125, January, 1866.

Merivale's Roman Triumvirates. *Nation*, vol. xxv. p. 306, November, 1877.

Mommsen. *Nation*, vol. xlv. p. 412, November, 1887.†

Mommsen's Comites Augusti. *Nation*, vol. ix. p. 507, December, 1869.

Mommsen's History of Rome. *North American Review*, vol. lxxxiv. p. 226, January, 1857; *Christian Examiner*, vol. lxxxi. p. 284, September, 1866; *Nation*, vol. iv. p. 468, December, 1867; vol. xviii. p. 284, April, 1874; vol. xliv. p. 251, March, 1887.

Mommsen's Römische Forschungen. *Nation*, vol. xxxii. p. 61, January, 1881.

Mommsen's Römisches Staatsrecht. *Nation*, vol. xiv. p. 422, June, 1872; vol. xlvii. p. 500, December, 1888; *North American Review*, vol. cxvi. p. 447, April, 1873; vol. cxxi. p. 433, October, 1875.

Monetary Crisis in Rome, A.D. 33. *Transactions of the American Philological Association*, 1887, p. 5.†

Montesquieu's Grandeur et Décadence des Romains. *Dial*, vol. iii. p. 40, June, 1882.

Morgan upon Early Roman History. *Penn Monthly*, vol. x. p. 115.†

Napoleon's Cæsar. *Nation*, vol. iv. p. 85, 1867; *Christian Examiner*, vol. lxxxii. p. 255, March, 1867.

Nitzsch's Rome. *Nation*, vol. xlii. p. 509, June, 1886.

Ovid. Edited with J. H. Allen and J. B. Greenough. Boston, 1875. 12mo. pp. 282.*

Papillon's Virgil. *Nation*, vol. xxxv. p. 316, October, 1882.

Perrot's Mémoires d'Archéologie, etc. *Nation*, vol. xxi. p. 389, December, 1875.

Peter's Geschichte Roms. *North American Review*, vol. lxxxiv. p. 226, January, 1857.

Politics of Early Rome. *Christian Examiner*, vol. lxvii., p. 379, November, 1859.†

Pollard's Sallust. *Nation*, vol. xxxv. p. 228, September, 1882.

Preller's Roman Mythology. *Christian Examiner*, vol. lxvi. p. 296, March, 1859.

Preparatory Latin Course. Edited with J. H. Allen and J. B. Greenough. Boston, 1875. 12mo. pp. 301.*

Religion of the Romans. *North American Review*, vol. cxiii. p. 30, 1873.†

Réville's La Religion à Rome. *Nation*, vol. xliii. p. 314, September, 1886.

Richardson's Roman Orthoepy. *Christian Examiner*, vol. lxviii. p. 316, March, 1860.

Sallust's Catiline. Edited with J. H. Allen and J. B. Greenough. Boston, 1874. 12mo. pp. 84.*

Schaeffer's Latin Chart. *Nation*, vol. xi. p. 122. August, 1870.

Schmitz's History of Latin Literature. *Nation*, vol. xxvii. p. 103. August, 1878.

Schwartz's Der Ursprung der Stamm- und Gründungssage Roms, etc. *Nation*, vol. xxviii. p. 302, May, 1879.

Schwegler's Römische Geschichte. *North American Review*, vol. lxxxiv. p. 226, January, 1857; *Christian Examiner*, vol. lxiv. p. 137, January, 1858; vol. lxvi. p. 295, March, 1859; *North American Review*, vol. cxix. p. 182, July, 1874.

Searing's Æneid. *Nation*, vol. ix. p. 255, September, 1869.

Seeley's Livy. *North American Review*, vol. cxiv. p. 419, April, 1872.

Select Orations of Cicero. Edited with J. H. Allen and J. B. Greenough. Boston, 1889. 12mo. pp. 370.*

Shepard's History of Roman Empire. *Nation*, vol. xlii. p. 112, February, 1886.

Short History of the Roman People. Boston, 1890. 12mo. pp. 370.*

Shorter Course of Latin Prose. Edited with J. H. Allen and J. B. Greenough. Boston, 1873. 12mo. pp. 64.*

Smith's Latin Selections. *Nation*, vol. xxxvi. p. 262, March, 1883.

Smith's Rome and Carthage. *Dial*, vol. ii. p. 17, May, 1881 ; *Nation*, vol. xxxiii. p. 160, August, 1881.

Stuart's Select Orations of Cicero. *Nation*, vol. ix. p. 195, September, 1869.

Sturenberg's Zu den Schlachtfeldern am transimenischen See, und in den caudinischen Pässen. *Nation*, vol. xlix. p. 214, September, 1889.

Thompson's Scalæ Novæ. *Christian Examiner*, vol. lxxxv. p. 359, November, 1868.

Tighe's Development of the Roman Constitution. *Nation*, vol. xlv. p. 19, July, 1887.

Trollope's Cicero. *Nation*, vol. xxxiii. p. 75, July, 1881.

Utility of Classical Studies. *Wisconsin Journal of Education*, vol. iv. p. 11, 1874.†

Virgil. Edited with J. H. Allen and J. B. Greenough. Boston, 1875. 12mo. pp. 188.*

Wainwright's Julius Cæsar. *Nation*, vol. ix. p. 155, August, 1869.

Wallon's Slavery in Rome. *North American Review*, vol. xci. p. 90, July, 1860.†

Watson's Marcus Aurelius. *Nation*, vol. xxxviii. p. 529, June, 1884.

Wiedemeister's Insanity of the Cæsars. *Nation*, vol. xxi. p. 182, September, 1875.

Wilkinson's Preparatory Latin Course in English. *Nation*, vol. xxxviii. p. 473, May, 1884.

Willen's Le Sénat Romain. *Nation*, vol. xxviii. p. 420, June, 1879.

CLASSICAL HISTORY AND PHILOLOGY.

Abbott and Matheson's Skeleton Outline of Greek and Roman History. *Nation*, vol. xl. p. 81, January, 1885.

Anthon, Professor. *Nation*, vol. v. p. 104, August, 1867.†

Bigg and Limcox (Eds.), Catena Classicorum. *Nation*, vol. xiii. p. 41, July, 1871.

Corinthian Custom, A. *Aldine*, October, 1871.

Cruttwell's History of Roman Literature. *Nation*, vol. xxvii. p. 405, December, 1878.

Day in Athens with Socrates, A. *Nation*, vol. xxxviii. p. 283, March, 1884.

Gray's Classics for the Millions. *Nation*, vol. xxxiv. p. 366, April, 1882.

Hand-book of Classical Geography, Chronology, Mythology, and Antiquities. Prepared for the use of schools by T. P. Allen and W. F. Allen. Boston, 1861.*

Jenning and Johnstone's Half-hours with Greek and Latin Authors. *Nation*, vol. xxxiii. p. 498, December, 1881.

Louage's History of Classical Literature. *Nation*, vol. xvii. p. 198, September, 1873.

Marcel's Study of Language. *North American Review*, vol. cix. p. 285, July, 1869.

Morris's Classical Literature. *Nation*, vol. xxxii. p. 18, January, 1881.
Perrot's Mémoires d'Archéologie, d'Épigraphie, et d'Histoire. *Nation*, vol. xxi. p. 389, December, 1875.
Reber's History of Ancient Art. *Dial*, vol. iii. p. 224, February, 1883.
Smith's Dictionary of Greek and Roman Geography. *North American Review*, vol. lxxxi. p. 268, July, 1855.

Taylor's Methods of Classical Study. *Christian Examiner*, May, 1862.
Teubner and Tauchnitz's Classics. *Christian Examiner*, January, 1858.
White's Classic Literature. *Nation*, vol. xxv. p. 290, November, 1877.
Wordsworth's Fragments, etc. *Nation*, vol. xx. p. 223, April, 1875.

MEDIÆVAL AND MODERN HISTORY.

Agriculture in the Middle Ages. *Transactions of Wisconsin State Agricultural Society*, 1876–77, p. 205.†
Church's Beginnings of Middle Ages. *Nation*, vol. xxvii. p. 200, September, 1878.
Coulanges's Origin of Feudality. *Nation*, vol. xix. p. 366, December, 1874.
Emerton's Middle Ages. *Nation*, vol. xlvii. p. 217, September, 1888.
Hallam's Middle Ages. *Nation*, vol. xiii. p. 193, September, 1871.
Lodge's Modern Europe, *Nation*, vol. xliii. p. 165, August, 1886.

Michelet's Modern History. *Nation*, vol. xx. p. 428, June, 1875.
Myer's Outlines of Mediæval and Modern History. *Nation*, vol. xliii. p. 145, August, 1886; vol. xlvii. p. 152, August, 1888.
Nasse's Agricultural Communities of Middle Ages. *Nation*, vol. xviii. p. 204, March, 1874.
Stillé's Studies in Mediæval History. *Nation*, vol. xxxiv. p. 447, May, 1882; *Dial*, vol. iii. p. 6, May, 1882.
Thalheimer's Modern History. *Nation*, vol. xix. p. 189, September, 1874.

HISTORY OF ENGLAND, SCOTLAND, AND IRELAND.

Adams's Essays in Anglo-Saxon Law. *North American Review*, vol. xxiv. p. 328, March, 1877.
Airy's English Restoration and Louis XIV. *Nation*, vol. xlviii. p. 293, April, 1889.
Airy's Romans in Britain. *Nation*, vol. xliv. p. 511, June, 1887.
Anmerkung zur Macaulay's History of England. *Nation*, vol. xxxvi. p. 38, January, 1883.
Archer's Crusade of Richard I. *Nation*, vol. xlviii. p. 387, May, 1889.

Armitage's English Nation. *Nation*, vol. xxv. p. 77, August, 1877.
Axon's Cheshire Gleanings. *Nation*, vol. xxxix. p. 32, July, 1884.
Axon's Lancashire Gleannigs. *Nation*, vol. xxxvii. p. 300, October, 1883.
Bailey's Succession to the English Crown. *Nation*, vol. xxx. p. 274, April, 1880.
Baker's Chronicon, etc. *Nation*, vol. xlix. p. 254, September, 1889.

Ball's Historical Review of the Legislative Systems Operative in Ireland, etc. *Dial,* vol. ix. p. 153, November, 1888.

Bémont's Simon de Montfort. *Nation,*vol. xliii. p. 124, August, 1886.

Besant and Rice's Whittington. *Nation,* vol. xxxiv. p. 62, January, 1882.

Bigelow's Placita Anglo-Normannica. *Nation,* vol. xxix. p. 298, October, 1879.

Bloomfield's Reminiscences of Court and Diplomatic Life. *Nation,* vol. xxxvi. p. 109, February, 1883.

Bright's History of England. *Nation,* vol. xxiii. p. 201, September, 1876; vol. xxv. p. 245, October, 1877; vol. xlviii. p. 414, May, 1889.

Bright's School History of England. *Nation,* vol. xxii. p. 86, February, 1876.

Bright's Speeches. *Nation,* vol. xxix. p. 409, December, 1879.

Browning's Gower's Dispatches. *Nation,* vol. xliii. p. 36, July, 1886.

Burt's Synoptical History of England. *Nation,* vol. xx. p. 211, March, 1875.

Burton's History of Scotland. *Nation,* vol. xvi. p. 301, May, 1873; vol. xix. p. 41, July, 1874.

Calcott's Little Arthur's History of England. *Nation,* vol. xxxix. p. 403, November, 1884.

Cavalier Playing Cards. *Nation,* vol. xliii. p. 56, July, 1886.

Chancellor's Life of Charles I. *Nation,* vol. xliii. p. 258, September, 1886.

Collins's Bolingbroke. *Nation,* vol. xliii. p. 164, August, 1886.

Cooper's Topics in English History. *Nation,* vol. xlviii. p. 119, February, 1889.

Cordery and Phillpott's King and Commonwealth. *Nation,* vol. xxii. p. 296, May, 1876.

Creasy's History of England. *Nation,* vol. viii. p. 497, June, 1869; *Old and New,* vol. iv. p. 99, July, 1871.

Creighton's Cardinal Wolsey. *Nation,* vol. xlvii. p. 343, October, 1888.

Creighton's Edward the Black Prince. *Nation,* vol. xxiv. p. 152, March, 1877.

Creighton's Raleigh. *Nation,* vol. xxvi. p. 249, April, 1878.

Creighton's Simon de Montfort. *Nation,* vol. xxiv. p. 152, March, 1877.

Cusack's Patriot's History of Ireland. *Nation,* vol. ix. p. 393, November, 1869.

Domesday Book (note). *Nation,* vol. xiv. p. 24, January, 1872.

Dove's Domesday Studies. *Nation,* vol. xlvii. p. 155, August, 1888.

Earle's Land Charters. *Nation,* vol. xlvii. p. 523, December, 1888.

Edwards's Life of Raleigh. *Nation,* vol. viii. p. 456, June, 1869.

Elliot's Life of Godolphin. *Nation,* vol. xlix. p. 238, September, 1889.

Elton's Origins of English History. *Nation,* vol. xxxiv. p. 255, March, 1882.

English Cottagers of the Middle Ages, The. *Transactions of Wisconsin Academy of Sciences, Arts, and Letters,* vol. v.†

English History in Short Stories. *Nation,* vol. xxviii. p. 273, April, 1879.

Epping Forest Survey. *Nation,* vol. xxiii. p. 314, November, 1876.

Ewald's Stories from the State Papers. *Nation,* vol. xxxiv. p. 550, June, 1882.

Ferguson's Laird of Lag. *Nation,* vol. xliii. p. 62, July, 1886.

Fisher's Land-holding in Ireland. *Nation,* vol. xxvii. p. 98, August, 1878.

Fonblanque's Life of General Burgoyne. *Nation,* vol. xxii. p. 250, April, 1876.

Fortesque's Governance of England. *Dial,* vol. vii. p. 42, June, 1886.

Freeman's Lectures. *Nation*, vol. xlvii. p. 79, July, 1888.

Freeman's Norman Conquest. *North American Review*, vol. cx. p. 349, April, 1870; *Nation*, vol. ix. p. 31, July, 1869; vol. x. p. 45, January, 1870; vol. xiv. p. 341, May, 1872; vol. xxiii. p. 331, November, 1876.

Freeman's Old English History. *Old and New*, vol. i. p. 258, February, 1870.

Freeman's Short History of the Norman Conquest. *Nation*, vol. xxxi. p. 295, October, 1880.

Friedman's Anne Boleyn. *Nation*, vol. xl. p. 307, April, 1885.

Froude's Last Volumes. *Nation*, vol. x. p. 323, May, 1870.

Gädeke's Mary Queen of Scots. *Nation*, vol. xxxvii. p. 57, July, 1883.

Gairdner's England : Early Chroniclers of Europe Series. *Nation*, vol. xxxi. p. 101, August, 1880.

Gairdner's Houses of Lancaster and York. *Nation*, vol. xx. p. 206, April, 1875.

Gairdner and Speddings's Studies in English History. *Nation*, vol. xxxiv. p. 364, April, 1882.

Gardiner's English Histories. *Nation*, vol. xxxiii. p. 377, November, 1881.

Gardiner's History of England. *Nation*, vol. xxxvii. p. 449, November, 1883.— Vols. V. and VI. *Nation*, vol. xxxviii. p. 189, February, 1884.—Vol. VII. *Nation*, vol. xxxviii. p. 295, April, 1884.— Vol. VIII. *Nation*, vol. xxxviii. p. 484, June, 1884.— Vol. IX. *Nation*, vol. xxxix. p. 13, July, 1884.—Vol. X. *Nation*, vol. xxxix. p. 288, October, 1884.

Gentleman's Magazine Library. *Nation*, vol. xlv. p. 396, November, 1887.

Gneist's English Parliament. *Nation*, vol. xlv. p. 139, August, 1887; vol. xlv. p. 274, October, 1887; *Dial*, vol. vii. p. 185, December, 1886.

Great Case of the Impositions, The. *Nation*, vol. xxxvi. p. 173, February, 1883.

Green's Conquest of England. *Dial*, vol. iv. p. 280, March, 1884.

Green's (Mrs.) Henry II. *Nation*, vol. xlvii. p. 422, November, 1888.

Green's Short History of the English People. *Nation*, vol. xx. p. 226, April, 1875.

Gross's Gilda Mercatoria. *Nation*, vol. xxxviii. p. 15, January, 1884.

Guest's Handbook of English History. *Nation*, vol. xliii. p. 202, September, 1886.

Guest's Lectures on English History. *Nation*, vol. xxix. p. 164, September, 1879.

Hall's Society in the Elizabethan Age. *Nation*, vol. xlv. p. 358, November, 1887.

Higginson's English Statesmen. *Nation*, vol. xx. p. 367, May, 1875.

Hood's Life of Oliver Cromwell. *Nation*, vol. xxxvii. p. 146, August, 1883.

Hosmer's Life of Sir Henry Vane. *Nation*, vol. xlviii. p. 371, May, 1889.

Hughes's Alfred the Great. *Nation*, vol. x. p. 325, May, 1870.

Hutchinson's Memoirs of Colonel Hutchinson. *Nation*, vol. xlii. p. 453, May, 1886.

Innes's Scotch Antiquities. *Nation*, vol. xx. p. 223, April, 1875.

Jessop's Coming of the Friars. *Nation*, vol. xlviii. p. 532, June, 1889.

Jewett's Normans. *Nation*, vol. xliv. p. 477, June, 1887.

Kautman's Queens of England. *Nation*, vol. xxxvii. p. 508, December, 1883.

Lancaster's English History. *Nation*, vol. xxv. p. 126, August, 1877.

Lappenberg's England under Anglo-Saxon Kings. *Nation*, vol. xxxii. p. 285, April, 1881.

Leader's Mary Queen of Scots. *Nation*, vol. xxxiii. p. 200, September, 1881.

Lecky's History of England. *Nation*, vol. xxxv. p. 160, August, 1882.

Lee's Reginald Pole. *Nation*, vol. xlvi. p. 393, May, 1888.

Lenz's König Sigismund und Heinrich der Fünfte von England. *Nation*, vol. xx. p. 226, April, 1875.

Location of Clovesho. *Nation*, vol. xliv. p. 491, June, 1887.

Loci e Libro Veritatum. *Nation*, vol. xxxiii. p. 360, November, 1881.

Lossing's History of England. *Nation*, vol. xiii. p. 311, November, 1871.

Luckock's The Bishops in the Tower. *Nation*, vol. xliv. p. 302, April, 1887.

Lupton's History of England. *Nation*, vol. xxxvi. p. 476, May, 1883.

Macarthur's History of Scotland. *Nation*, vol. xviii. p. 95, February, 1874.

Manchester (England), "Chetham Society" of. Literary and Historical Remains of Lancaster and Chester Counties. *Nation*, vol. xlvii. p. 113, August, 1888.

Markham's "The Fighting Veres." *Nation*, vol. xlvii. p. 199, September, 1888.

Masson's Life of Milton. *Nation*, vol. xiii. p. 91, August, 1871; vol. xvii. p. 165, September, 1873; vol. xxxi. p. 15, July, 1880.

McCalman's History of England. *Nation*, vol. xxxii. p. 65, January, 1881.

McCarthy's Epoch of Reform. *Nation*, vol. xxxv. p. 120, August, 1882; *Dial*, vol. iii. p. 79, August, 1882.

McCarthy's History of Ireland. *Nation*, vol. xxxvii. p. 193, August, 1883.

McCarthy's History of Our Own Times. *Dial*, vol. i. p. 196, January, 1881.

Michell's Scottish Expedition to Norway. *Nation*, vol. xliii. p. 220, September, 1886.

Moberly's Early Tudors. *Nation*, vol. xlv. p. 139, August, 1887.

Morris's Claverhouse. *Nation*, vol. xlvi. p. 39, January, 1888.

Morris's Early Hanoverians. *Nation*, vol. xlii. p. 346, April, 1886.

Morris's History of England. *Nation*, vol. xxx. p. 293, April, 1880.

Nicholas's British Ethnology. *Nation*, vol. xx. p. 226, April, 1875.

Norgate's England under the Angevin Kings. *Nation*, vol. xlv. p. 139, August, 1887.

Ochenkowski's England's Gesetzgebung. *Nation*, vol. xxviii. p. 102, February, 1879.

Origin of the Freeholders. *Transactions of Wisconsin Academy of Sciences, Arts, and Letters*, vol. iv. p. 19.†

Outline Studies in the History of Ireland. Chicago, 1887. 32mo. pp. 7.*

Pearson's English History in Fourteenth Century. *Nation*, vol. xxiii. p. 261, October, 1876.

Picton's Life of Oliver Cromwell. *Nation*, vol. xxxvii. p. 146, August, 1883; *Dial*, vol. iv. p. 14, May, 1883.

Preston's Yeomen of the Guard. *Nation*, vol. xliii. p. 84, July, 1886.

Ranks and Classes among the Anglo-Saxons. *Transactions of Wisconsin Academy of Sciences, Arts, and Letters*, vol. ii. p. 234.†

Ransome's History of England. *Nation*, vol. xlv. p. 444, December, 1887.

Reader's Guide to English History, The, with supplement extending the plan to other countries and periods. Boston, 1888. 12mo. pp. 49.*

Rhys's Celtic Britain. *Nation*, vol. xxxvii. p. 60, July, 1883.

Rideing's Young Folks' History of London. *Nation*, vol. xxxix. p. 487, December, 1884.

Round's Domesday of Colchester. *Nation*, vol. xxxvi. p. 213, March, 1883.

Rural Classes of England in the Thirteenth Century, The. *Transactions of Wisconsin Academy of Sciences, Arts, and Letters,* vol. ii. p. 220.†

Rural Population of England, The, as classified in Domesday Book. *Transactions of Wisconsin Academy of Sciences, Arts, and Letters,* vol. i. p. 167.†

Sadlier's History of Ireland. *Nation,* vol. xli. p. 450, November, 1885.

Schiern's Earl of Bothwell. *Nation,* vol. xxx. p. 389, May, 1880.

Seebohm's English Village Communities. *Nation,* vol. xxxviii. p. 78, January, 1884; *Science,* vol. iii. p. 786, June, 1884.

Smith's Hallam's England. *Nation,* vol. xvi. p. 222, March, 1873.

Smith's History of English Institutions. *Nation,* vol. xviii. p. 209, March, 1874.

Smith's Story of the English Jacobins. *Nation,* vol. xxxiii. p. 381, November, 1881.

Stubbs's Constitutional History of England, Vol. II. *North American Review,* vol. cxxiii. p. 161, July, 1876.

Stubbs's Early Plantagenets. *Nation,* vol. xxiv. p. 198, March, 1877.

Stubbs's Lectures. *Nation,* vol. xliv. p. 193, March, 1887.

Taswell-Langmead's English Constitutional History. *Nation,* vol. xxii. p. 284, April, 1876.

Thalheimer's History of England. *Nation,* vol. xxi. p. 252, October, 1875.

Towle's Drake, the Sea King of Devon. *Nation,* vol. xxxv. p. 384, November, 1882.

Towle's History of England. *Nation,* vol. xliii. p. 165, August, 1886.

Towle's Raleigh. *Nation,* vol. xxxiii. p. 456, December, 1881.

Traill's Shaftesbury. *Nation,* vol. xliii. p. 220, September, 1886.

Trial of King John. *Nation,* vol. xliii. p. 544, December, 1886.

Village Community and Serfdom in England. *Transactions of Wisconsin Academy of Sciences, Arts, and Letters,* vol. vii. p. 130.†

Walpole's History of Ireland. *Dial,* vol. iii. p. 133, November, 1882.

Warburton's Edward III. *Nation,* vol. xxxvi. p. 68, January, 1883.

Wheeler's Sketches from English History. *Nation,* vol. xliv. p. 151, February, 1887.

Yeatman's Introduction to the Study of Early English History. *Nation,* vol. xx. p. 226, April, 1875.

Yonge's History of England. *Nation,* vol. xxix. p. 354, November, 1879.

Yonge's Jubilee Book. *Nation,* vol. xliv. p. 470, June, 1887.

GERMANIC HISTORY.

Arnold's Deutsche Urzeit. *Nation,* vol. xxxi. p. 210, September, 1880.

Arnold's Wanderungen, etc. *North American Review,* vol. cxxiii. p. 151, July, 1876.

Baring-Gould's Germany. *Nation,* vol. xliii. p. 202, September, 1886.

Bebel's Der deutsche Bauernkrieg. *Nation,* vol. xxiv. p. 222, April, 1877.

Bezold's König Sigmund. *Nation,* vol. xxii. p. 291, May, 1876; vol. xxv. p. 288, November, 1877.

Böhm (Ed.), Reformation of Emperor Sigismund. *Nation,* vol. xxiv. p. 75, February, 1877.

Brackenbury's Frederick the Great. *Nation,* vol. xxxviii. p. 454, May, 1884.

Bradley's Story of the Goths. *Nation*, vol. xlvi. p. 475, June, 1888.

Brülcke's Germanic Diet. *Nation*, vol. xxxix. p. 13, July, 1884.

Bryce's Holy Roman Empire. *North American Review*, vol. cxii. p. 455, April, 1871.

Döbner's Die Auseinandersetzung zwischen Ludwig IV. dem Bayer und Friedrich dem Schönen von Oesterreich im Jahre 1325. *Nation*, vol. xxv. p. 198, September, 1877.

Duc de Broglie's Frederick II. and Maria Theresa. *Nation*, vol. xxxvii. p. 185, August, 1883.

Ebrard's Der erste Annäherungsversuch König Wenzels an dem schwäbisch-rheinischen Städtebund. *Nation*, vol. xxvii. p. 85, August, 1878.

Eggert's Geschichte Landfrieden. *Nation*, vol. xxvii. p. 351, December, 1878.

Friedjung's Kaiser Karl IV. und sein Antheil am geistigen Leben seiner Zeit. *Nation*, vol. xxiv. p. 15, January, 1877.

Geffroy's article in Revue des Deux Mondes. *Nation*, vol. xvii. p. 291, October, 1873.

Gengler's Deutsche Rechtsdenkmäler. *Nation*, vol. xxiv. p. 236, April, 1877.

Gierke's Untersuchungen, etc. *Nation*, vol. xxx. p. 455, June, 1880.

Giesebrecht's Geschichte der Kaiserzeit. *Nation*, vol. xix. p. 45, July, 1874.

Gindely's Thirty Years' War. *Nation*, vol. xxxv. p. 424, November, 1882.

Hausischer Geschichtsverein. *Nation*, vol. xxv. p. 27, July, 1877.

Hegel's Verfassungsgeschichte von Cöln. *Nation*, vol. xxvii. p. 26, July, 1878.

Heidemann's Peter von Aspelt als Kirchenfürst und Staatsmann. *Nation*, vol. xxiv. p. 14, January, 1877.

Historical Commission. *Nation*, vol. xiv. p. 322, May, 1872; vol. xviii. p. 11, January, 1874.

Inama-Sternegg's Wirthschaftsgeschichte. *Nation*, vol. xxxii. p. 45, January, 1881.

Johnson's Peasant Life in Germany. *Christian Examiner*, vol. lxvi. p. 147, January, 1859.

Knoke's Kriegszüge des Germanicus in Deutschland. *Nation*, vol. xlv. p. 461, December, 1887.

Kopp's Geschichte der eidgenössischen Bünde. *Nation*, vol. xxxv. p. 13, July, 1882.

Krause's Beziehungen zwischen Hapsburg und Burgund bis zum Ausgang der Trierer Zusammenkunft im Jahre 1473. *Nation*, vol. xxvii. p. 85, August, 1878.

Krone and Mayer's Austria. *Nation*, vol. xxix. p. 79, July, 1879.

Laurent's Aachene Zustände. *Nation*, vol. xxiv. p. 59, January, 1877.

Leding's Die Freiheit der Friesen, etc. *Nation*, vol. xxx. p. 177, March, 1880.

Lenz's König Sigismund und Heinrich der Fünfte von England. *Nation*, vol. xx. p. 226, April, 1875.

Lewis's History of Germany. *Nation*, vol. xix. p. 369, December, 1874.

Lindner's Geschichte des deutschen Reiches, etc. *North American Review*, vol. cxxiii. p. 165, July, 1876.

Lochner's Geschichte der Reichsstadt Nürnberg zur Zeit Kaiser Karls IV. *Nation*, vol. xxiv. p. 15, January, 1877.

Longman's Frederick the Great. *Dial*, vol. i. p. 238, March, 1881; *Nation*, vol. xxxii. p. 376, May, 1881.

Lorenz's Geschichtsquellen, etc. *Nation*, vol. xxvi. p. 10, January, 1878.

Loserth's Beiträge zur Geschichte der hussitischen Bewegung. *Nation*, vol. xxvii. p. 85, August, 1878.

Müller's Der Kampf Ludwigs des Baiern mit der römischen Curie. *Nation*, vol. xxxv. p. 13, July, 1882.

Peake's Emperors of Germany. *Nation*, vol. xix. p. 290, October, 1874.

Ropp, von der, Deutsch-skandinavische Geschichte. *Nation*, vol. xxvi. p. 27. January, 1878.

Schmoller's Strassburgs Blüte, etc. *Nation*, vol. xxi. p. 419, December, 1875.

Schroller's Die Wahl Sigmunds zum römischen Könige., *Nation*, vol. xxv. p. 198, September, 1877.

Schweizer's Schwäbischer Bund. *Nation*, vol. xxiv. p. 209, April, 1877.

Steven's Gustavus Adolphus. *Nation*, vol. xl. p. 267, March, 1885.

Stockmar's Memoirs of Baron Stockmar. *Nation*, vol. xvii. p. 9, July, 1873.

Territorial Development of Prussia. *Aldine*, September, 1871.†

Territorial Growth of Austria. *Aldine*, July, 1871.†

Thomas's Zur Königswahl des Grafen Heinrich von Luxemburg im Jahre 1308. *Nation*, vol. xxiv. p. 14, January, 1877.

Topelius's Times of Frederick I. *Nation*, vol. xxxix. p. 18, July, 1884.

Treitschke's Germany in Nineteenth Century. *Nation*, vol. xxix. p. 131, August, 1879.

Usinger's Territory of German Empire. *Nation*, vol. xiv. p. 355, May, 1872.

Waitz's Deutsche Verfassungsgeschichte. *Nation*, vol. xxi. p. 265, October, 1875; vol. xxii. p. 195, March, 1876; vol. xxxiii. p. 135, August, 1881; *International Review*, vol. vii. p. 576, November, 1879.

Waitz and Mommsen (Eds.), Monumenta Germaniæ. *Nation*, vol. xxi. p. 262, October, 1875.

Ward's Experiences of a Diplomatist. *Nation*, vol. xv. p. 190, September, 1872.

Wenck's Clemens V. und Heinrich VII. *Nation*, vol. xxxv. p. 13, July, 1882.

Wenck's Die Wettiner im XIV. Jahrhundert. *Nation*, vol. xxv. p. 198, September, 1877.

Worthmann's Die Wahl Karls IV. zum römischen Könige. *Nation*, vol. xxiv. p. 15, January, 1877.

Yonge's History of Germany. *Nation*, vol. xxviii. p. 375, May, 1879.

HISTORY OF FRANCE.

Baird's Huguenots, etc. *Nation*, vol. xliv. p. 433, May, 1887.

Baker's Montesquieu. *Nation*, vol. xxxiv. p. 549, June, 1882.

Bancroft's (J.) Parliament of Paris. *Nation*, vol. xxxix. p. 222, September, 1884.

Bonnenière's Histoire des Paysans. *North American Review*, vol. cxxi. p. 202, July, 1875.

Bourgeois's Neuchâtel et la Politique Prussienne en Franche-Comté. *Nation*, vol. xlv. p. 527, December, 1887.

Brooks's French History. *Nation*, vol. xxxiii. p. 456, December, 1881.

Chenon's Étude sur l'Histoire des Alleux en France. *Nation*, vol. xlvii. p. 417, November, 1888.

Christie's Étienne Dolet. *Nation*, vol. xxxii. p. 266, April, 1881.

Commune. *Nation*, vol. xii. p. 360, May, 1871.

Coulanges's Recherches sur Histoire. *Nation*, vol. xliii. p. 161, August, 1886.

Cutts's Charlemagne. *Nation*, vol. xxxiv. p. 550, June, 1882.

Däudliker's Charles the Bold. *Nation*, vol. xxiv. p. 251, April, 1877.

Deloche's La Trustis et l'Antrustion-royal. *Nation*, vol. xviii. p. 266, April, 1874.

Duc des Cars's Memoirs of the Duchess de Tourzel. *Nation*, vol. xliii. p. 528, December, 1886.

Duruy's Histoire de France. *Nation*, vol. xlix. p. 434, November, 1889.

Fagniez's Journal of Jean Maupoint. *Nation*, vol. xxvii. p. 303, November, 1878.

Fahlbeck's Frank Monarchy. *Nation*, vol. xxxvii. p. 436, November, 1883.

Farmer's History of the French Revolution. *Nation*, vol. xlix. p. 415, November, 1889.

Fauriel's Last Days of the Consulate. *Nation*, vol. xliii. p. 239, September, 1886.

Flammermont's Jacquerie in Beauvaisis. *Nation*, vol. xxviii. p. 420, June, 1879.

Fredericq's Ducs de Bourgogne. *Nation*, vol. xxvi. p. 249, April, 1878.

Gerard's Peace of Utrecht. *Nation*, vol. xliii. p. 103, July, 1886.

Gower's Last Days of Marie Antoinette. *Nation*, vol. xliii. p. 498, December, 1886.

Guizot's History of France. *Nation*, vol. xii. p. 385, June, 1871.

Hamley's Life of Voltaire. *Nation*, vol. xxvi. p. 102, February, 1878.

Kindersley's Bayard. *Nation*, vol. xxxix. p. 488, December, 1884.

Kirkland's History of France. *Nation*, vol. xxvii. p. 389, December, 1878.

Knights Templars. *Nation*, vol. xxxi. p. 428, December, 1880.

Lady Jackson's Old Régime. *Nation*, vol. xxxiv. p. 550, June, 1882.

Little Arthur's History of France. *Nation*, vol. xl. p. 309, April, 1885.

Longnon's Atlas Historique de la France. *Nation*, vol. xl. p. 203, March, 1885.

Masson's France: Early Chroniclers of Europe. *Nation*, vol. xxxi. p. 101, August, 1880.

Masson's Mediæval France. *Nation*, vol. xlviii. p. 60, January, 1889.

Masson's Richelieu. *Nation*, vol. xl. p. 309, April, 1885.

Mombert's Charlemagne. *Nation*, vol. xlviii. p. 144, February, 1889.

Monnier's Charlemagne. *Nation*, vol. xvi. p. 115, February, 1873.

Pardoe's Francis I. *Nation*, vol. xlvi. p. 225, March, 1888.

Perkins's France under Mazarin. *Nation*, vol. xliii. p. 215, September, 1886.

Perren's La Démocratie en France. *North American Review*, vol. cxix. p. 185, July, 1874.

Robinson's Margaret of Angoulême. *Nation*, vol. xlv. p. 79, July, 1887.

Seignobos's La Régime Féodale en Bourgogne jusqu'en 1360. *Nation*, vol. xxxvi. p. 106, February, 1883.

Taine's French Revolution. *Dial*, vol. ii. p. 91, September, 1881.

Territorial Growth of France. *Aldine*, April, 1871.†

Thackeray's (Miss) Madame de Sévigné. *Nation*, vol. xxxiii. p. 381, November, 1881.

Van Laun's French Revolutionary Epoch. *Nation*, vol. xxviii. p. 88, January, 1879.

Vizetelly's Diamond Necklace. *Nation*, vol. xxxii. p. 139, February, 1881.

Wauter's Les Libertés Communales. *Nation*, vol. xxx. p. 387, May, 1880.

Yonge's History of France. *Nation*, vol. xxix. p. 373, November, 1879.

Yonge's Marie Antoinette. *Nation*, vol. xxiv. p. 224, April, 1877.

Yonge's Wars in France. *Nation*, vol. xiii. p. 278, October, 1871.

HISTORY OF ITALY.

Bent's Genoa. *Nation*, vol. xxxii. p. 447, June, 1881.
Diary of Marino Sanudo. *Nation*, vol. xxvi. p. 374, June, 1878.
Gretton's Vicissitudes of Italy. *Christian Examiner*, vol. lxvii. p. 466, November, 1859.
Hodgkin's Invaders of Italy. *Nation*, vol. xxxii. p. 29, January, 1881 ; vol. xlii. p. 409, May, 1886.

States of the Church. *Nation*, vol. xxii. p. 47, January, 1876.
Symonds's Renaissance in Italy. *Nation*, vol. xxxiv. p. 298, April, 1882.
Thomas's Commission des Dogen Andreas Dandolo, etc. *Nation*, vol. xxvii. p. 26, July, 1878.

HISTORY OF SPAIN.

Coppée's Moors in Spain. *Dial*, vol. i. p. 257, April, 1881.
Dezert's Don Carlos. *Nation*, vol. xlix. p. 254, September, 1889.
Harrison's Spain. *Nation*, vol. xxxiii. p. 498, December, 1881.
Höfler's Castilianische Städte. *Nation*, vol. xxiv. p. 75, February, 1877.

Noble's Spanish Armada. *Nation*, vol. xliii. p. 380, November, 1886.
Prescott's Revised Works. *Nation*, vol. xviii. p. 252, April, 1874.
Yonge's Christians and Moors in Spain. *Nation*, vol. xxviii. p. 57, January, 1879.

EASTERN EUROPE.

Bachmann's George von Podiebrad. *Nation*, vol. xxiv. p. 90, February, 1877.
Beaure and Mathorei's La Roumanie. *Nation*, vol. xxvii. p. 273, October, 1878.
Bibliotheca Corvina. *Nation*, vol. xxv. p. 27, July, 1877.
Caro's Geschichte Polens. *Nation*, vol. xxi. p. 231, October, 1875.
Dole's History of Russia. *Nation*, vol. xxxiv. p. 84, January, 1882.
Fessler's History of Hungary. *Nation*, vol. xxii. p. 47, January, 1876.
Freeman's History of the Saracens. *Nation*, vol. xxiv. p. 63, January, 1877.
George von Podiebrad. *Nation*, vol. ix. p. 92, July, 1869; vol. xii. p. 322, May, 1871.

Hapgood's Epic Songs of Russia. *Dial*, vol. vii. p. 11, May, 1886.
Helfert's Böhmische Frage. *Nation*, vol. xix. p. 155, September, 1874.
Kállay's Geschichte der Serben. *Nation*, vol. xxvi. p. 293, May, 1878.
Krause's Taking of Constantinople. *Nation*, vol. xii. p. 322, May, 1871.
Leger's Études Slaves. *Nation*, vol. xxi. p. 342, November, 1875.
Pear's Fall of Constantinople. *Nation*, vol. xlii. p. 63, January, 1886.
Roesler's Origin of Wallachians. *Nation*, vol. xiv. p. 106, February, 1872.
Schlesinger's Geschichte Böhmen. *Nation*, vol. xiii. p. 338, November, 1871.

Szalay's History of Hungary. *Nation*, vol. xxii. p. 47, January, 1876.
Territorial Development of Russia. *Aldine*, November, 1871.
Völker Oesterreich-Ungarns. *Nation*, vol. xxxv. p. 202, September, 1882.

Wratislaw's Bohemian Literature. *Nation*, vol. xxvii. p. 117, August, 1878.
Wurstemberger's Russia. *Nation*, vol. xvii. p. 194, September, 1873.

AMERICAN HISTORY.

Adams's Maryland's Influence on the Land Cessions to the United States. *Nation*, vol. xl. p. 155, February, 1885.
Alden's Christopher Columbus. *Nation*, vol. xxxiv. p. 130, February, 1882.
Allen's (J. G.) Topical Studies in American History. *Nation*, vol. xlii. p. 99, February, 1886.
Anderson's Soldier and Pioneer. *Nation*, vol. xxviii. p. 358, May, 1879.
Armstrong's Primer of United States History. *Nation*, vol. xxxiii. p. 381, November, 1881.
Ballance's History of Peoria, Ill. *Nation*, vol. xiii. p. 148, August, 1871.
Bancroft's History of the United States, Vol. X. *Nation*, vol. xx. p. 80, February, 1875.
Bancroft's History of the United States. *Nation*, vol. xxii. p. 263, April, 1876.
Bancroft's History of the United States. *Dial*, vol. iii. p. 249, March, 1883.
Bancroft's History of the United States. Vol. I. *Nation*, vol. xxxvi. p. 127, February, 1883.— Vol. II. *Nation*, vol. xxxvii. p. 11, July, 1883.— Vol. III. *Nation*, vol. xxxvii. p. 431, November, 1883.— Vol. IV. *Nation*, vol. xxxviii. p. 276, March, 1884. — Vol. V. *Nation*, vol. xxxix. p. 544, December, 1884.— Vol. VI. *Nation*, vol. xl. p. 202, March, 1885.
Baxter's Pea Ridge and Prairie Grove. *Christian Examiner*, vol. lxxviii. p. 136, January, 1865.

Boys and Girls of the Revolution. *Nation*, vol. xxiii. p. 345, December, 1876.
Browne's Maryland. *Nation*, vol. xxxix. p. 484, December, 1884.
Bryant's Popular History of the United States. Vol. I. *Nation*, vol. xxiii. p. 274, November, 1876.— Vol. II. *Nation*, vol. xxvii. p. 167, September, 1878.— Vol. III. *Nation*, vol. xxix. p. 410, December, 1879.— Vol. IV. *Nation*, vol. xxxii. p. 247, April, 1881.
Butler's History of the United States. *Nation*, vol. xxi. p. 186, September, 1875.
Butterfield's Washington-Irvine Correspondence. *Nation*, vol. xxxvi. p. 476, May, 1883.
Butterworth's History of America. *Nation*, vol. xxxiii. p. 160, August, 1881.
Campbell's History of Michigan. *Nation*, vol. xxiv. p. 270, May, 1877.
Champlin's Young Folks' History of the War for the Union. *Nation*, vol. xxxiii. p. 419, November, 1881.
Channing's Town and County Government. *Nation*, vol. xxxix. p. 378, October, 1884.
Cheney's History of the Civil War. *Nation*, vol. xxxvii. p. 508, December, 1883.
Coffin's Story of Liberty. *Nation*, vol. xxvii. p. 389, December, 1878.
Cooke's Virginia. *Dial*, vol. iv. p. 131, October, 1883.
Cooper's Virginia. *Nation*, vol. xxxvii. p. 318, October, 1883.

Crooker's John Wise. *Nation*, vol. xlvii. p. 296, October, 1888.

De Vere's Romance of American History. *Nation*, vol. xv. p. 354, November, 1872.

Deane on Burgoyne. *Nation*, vol. xxvi. p. 418, June, 1878.

Dexter's As to Roger Williams. *Nation*, vol. xxiii. p. 171, September, 1876.

Doddridge's Indian Wars. *Nation*, vol. xxv. p. 141, August, 1877.

Doyle's History of the United States. *Nation*, vol. xxii. p. 296, May, 1876.

Draper's History of the Civil War. *Christian Examiner*, vol. lxxxvi. p. 115, January, 1869.

Eggleston's First Book in American History. *Nation*, vol. xlix. p. 415, November, 1881.

Eggleston's Land Systems of the New England Colonies. *Nation*, vol. xliv. p. 34, January, 1887.

Eggleston's Pocahontas. *Nation*, vol. xxix. p. 391, November, 1879.

Fisher's The Californians. *Nation*, vol. xxiv. p. 47, January, 1877.

Foster's Stephen Hopkins. *Nation*, vol. xxxix. p. 117, August, 1884.

Frothingham's Gerrit Smith. *Nation*, vol. xxvi. p. 173, March, 1878.

Frothingham's Rise of the Republic. *Nation*, vol. xv. p. 318, November, 1872.

Garrett's Boundary of South Carolina. *Nation*, vol. xlii. p. 447, May, 1886.

Gay's Life of Madison. *Nation*, vol. xxxix. p. 383, October, 1884.

Gilman's Life of Monroe. *Nation*, vol. xxxvi. p. 347, April, 1883.

Godfrey's Nantucket. *Nation*, vol. xxxv. p. 119, August, 1882.

Goodrich's Life of Columbus. *Nation*, vol. xix. p. 442, December, 1874.

Grant's Memoirs of an American Lady. *Nation*, vol. xxiv. p. 342, June, 1877.

Greene's Life of General Greene. *Nation*, vol. vi. p. 92, January, 1868; vol. xii. p. 323, May, 1871; vol. xii. p. 450, June, 1871.

Habberton's Washington. *Nation*, vol. xxxviii. p. 218, March, 1884.

Harrison's Memoir of Tench Tilghman. *Nation*, vol. xxv. p. 30, July, 1877.

Historische Zeitschrift Articles on American War. *Nation*, vol. xxvi. p. 309, May, 1878.

Ingle's Local Institutions of Virginia. *Nation*, vol. xl. p. 280, April, 1885.

Instruction in American History. *Wisconsin Journal of Education*, N.S., vol. iv. p. 380, 1874.†

Jay's Address to the New York Historical Society. *Nation*, vol. xl. p. 155, February, 1885.

Johns Hopkins Publications. *Nation*, vol. xlv. p. 460, December, 1887.

Kinzie's Waubun. *Nation*, vol. xvii. p. 134, August, 1873.

Ladd's War with Mexico. *Nation*, vol. xxxvii. p. 493, December, 1883.

Lalor's Translation of Von Holst's United States. *Nation*, vol. xxix. p. 78, July, 1879.

Leed's History of the United States. *Nation*, vol. xxvi. p. 30, January, 1878.

Leland's Fusang. *Nation*, vol. xxi. p. 138, August, 1875.

Lossing's Two Spies. *Nation*, vol. xliv. p. 151, February, 1887.

Lunt's Old New England Traits. *Nation*, vol. xvii. p. 119, August, 1873.

MacCoun's Historical Atlas of the United States. *Nation*, vol. xlix. p. 72, July, 1889.

Mackay's Founders of the American Republic. *Nation*, vol. xlii. p. 16, January, 1886.

Mackenzie's America. *Nation*, vol. xxxiv. p. 152, February, 1882.

Markham's King Philip's War. *Nation*, vol. xxxvii. p. 493, December, 1883.

Montauk and the Common Lands at Easthampton. *Nation*, vol. xxxvi. p. 403, May, 1883.

Moore's (Ed.) Rebellion Record, Parts I.–IV. *Christian Examiner*, vol. lxxi. p. 283, September, 1861.

Parkman's Conspiracy of Pontiac. *Nation*, vol. xii. p. 239, April, 1871.

Parkman's Frontenac. *Nation*, vol. xxv. p. 259, October, 1877.

Parkman's Montcalm and Wolfe. *Nation*, vol. xxxix. p. 506, December, 1884.

Pennypacker's Historical Sketches. *Nation*, vol. xxxvii. p. 214, September, 1883.

Pickering's Timothy Pickering. *Nation*, vol. v. p. 450, December, 1867.

Pierson's Lives of the Presidents of the United States. *Nation*, vol. xli. p. 450, November, 1885.

Place of the North-west in General History. *Papers of the American Historical Association*, vol. iii. p. 87, 1889.†

Porter's Constitutional History of the United States. *Nation*, vol. xxxvii. p. 104, August, 1883.

Prescott's Revised Works. *Nation*, vol. xviii. p. 252, April, 1874.

Read's Life of George Read. *Nation*, vol. xii. p. 12, January, 1871.

Recent Foreign Works on America. *Nation*, vol. xxiii. p. 61, July, 1876.

Sargent's Political Reminiscences. *Nation*, vol. xx. p. 427, June, 1875.

Schlief's Verfassung der Nordamerikanischen Union. *Nation*, vol. xxxi. p. 136, August, 1880.

Schurz's Henry Clay. *Nation*, vol. xliv. p. 536, June, 1887.

Scott's Development of Constitutional Liberty. *Nation*, vol. xxxvi. p. 176, February, 1883.

Shaler's Kentucky. *Nation*, vol. xl. p. 289, April, 1885.

Somer's Southern States. *Nation*, vol. xv. p. 44, July, 1872.

Stephen's History of the United States. *Nation*, vol. xv. p. 156, September, 1872.

Sterne's Constitutional History of the United States. *Dial*, vol. iii. p. 138, November, 1882.

Stillman's Seeking the Golden Fleece. *Nation*, vol. xxiv. p. 387, June, 1877.

Story's Life of William Carstares. *Nation*, vol. xix. p. 62, July, 1874.

Sumner's Andrew Jackson. *Nation*, vol. xxxv. p. 407, November, 1882.

Survival of Land Community in New England. *Nation*, vol. xxvi. p. 22, January, 1878.†

Talleyrand's Study upon the United States. *Nation*, vol. xxiv. p. 44, January, 1877.

Tarbox's Life of Israel Putnam. *Nation*, vol. xxiii. p. 216, October, 1876.

Towle's Magellan. *Nation*, vol. xxix. p. 391, November, 1879.

Towle's Montezuma. *Nation*, vol. xxxi. p. 364, November, 1880.

Towle's Pizarro. *Nation*, vol. xxviii. p. 273, April, 1879.

Town Nomenclature. *Nation*, vol. vii. p. 490, December, 1868.†

Town, Township, and Tithing. *Transactions of the Wisconsin Academy of Sciences, Arts, and Letters*, vol. vii. p. 141.†

Trumbull's Blue Laws of Connecticut. *Nation*, vol. xxiv. p. 269, May, 1877.

Twiss's Burial Place of Columbus. *Nation*, vol. xxix. p. 143, August, 1879.

Tyler's Letters and Times of the Tylers. *Nation*, vol. xl. p. 287, April, 1885; vol. xli. p. 364.

Tyler's Life of Patrick Henry. *Nation*, vol. xlvi. p. 306, April, 1888.

Upham's Life of Pickering. *Nation*, vol. xviii. p. 93, February, 1874.

Von Holst's Andrew Jackson. *Nation*, vol. xix. p. 301, November, 1874.

Von Holst's Calhoun. *Nation*, vol. xxxv. p. 79, July, 1882.

Von Holst's Constitutional History of the United States. *Nation*, vol. xviii. p. 364, June, 1874.

Von Holst's Constitutional History of the United States, Vol. II. *Nation*, vol. xxviii. p. 185, March, 1879.

Von Holst's Constitutional History of the United States, Vol. III. *Nation*, vol. xxxii. p. 280, April, 1881.

Von Holst's Constitutional History of the United States (Lalor's translation). *Nation*, vol. xxix. p. 78, July, 1879.

Von Holst (Note on). *Nation*, vol. xviii. p. 380, June, 1874.

Von Holst on H. B. Adams. *Nation*, vol. xxvii. p. 365, December, 1878.

Von Holst on Jameson's Constitutional Convention. *Nation*, vol. xx. p. 77, February, 1875.

Winsor's Handbook of the American Revolution. *Nation*, vol. xxx. p. 17, January, 1880.

Woodbury's Campaigns of the First Rhode Island Regiment. *Christian Examiner*, vol. lxxiii. p. 308, September, 1862.

THE SOUTH AFTER THE WAR.

Basis of Suffrage. *Nation*, vol. i. p. 363, September, 1865.†

Feeling of the South Carolinians. *Nation*, vol. i. p. 237, August, 1865.†

Feelings of the Southern Negroes. *Nation*, vol. i. p. 393, September, 1865.†

Free Labor in Louisiana. *Christian Examiner*, vol. lxxviii. p. 383, May, 1865.†

Freedmen and Free Labor in the South. *Christian Examiner*, vol. lxxvi. p. 344, May, 1864.†

Future of the South. *Christian Examiner*, vol. lxxiii. p. 435, November, 1862.†

Homesteads for Negroes. *Boston Advertiser*, July, 1866.†

Negro Dialect. *Nation*, vol. i. p. 744, 1865.†

Reconstruction. *Boston Advertiser*, September, 1866.†

Slave Songs of the United States. Compiled in connection with Charles P. Ware and Lucy M. Garrison. New York, 1867. 8vo, pp. 115.*

South Carolina. *Christian Examiner*, vol. lxxix. p. 226, September, 1865.†

Southern Whites. *Nation*, vol. i. p. 331, September, 1865.†

State of Things in South Carolina. *Nation*, vol. i. p. 172, August, 1865.†

Trip in South Carolina. *Nation*, vol. i. p. 106, July, 1865.†

Vote in South Carolina. *Advance*, December, 1868.†

MISCELLANEOUS HISTORIES.

Fredericq's Van Artevelde. *Nation*, vol. xxix. p. 227, October, 1879.

Leland's The Gypsies. *Dial*, vol. iii. p. 57, July, 1882.

Otte's Christian II. of Denmark. *Nation*, vol. xxi. p. 59, July, 1875.

Young's History of the Netherlands. *Nation*, vol. xl. p. 61, January, 1885.

Birckbeck's Distribution of Land. *Nation*, vol. xliii. p. 62, July, 1886.

Cobden Club Essays. Systems of Land Tenure. *Nation*, vol. xiv. p. 89, February, 1872.

Coulanges's Recherches sur Histoire. *Nation*, vol. xliii. p. 161, August, 1886.

Eggleston's Land System of New England Colonies. *Nation*, vol. xliv. p. 34, January, 1887.

Fenton's Early Hebrew Life. *Nation*, vol. xxxiii. p. 203, September, 1881.

Fisher's History of Land-holding. *Nation*, vol. xxii. p. 233, April, 1876.

Land Communities among the Ancient Germans. *Transactions Wisconsin Academy of Sciences, Arts, and Letters*, vol. vi. p. 28.†

Laveleye's Primitive Property. *Nation*, vol. xxvi. p. 375, June, 1878.

Maine's Ancient Law. *Nation*, vol. xi. p. 192, September, 1870.

Maine's Early Law and Custom. *Science*, vol. iii. p. 186, June, 1884.

Maine's Village Communities. *Nation*, vol. xiii. p. 370, December, 1871.

Montauk and the Common Lands at Easthampton. *Nation*, vol. xxxvi. p. 403, May, 1883.

Morgan's Ancient Society. *Penn Monthly*, vol. x. p. 115, February, 1879.

Pollock's Land Laws. *Nation*, vol. xxxviii. p. 489, June, 1884.

Primitive Communities. *Science*, vol. iii. p. 786, 1884.

Probyn's System of Land Tenure. *Nation*, vol. xxiii. p. 167, September, 1876.

Ross's Early History of Land-holding among the Germans. *Science*, vol. ii. p. 768, December, 1883; vol. iii. p. 786, June, 1884; *Nation*, xxxii. p. 260, April, 1881; vol. xxxviii. p. 78, January, 1884.

Seebohm's English Village Communities. *Science*, vol. iii. p. 786, June, 1884; *Nation*, vol. xxxviii. p. 78, January, 1884.

Survival of Land Community in New England. *Nation*, vol. xxvi. p. 22, January, 1878.†

Town, Township, and Tithing. *Transactions of the Wisconsin Academy of Sciences, Arts, and Letters*, vol. vii. p. 141.†

Tylor's Primitive Culture. *Nation*, vol. xviii. p. 161, March, 1874.

Village Community and Feudal Manor (A review of Earle's Land Charters). *Nation*, vol. xlvii. p. 523, December, 1888.

Village Community and Serfdom in England. *Transactions of the Wisconsin Academy of Sciences, Arts, and Letters*, vol. vii. p. 130.†

MILITARY ART.

Estvàn's War Pictures. *Christian Examiner*, vol. lxxv. p. 290, September, 1863.

Halleck's Art of War. *Christian Examiner*, vol. lxxii. p. 456, May, 1862.

Jomini's Art of War. *Christian Examiner*, vol. lxxiii. p. 154, July, 1862.

Judson's Cæsar's Army. *Nation*, vol. xlvii. p. 237, September, 1888.

Marmont's Spirit of Military Institutions. *Christian Examiner*, vol. lxxiii. p. 154, July, 1862.

Militia System. *Christian Examiner*, vol. lxxix. p. 428, November, 1865.

REVIEWS OF HISTORICAL MAGAZINES.

Annales de l'École Libre des Sciences Politiques. *Nation*, vol. xliv. p. 187, March, 1887.

Antiquary. *Nation*, vol. xxxiii. p. 375, November, 1881 ; vol. xxxvi. p. 511, June, 1883 ; vol. xxxvii. p. 163, August, 1883 ; vol. xxxvii. p. 528, December, 1883 ; vol. xxxviii. p. 99, January, 1884 ; vol. xxxviii. p. 257, March, 1884 ; vol. xxxviii. p. 363, April, 1884 ; vol. xxxviii. p. 406, May, 1884 ; vol. xxxix. p. 72, July, 1884 ; vol. xxxix. p. 201, September, 1884 ; vol. xxxix. p. 266, September, 1884 ; vol. xxxix. p. 353, October, 1884 ; vol. xxxix. p. 418, November, 1884 ; vol. xlii. p. 130, February, 1886 ; vol. xlii. p. 217, March, 1886 ; vol. xlii. p. 261, March, 1886 ; vol. xlii. p. 385, May, 1886 ; vol. xlii. p. 488, June, 1886 ; vol. xliii. p. 97, July, 1886 ; vol. xliii. p. 269, September, 1886 ; vol. xliii. p. 374, November, 1886 ; vol. xliv. p. 35, January, 1887 ; vol. xliv. p. 99, February, 1887 ; vol. xliv. p. 364, April, 1887 ; vol. xliv. p. 273, March, 1887 ; vol. xliv. p. 471, June, 1887 ; vol. xliv. p. 553, June, 1887 ; vol. xlv. p. 480, December, 1887 ; vol. xlvi. p. 200, March, 1888.

East Anglian. *Nation*, vol. xli. p. 465, December, 1885.

English Historical Review. *Nation*, vol. xlii. p. 101, February, 1886 ; vol. xlii. p. 509, June, 1886 ; vol. xliii. p. 138, August, 1886 ; vol. xliii. p. 456, December, 1886 ; vol. xliv. p. 187, March, 1887 ; vol. xliv. p. 450, May, 1887 ; vol. xlv. p. 481, December, 1887 ; vol. xlvi. p. 200, March, 1888 ; vol. xlvii. p. 417, November, 1888 ; vol. xlviii. p. 247, March, 1889 ; vol. xlix. p. 171, August, 1889.

Historical Reviews. *Nation*, vol. xxiv. p. 165, March, 1877.

Historische Zeitschrift. *Nation*, vol. xiii. p. 290, November, 1871.

Historische Zeitschrift. *Nation*, vol. xv. p. 428, December, 1872.

Jahresberichte der Geschichtwissenschaft. *Nation*, vol. xxxiv. p. 210, March, 1882.

La Référence Sociale (Journal). *Nation*, vol. xliv. p. 251, March, 1887.

Latine. *Nation*, vol. xxxv. p. 464, November, 1882.

Revue des Deux Mondes (note or.). *Nation*, vol. xv. p. 252, October, 1872.

Revue des Questions Historiques. *Nation*, vol. xxii. p. 291, May, 1876.

Revue Historique. *Nation*, vol. xxii. p. 131, February, 1876.

Walford's Antiquarian. *Nation*, vol. xliv. p. 164, February, 1887 ; vol. xliv. p. 364, April, 1887.

Zeitschrift für vergleichende Rechtswissenschaft. *Nation*, vol. xxviii. p. 217, March, 1879.

ANNUAL REVIEWS OF HISTORICAL LITERATURE.

Bulletin Historique. États-Unis. *Revue Historique*, vol. xiii. p. 372, 1880 ; vol. xx. p. 159, 1882 ; vol. xxvi. p. 108, 1884 ; vol. xxix. p. 124, 1885 ; vol. xxxii., 1886.

Historical Literature of 1870. *Nation*, vol. xii. p. 90, February, 1871.

Historical Literature of 1871. *Nation*, vol. xiv. p. 138, February, 1872.

Historical Literature of 1872. *Nation*, vol. xvi. p. 253, April, 1873.

Historical Literature of 1873. *Nation*, vol. xviii. p. 173, March, 1874.

Historical Literature of 1874. *Nation*, vol. xx. p. 97, February, 1875.

Historical Review of 1875. *Nation*, vol. xxii. p. 81, February, 1876.

Historical Literature of 1876. *Nation*, vol. xxiv. p. 149, March, 1877.

Historical Literature of 1877. *Nation*, vol. xxvi. p. 116, February, 1878.

Historical Literature of 1878. *Nation*, vol. xxviii. p. 166, March, 1879.

Historical Literature of 1879. *Nation*, vol. xxx. p. 156, February, 1880.

HISTORICAL AIDS.

Adams's Manual of Historical Literature. *Nation*, vol. xxxiv. p. 387, May, 1882; *Dial*, vol. ii. p. 290, April, 1882.

Atkinson's History and the Study of History. *Nation*, vol. xxxix. p. 222, September, 1884.

Diesterweg's Teaching History. *Nation*, vol. xxxviii. p. 197, February, 1884.

Fredericq on Historical Instruction. *Nation*, vol. xxxv. p. 203, September, 1882.

Fredericq's Historical Instruction in Holland. *Nation*, vol. xlix. p. 254, September, 1889.

Fredericq's Travaux du Cours Pratique d'Histoire Nationale. *Nation*, vol. xxxix. p. 14, July, 1884.

Fredericq's Works. *Nation*, vol. xli. p. 512, December, 1885.

Freeman's Methods of Historical Study. *Nation*, vol. xliii. p. 358, October, 1886.

Gage's Historical Atlas. *North American Review*, vol. cviii. p. 66, April, 1869.

Gilman's Historical Readers. *Nation*, vol. xlv. p. 313, October, 1887.

Gradation and the Topical Method of Historical Study, and History Topics. In *Hall's Methods of Teaching and Studying History.* Boston, 1885. 8vo, pp. 106.*

Grote's Stammtafeln. *Nation*, vol. xxvii. p. 226, October, 1878.

Halsey's Historical Chart. *Nation*, vol. xviii. p. 129, February, 1874.

Heilprin's Historical Reference Book. *Nation*, vol. xl. p. 187, February, 1885.

Instruction in American History. *Wisconsin Journal of Education*, vol. iv. p. 380, 1874.†

Labberton's Historical Atlas. *Nation*, vol. xiii. p. 261, October, 1871; vol. xl. p. 165, February, 1885; vol. xli. p. 403, November, 1885; vol. xlv. p. 36, July, 1887.

Levermore and Dewey's Political History. *Nation*, vol. xlviii. p. 308, April, 1889.

Longnon's Atlas Historique. Part II. *Nation*, vol. xlvii. p. 337, October, 1888.

Morris's Epochs of History. *Nation*, vol. xix. p. 255, October, 1874.

Nichol's Chronological Tables. *Nation*, vol. xlvii. p. 114, August, 1888.

Recent Text-books of History. *Nation*, vol. xv. p. 75, August, 1872.

Sheldon's Studies in General History. *Nation*, vol. xliii. p. 164, August, 1886; vol. xliii. p. 373, November, 1886.

Study of History. University Press, 1874.†

Weisser's Bilderatlas, etc. *Nation*, vol. xl. p. 97, January, 1885.

HISTORY OF RELIGION.

Bezold's Geschichte des Hussitentums. *Nation,* vol. xx. p. 276, April, 1875.

Bigelow's Molinos the Quietist. *Nation,* vol. xxxvi. p. 22, January, 1883.

Böhm's Reformation of Emperor Sigismund. *Nation,* vol. xxiv. p. 75, February, 1877.

Boissier's La Religion Romaine. *North American Review,* vol. cxxi. p. 206, July, 1875.

Breed's Presbyterians and the Revolution. *Nation,* vol. xxii. p. 183, March, 1876.

Channing, sa Vie et sa Doctrine. *Nation,* vol. xxii. p. 216, March, 1876.

Christ's Ministry. *Nation,* vol. xiv. p. 275, April, 1872.

Church Goods. *Nation,* vol. xlvii. p. 153, August, 1888.

Clodd's Childhood of Religions. *Nation,* vol. xxi. p. 266, October, 1875.

Cox's Mythology. *Nation,* vol. vii. p. 419, November, 1868.

Coxe's Moral Reforms. *Nation,* vol. ix. p. 486, December, 1869.

Creighton's History of the Papacy. *Dial,* vol. viii. p. 35, June, 1887.

Dupuis's Origin of Religious Worship. *Nation,* vol. xvii. p. 46, July, 1873.

Free Religion. An Address before the Free Religious Association of the University of Wisconsin, 1880.†

Geike's English Reformation. *Nation,* vol. xxviii. p. 338, May, 1879.

Gladstone's Juventus Mundi. *Nation,* vol. ix. p. 254, September, 1869.

Gubertatis's Zoölogical Mythology. *Nation,* vol. xvi. p. 253, April, 1873.

Hardwick's History of the Christian Church. *Nation,* vol. xv. p. 334, November, 1872.

Hartung's Religion der Griechen. *Nation,* vol. xix. p. 422, December, 1874; *Christian Examiner,* vol. lxxxii. p. 118, January, 1867.

Hauréau's Bernard Délicieux et l'Inquisition Albigeoise. *Nation,* vol. xxvii. p. 30, July, 1878.

Hefele's Council of Constance. *Nation,* vol. xii. p. 437, June, 1871.

Herrick's Some Heretics. *Nation,* vol. xl. p. 268, March, 1885.

Höfler's Avignonese Popes. *Nation,* vol. xiv. p. 322, May, 1872.

Hubert's Protestants. *Nation,* vol. xxxv. p. 403, November, 1882.

Hübner's Sixtus the Fifth. *Nation,* vol. xvi. p. 136, February, 1873.

Hurst's Reformation. *Nation,* vol. xxxix. p. 250, September, 1884.

Jundt's Les Amis de Dieu. *Nation,* vol. xxxiv. p. 502, June, 1882.

Keary's Primitive Belief. *Nation,* vol. xxxvi. p. 110, February, 1883.

Kip's Jesuit Missions. *Nation,* vol. xxii. p. 35, January, 1876.

Lang's Custom and Myth. *Nation,* vol. xl. p. 307, April, 1885.

Lea's Inquisition in the Middle Ages. *Dial,* vol. ix. p. 34, June, 1888.

Luther (note on). *Nation,* vol. xiii. p. 144, August, 1871.

Murray's Mythology. *Nation,* vol. xx. p. 83, February, 1875.

Oliver's Church Music. *Christian Examiner,* vol. lxxii. p. 306, March, 1862.

Preller's Roman Mythology. *Christian Examiner,* vol. lxvi. p. 296, March, 1859.

Religion of Ancient Greece. *North American Review,* vol. cix. p. 106, July, 1869.†

Religion of Ancient Romans. *North American Review,* vol. cxiii. p. 30, July, 1871.†

Réville's La Religion à Rome. *Nation*, vol. xliii. p. 314, September, 1886.

Schweinitz's Unitas Fratrum. *Nation*, vol. xli. p. 473, December, 1885.

Thompson's Nineteen Christian Centuries. *Nation*, vol. xxxiii. p. 400, November, 1881.

Tollin's Michael Servetus. *Nation*, vol. xxx. p. 269, April, 1880.

Treadwell's Martin Luther. *Nation*, vol. xxxiii. p. 421, November, 1881.

Trench's Mediæval Church History. *Nation*, vol. xxvii. p. 323, November, 1878.

Tschackert's Peter von Ailli. *Nation*, vol. xxv. p. 381, December, 1877.

Tyler's Theology of the Greek Poets. *Nation*, p. 291, No. 119, 1867.

Wattenbach's Geschichte des römischen Papstthums. *Nation*, vol. xxv. p. 229, October, 1877.

Werner's Bonifacius. *Nation*, vol. xxii. p. 98, February, 1876.

Werunsky's Politik Papst Innocenz VI. *Nation*, vol. xxx. p. 370, May, 1880.

Witt's Classic Mythology. *Nation*, vol. xxxvii. p. 19, July, 1883.

Wylie's History of the Waldenses. *Nation*, vol. xxxi. p. 314, October, 1880.

Yonge's Pioneers and Founders. *Nation*, vol. xiii. p. 149, August, 1871.

POLITICS.

Alden's Science of Government. *Nation*, vol. ix. p. 236, September, 1869.

Alton's Among the Law-makers. *Nation*, vol. xliii. p. 504, December, 1886.

American Executive. *Christian Examiner*, vol. lxxx. p. 174, January, 1866.†

Basis of Suffrage. *Nation*, vol. i. p. 363, 1865.†

Buckalew's Proportional Representation. *Nation*, vol. xvi. p. 185, March, 1873.

Brunner's Trial by Jury. *Nation*, vol. xvi. p. 270, April, 1873.

Campbell's Civil Service Reform in New York. *Nation*, vol. xxxiii. p. 154, August, 1881.

Capen's History of Democracy. *Nation*, vol. xx. p. 351, May, 1875.

Caucus System. *Christian Examiner*, vol. lxxxvii. p. 137, September, 1869.†

City Government in Massachusetts. *Nation*, vol. xxxiii. p. 169, September, 1881.†

Coming Administration. *Christian Examiner*, vol. lxxxvi. p. 30, January, 1869.†

Congressional Districts. *Nation*, vol. xxxii. p. 59, January, 1881.†

Dangers of the Republican Party. *Nation*, vol. v. p. 232, 1867 (joint author).†

Dean's British Constitution. *Nation*, vol. xxxvii. p. 471, December, 1883.

Defeat of Mr. Milo. *Advance*, December, 1868.

Democracy on Trial. *Christian Examiner*, vol. lxxiv. p. 262, March, 1863.†

Election of Postmasters. *Nation*, vol. xiv. p. 302, May, 1872.†

Fawcett's Speeches on Current Political Questions. *Nation*, vol. xviii. p. 14, January, 1874.

Fisher's Trial of the Constitution. *Christian Examiner*, vol. lxxv. p. 286, September, 1863.

Gneist's Self-government. *Nation*, vol. xvi. p. 151, February, 1873.

Guiraud's Assemblées Provinciales. *Nation*, vol. xlviii. p. 180, February, 1889.

Impeachment. *Nation*, vol. vi. p. 490, June, 1868.†

Ingersoll's Fears for Democracy. *Nation*, vol. xxi. p. 75, July, 1875.

Macy's Our Government. *Nation*, vol. xliii. p. 399, November, 1886.

Man on Horseback. *International Review*, vol. vii. p. 33, July, 1879.†

Mas Latrie's Du Droit de Marque. *Nation*, vol. xxv. p. 27, July, 1877.

McMillan's Elective Franchise. *Nation*, vol. xxxi. p. 100, August, 1880.

Minority Representation. *Nation*, vol. ix. p. 556, December, 1869; vol. xliii. p. 229, September, 1886.†

Mob Spirit. *Nation*, vol. vii. p. 410, November, 1868.†

Personal Representation. *Nation*, vol. v. p. 130, 1867; vol. x. p. 69, February, 1870; *Oshkosh Northwestern*, 1870.

Pomeroy's Constitutional Law. *Christian Examiner*, vol. lxxxvii. p. 99, July, 1869.

Porter's Constitutional History of United States. *Nation*, vol. xxxvii. p. 104, August, 1883.

Post-office Reform. *Boston Advertiser*, November, 1866.

Probyn's Local Government and Taxation. *Nation*, vol. xxi. p. 170, September, 1875.

Re-election. *Boston Advertiser*, December, 1866.

Skinner's American Politics. *Nation*, vol. xv. p. 336, November, 1872.

Tenure in Civil Service Reform. *Nation*, vol. xxiii. p. 37, July, 1876.†

Town Meetings for Great Cities. *Nation*, vol. ii. p. 684, 1866.†

Townsend's Civil Government. *Nation*, vol. viii. p. 56, July, 1869.

Use of Mr. Johnson's Folly. *Nation*, vol. v. p. 170, 1867.†

Williams's Constitution of the United States. *Christian Examiner*, vol. lxxi. p. 444, November, 1861.

Young's Civil Government. *Nation*, vol. ix. p. 137, August, 1869.

SOCIOLOGY AND ECONOMICS.

Agriculture in the Middle Ages. *Transactions of Wisconsin State Agricultural Society*, 1876–77, p. 205.†

Brentano's History of Gilds. *Nation*, vol. xi. p. 354, November, 1870.

Essays by a Pupil of Cobden. *Nation*, vol. xviii. p. 94, February, 1874.

Fagniez's Études sur l'Industrie, etc. *Nation*, vol. xxvii. p. 85, August, 1878.

Fawcett's Essays. *Nation*, vol. xv. p. 203, September, 1872.

Gross's Gilda Mercatoria. *Nation*, vol. xxxviii. p. 15, January, 1884.

Holyoake's History of Co-operation. *Nation*, vol. xxi. p. 315, November, 1875; vol. xxix. p. 163, September, 1879.

Inama-Sternegg's Wirtschaftsgeschichte. *Nation*, vol. xxxii. p. 45, January, 1881.

Kenny's Essay on Primogeniture. *Nation*, vol. xxix. p. 367, November, 1879.

Laurence's Essay on Primogeniture. *Nation*, vol. xxix. p. 367, November, 1879.

Lüder's Convention at Geneva. *Nation*, vol. xxv. p. 10, July, 1877.

Pearson's Theories of Usury. *Nation*, vol. xxvi. p. 342, May, 1878.

Perry's Political Economy. *Christian Examiner*, vol. lxxxv. p. 112, July, 1868; *Nation*, vol. viii. p. 55, January, 1869.

Rae's Contemporary Socialism. *Dial*, vol. v. p. 166, November, 1884.

Rogers's Social Economy. *Nation*, vol. xvi. p. 78, January, 1873.

Rogers's Work and Wages. *Nation*, vol. xxxix. p. 77, July, 1884; *Dial*, vol. v. p. 33, June, 1884.

Roscher's Ideas on Free Trade. *Nation*, vol. xxvi. p. 114. February, 1878.†

Roscher's Nationalökonomie des Ackerbaus. *Nation*, vol. xxi. p. 357, December, 1875.

Schanz's Zur Geschichte der deutschen Gesellen - Verbände im Mittelalter. *Nation*, vol. xxiv. p. 367, June, 1877.

Schmoller's Staats- und social-wissenschaftliche Forschungen. *Nation*, vol. xxx. p. 62, January, 1880.

Stieda's Zur Entstehung des deutschen Zunftwesens. *Nation*, vol. xxiv. p. 367, June, 1877.

Taylor's Introduction to History of Factory System. *Nation*, vol. xliv. p. 85, January, 1887.

Thornton's Labor. *Financier*, December 19, 1874.

Tourmagne's Histoire du Servage. *Nation*, vol. xxx. p. 420, June, 1880.

Waring's Village Improvements and Farm Villages. *Nation*, vol. xxv. p. 336, November, 1877.

GENERAL BIOGRAPHY.

Allin, Rev. John. *New England Register*, January, 1887.

Anthon, Professor. *Nation*, vol. v. p. 104, August, 1867.†

Beardsley's Life of William Samuel Johnson. *Nation*, vol. xxiv. p. 135, March, 1877.

Clarke's Memorial and Biographical Sketches. *Nation*, vol. xxvi. p. 408, June, 1878.

Delafield's Lives of Francis and Morgan Lewis. *Nation*, vol. xxvi. p. 425, June, 1878.

Emerson. *Dial*, vol. iii. p. 1, May, 1882.†

Farmer's Famous Queens. *Nation*, vol. xlv. p. 275, October, 1887.

Finney's Life of Rev. C. G. Finney. *Nation*, vol. xxii. p. 216, March, 1876.

Holmes's Life of Motley. *Nation*, vol. xxviii. p. 139, February, 1879.

Keary's Life of Annie Keary. *Nation*, vol. xxxvi. p. 388, May, 1883.

Lee's Lord Herbert of Cherbury. *Nation*, vol. xlv. p. 79, July, 1887.

Mommsen. *Nation*, vol. xlv. p. 412, November, 1887.†

Santvoord's Life of Eliphalet Nott. *Nation*, vol. xxii. p. 234, April, 1876.

Scudder's Breck's Recollections. *Nation*, vol. xxv. p. 31, July, 1877.

Spalding's Life of Archbishop Spalding. *Nation*, vol. xviii. p. 208, March, 1874.

Todd's Life of John Todd. *Nation*, vol. xxi. p. 424, December, 1875.

Water's Cobbett's How to Get on, etc., as illustrated by the Life of William Cobbett. *Nation*, vol. xxxvii. p. 300, October, 1883.

MISCELLANEOUS PHILOLOGY.

Fiske's Celtic Views. *Nation*, vol. x. p. 406, June, 1870.

Key's Philological Essays. *Nation*, vol. vii. p. 251, September, 1868.

Meyer's Vergleichische Grammatik. *Christian Examiner*, vol. lxxiii. p. 140. July, 1862.

Müller's Chips. *Nation*, vol. viii. p. 317, April, 1869.

Müller's Science of Language. *Christian Examiner*, vol. lxxiii. p. 140, July, 1862.

Negro Dialect. *Nation*, vol. i. p. 744, 1865.†

Philological Convention at Easton, Pa. *Nation*, vol. xvii. p. 71, July, 1873.

Philological Convention at Hartford. *Nation*, vol. xix. p. 59, July, 1874.

Poughkeepsie Convention of Philologists. *Nation*, vol. ix. p. 109, August, 1869.

Skeat's Etymological Dictionary. *Dial*, vol. iii. p. 59, July, 1882.

Wheeler's Our Spoken English. *Nation*, vol. xi. p. 312, November, 1870.

Whitney's Science of Language. *Christian Examiner*, vol. lxxxiv. p. 373, May, 1868.

EDUCATION.

Antioch College. *Nation*, vol. xxxiv. p. 146, February, 1882.

Bloxam's Magdalen College. *Nation*, vol. xliv. p. 509, June, 1887.

Brodrick's History of the University of Oxford. *Nation*, vol. xlv. p. 280, October, 1887.

Brodrick's Memorials of Merton College. *Nation*, vol. xliii. p. 42, July, 1886.

Budinszky's University of Paris. *Nation*, vol. xxv. p. 137, August, 1877.

Coeducation in the University of Wisconsin. *Nation*, vol. xxv. p. 228, October, 1877.

Bishop Dupanloup's The Child. *Nation*, vol. xxi. p. 234, October, 1875.

Fredericq's Calvinist University. *Nation*, vol. xxvii. p. 71, August, 1878.

Lyte's History of the University of Oxford. *Nation*, vol. xlv. p. 179, September, 1887.

Mullinger's History of University of Cambridge. *Nation*, vol. xlix. p. 80, July, 1889.

Our Colleges. *Christian Examiner*, vol. lxxxiii. p. 47, July, 1867.†

Parker's Early History of Oxford. *Nation*, vol. xliii. p. 63, July, 1886.

Plummer's Elizabethan Oxford. *Nation*, vol. xlvi. p. 342, April, 1888.

Practical Education. An address before the University of Nebraska, 1876. pp. 22. Printed for the University of Nebraska, 1876.†

Von Raumer's German Universities. *Christian Examiner*, vol. lxviii. p. 147, January, 1860.

Rein's Pädagogische Studien. *Nation*, vol. xxv. p. 106, August, 1877.

Routine in Education. *Boston Advertiser*, August, 1866.†

Sexes in Colleges. *Nation*, vol. x. p. 134, March, 1870.†

Spear's Religion and the State. *Nation*, vol. xxiv. p. 78, February, 1877.

Staunton's Great Schools of England. *Christian Examiner*, vol. lxxxii. p. 256, March, 1867.

Two Dangers threatening our Schools. *Nation*, vol. xv. p. 103, August, 1872.†

University of Wisconsin. *Old and New*, vol. iv. p. 137, July, 1871.†

University Reform. *Boston Advertiser*, August, September, 1866.†

Utility of Classical Studies as a Means of Mental Discipline. *Wisconsin Journal of Education*, vol. iv. p. 11, 1874.

MISCELLANEOUS TEXT-BOOKS.

Arnold-Foster's Citizen Reader. *Nation*, vol. xliv. p. 144, February, 1887.

Educational Text-books. *Nation*, vol. xiv. p. 219, April, 1872.

Geikie's Teaching of Geography. *Nation*, vol. xlv. p. 319, October, 1887.

Haven's Rhetoric. *Nation*, vol. ix. p. 345, October, 1869.

Magill's French Grammar. *Christian Examiner*, vol. lxxxii. p. 261, March, 1867.

Minto's Manual of English Prose Literature. *Nation*, vol. xxxii. p. 430, June, 1881.

Pearson's English Grammar. *Nation*, vol. xxiii. p. 304, November, 1876.

Recent Text-books. *Nation*, vol. x. p. 275, April, 1870.

Richardson's English Literature. *Nation*, vol. xxxii. p. 139, February, 1881.

Sanborn's " Round Table Series " of Literature Lessons. *Nation*, vol. xxxv. p. 443, November, 1882.

Taber's Puzzle Primer. *Nation*, vol. xli. p. 465, December, 1885.

Watson's Third Reader. *Nation*, vol. ix. p. 369, October, 1869.

Whitney's German Grammar. *Nation*, vol. x. p. 196, March, 1870.

JUVENILE LITERATURE.

Belt and Spur. *Nation*, vol. xxxv. p. 468, November, 1882.

Brooks's Chivalric Days. *Nation*, vol. xliii. p. 504, December, 1886.

Butterworth's Zigzag Journeys in Europe. *Nation*, vol. xxix. p. 427, December, 1879.

Eggleston's Strange Stories from History. *Nation*, vol. xli. p. 450, November, 1885.

Gilman's Short Stories. *Nation*, vol. xliv. p. 53, January, 1887.

Hanson's Stories from the Days of King Arthur. *Nation*, vol. xxxv. p. 428, November, 1882.

Harris's Uncle Remus. *Dial*, vol. i. p. 183, January, 1881.

Jenkin's Little Hodge. *Nation*, vol. xvi. p. 220, March, 1873.

Laing's Heroes of Seven Hills. *Nation*, vol. xix. p. 13, July, 1874.

Lanier's Boy's Froissart. *Nation*, vol. xxix. p. 392, November, 1879.

Lanier's Boy's Mabinogion. *Nation*, vol. xxxiii. p. 419, November, 1881.

Leland's Johnnykin and the Goblins. *Nation*, vol. xxiii. p. 359, December, 1876.

MISCELLANEOUS.

American Good Nature. *Boston Advertiser*, June, 1866.†

Blaine's Popularity at the West. *Nation*, vol. xxii. p. 412, June, 1876.†

Bowen's Coal and Coal-oil. *Christian Examiner*, vol. lxxviii. p. 447, May, 1865.

Burroughs's Wake-Robin. *Nation*, vol. xiii. p. 79, August, 1871.

Clough's Poems. *Christian Examiner*, vol. lxxiii. p. 307, September, 1862.

Fairchild's Moral Philosophy, *Nation*, vol. ix. p. 393, November, 1869.

Feuling's Phocydidis. *Nation,* vol. ix. p. 321, October, 1869.

Habits of Good Society. *Christian Examiner,* vol. lxix. p. 147, July, 1860.

Historical Fiction. *Unitarian Review,* vol. xxxiii. p. 447, May, 1890.

Holland's Timothy Titcomb's Letters to Young People. *Christian Examiner,* vol. lxvi. p. 144, January, 1859.

International Copyright. *Lippincott,* vol. xxv. p. 102, January, 1880.†

Johnson's Lectures, Essays, etc. *Nation,* vol. xxxvii. p. 63, July, 1883.

Kirke's Among the Pines. *Christian Examiner,* vol. lxxiii. p. 295, September, 1862.

Lewis's Natural History of Birds. *Nation,* vol. vii. p. 335, October, 1868.

Lubbock's Addresses. *Nation,* vol. xxx. p. 48, January, 1880.

Margaret Howth. *Christian Examiner,* vol. lxxii. p. 449, May, 1862.

Morgan's Representative Names. *Nation,* vol. xxiv. p. 47, January, 1877.

Palace Cars. *Nation,* vol. xxv. p. 380, December, 1877.†

Progress of Public Opinion. *Boston Advertiser,* August, 1866.†

Reusch's Process of Galileo. *Nation,* vol. xxi. p. 214, September, 1875.

Ruskin's Letters. *Dial,* vol. i. p. 228, March, 1881.

Samuels's Ornithology. *Nation,* vol. v. p. 108, August, 1867.

Topelius's Times of Alchemy. *Nation,* vol. xxxix. p. 116, August, 1884.

Two Years behind the Plough. *Nation,* vol. xxvi. p. 140, February, 1878.